More praise for
Dragonshadow

"With its resourceful, forty-five-year-old heroine who must make difficult choices, face both emotional and demonic challenges and deal with the pain of her past, Hambly's novel should appeal to mature readers who seek more than flashing swords and simple sorcery . . . This novel excels as a sequel but readers new to the story won't miss a beat."
—*Publishers Weekly* (starred review)

"Beautifully concise, adroitly plotted, inventive, and insightful; a wrenching affair that works its barbed pleasures ever deeper into the enthralled, horrified reader."
—*Kirkus Reviews* (starred review)

"Hambly creates a believable setting and compellingly real characters without sacrificing the sense of a truly magical world, both beautiful and deadly. This is *not* yet another predictable sword and sorcery tale. This story concerns the temptations of power and the cost of resisting evil. Grief and loss are inescapable. Unlike *Dragonsbane*, however, *Dragonshadow* promises readers another book in which, perhaps, the protagonists will find peace and healing."
—Amazon.com

By Barbara Hambly
Published by Ballantine Books:

The Darwath Trilogy
THE TIME OF THE DARK
THE WALLS OF AIR
THE ARMIES OF DAYLIGHT

MOTHER OF WINTER
ICEFALCON'S QUEST

Sun Wolf and Starhawk
THE LADIES OF MANDRIGYN
THE WITCHES OF WENSHAR
THE DARK HAND OF MAGIC

The Windrose Chronicles
THE SILENT TOWER
THE SILICON MAGE
DOG WIZARD

STRANGER AT THE WEDDING

Sun-Cross
THE RAINBOW ABYSS
THE MAGICIANS OF NIGHT

THOSE WHO HUNT THE NIGHT
TRAVELING WITH THE DEAD

SEARCH THE SEVEN HILLS

BRIDE OF THE RAT GOD

DRAGONSBANE
DRAGONSHADOW

Books published by The Ballantine Publishing Group are available at quantity discounts on bulk purchases for premium, educational, fund-raising, and special sales use. For details, please call 1-800-733-3000.

DRAGONSHADOW

Barbara Hambly

A Del Rey® Book
THE BALLANTINE PUBLISHING GROUP • NEW YORK

A Del Rey® Book
Published by The Ballantine Publishing Group
Copyright © 1999 by Barbara Hambly

All rights reserved under International and Pan-American Copyright Conventions. Published in the United States by The Ballantine Publishing Group, a division of Random House, Inc., New York, and simultaneously in Canada by Random House of Canada Limited, Toronto.

Del Rey is a registered trademark and the Del Rey colophon is a trademark of Random House, Inc.

www.randomhouse.com/delrey/

Library of Congress Catalog Card Number: 99-091140

ISBN 0-345-42188-4

Manufactured in the United States of America

First Hardcover Edition: March 1999
First Mass Market Edition: January 2000

10 9 8 7 6 5 4 3 2 1

For
J.W.L.

THE MARCHES

NAST WALL

Imperteng Woods

Ernine

Jotham

CITADEL OF HALNATH

DEEP OF YLFERDUN

Core Bridge

Tanner's Rise

Great Gates
Market Hall

Claekith Harbor

BEL

Royal Palace

Dockmarket

Urrate

Silver Isle

Somanthus

The Seven Isles

BEL
and
ENVIRONS

Book One

THE SKERRIES
OF LIGHT

CHAPTER ONE

Dragonsbane, they called him.

Slayer of dragons.

Or *a* dragon, anyway. And, he'd later found out, not such a very big one at that.

Lord John Aversin, Thane of the Winterlands, leaned back in the mended oak chair in his library as the messenger's footfalls retreated down the tower stairs, and looked across at Jenny Waynest, who was curled up on the windowsill with a cat dozing in her lap.

"Bugger," he said.

The night's first appreciable breeze—warm and sticky as such things were in the Winterlands in summer—brought the grit of woodsmoke through the open window and made the candle flames shudder among the heaped books.

"A hundred feet long," Jenny murmured.

John shook his head. "Gaw, any dragon looks a hundred feet long if you're under it." He pushed his round-lensed spectacles more firmly onto the bridge of his long nose. "Or in a position where you have to think about bein' under it in the near future. I doubt it's over fifty. That one we slew over by Far West Riding wasn't quite thirty . . ." He nodded to the cold fireplace, where the black spiked mace of the golden dragon's tail-tip hung. "And Morkeleb the Black was forty-two, though I thought he'd whack me over the back of the head when I asked could I measure him." He grinned at the memory, but behind the spectacles Jenny could see the fear in his eyes.

Almost as an afterthought he added, "We'll have to go after it."

Jenny stroked the cat's head. "Yes." Her voice was inaudible. The cat purred and made bread on her knee.

"Funny, that." John got to his feet and stretched to get the crick out of his back. "I've put together every account I can find of past Dragonsbanes—all them old ballads and tales—and matched 'em up as well as I could with the King-lists." He gestured to the vast rummage that covered desk and floor and every shelf of the low-vaulted study: bound bundles of notes, parchments half copied from waterstained books found in the ruins south of Wrynde. Curillius on *The Deeds of the Ancient Heroes*, Gorgonimir's *Creatures and Phenomena*. A fair copy of a fragment of the old *Liever Draiken* sent by the Regent of Bel, a connoisseur of both ancient manuscripts and the tales of Dragonsbanes. Notes yet to be copied—he'd jotted them down two years ago—of a dragon-slaying song sung by one of the garrison at Cair Corflyn, all mixed up with wax note tablets, candles, inkwells, scrapers, prickers, pumice, candle scissors, and dismantled clocks. For the fourteen years they'd been together, Jenny had heard John swear every year or two he'd put the place in order, and she knew that the phrase "put together" must not be taken too literally.

Magpie gleanings of learning by a man whose curiosity was an unfilled well; accretions of useful, interesting, or merely frivolous lore spewed back at random by circumstance and the mad God of Time.

"Some Dragonsbanes slay one dragon and that's that, they're in the ballads for good," mused John. "Others slay two or three, and two of those, as far as I can figure 'em, are within ten years of the singletons. Then you'll get generations, fifty, sixty, seventy years, when the dragons mind their own business, whatever that is, and nobody slays anybody. This is three for me. How'd I get so lucky?"

"The North is being settled again." Jenny set Skinny Kitty aside and went to stand behind John, her arms around his waist. Through his rough red wool doublet and patched linen shirt she felt the ribs under the hard sheath of muscle, the warmth of his flesh. "It was the cattle herd at Skep Dhû garrison that the dragon hit. There probably hasn't been this much livestock in the North since the Kings left. It may have drawn this one."

"Gaw," he said again, and set his hand over the folded knot of hers. An oddly deft hand for a warrior's, inkstained and blistered in two places from a chemical experiment that took an unexpected turn. But thick, like his forearm, with the muscle of a lifetime of wielding a sword. In profile his was the face of a scholar. In his reddish-brown hair, hanging loose to his shoulders, the candlelight gilded the first flecks of gray.

He'd been twenty-four when he'd gone against the gold Dragon of Wyr, and his side still hurt like a knife-thrust from the damaged ribs whenever the weather turned. Jenny's fingers could detect the ridge of the biggest scar he'd taken when he fought Morkeleb the Black in the burned-out Deep beneath Nast Wall. *Life is fragile,* she thought. *Life is precious, and life is short.* "How many is the most any Dragonsbane has been able to slay?" she asked, and John half-turned his head to grin down over his shoulder at her.

"Three. That was Alkmar the Godborn. His third dragon killed him."

In the hour or so that separated them from moonrise, John and Jenny mustered all they would need for the slaying of the Dragon of Skep Dhû, such of them as were stored at the Hold. John's battle armor, almost as battered and sorry as the doublet of black leather and iron in which he was wont to patrol his lands. Two axes, one a short, single-grip weapon that could be wielded from the back of a horse, the other longer and heavier, a two-handed thing for finishing a creature dying on the ground. Eight harpoons, like boar spears but larger, barbed and massive and written over with spells of death and ruin.

John's half-brother Muffle, sergeant of the local militia and smith of the village of Alyn, had forged the first two in a hurry, when the Dragon of Wyr had descended on the herds of Great Toby fourteen years ago, and the others had been made a few weeks after that. Jenny had put spells of death on them all. In those days her powers had been small, hedge-witch magics taught her by old Caerdinn, who had once been tutor at Alyn

Hold, and she had known little of dragons, only scraps and snippets culled from John's books. Killing the golden dragon had taught her something of a dragon's nature, so when Prince Gareth of Magloshaldon, later Regent for the King of Belmarie, had come begging John's help against the Dragon of Nast Wall, she had been able to weave more accurate spells. Her magic was still, at that time, small.

Now she sat on the wooden platform that John and Muffle had built at the top of the tower for John's telescope. The eight harpoons lay before her on the planks. Far below she heard John's voice, and Muffle's, distant as birdsong but far more profane, as they dragged out cauldrons and wood. She heard Adric's voice, too, a gay treble—her second son, at eight burly and red-haired and every inch the descendant of John's formidable, bearlike father: *He should be in bed!* Beyond a doubt three-year-old Mag was trailing, silent as a marsh fey, at his heels.

For a moment she felt annoyed at John's Cousin Dilly, who was supposed to be looking after the children, and then let all thought of them slip away with the releasing of her breath. *You cannot be a mage,* old Caerdinn had said to her, *if your thoughts are ever straying: to your supper, to your child, to whether you will have the next breath of air after this one is gone from under your ribs. The key to magic is magic. Never forget that.*

And though she had found that magic's key was something else, in many ways the old man had been correct. Her thought circled, like the power circle she had drawn on the platform around herself and the harpoons, and like the power that came down to her in silver threads from the shape of the stars, her thought took shape.

Cruelty. Uncaring. The quenching of life. The weary welcoming of the final dark.

Death-spells. And behind the death-spells, the gold fierce fire of dragon-magic.

For four years, now, that dragon-blaze had burned in her blood.

Morkeleb, she thought, *forgive me.*
Or was it not a thing of dragons to forgive?
Morkeleb the Black. The Dragon of Nast Wall.

She summoned the magic down from the stars, out of the air, called it from the core of fire within her that had burned into life when, by Morkeleb's power, she had been transformed to dragon-kind. Though she had returned to human form, abandoning the immortality of the star-drakes, part of her essence, her inner heart, had remained the essence of a dragon, and she understood power as dragons understood it. Since it was not a thing of dragons to think or care, she did not, as she wove her death-spells, think or care about Morkeleb, who had loved her.

Loved her enough to let her return to human form.

Loved her enough to return her to John.

But after the death-spells were wrought and bound into the harpoons, she sat on the rickety platform above the Hold, her arms clasped round her knees, listening to the far-off voices of her husband and her son and remembering the skeletal black shape in the darkness, the silver labyrinthine eyes.

Morkeleb.

"Mother?"

Starlight showed the trapdoor that opened among the slates of the turret roof, but it did not penetrate the shadow underneath. Mageborn, Jenny was able to see her elder son, Ian, a weedy twelve-year-old, her own night-black hair and blue eyes in John's beaky face. He stepped onto the steeply slanting roof and made to come down the stairs, and she said, "No, wait there." The weariness of working the death-songs dragged at her bones. "Let me gather these up and send them on their way."

Ian, she knew, would understand what she said. Only this year his own powers had started to manifest: small, as any teenager's were—the ability to call fire and find lost objects, to sometimes see in fire things far away. Ian sat on the trapdoor's sill and watched in fascination as she drew the glimmer from out of the circles, collecting it like cold spider-silk in her hands. All magic, Caerdinn had taught her, depended on Limitations. Before even beginning to lay down the circles of power, let alone summon the death-spells, she had cleansed the platform with rainwater and hyssop and laid on each separate rough-hewn plank such Words as would keep the vile magics from attaching to the place itself. Spells, too, were required to hold the wicked ferocity of what she had done within a small space, so it would not disperse over the countryside and cause ruin and death to everyone in the Hold, in the village, in the farms that nestled close to the walls. Like a miser picking up pinhead-sized crumbs of gold dust with his fingernails, so Jenny gathered into her palms each whisper and shudder of the death-spells' residue, named them and neutralized them and released them into the turning starlight.

"Can I help?"

"No, not this time. You see what I'm doing, though?" He nodded. As she worked, she felt, rising through her—as it always rose, it seemed to her, at the most inopportune of times—the miserable flush of heat, the reminder that the change of a woman's life was coming upon her. Patiently, wearily, she called upon other spells, little silvery cantrips of blood and time, to put that heat aside. "With spells of cursing you must be absolutely thorough, absolutely clean, particularly with spells worked in a high place," she said.

Ian's eyes went to John's telescope, mounted at the far side of the platform; she saw him read her thought. It would not take much, they both knew, for the rail to give way, or John to lose his balance. A fragment of curse, a stray shadow of ill will, would be enough to cause John or Ian or anyone else to forget to latch the trapdoor, or for the latch to stick, so that Adric or Mag, or one of Cousin Rowanberry's ever-multiplying brood, could come up here . . .

And even so, the platform was the safest place in all the Hold to work such spells.

As she and Ian bore the harpoons down the twisting stair, Jenny remembered what it had been, to be a dragon. To be a creature of diamond heart and limitless power. A creature to whom magic was not something that one *did*—well or less well—but the thing that one *was*: will and magic, flesh and bone, all one.

And not caring if a child fell from the platform.

With the moon's rising John and Jenny and Ian rode out from Alyn Hold to the stone house on Frost Fell, where Jenny had for so many years lived alone. It had been Caerdinn's house, and Jenny had lived as the old wizard's pupil from the time she was thirteen and the buds of power she'd had as a child began to blossom. A single big room and a loft, bookshelves, a table of pickled pine, a vast hearth, and a big bed. It was to this house that John had first come to her, twenty-two and needing help against one of the bandit hordes that had been the scourge of the Winterlands in the days before the King sent his protecting armies to them again. He'd been challenged, Jenny recalled, to single combat by some bandit chief—maybe the one who had slain his father—and had heard that no weapon could harm a man who'd lain with a witch.

But she'd remembered him from her own childhood and his. His mother had been Jenny's first teacher in the arts of power, a captive woman, an Icerider witch: The scandal when Lord Aver married her had been a nine days' wonder through the Winterlands. When her son was four and Jenny seven, Kahiera Night-raven had vanished, gone back to the Iceriders, leaving Jenny with no better instructor than Caerdinn, who had hated all Iceriders and Kahiera above the rest. From that time until his arrival at Frost Fell, she had seen Kahiera's son barely a score of times.

Riding up the fell now, she saw him in her mind as she had seen him then—cocky, quirky, aggressive, the scourge of maidens in five villages . . . And angry. It was his anger she remembered most, and the shy fleeting sweetness of his smile.

"Place needs thatching," he remarked now, standing in Battle-hammer's stirrups to pull a straw from the overhang of the roof. "According to Dotys' *Catalogues*, villagers on the Silver Isles used to braid straw into solid tiles and peg 'em to the rafterwork, which must have been gie heavy. Cowan"—the head stableman at the Hold—"says it can't be done, but I've a mind to try this summer, if I can find how they did the braiding. If we're all still alive by haying, that is." Chewing the straw, he dropped from the warhorse's back, looped the rein around the gate, and trailed Jenny and Ian into the house. "Garn," he added, sniffing. "Why is it no matter what kind of Weirds you lay around the house, Jen, to keep wanderers from even seein' the place, mice always seem to get in just fine?"

Jenny flashed him a quick glance by the soft blue radiance of the witchlight she called and bent to pull from under the bed the box of herbs she kept there. Hellebore, yellow jessamine, and the bright red caps of panther-mushroom, carefully potted in wax-stoppered jars. Jars and box were written around with spells, as the house walls were written, to keep intruders away, but there were two mice dead under the bed nevertheless.

Jenny traced the box with her blunt brown fingertips, automatically undoing the wards she had woven. Calabash gourds from the south contained the heads of water-vipers and the dried bodies of certain jellyfish. Nameless leaves were tied in ensorcelled thread, and waxed-parchment packets held deadly earths and salts. On the other side of the room Ian hunted among the few books still on the shelf; John caught Jenny around the waist, tripped her and tossed her onto the old flattened mattress, grinning impishly as she flung a spell across the room to keep Ian unaware of his parents' misbehavior . . .

"Behave yourself." She wriggled from his grasp, giggling like a village girl.

"It's been too long since we've come here." He let her up, but held her with one arm on either side of her, hands grasping the rough bedpost behind her back. Though only a little over medium height himself, John was easily a foot taller than she; the witchlight flashed silvery in his spectacles and in the twinkle of his eyes.

"And whose fault is that?" She kept her voice low—Ian was still preoccupied with his search. "*I* wasn't the one who made stinks and messes and explosions in quest of self-igniting kindling all spring. *I* wasn't the one who had to try to make a flying machine from drawings he'd found in some old book . . ."

"That was Heronax of Ernine," protested John. "He flew from Ernine to the Silver Isles in it—wherever Ernine was—and I've gie near got the thing working properly now. You'll see."

He gathered her hair up in his hands, an overflowing double handful of oceanic night, and bent to kiss her lips. His body pressed hers to the tall, smooth-hewn post, and her hand explored the leather of his doublet, the rough wool of the dull-colored plaid wrapped over his shoulder, the hard muscle beneath the linen sleeve. Ian apparently bethought himself of some ingredient hidden inexplicably in the garden, for he wandered unseeing outside; the scents of the old house wrapped them around, moldy thatch and mice and the wild whisper of summer night in the Winterlands.

The heat of her body's changing whispered to her, and she whispered back, *Go away.* It was not just the little cantrips, the knots of warding and change, that turned aside those migraines, those flashes of moodiness, those alien angers. It was this knowledge, this man, the lips that sought hers and the warmth of his flesh against her. The joy of a girl who had been ugly, who had been scorned and stoned in the village streets, who had been told, *You're a witch and will grow old alone.*

The knowledge that this was not true.

Later she breathed, "*And* your dragon-slaying machine."

"Aye, well." He straightened from hunting her fallen hairpins, and the hard line returned to crease the corner of his mouth. "That's near done, too. More's the pity I spent this past winter tryin' to learn to fly instead."

Early in the morning Jenny kindled fire under the cauldrons that Sergeant Muffle had set up in the Hold's old barracks court. She fetched water from the well in the corner and spent the day brewing poisons to put on the ensorcelled harpoons. In this she accepted Ian's help, and John's, too, and it was all John's various aunts could do to keep Adric and Mag from stealing into the court and poisoning themselves in the process of lending a hand. By the late-gathering summer twilight they were dipping the harpoons into the thickened black mess, and the messenger from Skep Dhû joined them in the court.

"It isn't just the garrison that relies on that herd," the young man said, glancing, a little uncertainly, from the unprepossessing, bespectacled form of the Dragonsbane, stripped to a rather sooty singlet, doeskin britches, and boots, to that of the Witch of Frost Fell. His name was Borin, and he was a lieutenant of cavalry at the garrison, and like most southerners had to work very hard not to bite his thumb against evil in Jenny's presence. "The manors the Regent is trying to establish to feed all the new garrisons depend on those cattle as well, for breeding and restocking. And we lost six, maybe eight bulls and as many cows, as far as we can gather—the carcasses stripped and gouged, the whole pasture swept with fire."

John glanced at Jenny, who could almost read his thoughts. Fifteen cattle was a lot.

"And you got a good look at it?"

Borin nodded. "I saw it flying away toward the other side of the Skepping Hills. Green, as I said to you last night. The spines and horns down its back, and the barb on its tail, were crimson as blood."

There was a moment's silence. Ian, on the other side of the court, carefully propped two of the harpoons against the long shed that served John as a workroom; Sergeant Muffle leaned against the side of the beehive-shaped clay furnace in the center of the yard and wiped the sweat from his face. John said softly, "Green with crimson horns," and Jenny knew why that small upright line appeared between his brows. He was fishing through his memory for the name of a star-drake of those colors in the old dragon-lists. *Teltrevir, heliotrope,* the old list said, the list handed down rote from centuries ago, compiled by none knew whom. *Centhwevir blue, knotted with gold.*

"Only a dozen or so are on the list," said Jenny quietly. "There must be dozens—hundreds—that are not."

"Aye." He moved two of the harpoons, a restless gesture, not meeting her eyes. "We don't even know how many dragons there are in the world, or where they live—or what they eat, for that matter, when they're not makin' free with our herds." His voice was deep, like scuffed brown velvet; Jenny could sense him drawing in on himself, gathering himself for the fight. "In Gantering Pellus' *The Encyclopedia of Everything in the Material World* it says they live in volcanoes that are crowned with ice, but then again Gantering Pellus also says bears are born shapeless like dough and licked into shape by their fathers. I near got meself killed when I was fifteen, findin' out how much he didn't know about bears. The *Liever Draiken* has it that dragons come down from the north . . ."

"Will you want a troop of men to help you?" asked Borin. In the short time he'd been at the Hold he'd already learned that when the Thane of the Winterlands started on ancient writings it was better to simply interrupt if one wanted anything done. "Commander Rocklys said she could dispatch one to meet you at Skep Dhû."

John hesitated, then said, "Better not. Or at least, have 'em come, but no nearer than Wormwood Ford. There's a reason them old heroes are always riding up on the dragon's lair by themselves, son. Dragons listen, even in their sleep. Just three or four men, they'll hear 'em coming, miles off, and be in the air by the time company arrives. If a dragon gets in the air, the man going after it is dead. You *have* to take 'em on the ground."

"Oh." Borin tried hard to look unconcerned about this piece of news. "I see."

"At a guess," John added thoughtfully, "the thing's laired up in the ravines on the northwest side of the Skepping Hills, near where the herd was pastured. There's only one or two ravines large enough to take a dragon. It shouldn't be hard to figure out which. And then," he said grimly, "then we'll see who gets slain."

CHAPTER TWO

It was a ride of almost two days, east to the Skepping Hills. John and Jenny took with them, in addition to Borin and the two southern soldiers who'd ridden with him—a not-unreasonable precaution in the Winterlands—Skaff Gradely, who acted as militia captain for the farms around Alyn Hold, and two of Jenny's cousins from the Darrow Bottoms, all of whom were unwilling to leave their farms this close to haying-time but equally unwilling to have the dragon move west. Sergeant Muffle was left in command of the Hold.

"There's no reason for it," argued Borin, who appeared to have gotten the Hold servants to launder and press his red military tunic and polish his boots. "There's been no sign of bandits this spring. Commander Rocklys has put this entire land under law again, so there's really no call for a man to walk armed wherever he goes." He almost, but not quite, looked pointedly at Gradely and the Darrow boys, who, as usual for those born and bred in the Winterlands, bristled with knives, spiked clubs, axes, and the long slim savage northern bows. Jenny knew that in the King's southern lands, farmers did not even carry swords—most of the colonists who had come in the wake of the new garrisons were, in fact, serfs, transplanted by royal fiat to these manors and forbidden to carry weapons at all.

"There's never any sign of bandits that're good at their jobs." John signaled a halt for the dozenth time and dismounted to scout, though by order of the Commander of the Winterlands, roads in this part of the country had been cleared for a bow shot's distance on either side. In Jenny's opinion, whoever had done the clearing had no idea how far a northern longbow could shoot.

Borin said, "Really!" as John disappeared into the trees, his green and brown plaid mingling with the colors of the thick-matted brush. "Every one of these stops loses us time, and . . ."

Jenny lifted her hand for silence, listening ahead, around, among the trees. Stretching out her senses, as wizards did. Smelling for horses. Listening for birds and rabbits that would fall silent at the presence of man. Feeling the air as a wealthy southern lady would feel silk with fingers white and sensitive, seeking a flaw, a thickened thread . . .

Arts that all of Jenny's life, of all the lives of her parents and grandparents, had meant the difference between life and death in the Winterlands.

In time she said, quietly, "I apologize if this seems to discount Commander Rocklys' defenses of the Realm, Lieutenant. But Skep Dhû is the boundary garrison in these parts, and beyond it, the bandit troops might still be at large. The great bands, Balgo-dorus Black-Knife's, or that of Gorgax the Red, number in hundreds. If I know them, they've been waiting all spring for a disruption such as a dragon would cause to raid the new manors while your captain's attention is elsewhere."

The lieutenant looked as if he would protest, then simply looked away. Jenny didn't know whether this was because she carried her own halberd and bow slung behind Moon Horse's saddle—women in the south did not customarily go armed, though there were some notable exceptions—or because she was a wizard, or for some other reason entirely. Many of the southern garrisons were devout worshipers of the Twelve Gods and regarded the Winterlands as a wilderness of heresy. In any case, disapproving silence reigned for something like half an hour—Gradely and the Darrow boys sitting their scrubby mounts ten or twelve paces away, scratching under their plaids and picking their noses—until John returned.

They camped that night in the ruins of what had been a small village or a large manor farm three centuries ago, when the Winterlands still supported such things. A messenger met them there with word that the dragon was in fact laired in the largest of the ravines east of the Skepping Hills—"The one with the oak wood along the ridge at its head, my lord"—and that

Commander Rocklys had personally led a squadron of fifty to meet them at Wormwood Ford.

"Gaw, leavin' who to garrison Cair Corflyn, if they get themselves munched up?" demanded John, horrified. "You get back now, son, and tell the lot of 'em to stay put. Do they think this is a bloody fox-hunt? The thing'll hear 'em coming ten miles off!"

The second night they made camp early, while light was still high in the sky, in a gully just west of the Skepping Hills. Beyond, the northern arm of the Wood of Wyr lay thick, a land of knotted trees and dark, slow-moving streams that flowed down out of the Gray Mountains, a land that had never been brought under the dominion of the Kings. Lying with John under their spread-out plaids, Jenny felt by his breathing that he did not sleep.

"I hate this," he said softly. "I'd hoped, after meeting Morkeleb—after speaking with him, touching him . . . hearing that voice of his speak in me mind—I'd hoped never to have to go after a dragon again in me life."

Jenny remembered the Dragon of Nast Wall. "No."

He sat up, his arms wrapped around his knees, and looked down at her, knowing how her own experience of the dragon-kind had touched her. "Don't hate me for it, Jen."

She shook her head, knowing that she so easily could. If she didn't understand about the Winterlands, and about what it was to be Thane. "No." John loved wolves, too, and studied every legend, every hunter's tale: He'd built a blind for himself so he could sit and watch them for hours at their howlings and their hunts. He'd drive them away sooner than kill them, if they preyed on the cattle. But he'd kill them without compunction if he had to.

He was Thane of the Winterlands, as his father had been. He could no more turn his back on a fight with a dragon than he could turn his back should a bandit chief, handsome and wise as the priests said gods were, start raiding the farms.

Jenny supposed that if a god were to come burning the fields and killing the stock, exposing the people to the perils of these terrible lands, John would read everything he could on the subject, pick up whatever weapon seemed appropriate, and try to take it on.

The fact that he'd never wanted any of this was beside the point.

An hour after midnight he rose for good, ate cold barley bannocks—none of them had been so foolish as to suggest cooking, within a few miles of a dragon's lair—and armed himself in his fighting doublet, his close-fitting helmet, and iron-backed gloves. Jenny knew that dragons were neither strictly nocturnal nor diurnal, but woke and slept like cats; still, she also knew that most dragons were aground and asleep in the hours just before dawn. She flung a little ravel of witchlight close to the ground, just enough for the horses to see the trail, and led the way toward the razor-backed hunch of the Skepping Hills and the oak-fringed ravine.

Mist swirled around the knees of the horses, floated like rags of silk among the heather. They left Borin on the edge of the heath, to watch from afar. Stretching her senses, Jenny felt everywhere the tingle and touch of magic. Had the dragon summoned these unseasonable mists for protection? she wondered. Would it sense her, sense them, if she raised a counterspell to send them away?

For a star-drake's body to be simply of one color, she thought, it must be either very young or very old, and if very old, its senses would fill the lands around, like still water that would carry the slightest ripple to its dreams. But this she did not feel. She had sensed Morkeleb's awareness when she and John had first ridden to do battle with the black dragon under the shadows of the Deep of Ylferdun . . . The red horns and spikes and tail seemed to argue for a young dragon anyway, but would a youngster be large enough to be mistaken for something a hundred feet long?

She touched John's wrist and whispered, though they were close enough now to the head of the ravine to need absolute silence, "John, wait. There's something wrong."

The ravine before them was a drift of gray mist. His spectacles, framed by his helmet, glinted like the eyes of an enormous moth. In a hunter's whisper, he asked, "Can it hear us? Feel us?"

"I don't know. But I don't . . . I don't feel it. At all."

He tilted his head, inquiring.

"I don't know. Get ready to run or to charge."

Then she reached out with her mind, her will, her dragon-heart and dragon-spells, and tore the mists from the ravine in a single fierce swirl of chilling wind.

The slice and flash of early light blinked on metal in the oak woods above the ravine, and a second later something came roaring and flapping up from between the hills: green, red-horned, bat-winged, snake-headed, serpentine tail tipped with something that looked like a gargantuan crimson arrowhead and absolutely unlike any dragon Jenny had ever seen outside the illuminations of John's old books. John said, "Bugger all!" and Jenny yelled, "John, look out, it's an illusion . . . !"

Unnecessarily, for John was turning already, sword drawn, spurring toward the nearest cover. Jenny followed, flinging behind her a blast and hammer of fire-spells, ripping up from the heather between them and the riders that galloped out of the woods.

Bandits. The illusory dragon dissolved in midair the moment it was clear that neither John nor Jenny was distracted by its presence, and the bearded attackers in makeshift panoplies of hunting leathers and stolen mail converged on the cut overhang of a streambank that provided the only defensible ground in sight.

Jenny followed the fire-spells with a sweeping Word of Poor Aim, and to her shock felt counterspells whirl and clutch at her. Beside her, John cursed and staggered as an arrowhead slashed his thigh. She felt fire-spells in the air around them and breathed Words of Limitation and counterspells herself, distracting her mind from her own magics. Behind the spells she felt the mind of the wizard: an impression of untaught power, of crude talent without training, of enormous strength. She felt stunned, as if she'd walked into a wall in darkness.

John cursed again and nocked the arrows he'd pulled down with him when he'd dismounted; at least, thought Jenny, casting her mind to the head of the stream that the outlaws would have to cross to get at them, their attackers could only come at them from two sides. She tried to call back the mists, to make them work for her and John as they'd concealed the bandits before, but again the counterspells of the other wizard twisted and grabbed at her mind. Fire in the heather, at the same time damping the fire-spells that filled the cut under the bank with smoke; spells of breaking and damage to bowstrings and arrows . . .

And then the bandits were on them. Illusion, distraction—Jenny called them into being, worked them on the filthy, scarred, furious men who waded through the rising stream. Swords, pikes, the hammering rain of slung stones, some of which veered aside with her warding-spells, some of which punched through them as if they had not been there. A man would stop, staring about him in confusion and horror—Jenny's spells of flaring lights, of armed warriors around herself and John taking effect . . . John's sword, or Jenny's halberd, would slash into his flesh. But as many times as not the man would spring back with a cry, seeing clearly, and Jenny would feel on her mind the cold grip of the other mage's counterspell. Illusion, too, she felt, for there were bandits who simply dissolved as the illusion of the dragon had dissolved . . .

And through it all she thought, *The bandits have a wizard! The bandits have a wizard with them!*

In John's words: *Bugger, bugger, bugger.*

Jenny didn't know how long they held them off. Certainly not much longer than it would take to hard-boil an egg, though it seemed far longer. Still, the sun had just cleared the Skepping Hills when she and John first saw the bandits, and when the blare of trumpets sliced golden through the ruckus and Commander Rocklys and her troops rode out of the hills in a ragged line, the shadows hadn't shortened by more than a foot. Jenny felt the other wizard's spells reach out toward the crimson troopers and threw her own power to intercept them, shattering whatever illusions the rescuers would have seen and attacked. Rocklys, standing in her stirrups, drew rein and fired into the thick of the outlaw horde; Jenny saw one of the leaders fall. Then a great voice bellowed, "Out of it, men!" and near the head of the ravine a tall man sprang up on a boulder, massive and black-bearded, like a great dirty bear.

John said, "Curse," and Rocklys, whipping another arrow to her short black southern bow, got off a shot at him. But the arrow went wide—Jenny felt the Word that struck it aside—and then battle surged around them, mist and smoke rising out of the ground like dust from a beaten rug. The spells she'd called onto the stream were working now and the water rushed in furious spate, sweeping men off their feet, the water splashing icy on John's boots and soaking the hem of Jenny's skirt. Then the bandits fled; Rocklys and her men in pursuit.

"Curse it," said John. "Balgodorus Black-Knife, damn his tripes, and they had a wizard with 'em, didn't they, love?" He leaned against the clay wall of the bank, panting; Jenny pressed her hand against his thigh, where the first arrowhead had cut, but felt no poison in the wound.

"Somebody who knew enough about dragon-slaying to know we'd have to attack it alone, together."

"Maggots fester it—ow!" he added, as Jenny applied a rough bandage to the wound. "Anybody'd know that who's heard me talk about it, or talked to someone who had. Anyway, it wasn't me they was after, love." He reached down and touched her face. "It was you."

She looked up, filthy with sweat and soot, her dark hair unraveled: a thin small brown woman of forty-five, flushed—she was annoyed to note—with yet another rise of inner heat. She sent it away, exasperated at the untimeliness and the reminder of her age.

"Me?" She got to her feet. The rush of the stream was dying as quickly as it had risen. Bandits slain by John's sword, or her halberd, or by the arrows of Rocklys' men, lay where the water had washed them.

"You're the only mage in the Winterlands." John tucked up a wet straggle of her hair into a half-collapsed braid, broke off a twig from a nearby laurel bush and worked it in like a hairpin to hold it in place. "In the whole of the King's Realm, for all I know. Gar"—that was the Regent—"told me he's been trying to find wizards in Bel and Greenhythe and all around the Realm, and hasn't located a one, bar a couple of gnomes. So if a bandit like Balgodorus Black-Knife's got a wizard in his troop, and we have none . . ."

"We'd have been in a lot of trouble," Jenny said softly, "had this ambush succeeded."

"And it might have," mused John, "if their boy—"

"Girl."

"Eh?"

"Their mage is a woman. I'm almost certain of it."

He sniffed. "Girl, then. If their girl had known the first thing about star-drakes, beyond that they have wings and long tails, you might not have twigged soon enough to keep us out of the jaws of the trap. Which goes to demonstrate the value of a classical education . . ."

Commander Rocklys returned in a clatter of hooves, Borin at her side. "Are you all right?" She sprang down from her tall bronze-bay warhorse, a lanky powerful woman of thirty, gold-stamped boots spattered with mud and gore. "We were saddled and ready to ride to your help with the dragon when Borin charged into camp shouting you were being ambushed."

"The dragon was a hoax," John said briefly. He wiped a gout of blood from his cheekbone and scrubbed his gloved fingers with the end of his plaid. "Better if it had been a real drake than what's really going on."

Rocklys of Galyon listened, arms folded, to his account. It was a rare woman, Jenny knew, who could get men to follow her into combat; on the whole, most soldiers knew of women only what they saw of their victims during the sack of farmsteads or towns, or what they learned from the camp whores. Some, like John, were willing to learn different. Others had to be strenuously taught. Though the women soldiers Jenny had met—mostly bandits—tended to gang together to protect one another in the war camps, a woman commander as a rule had to be large and strong enough to take on and beat a good percentage of the men under her command.

Rocklys of the House of Uwanë was such a woman. The royal house of Bel was a tall one, and she was easily John's nearly six-foot height, with powerful arms and shoulders that could only have been achieved by the most strenuous physical training. As a cousin of the King, Jenny guessed she would have been granted a position as second-in-command or a captaincy of royal guards regardless, but it was clear by the set of her square chin that an honorary post was not what she wanted.

For the rest, she was fair-haired, like her cousin the Regent Gareth—though the last time Jenny had seen Gareth, two years ago, he'd still affected a dandy's habit of dyeing portions of his hair blue or pink or whatever the fashionable shade was that year. Her eyes, like Gareth's, were a light, cold gray. She neither interrupted nor reacted to John's tale, only stood with the slight breezes moving the gold tassels on her sword-belt and on the red wool oversleeves that covered her linen shirt. At the end of his recital she said, "Damn it." Her voice was a sort of husky growl, and Jenny guessed she'd early acquired the habit of deepening it. "If I'd known there was a wizard with them I'd never have called off the men so soon. You're sure?"

"I'm sure." Jenny stepped up beside John. "Completely aside from the green dragon, which was sheer illusion—only created to lure John and me—I could feel this mage's mind, her power, with every spell I tried to cast. There's a wizard with Balgodorus, and a strong one."

"*Damn* it." Rocklys' mouth hardened, and for a moment Jenny saw a genuine fury in her eyes. Then they shifted, thoughtful, considering the two people before her: the bloodied and shabby Dragonsbane and the Witch of Frost Fell. Jenny knew the look in her eyes, for she'd seen it often in John's. The look of a commander, considering the tools she has and the job that needs to be done.

"Lady Jenny," she said. "Lord John."

"Now we're in trouble." John looked up from polishing his spectacles on his shirt. "Anytime anyone comes to me and says . . ." He shifted into an imitation of that of the Mayor of Far West Riding, or one of the councilmen of Wrynde, when those worthies would come to the Hold asking him to kill wolves or deal with bandits, " 'Lord John'—or worse, 'Your lordship.' "

Commander Rocklys, who didn't have much of a sense of humor, frowned. "But we are in trouble," she said. "And we shall be in far worse trouble should Balgodorus Black-Knife continue at large, with a witch . . ." She hesitated—she'd used a southern word for the mageborn that had pejorative connotations of evil and slyness—and politely changed it. ". . . with a wizard in his band. Surely you agree."

"And you want our Jen to go after 'em."

Rocklys looked a little surprised to find her logic so readily followed. As if, thought Jenny, the necessity for her to pursue the renegade mage was not obvious to all. "For the good of all the Winterlands, you must agree."

John glanced at Jenny, who nodded slightly. He sighed and said, "Aye." The good of all the Winterlands had ruled his life for twenty-two years, since his father's death. Even before that, when as his father's only son he had been torn from his books and his music and his tinkerings with pulleys and steam, and had a sword thrust into his hand.

Four years ago it had been the good of all the Winterlands that took him south, to barter his body and bones in the fight against Morkeleb the Black, so the King would in return send troops to garrison those lost territories and bring them again under the rule of law.

"Aye, love, you'd best go. God knows if you don't we'll only have 'em besiegin' the Hold in the end."

"Good." Rocklys nodded briskly, though she still looked vexed. "I've already sent one of the men back to Skep Dhû, with orders to outfit a pack-train, Lady Jenny; you'll ride with twenty-five of my men here."

"Twenty-five?" said John. "There were at least twenty in the band that attacked us, and rumor has it Balgodorus commands hundreds these days."

Rocklys shook her head. "My scouts report no more than forty. Untrained men at that, scum and outlaws, no match for disciplined troops.

"If at all possible," she went on, "bring the woman back alive. The Realm needs mages, Lady Jenny. You know that, you and I have talked of this before. It is only the most appalling prejudice that has caused wizardry to fall into disrepute, so that the Lines of teaching died out or went underground. I am told the gnomes have wizards: That alone should have convinced my uncle and his predecessors to foster, rather than forbid, the study of those arts. Instead, what did they do? Simply crippled themselves, so that four years ago when an evil mage like the Lady Zyerne rose up, no one was prepared to deal with her. That situation cannot be allowed to repeat itself. Yes, Geryon?"

She turned as an orderly spoke to her; John put his hands on Jenny's shoulders.

"Will you be all right?" she asked him, and he bent to kiss her lips. She tasted blood on his, and sweat and dirt; he must have tasted the same.

"Who, me? With Muffle and Ian and me aunties to defend the Hold if we're attacked? Nothing to it." Deadpan, he propped his spectacles more firmly onto the bridge of his long nose. "Shall I send a messenger after you with your good shoes and a couple of silk dresses just in case you want a change?"

"I'll manage with what I have," said Jenny gravely. "Borin was right, you know, " she added. "The garrisons may be a nuisance, and the farmers may grumble about the extra taxes, but there hasn't been a major bandit attack since their coming. I'll scry you, and the Hold, in my crystal every night—a pity Ian's powers haven't grown strong enough yet for him to learn to speak with me through a crystal or through fire. But he's a fair healer already. And if there's trouble . . ." She raised her hand, touched the long hair where it straggled, pointy with sweat, over his bruised face. "Braid a red ribbon into your hair. I'll see it when I call your image. If I can, I'll return to you."

John caught her hand as she would have lowered it and kissed her dirty fingers; and she drew down his in return, pressed her lips to the scruffy leather, the battered chain-mail of his glove. Skaff Gradely and the Darrow boys had come up by this time, arguing all the way with Borin's fellow messengers, with the spare horses and the baggage, so there was little to stay for.

"Borin will ride with you," Commander Rocklys said, "and his fellows. Send one of them to me when you've come up with these bandits and their wizard. Let us know where you are and if you need troops. I'll dispatch as many as I can, as swiftly as I can. And bring the woman alive, at whatever the cost. We'll make it worth her while to pledge her services to the Realm."

"Even so." Jenny swung to Moon Horse's saddle again and adjusted her halberd and bow. She wondered what reward she herself would consider "worth her while" to betray John, to turn against him, to ride with his foes . . .

Or, she thought, as the twenty-five picked pursuers formed up around her, *to leave him and our children and the folk of Alyn Hold to their own devices, when I know there's a bandit wizard abroad in the lands?*

The good of all the Winterlands, maybe.

The good of the Realm, which John considered his first and greatest loyalty.

She lifted her hand to him as she and the men rode off. A little later, as they crested the rise above the ravine and approached the oak woods into which the bandits had fled, she looked back to see Commander Rocklys marshaling her forces to ride back to Cair Corflyn, the garrison on the banks of the Black River, which was the headquarters for the whole network of new manors and forts. John's doing, those garrisons, she thought. The protection he had bought with the blood he'd shed, dragon-fighting four years ago. His reward.

As the dragon-magic in her veins was hers.

John himself stood, a small tatty black figure on the high ground above the stream, watching her. She lifted her hand again to him, and his spectacles flashed like mirrors as he waved good-bye. The wasting moon still stood above the moors to the west, a pale crescent like a slice of cheese.

Less than three weeks later, before that moon waxed again to its full, a real dragon descended on the farms near Alyn Hold.

CHAPTER THREE

"A hundred feet long it was, my lord." Deke Brown from the Lone Steadings, a man John had known all his life, folded his hands together before his knees and leaned forward from the library chair in the flicker of the candlelight. His face was bruised, and there was a running burn on his forehead, the kind John knew was made by a droplet of the flaming acid that dragons spit. "Blue it was, but like as if it had gold flowers spread all over it, and golden wings, and the horns of it all black and white stripes, and maned like a lion. It had three of the cows, and I bare got April and the babies out'n the house and in the root cellar in time."

In the silence John was very conscious of the hoarseness of the man's breathing, and of the thumping of his own heart.

No illusion this time. Or a damn good one if it was.

Jenny, wherever you are, I need you. I can't handle this alone.

"I heard down in the village that Ned Wooley was up here yesterday, from Great Toby." Brown spoke diffidently, trying to word it without sounding accusing. "They said this thing killed his horse and his mule on the road to the Bottom Farms, and near as check killed him."

John said, "Aye." He swallowed hard, feeling very cold inside. "We've been makin' up the poisons and gettin' ready to go all day. You didn't happen to see which way it went?"

"I didn't, no, my lord. I was that done up about the cows. They're all we've got. But April says it went off northwest. She says to tell you she saw it circling above Cair Dhû."

"You give April a kiss for me." He knew the ruins of the old watchtower, every ditch, bank, and clump of broken masonry; he'd played there as a child, risking life and soul because blood-

26

devils haunted them at certain times of the year. He'd hunted rabbits there, too, and hidden from his father. *At least I'll be fighting it on familiar ground.* "Get Cousin Dilly to give you something from the kitchen, you look fagged out. I'll be going there in the morning."

He drew a deep breath, trying to put the thought of the dragon from his mind. "We'll see about getting you another cow. One of the Red Shaggies is heavy with calf; I could probably let you have the both of them. Clivy writes that red cows give more wholesome milk that's higher in butter, but I've never measured—still, it's the best I can do. We'll talk about it when I get back."

If I get back.

Brown disappeared down the tower stair.

Jenny, I need you.

Behind him a clock chimed the hour, amid a great parade of mechanical lions, elephants, trumpeters, and flying swans. The moon turned its phases, and an allegorical representation of Good thumped Evil repeatedly over the head with a golden mallet. John watched the show with his usual grave delight, then got up and consulted the water-clock that gurgled quietly in a corner of the study.

Not even close.

Shaking his head regretfully, he descended the tower stair.

He passed the kitchen, where Dilly, Rowan, and Jane clustered around Deke Brown, exclaiming over his few bruises and filling him in on what had befallen Ned Wooley—"A hundred feet long, it was, and breathed green fire . . ."

Ian was in the old barracks court, the firelight under the cauldrons gleaming on the sweat that sheathed his bare arms. Tawny light tongued Jenny's red and black poison pots, carefully stoppered and arranged along a wall out of all possible chance of being tripped over, broken, or gotten into by anything or anyone. The fumes burned John's eyes. It was all a repeat of the scene three weeks ago.

He hoped to hell the stuff would work.

"Father." The boy laid his stirring stick down and crossed the broken and weedy pavement toward him. Muffle and Adric put down their loads of wood and followed, stripped, like Ian, to their breeches, boots, and knitted singlets in the heat; clothed like Ian in sweat. "That messenger wasn't . . . ?"

"Deke Brown. It hit his farm."

"Devils bugger it," Muffle said. He hitched his belt under the muscled roll of his huge belly. "April and the children . . . ?"

"Are fine. April saw the thing to ground at Cair Dhû."

"Good for April." John's half-brother regarded him for a moment, his thick, red-stubbled face eerily like their father's, trying to read his thoughts. "No word from Jenny?"

John shook his head, his own face ungiving: a holdover, he supposed, from growing up with his father's notions about what a man and the Lord of Alyn Hold must and must not feel. It would never have occurred to him to beat Adric for showing fear—not that Adric had the slightest concept of what the word meant. And Ian . . .

Mageborn children feared different things.

"Wherever she is, she can't come." The bloody light darkened the red ribbon he'd braided yesterday into his hair. *I'll scry every evening in my crystal* . . . "Or she can't come in time."

"I could go to the house on Frost Fell." Ian wiped his face with the back of his arm. "Mother's books—old Caerdinn has to have written down how to do . . ." he hesitated, "how to do death-spells."

"No." John had thought of that yesterday.

"I don't think these poisons are going to work against a dragon unless there are fresh death-spells put into their making." Returning from the false alarm and ambush, John had cleansed the harpoons with water and with fire, as Jenny had instructed him to do: a necessary precaution given little Mag's eerie facility with locks, bolts, and anything else she was particularly not supposed to get into. Jenny, he knew, was conscientious about the Limitations she put on the death-spells. It had never occurred to either of them that they'd be needed again so soon. "We need to put death-spells on the harpoons as well."

"No." John had thought of that, too. "I don't want you touching such stuff."

"But *we* don't want *you* to die!" protested Adric reasonably.

Muffle raised his brows and looked away in a fashion that said, *The boy's got a point.*

"Mother uses them."

"You're twelve years old, Ian." John swallowed hard, hoping by all the gods that his own fear didn't show. "Leavin' out the fact that certain spells can be too strong for an inexperienced mage to wield—"

"I'm not inexperienced."

"—you haven't learned near all there is to know about Limitations, and I for one don't want to end up havin' one of me feet fall off from leprosy in the middle of the fight because you got a word wrong."

Surprised into laughter, Ian looked quickly aside, mouth pursed to prevent it. Like many boys he had the disapproving air of one who feels that laughter is not the appropriate response to facing death, especially not for one's father. John had suspected for some time that both his sons regarded him as frivolous.

"Now, get back to stirring," he ordered. "Is that stuff settin' up at all like it's supposed to? Adric, as long as you're down here you might as well stir that other cauldron, but for God's sake put gloves on . . . We've got a long night." He stripped off his old red doublet and his shirt and hung both on pegs on the work shed wall. The smell of summer hay from the fields beyond the Hold filled the night. Though midnight lay only a few hours off, the sky still glowed with light. As he pulled on his gloves, John watched them all in the firelit court: his sons, his brother—his aunts, Jane and Rowe and Hol, and Cousin Dilly, coming down with gingerwater and trying to tell Adric it was time for him to go to bed. Seeing them as Jenny would be seeing them, wherever the hell she was, gazing into her crystal. Rowe with her long untidy braids of graying red and Dilly peering shortsightedly at Muffle, and all of them chatting like a nest of magpies—the real rulers, if the truth be told, of Alyn Hold.

She has to know what all this means. He closed his eyes, desperately willing that Jenny be on her way. *I'm sorry. I waited as long as I could.*

Teltrevir, heliotrope . . . His mind echoed the fragments of the old dragon-list. *Centhwevir is blue knotted with gold. Nymr blue violet-crowned, Glammring Gold-Horns bright as emeralds . . .* Scraps of information and old learning:

Maggots from meat, weevils from rye,
Dragons from stars in an empty sky.
And, *Save a dragon, slave a dragon.*

Secondhand accounts, most of them a mash of broken half-volumes; notes of legends and granny rhymes; jumbled ballads that Gareth collected and sent copies of. Everything left of learning in the Winterlands, after the King's armies had abandoned them to bandits, Iceriders, cold, and plague. He'd gathered them painfully from ruins, collated them in those few moments between fighting for his own life and the lives of those who depended on him . . . Secondhand accounts and the speculations of scholars who'd never come closer to a dragon than the sites of old slayings, or a nervously cursory inspection of torn-up, blood-soaked, acid-burned ground.

Something in there might save his life, but he didn't know what.

Antara Warlady was supposed to have gotten right up next to the Worm of Wevir by wrapping herself in a fresh-flayed pig hide, according to the oldest Drymarch version of her tale; Grimonious Grimblade had supposedly put out live lambs as bait.

Alkmar the Godborn had been killed by the third dragon he fought.

Selkythar of golden curls and sword of sunlight flashing,
Seeking meed of glory through the dragon's talons lashing.
Cried he, "Strike again, foul worm, my bloody blade is slashing . . ."

John shook his head. He'd never sought a meed of glory in his life, and if he ever decided to start, it wouldn't be by riding smack up a long hill in open daylight as Selkythar had reportedly done, armed with only a sword—well, a shield, too, as if a shield ever did any good against a thirty-foot hellstorm of spitting acid and whirling spikes.

"The boy may be right." Muffle's voice pulled him out of his memories of the Dragon of Wyr, of Morkeleb's black talons sweeping down at him from darkness . . .

John dipped the harpoon he held into the cauldron and watched the liquid drip off the iron, thin as water.

"Stuff ain't thickenin' up," he sighed. "Maybe I should get Auntie Jane back here. Her gravies always set."

Muffle caught his arm. "Be serious, son."

"Why?" John rested the harpoon's spines on the vat's edge and coughed in the smoke. "I may be dead twenty-four hours from now."

"So you may," replied the blacksmith softly, and glanced across at Ian in the amber glare. "And what then? Four years ago you bargained with the King to send garrisons. Well, they've been gie helpful, but you know there's a price. If you die, d'you think your boys are going to be let to inherit? In the south they've laws against wizards holding property or power, and Adric's but eight. You think the King's council's going to let a witch be Regent of Wyr? Especially if they think they can get tax money by ruling here themselves?"

"I'm the King's subject." John stepped back from the fire, hell-mouth hot on his bare arms. "And the King's servant, and the Regent's me friend. What're you askin'? That I not fight this drake?"

"I'm asking that you let Ian do what he's asked to do."

"No."

Muffle pursed his lips, which made him look astoundingly like their father. Except, thought John, that their father had never let things stop with pursed lips, nor would he have reacted to *No* with that simple grimace. The last time John had said a flat-out *No* to old Lord Aver, at the age of twelve, he'd been lucky his collarbone had set straight.

"In the village they say the boy's good. He goes over those magic-books in your library like you go over the ones on steam and smokes and old machines. He knows enough . . ."

"No," said John. And then, seeing the doubt, the fear for him in the fat man's small brown eyes, he said, "There's things a boy his years shouldn't know about. Not so soon."

"Things you'd put your life at risk—your people at risk—to spare him?"

John thought about them, those things Jenny had told him lay in old Caerdinn's crumbling books. Things he'd read in the books that had been part of his bargain with Prince Gareth to fight the Dragon of Nast Wall. Things he read in Jenny's silence when he surprised her sometimes in her own small study, studying in the deep of night.

He said, "Aye." And saw the shift in Muffle's eyes.

"People hereabouts know the magic Jen does for them." John picked up the harpoon and turned the shaft in his hands. "Or what old Caerdinn did. Birthin' babies, and keepin' the mice out of the barns in a bad year, or maybe buyin' an hour on the harvest when a storm's coming in. Those that remember me mother are mostly dead." He glanced up at Muffle over the rims of his spectacles. "And anyway, by what I hear from our aunties, me mother never did the worst she could have done."

Except maybe only once or twice, he thought, and pushed those barely coherent recollections from his mind.

"People here don't know what magic really is," John went on. "They haven't seen what it can do, and they haven't seen what it can do to those that do it. You always pay for it somehow, and sometimes other people besides you do the payin'. Gaw," he added, turning back to the cauldron and dipping the harpoon once more, "this's blashier than Cousin Rowanberry's tea. Let's put some flour in it, see if we can get it thick enough to do us some good."

Ian's heart beat hard as he kicked his scrubby pony to a gallop up Toadback Hill.

Death-spells.

And the dragon.

He'd always hated the harpoons with which his father had killed the Dragon of Wyr, two years before he was born. He had instinctively avoided the cupboard in his father's cluttered study in which they were locked. If he touched the wood he could feel them, even before he realized that he had magic in him. Sometimes he dreamed about them, each barbed and pronged shaft of iron its own ugly entity, whispering in the darkness about pain and cold and giving up.

His mother had wrought well.

Ian shivered.

For the first eight years of Ian's life he had only seen her now and then, for she'd lived alone with her cats on the Fell, coming to be with his father at the Hold for a few days together. She had told him later—when his own powers had crossed through that wall from dreaming to daytime reality—that in those days her powers were small. She had kept herself apart to study and meditate, to work on what little she had. There was only so much time in her life to give.

And then had come the Dragon of Nast Wall.

His parents had gone away to the south together to fight it, along with the messenger who'd fetched them, a gawky near-sighted boy in spectacles. That boy had turned out to be Prince Gareth, later Regent for the ailing King Uriens of Belmarie. At that time Ian had accepted without question that his father could easily slay a dragon and hadn't been particularly concerned. As if to confirm him in this opinion, his parents had returned more or less unharmed, and he didn't learn until much later how close both had come to not returning at all.

After that, Jenny had lived at the Hold. But she still went sometimes to meditate in the stone house on Frost Fell, and it was there that she'd begun to teach Ian, away from the Hold's distractions. In that quiet house he did not need to be a brother or a nephew or a father's firstborn son.

Even had Ian not been mageborn and able to see easily in the clear blue darkness, he could have followed the path that led away from the village fields over Toadback Hill. Ruins dotted the far slope, one of the many vanished towns that spoke of what the Winterlands had been and had become. Shattered walls, slumped puddles where wells had been, all were nearly drowned now in the mists that rose from the cranberry bog.

From the hill crest he looked back and saw his father and his uncle by the village gates, talking with Peg the Gatekeeper. The gates were squat and solid, built up of rubble filched from the broken town. Lanterns burned over them, but Ian did not need those dim yellow smudges to see how his father turned in Battle-hammer's saddle, searching the formless swell of the hills, gesturing as he spoke.

He knows I'm gone. Ian felt a stab of guilt. He'd laid a word on Peg, causing her to rise from her bed in the turret and lower the drawbridge to let him pass. This cantrip wasn't something his mother had taught him, but he'd learned it from one of Caerdinn's books and had experimented, mostly on the unsuspecting

Adric. He knew perfectly well that such magic was an act of betrayal, of violation, and he squirmed with shame every time he did it, but as a wizard, he felt driven to learn.

He was glad he'd practiced it, now.

It was still too dark to distinguish his pony's hoofprints in the mud. In any case, he guessed his father had no time to search. Nor had he, Ian, any to linger. He shrugged his old jacket closer around him and put his pony to a fast trot through the battered walls, and the rags of bog mist swallowed them.

Death-spells. His palms grew clammy at the thought. In a corner of his mind he knew perfectly well that he might not have the strength to wield them, certainly not to wield the dreadful power he sensed whenever he touched the harpoons. But he could think of no other way to help. Since the coming of that first word of the dragon yesterday, he'd tried desperately to make contact with his mother in the ways she'd told him wizards could, by looking into fire or water or chips of ensorcelled crystal or glass. But he had seen only confusing images of trees, and once a moss-covered standing stone, and water glimmering in the moon's waxing light.

Remember the Limitations, he told himself, ticking over his mother's instructions in his mind. *And gather up the power circles afterward and disperse them. Don't work in a house. Don't work near water . . .*

There had to be something in the house at Frost Fell that he could use to save his father's life.

Frost Fell was a hard gray skull of granite, rising nearly two hundred feet above waterlogged bottomlands—enough to be free of the mosquitoes that made the summers of Winterlands such a horror. In spring, huge poppies grew there, and in fall, yellow daisies. Most of the other fells were barren of anything but heather and gorse, but Frost Fell boasted a modest pocket of soil at its top, where centuries ago some hardy crofter had cultivated oats. These days it was his mother's garden, circled like the house in wardings and wyrd-lines. Ian reviewed these in his mind, hoping he'd be able to get past the gate, hoping he could open the doors. *Triangle, triangle, rune of the Eye . . .* The last two times he'd been there she'd simply stood back and let him do it, so there was a chance . . .

Light burned in the house.

She's back! Exultation, and blinding relief. A dim glow of candle flame, like a stain on the blue bulk of shadow. The rosy flicker of hearth-fire glimpsed through half-open doors. He wrapped the pony's rein hastily around the gate, ran up the path. *She's back, she'll be able to help!*

It wasn't until his foot was on the step that he thought, *If it was Mother, she'd have ridden at once to the Hold.*

And at that moment, he saw something bright on the step.

He stopped and knelt to look at it. Like a seashell wrought of glass, thin as a bubble, broken at one end. A little beyond the broken end lay what appeared to be a blob of quicksilver, glistening on the wet stone in the reflected candle-glow.

"Go ahead." A deep, friendly voice spoke from within the house. "It's all right to touch it. It's perfectly safe."

Looking up Ian saw a man sitting by his mother's hearth, a man he'd never seen before. Big and square and pleasant-faced, he was clothed like the southerners who came from the King's court, in a short close coat of quilted violet silk lined with fur, and a fur-lined silk cap embroidered with violets. Expensive boots sheathed his calves and a pair of black kid gloves lay across his knee, and in his pale fingers he turned a jewel over and over, a sapphire dark as the sea. Ian knew he had to be a wizard, because he was in the house, but he asked, "Are you a mage, sir?"

"I am that." The man smiled again and gestured with his finger to the frail glass shell, the bead of quicksilver on the step. "And I'm here to help you, Ian. Bring that to me, if you would, my boy."

Ian reached toward it and hesitated, for he thought the quicksilver moved a little on the stone of the step. For an instant he had the impression that there were eyes within it, looking up at him. Bright small eyes, like a lizard or a crab. That it had its own name, and moreover that it knew his. But a moment later he thought, *It has to be just the light.* He carefully scooped the thing up in his hand.

CHAPTER FOUR

Alkmar the Godborn, greatest of the heroes of antiquity (it was said), slew two dragons while serving the King of Ernine—though according to Prince Gareth there was a late Imperteng version of the legend that said four—using a lasso made of chain and an iron spear heated red-hot, which he threw down each dragon's throat. *Must have been on a cable,* thought John, though of course Alkmar had been seven and a half feet tall, thewed like an ox, and presumably had a lot of time to spend at throwing practice.

For someone a thumb's breadth under six feet and thewed like a thirty-eight-year-old man who's spent most of his life riding boundary in cold weather, other strategies would probably be required.

John Aversin flexed his shoulders and listened, hoping to hell Sergeant Muffle and the spare horses were keeping absolutely quiet in the base camp at Deep Beck. Was three and a half miles far enough?

Morning stillness lay on the folded world of heather and stone, broken only by the hum of mosquitoes and bees. Even the creak of his stirrup leather seemed deafening, and the dry swish of Battlehammer's tail.

Interesting that the greatest hero of legend was described as throwing something at the dragon, rather than nobly slicing its head off with a single blow of his mighty sword and to hell with Selkythar and Antara Warlady and Grimonious Grimblade, thank you very much.

Battlehammer snuffled and flattened his ears. Though the

wind blew south off the ruins of Cair Dhû, if the stallion could smell the dragon from here, could the dragon smell them?

Or hear them, in the utter absence of the raucous dawn chitter of birds?

Dragonsbane. He was the one who was supposed to know all this.

John flexed his hands. The walls of the gorge still protected him, and the purl of the stream might conceivably cover the clack of Battlehammer's hooves. The problem with dragons was that, mostly, nobody knew what worked.

He slid from the saddle, checked the girths, checked the harpoons in their holsters. Lifted each of the warhorse's four feet to make sure he hadn't picked up a stone. *That's all I'd need.* While he did this, in his mind he reviewed the ruins. He'd checked them a few months ago; there couldn't have been much change. The dragon would be lairing in the crypt.

He'd have to catch it there, before it got into the air.

Stair, hall, doorway, doorway . . . How fast did dragons move? Morkeleb had come out of the dark of Ylferdun Deep's great markethall like a snake striking. Broken walls, the drop of a slope, everything tangled with heather and fallen masonry. Ditches invisible where weeds grew across them . . . *What a place for a gallop.* At least he knew the ground.

He settled his iron cap tighter on his head, the red ribbon still fluttering in his hair. *Jen, I'm in trouble, I need you, come at once.*

Though he supposed if she scried him now she'd get the idea without the ribbon.

He propped his spectacles again, dropped his hand back to touch the first of the harpoons in their holsters, and took a deep breath.

"*Strike again, foul worm,*" he whispered, and drove in his heels.

At five hundred yards, they knew you were coming, upwind, downwind, dark or storm. That seemed to be the consensus of the ballads. Maybe more than five hundred. Maybe a lot more.

Battlehammer hit open ground at a dead gallop and John watched the walls pour toward him: broken stone, stringers of outwalls, craggy pine and dwarf willow spreading around the ground. Everything broken now and burned with dragon-acid and the poisons of its breath. He saw it in his mind, slithering up those shattered stairways. A hundred feet long . . . *God of the Earth, let them be wrong about that . . .*

It was there in the riven gate. *Centhwevir is blue knotted with gold.* Fifty feet in front of him, rising on long hind legs to swing that birdlike head. Blue as gentian, blue as lapis and morning glories, iridescent blue as the summer sea all stitched and patched and flourished with buttercup yellow, and eyes like twin molten opals, gold as ancient glass. The beauty of it stopped his breath as his hand went back, closed around the nearest harpoon, knowing he was too far yet for a throw and thinking, *Sixty feet if it's an inch . . .*

Centhwevir is blue knotted with gold.

The thing came under the gate and the wings opened and John threw: arm, back, thighs, every muscle he possessed. The harpoon struck in the pink hollow beneath the right wing where the skin was delicate as velvet, and he was reining Battlehammer hard away and angling for distance, catching up another weapon, swinging to throw for the mouth.

Alkmar, if you're there among the gods, I could use the help . . .

That one missed as the snakelike neck struck at him, huge narrow head framed in its protective mane of black and white, primrose and cyan. Battlehammer screamed and fell and rolled, lifted from his feet by the hard counterswipe of the dragon's tail, and John kicked free of the stirrups and tumbled almost by instinct. Yellow-green acid slapped the heather at his feet, the stiff brush bursting into flame.

Battlehammer. He could hear the horse scream again in pain but didn't dare turn to look, only scooped up four harpoons from the ground—as many as he could reach—and ran in.

Keep it under the gate. Keep it under the gate. If it stays on the ground, you've a chance.

The star-drake struck at him again, head and tail, spitting acid that ignited in the air. John flung himself under the shelter of a broken wall, then rolled clear, coming in close, fast, striking up at the rippling wall of blue-and-golden spikes. The heather around them blazed, smoke searing his eyes. The dragon snapped, slashed, drove him back, slithered free of the confining walls. He struck with the harpoon, trying to hold it; talons like gold-bladed daggers snagged his leg, hurling him off balance. He struck up with the harpoon again as the head came down at him, teeth like dripping chisels, the spattering sear of blood.

Blind hacking, heat, fighting to get free. Once he fell and rolled into an old defensive ditch only seconds before the spiked knob at the end of the dragon's tail smote the earth. He was aware he was hurt and bleeding badly and didn't know when or how it had happened. Only pain and the fact that he couldn't breathe. He drove in a second harpoon, and a third, and then there was that great terrible leathery crack of wings, and he saw sunlight through the golden membranes, shining crimson veins, as the dragon lifted, lifted weightless as a blown leaf. Desperate, John flung himself for the shelter of a fallen wall and rather to his surprise found he couldn't stand up.

Buggery damn.

He threw himself under the stone a second before the acid drench of fire poured on top of him: smoke and suffocation, poison. Mind clouded, he fought and wriggled farther into the crack, tallying where he could go from here, how he could get away and wait for the poison to work. Would the flour he'd used to thicken it keep it from doing its job? Pain in his calf and thigh and dizzying weakness told him where he'd been slashed. He fumbled from his pocket one of Jenny's silk scarves, twisted the tourniquet around his leg, and then fire, acid, poison streamed down again on the stone above him. Smoke. Heat.

It'll tear the stone away from the top . . .

He had a belt-ax and pulled it free, cut at the claws that ripped down through the stone and roots above his head. A huge five-fingered hand, eighteen inches across, and he struck at it with all his strength, the blood that exploded out scorching his face. Above him, above the protecting stones, he heard Centhwevir scream, and the stones caved on top of him, struck by that monstrous tail.

Damn it, with all that poison in you, you should at least be feeling poorly by now!

The wall above him gave way. Darkness, pain, fire devouring his bleeding flesh.

Stillness.

His hold on consciousness slipped, as if he clung to rock above an abyss. He knew what lay in that abyss and didn't want to look down.

Ian's face, wreathed in woodsmoke and poison fumes, glistening with tears. He couldn't imagine shedding tears for his own father, not at twelve, nor at sixteen when that brawling, angry, red-faced man had died, nor indeed at any other time. The dreams shifted and for a time the smoke that burned his eyes was that of parchment curling and blackening in the hearth of Alyn Hold. The pain was the pain of cracked ribs that kept him from breathing, as he watched that big bear-shape black against the hall fireplace where his books burned: an old copy of Polybius he'd begged a trader to sell him, two volumes of the plays of Darygambe he'd ridden a week out to Eldsbouch to buy . . .

His father's brawling voice. "The people of the Hold don't need a bloody schoolmaster! They don't want some prig who can tell them about how steam can turn wheels or what kind of rocks you find at the bottom of the maggot-festerin' sea! What the hell good is that when the Iceriders come down from the north or the black wolves raid in winter's dead heart? This is the Winterlands, you fool! They need someone who'll defend 'em, body and bones! Who'll die defendin' 'em!"

Beyond him in a wall of blurred fire—all things were blurred in that chiaroscuro of hearthlight and myopia—John's books burned.

In the fire he saw still other things.

A distant vision of a tall thin woman, black-haired, frost-eyed, standing on the Hold's battlement with a gray wolf at her side. Wind frayed at the fur of her collar, and she gazed over the moors and streams of that stony thankless desolation that had been the frontier of the King's realm. His mother, though he could not remember her voice, nor her touch, nor anything about her save that for years he had dreamed of seeking her, never finding her again. One of the village girls had been her apprentice, skinny, tiny, with a thin brown face half-hid in an oceanic night of hair and a quirky triangular smile.

He seemed to hear her voice speaking his name.

"The poison won't keep him down for long," she seemed to be saying. "We have to finish him."

It wasn't the blue and gold dragon she was talking about. It was the first dragon, the golden dragon, the beautiful creature of sunlight and jewel-bright patterns of purple and red and black.

And she was right. He'd been hurt in that first fight, too, in the gully on the other side of Great Toby. She'd brought him to with those words. There was no way of knowing whether the poisons would kill a dragon or only numb it temporarily. He still didn't know. Now as then, he had to finish the matter with an ax.

It took everything he had to drag himself back to consciousness. The mortar that had held together the wall above him had perished with time. Acrid slime leaked through, staining the granite; bits of scrub and weed smoldered fitfully. His body hurt as if every bone were broken, and he felt weak and giddy, but he knew he'd better get the matter done with if he didn't want to go through all this again.

Body and bones, his father had said. *Body and bones.*

Maggot-festering old bastard.

He brought up his hand and fumbled at his spectacles. The slab of stone that had knocked him out had driven the steel frame into the side of his face, but the glass hadn't broken. The spell Jenny had put on them worked so far. He drew breath and cold agony sliced from toes to crown by way of the belly and groin.

No sound from outside. Then a dragging rasp, a thick scratching, metal on stone.

The dragon was still moving. But it was down.

No time. No time.

It took all his strength to shift the stone. Acid burned his hands through the charred remains of his gloves. Broken boulders, knobs of earth rained in his eyes. He got an elbow over the granite foundation, inched himself clear, like pulling his bones out of his flesh in splinters.

The ax, he thought, fighting nausea, fighting the gray buzzing warmth that closed around his vision. *The ax. Jenny, I can't do this without you.*

The sunlight was like having a burning brand rammed through his eyes into his brain. He waited for his head to clear.

Centhwevir lay before him, fallen among the ruins, a gorgeous tesselation of blue and gold. Striped wings spread, patterned like a butterfly's: black blood leaked from beneath one of them. A wonderment of black and white fur pillowed the birdlike head: long scales like sheet-gold ribbons, horns striped lengthwise and crosswise, antennae tipped in glowing, jeweled bobs. Spikes and corkscrews and razor-edged ridges of scales rose through it along the spine, glistened on the joints of those thin deadly forepaws, on the enormous narrow hindquarters, down the length of the deadly tail. It was, John estimated, some sixty-five feet in length, with a wingspan close to twice that, the biggest star-drake he had ever seen.

Music returned to his mind through a haze of exhaustion and smoke. Delicate airs and snippets of tunes that Jenny played on her harp, fragments of the forgotten songs that were the true names of the dragons. With them the memory of Jenny's ancient lists: *Teltrevir heliotrope; Centhwevir is blue knotted with gold* . . .

Ancient beings, more ancient than men could conceive, the foci of a thousand strange legends and broken glints of song.

Wings first. He forced his mind from his own sickened horror, his disgust at himself for butchering such beauty. A dragon could in a few short weeks destroy the fragile economy of the Winterlands, and there was no way of driving a dragon away as one could drive away bandits or wolves. Jenny was right. The dragons would seek to feed on the garrison herds. Bandits and Iceriders would be watching for any slackening in the garrison's strength. To drive the King's men, and the King's law, out; to have the lands as their own to prey on once more.

Moving as in a dream he found his ax, worked it painfully from beneath the rocks that had protected him. The stench of burned earth and acid numbed him. He could feel his hands and feet grow cold, his body sinking into shock. *Not now,* he thought. *Damn it, not now!*

Centhwevir moved his head, regarded him with those molten aureate eyes.

John felt his consciousness waver and begin to break up, like a raft coming to pieces in high seas.

Rock scraped. A slither of falling fragments on the other side of the old curtain wall.

Muffle! John's heart leaped. *You disobeyed and came after me! I could kiss you, you great chowderheaded lout!*

But it was not the blacksmith who stood framed, a moment later, against the pallid morning sky.

A man John had not seen before, a stranger to the Winterlands. He seemed in his middle fifties, big and broad-shouldered, with a calmly smiling face. John thought, through a haze of crimson agony that came and went, that he was wealthy. Though he did not move with a courtier's trained grace, neither had he the gait of a man who fought for his living, or worked. The violet silk of his coat was a color impossible without the dye-trade of the south. The curly black fur of his collar a southerner's bid for warmth. His hair was gray under an embroidered cap, and he bore a staff carved with a goblin's head, a white moonstone glowing in its mouth.

If this was a hallucination, thought John giddily, trying to breathe against the sinking cold that seemed to spread through his body, it was a bloody precise one. Had the fellow fallen out of the air? Did he have a horse cached somewhere out of sight? He carried a saddlebag at any rate, brass buckles clinking faintly as he picked his way down the slope. Halfway down the jumble of the broken wall he paused and turned his head in John's direction. He did not appear to be surprised, either by the dragon, dying, or by the broken form of the man.

Though the distance between them was probably a dozen yards, John could see in the set of his shoulders, in the tilt of that sleek-groomed head, the moment when the stranger dismissed him. Not important. Dying, and to be disregarded.

The stranger walked past him to the dragon.

Centhwevir lashed his tail feebly, hissed and moved his head. The man stepped back. Then, cautiously, he worked his way around to the other side—*Yes,* thought John, irritated despite the fact that he was only half-conscious. *That ball of spikes on the end of the tail isn't just to impress the she-dragons, you stupid oic.* Was this a dream?

He couldn't be sure. Pain grew and then seemed to diminish as images fragmented through the smoke. He saw his father again, belting him with a heavy wooden training-sword, yelling, "Use the shield! Use the shield, damn you!" A shield the child could barely lift . . . Probably a dream. He wasn't sure what to make of the image of that prim gentleman in the violet silk coat sliding a spike from the saddlebag, holding it up to the sun. Not a spike, but an icicle with a core of quicksilver . . . Now where would he have gotten an icicle in June?

John's mind scouted the trail of something he'd read in Honoribus Eppulis about the manufacture of ice from salt, trying to track down the reference, and for a time he wandered in smoky hallucinations of vats and straw and cold. So cold. He came out with the music of Jenny's harp in his mind again and saw he hadn't been unconscious for more than a moment, for the gentleman in purple was standing on the dragon's neck, straddling its backbone. Wan moorland sunlight caught in the frost-white icicle as the man drove it into the back of the dragon's skull.

Centhwevir opened his mouth and hissed again—*Missed the spinal cord, you silly bugger.* John wanted to go over and take it from him and do it right. *It's right there in front of you. Hope you've got another one of those.*

But the stranger stepped away, tucked his staff beneath his arm, and took from his bag things John recognized: vials of silver and blood, wands of gold and amethyst. The paraphernalia of wizardry. *I thought Jen said you were a girl.* Of healing. Centhwevir lay still, but his long spiked tail moved independently, like a cat's—*Dammit, the poison would have worked!*—as the man spread a green silk sheet upon the ground and began to lay out on it a circle of power. Despairing, feeling his own life seeping away, John watched him make the spells that would call back life from the frontiers of darkness.

No! John tried to move, tried to gather his strength to move, before he realized what a stupid thing that would have been. *Dammit, no!* It was a moot point anyway, since he couldn't summon the strength to so much as lift his hand. He felt the hopeless urge to weep. *Don't make me do all this again!*

Was this hell? Father Anmos, the priest at Cair Corflyn, would say so. Some infernal punishment for his sins, that he had to go on slaying the same dragon over and over? And would the gent in the violet coat come over and heal him next, and hand him his ax and a couple of harpoons and say, *Sorry, lad, up and at 'em.* Was he going to resurrect Battlehammer? What had poor Battle-hammer done to deserve getting killed over and over again in the same fight with the same dragon through eternity?

This ridiculous vision occupied his mind for a time, coming and going with the braided golden threads of that remembered music—or was the mage in the heather playing a flute?—and with the thought of darkness and of stars that did not twinkle but blazed with a distant, steady light.

Then from a great distance he seemed to see Ian, standing where the unknown wizard had stood at the top of the broken wall.

Can't be a hallucination, John found himself thinking. *That's his old jacket he's wearing*—the sleeve was stained with poisons from last night.

At the dragon's side, the wizard held out his hand.

Ian jumped lightly down from the wall, strode across the scorched and smoking ground without a blink, without a hesita-tion, grimy plaid fluttering in the morning breeze. The dragon raised its head, and the mage smiled, and John thought suddenly, *Ian, run!* Panic filled him, for no good reason, only that he knew this man in his embroidered cap was evil and that he was saving the dragon's life with ill in mind.

The dragon sat up like a dog on its haunches: its brilliant, bloodstained wings folded. Its injured foot it held a little off the ground. John could see where the slash had been stitched to-gether again. The wizard who had saved its life set aside the flute of bone and ivory.

It was said that if you saved a dragon's life it was your slave. It was true that when Jenny had saved the life of Morkeleb the Black, the Dragon of Nast Wall, she had done so by means of the dragon's name. That music, salvaged from ancient lore, had given her power. *Save a dragon, slave a dragon . . .*

Ian, go back!

He tried to scream the words, and his breath would not come. *Ian, no!*

John raised himself on his elbows, then his hands. It was as if every cord and muscle of his flesh tore loose. *Ian . . . !*

The boy paused, as if he'd heard his voice. Turning, he walked over to where John lay and stood looking down at him, and his bright sapphire eyes were no longer his own eyes, no longer Jenny's. No longer anything human.

With a smile on his face that was almost friendly, he kicked John in the side as a man would kick a dying dog that had bitten him.

Then he walked away.

When John's eyes cleared, he saw the dragon Centhwevir lowering himself to the earth, saw the strange wizard settling himself a little uneasily among the bristling ridges of the dragon's back. He stretched down a hand and helped Ian up behind him. Like a dream of cornflowers and daffodils, like lapis and golden music, the star-drake spread his wings.

"Ian . . ." It was like falling onto a harrow, but John tried to make himself crawl, as if he could somehow reach them, somehow snatch his son back.

The moonstone flashed in the wizard's staff. The dragon loosed its hold on the world, like the wind taking a kite. Weightless and perfect in its beauty it rose, and John tried and failed to call his son's name, though what he thought that would accomplish he knew not.

He only knew that the dragon was taking his son.

A dream, he thought, seeing again Ian's face and the flame of hell in those blue eyes. *It has to be a dream.*

Darkness took him.

CHAPTER FIVE

"Damn you, John." Jenny Waynest sank back on the straw tick and covered her mouth with her hands. She was trembling. "*Damn* you." For a moment more the images glowed in the fire's core: the blue and gold dragon stretched dying in its blood, the crumpled form of the man in his battered doublet of black leather and iron plate. Then they faded.

Ian, she thought. *Ian must have come.* Mages cannot see mages, in fire, water, stone, unless they consent to be seen. *Goddess of Earth, let it be that I can't see now because Ian has come.*

Ian was already a good enough healer that it might be just possible for him to save a man's life. To stop bleeding, anyway; to keep the lungs drawing air. To keep the cold of shock from reaching the heart. John would have forbidden him to follow, but knowing Ian there was a good chance that he had.

She closed her eyes, trying to breathe, trying to abate the shaking that racked her flesh. *God of the Earth, help him . . .*

Voices came to her through the window behind her head. Soldiers in the courtyard. "By the gods, I thought he had us last night." "Not a chance." A southerner's voice, one of the surviving dozen of the twenty-five who'd ridden with her from the Skepping Hills. "He's just a robber, when all's said."

But he wasn't. Or more properly, someone in his band was more than just a robber's follower. And it was abundantly clear that John's information concerning the band's numbers—and capabilities—was far more accurate than Rocklys'. Well, the southerners would learn—if they lived long enough.

Smoke from breakfast fires stung Jenny's nostrils, reminding her of her hunger. They had been at Palmorgin, the largest of the

47

new fortified manors in the deeps of the Wyrwoods, when Balgodorus turned and attacked. Fortunately there had been surplus grain in the storerooms. That probably had a good deal to do with the bandit's choice of target, though Jenny wasn't sure. They'd have to have known she was following them, and their goal, it was clear, was to eliminate her; to knock magic from John's—and Rocklys'—armory of resources. Then, too, the fine southern swordblades, arrowheads, and spears stored at Palmorgin made it a target. Early summer—before the harvest was in—was a hard time for bandits as for everyone else. The families from the outlying farms had managed to bring in the remnants of last year's oats and barley, and a handful had rescued pigs, cows, and chickens, but Palmorgin's lord Pellanor had nevertheless confiscated the lot and put everything under armed guard. After a week of siege, and no help in sight, Jenny was glad the elderly baron had taken this precaution.

Things were bad enough without starvation.

With her mind she walked from the storeroom where she slept down the corridor, past the guard and out onto the parapet that ran around the whole of the manor's outer wall. Testing and listening, smelling at every mark of ward and guard she had put on the place, to see if counterspells had probed them in her few hours of sleep since last night's attack. She'd have to make the walk in person as soon as she got up, but this probing had on a dozen occasions alerted her to trouble spots that she might not have reached for an hour or more: fires starting in the stables or under the kitchen roof, spells of sleep or inattention muttering to the guards.

Balgodorus' witch was good.

And under her mental probes, Jenny heard other voices. Women in the kitchen, chatting of commonplaces or gossiping of those not present—"She's been carrying on with Eamon like a common whore . . ." "Well, what do you suppose her mother was? And Eamon's wife with child!" None of them dared to speak of what filled all their minds: *What if Balgodorus breaks the gate?*

There were women in the eastern villages, women who had been through Balgodorus' raids, who still wore masks and would do so until they died. Those were the ones who had been deemed not pretty enough or strong enough to be sold as slaves in the far southeast.

Somewhere a child laughed, and a small girl patiently explained to a playmate the only correct rules for Hide-the-Bacon. Many bandit troops killed children as a matter of course: too expensive to feed. Balgodorus' was one of these.

Ian . . .

Jenny forced herself to concentrate.

Walls, kitchen, barracks. "Three years sweating it out in this godsforsaken wilderness, build this wall and clear that field and drink that cow-piss they call wine hereabouts." A man's voice, almost certainly one of the conscripts sent north from the King's lands in Greenhythe or Belmarie. "And for what? If the folk here had the sense Sister Illis gave to goats they'd have moved out a hundred years ago . . ."

Jenny sighed. Sister Illis was the southern name they gave to the Many-Colored Goddess. As for the sentiment, it was a common one among serfs who'd been uprooted from their villages and forcibly relocated. There were things that ending happily ever after did not address, and one of them was how everything got paid for.

"One of them's got to have gotten through." Very clearly she heard the Baron Pellanor's scratchy voice. At the same time she saw him in her mind, a tall, stringy, graying man of about her own age wearing serviceable back and breast-plate armor and a cloak of red wool, the color of the House of Uwanë.

So Grand John Alyn must have been, she thought, once upon a long-ago time. Another king had sent that ten-times removed ancestor north to govern and protect those who dwelled between the Gray Mountains and the bitter river Eld. A prosperous land it had been in those days. Caerdinn had told her of a land of rich barley and oats, of sheep and shaggy-coated cattle; a land of endlessly argumentative scholars, of strange heresies that sprang up among the silver miners in the Gray Mountains and the Skepping Hills; of ingenious weavers and bards and workers in silver and steel. That ancient king had told Grand John Alyn, *Hold the land, defend the law, protect my people with your life.*

And King Uriens—or rather Prince Gareth, who ruled in his father's mental absence—had given charge of these lands in the southeastern Wyrwoods to Pellanor, a minor cadet of the Lords of Grampyn, after twenty-seven years' service in arms.

"I don't know, m'lord," said a man-at-arms. "The bandits got men all through the forest. They got Kannid and Borin . . ."

Jenny saw Pellanor lift a hand and turn his face away. Borin had been sent for help four days ago. Yesterday his burned and emasculated body had been dumped in the open ground sixty feet from the gates. It was a difficult shot with an arrow, but after ten or twelve tries one of the men-at-arms had finally been able to kill him.

"Can't that witch-lady get a word to the Commander at Corflyn?" another soldier asked the baron. "With a talking bird, like in the stories?"

The Baron sighed. "Well, Ront, I'm sure if Mistress Jenny could do such a thing she would have, days ago. Wizards can get word to one another, but as far as I know there aren't any other wizards at Corflyn now."

There aren't any other wizards, Jenny thought wearily, *in the whole of the Winterlands. Nor have there been for many years.* Only herself. And Ian, not yet sufficiently versed in power to speak through crystal or fire.

And this woman in Balgodorus' band.

It was time to get up.

She opened her eyes. The fire had burned down low in the brazier, a jewel-box huddle of ember and coal. The heat seemed suddenly unbearable—she whispered the rush of it aside, dissolved with a Word that mimicked the echoes of youth.

John, she thought, staring again into the blaze's blue-glowing core. *John.*

The ruined walls of Cair Dhû formed themselves once more before her, sharp and tiny as the reflections in a diamond. Fumes of smoldering heather veiled her sight. John lay close to the broken mess of acid-scorched wall. The warhorse Battlehammer, bleeding from flanks and sides, stood over him, head down, favoring his right hind leg when he moved.

No dragon remained. Nor was there any sign of what had happened to it, neither bones nor tracks of dragging. *But John wounded it,* she thought, baffled. *Wounded it unto death.*

Somehow it had prevailed. It had won.

Then she saw Battlehammer raise his head, and from smoke and ruin Sergeant Muffle appeared, glancing warily about him, ax at his belt and his big hammer in hand, his own mount and a packhorse led by the reins.

Four years ago Cair Corflyn had been only a circle of broken walls, a stronghold for whatever bandit troop was powerful enough to hold it. In the twenty-two years he'd been Thane of the Winterlands, John Aversin had led three attacks against it, and it was there that his father had been killed.

The inhabitants of the current gaggle of thatch-roofed taverns, bordellos, shops, and shacks that circled Corflyn's new gates didn't take much notice of John and Muffle. Having left Battlehammer at Alyn Hold to recuperate ("You're the one who should be recuperating!" Muffle had scolded), he was mounted on his second-string warhorse, Jughead, a skillful animal in battle or ambush but hairy-footed, bony as a withy fence, and of a color unfashionable in the ballads. John's scuffed and mended gear, iron-plated here and there and with jangling bits of chainmail protecting his joints, was stained and old, and the plaids over it frayed. And Sergeant Muffle looked exactly what he was: a fat backcountry blacksmith.

The guards at the gate recognized them, though. "You did it, didn't you?" asked a hard-faced boy of not too many more than Ian's years. John had heard they recruited them as young as sixteen off the docks and taverns of Claekith, and drunk out of the slums. "Killed the dragon that cut up the Beck post so bad? Killed it by yourself? They say you did."

"They're lyin', though." John slid painfully from Jughead's back and clung for a moment to the saddle-bow until the grayness retreated from his vision. "God knows where the thing is now."

Commander Rocklys was waiting for him; he was shown directly in.

"Thunder of Heaven, man, you shouldn't even be on your

feet!" She crossed from the window and caught his arm in her heavy grip, to get him to a chair. "They say you slew the dragon of Cair Dhû . . ."

"So everybody's tellin' me." He sank into the carved seat, annoyed with the way his legs shook and how his ribs stabbed him under the plaster dressing every time he so much as turned his head. His breath was shallow from the pain. "But it's a filthy lie. I don't know where the beast is, nor if it'll be back."

A middle-aged chamberlain brought them watered southern wine in painted cups. With her back to the window that overlooked the camp parade ground it was hard to read Rocklys' expression, but when John was finished she said, "A wizard. *Damn.* Another wizard. A man . . . You're sure?"

"No," said John. "No, I'm not sure. I was far gone, and the very earth around me smoking, and some of what I saw I know wasn't real. Or if it was, then me dad sure fooled the lot of us at his funeral." Rocklys frowned. Like his sons, she disapproved on principle of frivolity under duress. "But Muffle tells me he saw no dragon when he reached the place an hour later and found me out colder than a sailor after a spree."

"And your son?"

John's jaw tightened. "Well," he said, and said nothing more. The Commander shoved away from the wall with her shoulders and went to a cupboard: She took out a silver flask and poured a quantity of brandy into his empty wine cup. John drank and looked out past her for a time, at two soldiers in the blue cloaks of auxiliaries arguing in the parade ground. Father Anmos and the cult flute player emerged from the shrine of the Lord of War, heads shrouded in the all-covering crimson hoods designed to blot out any sight or sound detrimental to the god's worship. Raised in the heresy of the Old God, John wondered who the god of dragons would be, and if he prayed for the return of his son whether it would do any good. He felt as if barbed iron was lodged somewhere inside him.

"Muffle doesn't know. *I* don't know. Ian . . ."

He took a deep breath and raised his head again to meet her eyes. "Adric—me other boy, you know—tells me Ian set off just after midnight for Jenny's house to get death-spells to lay on the dragon; somethin' I'd forbade him to do." He forced himself to sound matter-of-fact. "By the tracks next mornin'—or so says Jen's second cousin Gniffy, and he's a hunter—there'd been someone at the house, a man in new boots that looked like city work, who went off with Ian. Gniffy lost the tracks over the moors, but it's pretty clear where they ended up."

His jaw tightened, and he looked down into the cup, trying not to remember the look in Ian's eyes.

"Ian's powers aren't great. At least that's what Jen tells me. For me, anybody who can light a candle by just lookin' at the wick is far and away a marvel, and I wish I could do it. She says he'll never be one of the great ones, never one of those that can scry the wind or shift his shape or call down the magic of the stars. Which is no reason, she says, why he can't be a truly fine middlin'-strong wizard."

"Of course not." Rocklys set down the flask. "And by the Twelve, the world has more use for a well-trained and competent mediocrity than for half a cohort of brilliant fools. Which is why," she added gently, "I wish you had left your boy here."

"Well, be that as it may," sighed John. "Even if he'd been here, Ian would have stolen a horse and run away home at first word of the dragon, so it would all have come out the same." He ran his fingers through his hair. The red ribbon was still braided in it, faded and stained with blood. "But who this is, or if he's in league with Balgodorus as well . . . I take it you've no word from Jen?"

The Commander shook her head. Her eyes were troubled, resting on John's face. He must, he thought, look worse than he supposed.

"I got one message two weeks ago: Balgodorus seemed to be heading for the mountains. He has a stronghold there. I've sent search parties in that direction but they've found nothing, and frankly, in the Wyrwoods, unless you know what you're looking for you're not going to find it. You know those woods. Thickets that have been growing in on themselves since before the founding of the Realm; ranges of hills we've never heard of, swallowed in trees. They may be untrained scum, but they know the land, and they're rebellious, tricky, stopping at nothing . . ."

Her face suddenly set, grim anger in her eyes. "And some of the southern lords are as bad, or nearly so. Barons, they call themselves, or nobles—wolves tearing at the fabric of the Realm for their own purposes. Well"—she shook her head—"at least the likes of Balgodorus don't pretend allegiance and then make deals behind the Regent's back."

"Two weeks." John gazed into the dab of amber fluid at the bottom of his goblet. Two days' ride from Alyn, with Muffle scolding all the way. Ian had been gone for five days.

Old Caerdinn returned to his mind, as he had on and off since the strange mage's appearance. A vile old man, John remembered, dirty and obsessed. He had been John's tutor as well, and a quarter of the books at Alyn Hold had been dug from ruins by that muttering, bearded old bundle of rags, or bargained from any who had even the blackest scraps of paper to sell. He—and John's mother—were the only other wizards John had ever heard of north of the Wildspae, and they had hated one another cordially.

Had Caerdinn had other pupils? Pupils whose wizardry was stronger than Jenny's, maybe even stronger than Jenny's human magic alloyed with the alien powers of dragons? This woman of Balgodorus', or the person who had taught her. The man with the moonstone in his staff?

Somehow he couldn't see the gentleman in the purple coat taking instruction from a toothless dribbling old beggar, much less meekly letting Caerdinn beat him, as Jenny had done.

But there were other Lines of magic. Other provenances of teaching handed down in the south, in Belmarie or the Seven Isles. And as Rocklys had said, though their magic was very different from human magic, there were wizards also among the gnomes.

He sighed again and raised his head, to meet Rocklys' worried gaze. "I have to believe that I saw at least some of what I think I saw," he said simply. "I was flat on my back for three days after the fight, and it rained during that time. Gniffy had a look round but he said the tracks were so torn up, he couldn't be sure of anything. But Centhwevir's gone. And Ian's gone."

"Of this Centhwevir I've heard nothing." Rocklys walked to the niche in the wall, where in former centuries commandants had put the closed shrines of the gods. She had a shrine there to the Lord of War, and another to the Lord of Law, but where in the south he'd seen little charred basins of incense, and the stains of proffered wine and blood, was only clean-scrubbed marble. The rest of the niche held books, and his eye ran over the titles: Tenantius' *Theory of Laws*, Gurgustus' *Essays*, *The Liever Regulae*, and Caecilius' *The Righteous Monarch*. On the table before these books was a strongbox of silver pieces, and beside it a small casket containing half a handful of gems. He remembered the complaints that had come to him from the mayors of Far West Riding and Great Toby, how the King's commissioners demanded more to pay for the garrison than even the greediest thane ever had.

"Of this new wizard . . ." She shook her head. "Can Jenny have been mistaken? Or might the man you saw have been some kind of . . . of illusion, as the dragon was?"

"And be really this woman?" John shook his head. "But why? Why go to the trouble to fool me?"

"In any case," said the Commander, "all of this convinces me—well, I was convinced before—that we *must* establish this school I've spoken of, this academy of wizards, here in Corflyn. I hope now that when she returns, Jenny will agree to come here and teach others. We can't go on like this."

"No."

Save a dragon, slave a dragon . . . The old granny-rhyme drifted back through his mind, and the bodies he'd found the last time Balgodorus had raided a village.

And as he heard the words again he saw the wizard in his violet coat and embroidered cap mounting Centhwevir's back, holding out his hand to Ian.

His ribs ached where the boy's boot toe had driven in.

The Commander turned from the neglected shrines, the books of the Legalist scholars, very real distress on her face. "It isn't just bandit mages who are the danger. You know that! Look at the gnomes, operating what amount to independent kingdoms at the very heart of the King's Realm! Buying slaves, too, clean against the King's Law, no matter what they swear and claim! They have wizards among them, and who knows what or who they teach. Look at lords like the Master of Halnath, and the Prince of Greenhythe, and the merchant princes of the Seven Isles! Look at Tinán of Imperteng, claiming that his ancient title to the lands at the base of the mountains is equal in rank to that of the King himself!"

John propped his spectacles on his nose. "Well, accordin' to Dotys' *Histories*, it is."

"What kind of argument is that?!" Rocklys demanded angrily. "The revolt of the Prince of Wyr, four hundred years ago, broke the Realm in two! That should never have been permitted. And Prince Gareth—though I have nothing but respect for him as a scholar and an administrator—is letting it happen all over again!"

"Our boy Gar's not done so very ill," John pointed out quietly. "For one coming new to the game and untaught, he's doing gie well."

He smiled a little, remembering the gangly boy with the fashionable green streaks in his fair hair, broken glasses perched on the end of his long nose, delivering himself of an oratorical message from the King before collapsing in a faint in the Alyn Hold pigyard. Comic, maybe, thought John. But it had taken genuine courage to sail north to an unknown land; genuine courage to ride overland from the harbor at Eldsbouch to Alyn Hold. The boy was lucky he hadn't had his throat slit for his boots on the way.

Maybe luckier still that he'd set out on his journey when he had. In those days the witch Zyerne had been tightening her grip on the old King's mind and soul, draining his energy and looking about her for a new victim.

"That's exactly my point!" Rocklys drove her fist into her palm, her face hard. "His Highness the Prince is untaught. And inexperienced. And he's making mistakes that will cost the Realm dear. It will take years—decades—to repair them, if they can be repaired at all. His . . ." She stopped herself with an effort.

"I'm sorry," she said. "He's your friend, as he is my cousin. I suppose I can't get over my memories of him prancing along with his friends, wearing those silly shoulder-banners that were all the rage, and toe-points so long they had to be chained to his garters. You're not going to go seeking Jenny?" She came over to him and rested a big hand on his shoulder. John realized he was so tired it would cost him great effort to stand, and his hands were growing colder and colder around the painted rim of the cup.

"I'll ride on back to the Hold," he said. "Jenny'll know Ian's gone, and something's gie wrong. She'll be on her way back to the Hold as fast as she can."

"I thought mages couldn't scry other mages."

"Nor can they. So she'll know I haven't been next or nigh Ian in five days, and that I've got meself out of bed and down here before my cuts have fair scabbed. She'll put two and two together—she's good at that kind of addition, is Jenny. And it's as well," he added, setting the cup aside and rising cautiously from his chair. "For in truth, she can't return too soon for comfort."

"And if she doesn't return?" asked Rocklys. "If this bandit chief and his tame mage have found a way to imprison or destroy her?"

"Ah, well." John scratched the side of his long nose. "Then just us standin' off a couple of wizards, and a dragon, and all . . . I'd say we're in real trouble." He took three steps toward the door and fainted, as if struck over the head with a house beam.

CHAPTER SIX

Wait for me, you idiot! thought Jenny furiously, and let the images in the fire fade. *WAIT FOR ME!* She wondered why the Goddess of Women had seen fit to cause her to fall in love with a blockhead.

Moonlight streamed through the window, just tinged now with the smoke of far-off fires. Somewhere beyond the walls a whippoorwill cried. Jenny drew her plaid around her shoulders and wished with all that was in her that she could slip over the palisade, summon Moon Horse from her patient foraging in the woods, and ride for Alyn Hold as fast as she could go.

Or if all that were not possible—and it was not, not without leaving close to three hundred people to die—she wished that at least she knew what was going on.

Silence cupped Palmorgin manor in its invisible hand. Even the guards had nothing to say, focused through their exhaustion on the open ground beyond the moat. This was the dead hour of night that Balgodorus favored for his attacks. Mosquitoes whined in the darkness, but worn down as she was even the spells of "Go bite someone else" scraped at her, like a rough spot on the inside of a shoe after the tenth or twelfth mile.

No sign of Centhwevir. Under the best of circumstances it wasn't always possible to scry dragons, for their flesh, their very essence, was woven of magic. But over the past seven days, she had scried the outposts along the fell country, scried the towns of Great Toby and Far West Riding, scried Alyn itself.

No burned ground. No tangles of stripped and acid-charred bones.

And at the Hold, no mourning. But she saw Aunt Jane and

Aunt Rowan and Cousin Dilly weeping; saw Adric sitting alone on the battlements, looking out to the south. And John, after his brief interview with Rocklys, had refused to remain in bed, had instead dragged himself next morning back onto his horse and taken the road for home, Muffle behind him scolding all the way.

Ian.

Something had happened to Ian.

Wait till I get there, John. This can't last.

She slipped from the room.

Women and children slept rolled in blankets along the corridor outside her door. She picked her way among them, drawing her skirts aside. Pale blue light glowed around the door handles of other storerooms, warding away touch with spells of dread. Warding away, too, every spell of rats and mold and insects, leaks and fire, anything and everything Jenny could think of.

In the archway that led onto the palisade she nodded to the guard, and the night breeze lifted the dark hair from her face. Balgodorus' tame mage hadn't stopped with illusion. As she passed the roofs of the buildings around the court, Jenny checked the faint-glowing threads of ward-signs, of wyrds and counter-spells. In some places the fire-spells still lingered, the wood or plaster hot beneath her fingers. She scribbled additional marks, and in one place opened one of the several pouches at her belt and dipped her finger into the spelled mix of powdered silver and dried fox-blood, to strengthen the ward. She didn't like the untaught craziness of those wild spells, without Limitations to keep them from devouring and spreading where their sender had no intention of letting them go.

There had been other spells besides fire. Spells to summon bees from their hives and hornets from their nests in furious unseasonal swarms. Spells of sickness, of fleas, of unreasoning panic and rage. Anything to break the concentration of the defenders. The palisade and the blockhouses were a tangle of counterspells and amulets; the smelly air a lour of magic.

How could anyone, she wondered, born with the raw gold of magic in them, use it in the service of a beast like Balgodorus: slave trader, killer, rapist, and thief?

"Mistress Waynest?" Lord Pellanor appeared at the top of the ladder from the court below. He carried his helm under his arm, and the gold inlay that was its sole decoration caught the fire's reflection in a frivolous curlicue of light. Without it his balding, close-cropped head above gorget and collar looked silly and small. "Is all well?"

"As of sunset. I'm just starting another round."

"Can she see in?" asked the Baron. "I mean, look with a mirror or a crystal or with fire the way you do, to see where to plant those spells of hers?"

"I don't think so." Jenny folded her arms under her plaid. "She might be able to see in a room where I'm not, despite scry-wards I've put on everything I can think of. She's strong enough to keep me from looking into their camp. She's laying down spells at random, the way I've done: sickness on a horse or a man, fire in hay or wood, foulness in water. And she wouldn't know any more than I do how much effect those spells are having."

The Baron puffed his breath, making his long mustaches jump. "Where would she have learned, eh?" He started to bite his thumb against evil, then glanced at her and changed the gesture to simply scratching his chin. "I . . . er . . . don't suppose the man who taught you might still be about?"

Jenny shook her head.

"You're sure?"

She looked aside. "I buried him. Twenty-five years ago."

"Ah."

"I was the last of his students." Jenny scanned the formless yards of open ground below. They had fought, daily, over that ground, and daily, nightly, those ragged filthy foul-mouthed men had come back, with ladders, with axes, with brush to try to burn the gates or rams to try to break them. There were, she guessed, nearly twice as many bandits as there were defenders of fighting strength. They attacked in shifts.

Even now she could see the twinkle of lights from their camp and smell its stink on the breeze. Eating, drinking, resting up for another attack. Her bones ached with fatigue.

"He was very old," she went on, "and very bitter, I suppose through no fault of his own." She remembered the way his stick would whine as it slashed through the air, and the bite of the leather strap on her flesh. The better, he said, for her to remember her lessons. But she'd felt his satisfaction in the act of punishment alone, the relief of a frustration that ate him alive. She had wept for days, at the old man's lonely death. She still did not know why.

"He remembered the last of the King's troops, marching away to the south. That must have been the final garrison from Great Toby, because the others had gone centuries before that. He said his own teacher left with them, and after that he could only work at the books his teacher left. There was no one else in the north who could teach properly—not healing, not magic, not music. Nothing. Caerdinn was too young to follow the legions south, he said. Then the Iceriders came, and everything changed."

Pellanor cleared his throat apologetically, as if it were up to him to defend the decision of the man whom history knew as the Primrose King. "Well, Hudibras II was faced with a very difficult situation during the Kin-Wars. And the plague struck hardest among the armies. Your teacher seems to have learned enough on his own to have taught you well."

Jenny thought of all those things she'd learned in the south that Caerdinn hadn't known, the holes in his knowledge she'd struggled with all her life. Spells that could have saved lives, had she known them. But Pellanor had done her no harm, and didn't understand, so she only said, "So he did."

Had the old man's anger stemmed from that ancient desertion? she wondered, as she moved on into the corner turret. Under her touch the rough-dressed stone walls, the heavily plastered timbers, felt normal—no new spells embedded like embers within. Or had his rage at her been because she was herself untalented, born with only mediocre powers, when he considered himself fit to have instructed the great?

Had the masters of those ancient Lines truly had some method of raising small powers such as hers—and his—to primacy? Or was that just some fantasy of his own?

The fact remained that her greater powers had come from contact with the Dragon of Nast Wall. That dragon-magic she sent out now, flowing like thin blue lightning through rock and wood, thatch and tile, listening as dragons listened, sniffing and tasting for that other wizard's spells.

There. Summonings of rats, and fleas—good God, did that mage-born imbecile know nothing about the spread of plague? Another fire-spell . . . No, two. One under the rafters of the main hall. Another in the air in the courtyard, a stickiness waiting for someone to walk by. She probed at them, encysted them in Limits, pinched them dead.

Irresponsible. Foolish, insane. Bandit-magic. Like Balgodorus himself, uncaring what ill he caused as long as he got what he wanted.

Jenny renewed the Weirds on the turret and hastened, her soft sheepskin boots soundless on the rough dirty plank floors, to the places where the flea-spells had taken hold.

They were badly wrought, drifting patches of them scattered like seeds through the stable, through the kitchen corridor used as a barrack for Rocklys' men, and the dormitory set up among the arches under the main tower. It took Jenny weary hours to trace them down, to neutralize the knots and quirks of hunger and circumstance that would draw vermin to those places in swarms. They weren't strong enough to do any real damage under most circumstances, but still too strong to neglect. The foul, pissy smell of rodents was in any case stronger everywhere in the manor than she liked. A dangerous smell, with so many people crowded so close.

Did Balgodorus think he was immune? Did he think his tame mage's unhoned powers were up to combating full-scale plague?

As she traced the Runes and Circles and Summonings over and over, on walls and floors and furniture; as she called forth the power of the stars, of the earth, of water and moon-tide and air; as she wrought magic from her own flesh and bones and concentration, Jenny wanted to slap that ignorant, selfish, arrogant bandit-witch until her ears rang. Whatever Caerdinn's failings he had started his teaching with Limitations. The old man's tales had been filled with well-meaning adepts whose cantrips to draw wealth to the deserving had resulted in the deaths of moneyed but otherwise innocent relatives, and whose fever-cures slew their patients from shock or chill.

The short summer night was nearing its end when she finished. The warriors who'd watched around the courtyard fire had sought their rest. Somewhere in the dormitory a child cried out in her sleep, and Jenny heard a second child's whispering voice start a story about a wandering prince in exile, to beguile her sister back to sleep. The quarter moon stood high above the parapets: the Gray God, the mages' God of the High Faith. Jenny leaned her back against the stone arch and looked up at that neat white semi-circle, glowing so brightly that she could see the thin edge of light around the remainder of the velvety disc.

Listening as dragons listened, she felt the souls of Balgodorus' camp, a mile or so distant in the rock-girt clearing by Gan's Brook. Spirits like filthy laundry, grease-slick and reeking from short lifetimes of brutality, rape, and greed. She could scent the very blood of the camp horses and dogs.

So the star-drake had smelled John's blood as he'd ridden to meet it.

Had Ian ridden out after John?

He must have. She'd scried John and Muffle, at least until the bandits had attacked the manor again and she'd had to abandon her vision of the battle and turn to her own battle. Stumbling with exhaustion, she'd returned in time to see the confused vision of fire and blood that was the actual combat. Had Ian been there, she would have seen nothing. But had he followed? The wonder was that Adric hadn't found a way to get himself into trouble as well.

So what had happened?

Her mind returned, troubled, to the vision she'd had of John, only a few hours ago. John in that patched red robe of threadbare velvet he wore after a bath, sitting in his study once again, with every book on dragons and dragon-slaying that he owned heaped around him, his silly clocks chiming and whirling soundlessly in the dark at his back. He read, it seemed to her, with a concentrated, desperate energy, as she'd seen him read when he was trying to course out some half-remembered clue tossed to the surface of the magpie-nest of his memory.

Trying to find something before it was too late.

And at last, just as she let the vision fade, he took off his spectacles and sat with head bowed: weariness, desperation, and terrible knowledge in his immobile face.

He had found what he sought, whatever it was.

Wait for me.

She opened her eyes. Her head throbbed, but there was one more thing yet to do tonight.

She heard the breathing of Balgodorus Black-Knife's men, unseen in the misty eaves of the woods. Like a dragon, she smelled their blood. But in this dead hour of night, it was a good guess that the bandit-mage, whoever it was, slept.

Jenny hitched her plaids up over her shoulder and climbed the stair to the parapet again.

Pellanor was returning from his own rounds, craggy face drawn with strain. Jenny didn't know when the man slept last. He helped her fetch a rope and wrapped it around a post while she drew the signs of power in the air and on the stonework and wove about herself and the rope the signs of Look-Over-There. Even another wizard might easily miss her. Her mind still weaving those silvery webs about herself, she girdled up her faded blue skirts and let herself down over the wall.

She carried a long dagger and a short dagger, and her halberd slung over her back: slung also, awkward beside the weapon, was the small harp she'd borrowed from Pellanor. "Be careful," Pellanor whispered, when she knew he wanted to say *Come back soon*. In her absence anything could befall.

But this was something that had to be done.

Crossing the moat was easy. The bandits had been heaving rocks and dirt, broken trees and beams into it for weeks to provide their scaling ladders with footing. As she came under the trees of the woods that drew close to the wall at this point, she passed between two watchers, a woman and a man, ugly leathery brutes crouched like wolves waiting beside water for prey. Even if she had not been mageborn, she thought she would have been able to smell them in the dark. She'd walked one night to the edge of Balgodorus' camp, perhaps a mile and a half down the rough-sloping ground. Seen the shimmer of ward-sigils and elflight that fenced the place, guarding it as her own guarded Palmorgin's walls.

The clearing she sought tonight was half a mile from the bandit camp and long known to her. An ash tree stood in it, ruinously old, the sole survivor of some long-ago fire. The rock by which it grew could have been a natural one, unless you looked at it from a certain angle and realized it had been hewn into the shape of a crouching pig. There was a hollow in the top that collected dew. Around this hollow Jenny traced a circle with her fingers, her eyes slipping half-closed.

She formed in her heart the power of the moon, when it should lie one day closer to its dying than it lay tonight. The turning stars, white and cold and ancient. With her fingers she braided the moonlight, slippery-cold as heavy silk, and with a little spoon of crystal and silver drawn from her pocket she dipped up dew from the grass. Spiderweb and milkweed she bound into the spells and brushed them with the spoon-back into the air again: a whispering of longing and of pain. With the shadows of her hair she painted runes into the darkness, and from the pale starflash made sigils of pallid light.

Her knee braced on the rock, she slipped the harp free of its casing: balanced it in her arm as she had balanced her children when they were babies. There were barely strings for her two hands. The spells she wove she had learned from the Dragon of Nast Wall, and scarcely knew what emotion she wove into tomorrow's moonlight, tomorrow's stars, as she had woven it last night into the slant of tonight's milky shadows.

Hunger for what was gone forever. Heart-tearing sweetness glowing in the core of a bitter fruit. A hand curved around the illusion of fire or a jewel; books hidden long in the earth.

For two weeks she had come, while the silver coin of the moon swelled to fullness, then was clipped away bit by bit: the Gray God covering over with his sleeve the white paper he wrote on, they said, that men could not read what would work their ruin. For two weeks she had made this song of dreams of grief. Then in the silence that followed the song she waited.

Far off to her right one of the watchers around the manor swatted a gnat and cursed.

The stars moved. The moon rode high, singing its triumph. Bones and body ached. Moreover, the grief of the spell, as is the way of spells without words, was her own. Thin mists no higher than Jenny's knees stirred among the trees, and in time she smelled the change in the air that spoke of dawn.

She drew a mist about herself, and the changeable illusion of dreams. Like a deer wrought of glass, she picked her way back through thickets and dew-soaked ferns, through the dell where fey-lights danced among the mushrooms and the ringed stones. Those who crouched on picket, squinting across open ground to the new stone walls, the trash-filled moat and ruined outbuildings, didn't see her when she paused between them, looking at Pellanor's Hold.

A rough square of stone walls, perhaps sixty yards to the side, floating in a milky drift of mist. Turrets at each corner and a blockhouse on the west. Gate and gatehouse. Stables and granaries. Three hundred and fifty people—men, women, and children . . .

A gift, as Balgodorus would see it, of good southern weaponry and steel, of slaves for the selling and grain to feed his troops. And Jenny herself, a mageborn weapon in the Law's hand.

As this girl, whoever she was, was Black-Knife's weapon.

And against that she saw the burned-out havoc of Cair Dhû; Adric huddled alone among the sheepskins of the big curtained bed he and his brother shared. John in his study with his spectacles in his hand, reading one passage over and over, two times, three times, in the light of the candles, and then slowly leaning his forehead down on his hand.

She closed her eyes. She had only to whistle up Moon Horse and ride.

That fleck of light on the parapet would be Pellanor, waiting for her sign below to let down the rope.

Dawn rinsed the blackness over the walls with the thinnest pallor of gray.

Jenny sighed and wrapped invisibility around her. Like a shred of mist she moved among the ruins of the village, past the bandit watchers, to the beleaguered Hold once more.

CHAPTER SEVEN

"Maggots from meat, weevils from rye.
Dragons from stars in an empty sky."

John Aversin sat for a long time with the second volume of *The Encyclopedia of Everything in the Material World* open before him:

"Dragons come down out of the north, being formed in the hearts of the volcanoes that erupt in the ice. The combination of the heat and the cold, and the vapors from under the earth, give birth to eggs, and the eggs so to the dragons themselves. Being born not of flesh, they are invulnerable to all usages of the flesh . . ."

Among the green curlicues, gold-leaf flowers, and carmine berries of the marginalia could be found enlightening illuminations of perfectly conical mountains spitting forth orange dragon eggs as if they were melon seeds, accompanied by drawings of hugely grinning and rather crocodilian dragons.

"Teltrevir, heliotrope," whispered Jenny's voice in his mind and behind it the braided threads of music from her harp, the tunes that were joined to those names. "Centhwevir is blue knotted with gold. Nymr sea-blue, violet-crowned; Gwedthion ocean-green and Glammring Gold-Horns bright as emeralds . . ."

And each tune, each air, separate and alien and haunting. John closed his eyes, exhaustion grinding at his flesh, and remembered a round-dance he'd seen as a child. Its music had been spun from the twelfth of those nameless passages. The twelfth name on Jenny's list was Sandroving, gold and crimson. The girls had called the dance Bloodsnake. He could still whistle the tune.

Dotys had more to say. "The star-drakes, or dragons as such things are called, dwelt anciently in the archipelagoes of rock and ice that string the northern seas westward from the Peninsula of Tralchet, islands called by the gnomes the Skerries of Light. These skerries, or reefs, of rock are utterly barren, and so the dragons must descend to the lands of men to hunt, for they are creatures of voracious appetite, as well as archetypes of greed and lust and all manner of willfulness."

And they live on what between times? thought John.

On the corner of his desk Skinny Kitty woke long enough to scratch her ear and wash, then returned to sleep with her paw over her nose. In the cinder darkness beyond the window a cock crowed.

He touched the sheaf of parchment that the young Regent had sent him. The old ballads had been copied in beautiful bookhand by a court scribe. It was astonishing what coming to power could do for obsessions previously sneered at by the fashionable.

" 'For lo,' she quoth, 'do dragons sing
More beautifully than birds.' "

Who in their right mind would, or could, make up a detail like that?

"Southward-flying shadows of fire."

"From isles of ice and rock beneath the moon."

A candle guttered, smoking. John looked up in surprise and groped around until he found a pair of candle scissors to trim the wick. The sky in the stone window frame had gone from cinder to mother-of-pearl.

His body hurt, as if he'd been beaten with lengths of chain. Even the effort of sitting up for several hours made his breath short. Most of the candles had burned out, and their smutted light stirred uneasily in the networks of experimental pulleys and tackle that hung from the rafters. It would soon be time to go.

". . . isles of ice and rock . . ."

The other volume lay in front of him also. The partial volume of Juronal he had found in a ghoul's hive, near what had been the Tombs of Ghrai; the volume he had read on his return, two nights ago, as he searched for that half-remembered bit of information that told him what had become of Ian and why he could wait no longer to embark on his quest for help.

North, he thought. He took off his spectacles and leaned his forehead on his hand. *Alone. God help me.*

The key to magic is magic! Jenny flinched away from the hard knobbed hands striking her, the toothless mouth shouting abuse. The dirty, smoky stink of the house on Frost Fell returned to her through the dream's haze. Caerdinn's cats watched from the windowsills and doors, untroubled by the familiar scene. *The key to magic is magic!* The old man's grip like iron, he dragged her from the hearth by her hair, pulled the old harp from her hands, thrust her at the desk where the books lay, black lettering nearly invisible on the tobacco-colored pages.

The more you do, the more you'll be able to do! It's laziness, laziness, laziness that keeps you small!

It isn't true! She wanted to shout back at him, across all those years of life. *It isn't true.*

But at fourteen she hadn't known that. At thirty-nine she hadn't known.

In her dream she saw the summer twilight, the beauty of the nights when the sky held light until nearly midnight and breathed dawn again barely three hours later. In her dream she heard the sad little tunes she'd played on her master's harp, tunes that had nothing to do with the ancient music-spells handed down along the Line of Herne. Like all of Caerdinn's knowledge, those spells of music were maddeningly ambiguous, fragments of airs learned by rote.

In her dream Jenny thought she saw the black skeletal shape of a dragon flying before the ripe summer moon.

The key to magic was not magic.

Out of darkness burned two crystalline silver lamps. Stars that drank in the soul and tangled the mind in mazes of still-deeper dream. A white core of words forming in fathomless darkness.

What is truth, Wizard-woman? The truth that dragons see is not pleasant to the human eyes, however uncomfortably comprehensible it may be to their hearts. You know this.

The knots of colored music that were his true name.

The kaleidoscope of memory that she touched when she touched his mind.

The gold fire of magic that had flowed into her veins.

Plunging herself, dragon form, into the wind . . .

Mistress Waynest . . . !

This love you speak of, I do not know what it is. It is not a thing of dragons . . .

Mistress, wake up!

"Wake up!"

Gasping, she pulled clear of the mind-voice in the shadows. Raw smoke tore her throat; the air was a clamor of men shouting and the frenzied screams of cattle and horses in pain. "What is it?" She scrambled to a sitting position, head aching, eyes thick. Nemus, one of Rocklys' troopers, stood beside her narrow bed.

"Balgodorus . . ."

As if it would or could be anything else. Jenny was already grabbing for her halberd and her slingstones—she slept clothed and booted these days—trying to thrust the leaden exhaustion from her bones. Her mind registered details automatically: mid-morning, noise from all sides, concerted attack . . .

"—fire-arrows," the young man was saying. "Burning the blockhouse roof, but there's a storeroom in flames . . ."

Fire-spells.

". . . as if the animals have all gone mad . . ,"

Curse, thought Jenny. *Curse, curse, curse . . .*

The stables were in flames, too. She had no idea of the nature of the spell that had been put on the animals, but the horses, mules, and cattle were rushing crazily around the central court, charging and slashing at one another, kicking the walls, throwing themselves at the doors. Bellowing, shrieking, madness in their eyes. The smoke that rolled over the whole scene seemed to Jenny to be laden with magic, as if something foul burned and spread with the blaze.

Damn her, she thought, *who taught that bitch such a spell?*

Scaling ladders wavered and jerked beyond the frieze of palisade spikes. Arrows filled the air. On the north wall men were already being stabbed at and hacked by the defenders within. Slingstones cracked against the walls and an arrow splintered close to Jenny's head. Someone was bellowing orders. She got a brief glimpse of Pellanor in his steel-plated armor swaying hand-to-hand at the top of the wall with a robber in dirty leathers, as she sprang down the steps to the court.

"Watch out, m'lady!" yelled another soldier, racing along the catwalk. "Them horses is insane!"

Curse it, thought Jenny, trying to concentrate through exhaustion and the blurring blindness of a too-familiar migraine, trying to snatch the form and nature of the spell out of the air. There were panic-spells working, too, a new batch of them . . .

She banged on the shutters of the storerooms where the children hid during attacks. "It's me, Jenny Waynest!" she called out. "One of you, any of you . . ."

The shutters cracked. A girl's face showed in the slit.

"The names of the cows," said Jenny. She'd have to do this the hard way, with Limitations, not a counterspell. "Quick."

The girl, thank God, didn't ask her if she was insane, or if she meant what she said. "Uh—Florrie. Goddess. Ginger. You want me to point out which is which? They're moving awful fast."

"Just the names." Jenny already knew the names of the horses. "Give me a minute; I'll be back. Be thinking of all of them." She sprinted across the court, two cows and a mule turning, charging her. She barely reached the stair at the base of the east tower before them, leaped and scrambled up out of their reach, drew a Guardian on the stonework. Smoke poured like a river from under the eaves of the workrooms between the east tower and the north, but it was better than trying to get past the melee in the court. Jenny swung herself up, darted across the roof, forming counterspells to the fire as she ran and thanking the Twelve that the roof beneath her feet was tile. A man's body plunged from above, spraying blood.

Get the danger contained, thought Jenny. *Madness-spells, fire-spells, get those taken care of first.*

And then, by the Moon-Scribe's little white dog, you and I have a reckoning, my ill-instructed friend.

The Limitations quieted the maddened animals, exempting them one by one from the spell. It made Jenny's head ache to concentrate amid the chaos, the smell of smoke and the fear that any moment the bandits would come over the wall.

From the top of the west wall Jenny picked out Balgodorus

himself, a tall man, strong enough to dominate any of his men, dark and with a bristling beard. Men were rallying around him now, ready for another attack. They wound their crossbows, milled and shouted among themselves, working up their anger. Balgodorus was saying something to them, gesturing at the walls . . .

"Probably telling them about all the food and wealth we have in here," muttered Pellanor, his voice hollow within his steel helm as he came to Jenny's side. He was panting hard and smelled of sweat and the blood that ran down the steel.

Balgodorus gestured to the woman who stood near him.

Jenny said softly, "That's her."

"What?"

"The witch. She's wearing a skirt, and unarmed. Bandit women dress as men. Why else would she be at the battle? I'll need a rope." Jenny strode along the palisade, dark hair billowing in a crazy cloud behind her, Pellanor hurrying after. "I don't suppose there's a scaling ladder still standing."

On all the walls the defenders were panting, resting their spears and their swords against the palisade, wiping sweat or blood from their eyes. Children ran along the catwalk with water; a man could be heard telling them sharply to get back indoors and bar themselves in. Below, in the court, the horses stamped, restless at the smell of smoke and blood, and all around could be heard the faint, frenzied squealing of the mice, the cats the rats still under the influence of the mad-spell.

"Great Heaven, no!"

She felt for her stones and sling, shrugging her shoulder through the halberd's strap. "Go back. They're gathering for another try." She stepped over a dead bandit, kilting up her skirts.

"You can't seriously think of leaving in the middle of an attack! You'll be slaughtered!" Jenny had never used spells of illusion in or near the Hold, for fear of the effects they might have on the watchers on the wall, or on the counterspells against illusion with which she'd so carefully ringed the fortress. Last night she had renewed those counterspells after a scout told her there was untoward movement around the bandit camp. She'd had only time for a quick, disquieting glimpse of John, who should have been flat on his back in bed, loading provisions into that horror of an airship he'd built last spring. Muffle had been with him— *Muffle, for love of the Goddess, knock some sense into his head!*

"An attack is the only time she'll be concentrating on something else." Jenny found the rope down which Pellanor had let her climb two nights ago, still coiled just inside the door of the north turret. She checked the land below, and the ruined and trampled fields that lay to the east. No bandits in sight on that side of the keep. Arrows littered the ground, floated in the moat like straws. A single body, the legacy of an attack three days ago, bobbed obscenely among the half-sunk timbers and boughs.

"Whatever you do, hold them now," she said. "This shouldn't take long."

"What if she uses more spells?" asked the Baron worriedly. "Without you to counter them . . ."

"I'm counting on her to do just that," said Jenny. "It will give me a better chance at her. Hold fast and don't let anyone panic. I can't return until after the attack is driven off, but that shouldn't be long." She slithered under the dripping, charred spikes of the palisade, hanging onto the rope. "I'll be watching."

"May the gods of war and magic go with you, then." Pellanor saluted and snapped his visor down again. "Damn," he added, as the noise rose from the other side of the fortress. "Here they come."

Jenny dropped, playing the rope out fast, thankful that she and John still worked out against one another with halberd and sword. Still, she was forty-one and felt it. No sleep last night and precious little the night before, and when she did sleep, she saw in her mind what John was doing with that monstrosity he'd built . . .

She pushed away the images, her frantic fear and the desire to break her beloved's legs to keep him in bed until she got there, forced her thoughts to return to spells of protection, of concealment, as she ran for the fields. Broken crops offered some concealment from the men she could hear shouting beneath the walls.

"At 'em, men!" Balgodorus' voice clashed like an iron gong. "Make 'em wish they never been born!" He had come around with his forces, sword in hand, and now stood close to where Jenny lay in the broken stubble.

"And you, bitch—" He grabbed the arm of the woman beside him. Girl, Jenny saw now. No more than fifteen. Snarled chestnut hair and the kind of ill-fitting gown common to bandits' whores, expensive silk stamped with gold, black with sweat under the arms, kilted to show no petticoat beneath and quite clearly worn over neither corset nor shift. A thin little face like a shut door, dead eyes long past either tears or joy.

"You do your stuff or you'll feel it tonight, understand."

He thrust her off from him and ran to overtake his men, loping easily, like a big dark lion, sword raising high. A cheer greeted him. Some were already bracing themselves, letting fly arrows toward the walls, and the two or three warriors Balgodorus had left standing around the witch-girl watched, too, cursing and cheering and making jokes.

The girl closed her eyes and made the signs of power with her hands.

No Limitations, thought Jenny, disgusted. *No amplifications of power either—she must be calling it all out of her own bones and flesh.* The thin face was taut, lost in concentration, expressionless, though Jenny thought she saw the mouth tremble.

No older than she had been herself when Caerdinn had beaten the remnants of his learning into her.

And like her, probably starved for whatever craft she could learn.

It was too easy. Jenny slipped a stone from her purse and into the pocket of the sling, whipped it around her head as she rose to her knees. Timing, timing . . . The first of the scaling ladders went up against the manor wall, and Balgodorus scrambled up. One of the witch-girl's watchers yelled, "Have at 'em, Chief!" and raised his fist. The witch-girl's brows pulled hard together, pain in her face—as spent and battered, Jenny realized, as she was herself.

She felt a deep ache of pity as she let the sling-thong slip.

The girl twisted as if struck by invisible lightning and fell without a sound.

CHAPTER EIGHT

"You're mad, Johnny!"

Aversin turned from lashing the boxes, crates, and struts to the sides of what appeared to be a long, narrow boat wrought of wicker—curious enough given the distance Alyn Hold lay from any navigable water—and regarded his half-brother a moment in silence. Then he leaped over the boat's gunwale, scooped up a handful of packing straw from a broached barrel nearby, and, scrubbing it into his hair, executed a startling series of jigs and pirouettes without sound or change of expression. Sergeant Muffle stepped back in alarm.

"I'd get on me knees and bark like a dog," said John, catching the boat's railing for balance and panting, suddenly white, "but I've a touch of rheumatism." He was trembling all over, and Muffle strode forward and caught his arm to steady him.

"You've a touch of being torn up by a dragon, and lunacy into the bargain! You can't be serious about what you're going to do."

"Serious as falling over a cliff, son." He tried to draw his arm away. Despite the summer warmth condensed in the court, his bare flesh was cold against the blacksmith's big hand.

"Falling over a cliff would be a damned sight safer than what you're proposing. And more useful, too."

John had turned away, discreetly steadying himself on the half-carved, half-wickerwork figurehead on the boat's stern. He was stripped to his boots, doeskin breeches, and singlet; evening light gleamed on the round lenses of his spectacles as he dragged the boat nearer to the small furnace that had been burning for the past hour. The bandages on his chest and shoulder couldn't completely hide the bruised flesh; under the bruises, the scars taken in an encounter with another dragon shone dark.

Heavily loaded though it was, the boat moved easily. It was mounted on wheels wrought, like the machinery in its midsection, from the lightweight steels and alloys made by the gnomes. When the King's troops had arrived in the Winterlands two years ago, John had taken the occasion to ride to the gnomes' Deep at Wyldoom, having heard they needed a warrior to deal with a nest of cave-grues they'd disturbed in their digging. This machinery, made to John's specifications from designs he'd found in an ancient text of Heronax, had been his pay for two weeks of peril and horror in the dark.

"The year Adric was born, Jen and I were trapped by skelks and holed up for near two months in the Moonwood," he said to Muffle. "Jen'll be all right, wherever she is, but I can't wait for her to return. It's ten days that Ian's been gone."

"Ian'll be okay." Adric stepped close, a kind of bluff warrior's defiance in his stance. Mag toddled silently at his heels and began to examine the wicker boat with her usual careful intentness. The boy caught her hand and drew her back, having had plenty of experience with Mag's investigations. "And Mama can take care of any old crummy mage."

"Yeah." John grinned, and tousled his son's hair. "But it may take her a bit." He looked back at Muffle, eyes wary in his sweat-streaked face.

"There's something you're not telling me, Johnny."

John raised his eyebrows, looking surprised. "I'm not telling you to go take a long walk because none of this is your business, but that's 'cause you're me brother and bigger than me."

"John, you should be in bed!" Aunt Jane, the oldest and stoutest of old Lord Aver's three sisters, bustled down the broken stair from the courtyard above. "Muffle, I'm surprised at you for letting him be up!"

The blacksmith began to protest that he wasn't his brother's nursie, but Aunt Jane went on, "And mucking with all your heathen machinery when you should be resting!" She frowned disapprovingly at John's telescope, mounted on the rear gunwale. "And bringing the children, too! They'll end up as bad as you."

"Papa didn't bring us," Adric declared stoutly. "We snuck." He stepped to his father's side as though to defend him, still keeping a conscientious grip on his sister's hand.

"Honestly!" Aunt Jane paused and looked the boat up and down, though none of the aunts had much interest in their nephew's scholarly and mechanistic pursuits. She turned away with a shrug the next moment, scolding, as if the curious hybrid look of the thing had not struck her at all: boat-shaped, but, save for its bottom planking, made of lacquered wicker; wheeled and mounted with a whole array of sails, yards, booms, and masts as well as its strange clockwork and wires, fan-blades and springs. She did not seem to associate it with the framework of withes that stood above the furnace's stumpy chimney. Crates of folded silk lay open beside it, amid long skeins of gnome-woven cable, steel rings, and leather valves.

"Now you come upstairs," she ordered. "Come on! Gallivanting off all over the countryside when you should be resting . . ."

She reascended the stair, muttering, and Sergeant Muffle, with a worried glance back at John, picked up little Mag as if she'd been a single white poppy and carried her after. As soon as they were out of sight John sat down rather quickly on the pile of wood beside the furnace.

"Are you okay?" Adric came over to him, like John stripped to britches, boots, and singlet, hands folded over the hilt of the little sword that hung at his belt. It was only with difficulty that John persuaded him to take the weapon off when he went to bed.

"Just send me down another dragon," said John cheerily. "I'll wring his neck for him like a chicken."

Adric grinned and hoisted himself onto the woodpile at his father's side. "Are you going to go away and find Ian?"

"I've got to, son."

"Can I come with you? You're going to need help," added the boy, seeing his father draw breath for the inevitable refusal. "Even if you do take along all Mama's poisons and your dragon-slaying machine. You've never tried it out against a real dragon, you know. I can use a sword." He patted his blade confidently. "And I can shoot and rope and throw a javelin. You know I'm better than Ian."

This was true. Since the boys were small John had worked to teach them his skills with weapons, knowing they'd need them in the Winterlands, maybe long before they came to manhood. Where Ian learned intently, the younger boy devoured his lessons with a blithe ferocity that left John in no doubt as to who would take over as protector of the Winterlands when he himself was gone.

And probably do a better job of it, he reflected ruefully, than he ever had.

"You're going to tell me you'd really like to," sighed Adric, "but you can't. Is that right?"

"That's right, son," said John. He plucked a twig from the heap of logs and made mice-scampers for Skinny Kitty, who had come down to investigate the courtyard. The cat merely regarded it incuriously and settled herself to wash. "There'll be folk to supper, and for dancing, but if you could go up to my room while everyone's busy and bring my bundles down to the *Milkweed* here"—he jerked his thumb at the boat—"I'd take it as a favor; if me credit still runs to favors."

Adric's eyes sparkled, and he sprang down from the woodpile and raced up the stairs like a mountain goat. John followed more slowly, limping and holding on to the wall. He slept for a few hours, with Fat Kitty and Skinny Kitty somnolent gray lumps at his side, and waking, pulled on his jerkin and made a small bundle of clothes, spare boots, plaids, and his shaving razor. Beside this he set the satchel containing all the poisonous ingredients he and Ian had gleaned from Jenny's study and the house on Frost Fell, all those pots and packets either deadly or merely soporific; and a long bundle of parchment fragments begged from the scriptorium at Corflyn. Then despite the protests of his aunts he limped down to the noise and torchflame of the hall.

There was always someone from the village at the Hold for supper—Jane's legions of friends, or the brothers and sisters of the Hold servants, sometimes Jenny's sister Sparrow and her children or Muffle and his family or the long-suffering Father Hiero, whose attempts to perform the proper worship of the Gods in the village were met with universal indifference and a deep-seated stubborn faith in the Old God. John was obliged to retail for Sparrow and Aunt Hol and Cousin Rowanberry all that he'd seen and heard of Cair Corflyn, and all that Rocklys had said of the unrest in the south; the height of the corn and the progress of the new stone water mill and the numbers of the cattle ("What do you mean you don't know?" demanded old Cram Grabbitch from Ditch Farm. "Can't you count, boy?") and what the wives of the southern sergeants wore. It exhausted him, but he was loath to leave. He told himself that this was because it would be weeks before he saw them again, and he kept from even thinking, *Never.* After supper he brought out the hurdy-gurdy that had been part of his dragon-slayer's fee four years ago and played the four-hundred-year-old war songs, and children's rounds, and sentimental ballads he'd learned from a blackened book he found in the ruins of Eldsbouch. Muffle and Adric joined in on the hand drums and Aunt Jane on her wooden flutes. Aunt Rowan and Aunt Hol—Muffle's mother and his father's mistress for years—and Peg the gatekeeper danced with surprising lightness in a whirl of plaids and rags and long gray hair.

They were still at music when he said he was going to bed. But as he left the hall, he caught Adric's eye.

The boy joined him in the kitchen court a few minutes later. Together they descended the stair through warm blue darkness, seeing the smoldering amber eye of the furnace in the old barracks court below, laced and lidded with its frame of willow withe. The night was still and brought them the scents of ripening barley all around the Hold, and the great wet green pong of the marshes north and eastward. The music came to them still, faint and gay and wild, and with it the crying of crickets and frogs. The moon had just lifted clear of the broken horizon, waning but brave and yellow as a pumpkin's heart.

"They'll be after me hammer and tongs the minute they know I'm bound away," said John, as he checked the leather hose that led from the furnace to the great silvery masses of silk, laid out carefully on the broken pavement. During the past few hours they'd begun to lift and move, swelling upward . . .

In the crimson glare the boy's face quirked in his wide grin, "You mean you're afraid Aunt Jane won't let you go."

"I'm the Lord of the Hold, I'll thank you to remember, sir."

John chucked a short length of elm into the furnace, glad that he'd had servants bring out the cut wood earlier. "Show a bit of respect for an old, tired man."

But Adric only grinned wider. He knew all about the hammer and tongs. For a time they worked together, stoking the belly of the oven, the heat laving their faces and the gritty white smoke puffing out in the starlight. In time John kicked the door shut and dug in the pouch at his belt for the things he'd gotten from the gnomes of Wyldoom, two or three white stones about as big as crab apples, chalky and soft to the touch. The furnace had a sort of iron basket in the top of its chimney, and into this John put the stones, then checked again the great swelling sheets of gray silk. Ropes, valves, and hose were adjusted as the ancient books had said, and as John had figured out over months of experimentation and trial.

"Is it magic?" Adric whispered in time.

He was hard to impress. John felt a trifle pleased with himself for having done so.

"The balloons aren't, no." He stepped back and leaned unobtrusively against the boat for support. "Heronax of Ernine, twelve hundred years ago, used hot air to fill a silk bag and flew seventy-five miles in it, at least so he claims, all the way from Ernine, wherever that was, to the Silver Island. In Volume Four of Dotys' *Histories*—or is it in Polyborus?—there's talk of men building flying machines with the help of gnomes' magic, though whether they were balloons or like that winged machine I made a few years ago it doesn't say. *And* I'll thank you not to giggle about that machine," he added with dignity. "It nearly worked."

"So did your parachute," pointed out Adric, mispronouncing the archaic word. "And the glass bottle for going underwater. And the rockets. And . . ."

"Now, each and every one of those things worked in the past," retorted John, shedding his rough jerkin in the heat. "It's only me dragon-slayin' machine that's completely new, and all me own invention. If the ancients could do it, I can do it."

The silk billowed and shifted, like some huge version of the mice-feet he performed under the blankets of the bed to interest the torporous Fat Kitty—not that they ever did. Torchlight and moonlight flowed in watery patterns over the fabric. Slowly the silk began to rise, as if some great creature beneath were lifting itself out of the ground. Adric came around beside him, hands thrust casually through his sword-belt, trying to appear nonchalant but his eyes enormous.

"Hot air rises, y'see. That's what Cerduces says in the *Principia Mundis*, and it's true. If you put a bit of paper or a leaf on a fire, you've seen how it swirls up."

Adric nodded. He was generally less than interested in his father's scholarly pursuits, and he'd been hearing all his life about the flying machines without ever witnessing anything more impressive than the debacle of the winged vehicle the summer before last. "What happens when the air gets cool?" he asked.

"You come down. You can delay it a bit by takin' on more than you need and carryin' weights and such—accordin' to Cerduces, anyway—but in the end that's what happens. That's where the hothwais—them little rocks the gnomes gave me—come in. They charge the air to keep the heat. It's part of gnome-magic. Gnomes can charge rocks to hold certain kinds of light, to hold sounds, or even hold air around 'em, the same way your mum uses air-spells to swim underwater. I've heard rumor about other stuff as well, but the gnomes are damn chary about lettin' anybody know much of their magic. Now, in that fragment of Ibikus I found over in Eldsbouch it said . . ."

"And that's how you're going to go find the dragon that carried off Ian?"

John was silent. Aware of his son's eyes on his face; aware, too, that he had never lied to any of his children. Aware that his silence was too long.

Adric said, "You know what happened to Ian, don't you?"

Very quietly, John said, "No."

"But you think you know."

He closed his eyes, wishing he could lie. Wishing he could tell his son anything but what he suspected was the truth. "Yes." The wicker and withy binding of the boat's gunwales bit into his hands as he closed them hard, and his wounds ached—bled again, he thought, or else it was just exhaustion.

He wished it were possible to wait for Jenny.

Wished it were possible to do this any other way.

Wished he knew if what he was undertaking would even succeed.

Adric sounded scared. "Where are you going?"

"To find someone who can help me," said John.

If he doesn't kill me on sight.

In the days of the heroes a band of mages made slaves of dragons . . .

He closed his eyes, and the memory of what he had read in that battered half-volume of Juronal returned to him, as if it lay again before his eyes.

In the days of the heroes a band of mages made slaves of dragons.

He saw the blue-and-gold beauty of Centhwevir, bleeding on the black and smoking ground. The flash of crystal in the wizard's hand. *Save a dragon, slave a dragon . . .*

The southern mage's calm intent face. Ian's alien, hellish smile.

John slung his little bundle of clothes into the *Milkweed*, checked the masts and the rigging, and the machinery that would propel it in calm. He'd flown it before, or its earlier and less efficient brethren, but never so far, nor so heavily laden. The pieces of the dragon-slaying machine that he'd been tinkering with for the past three years, lashed among the foodstuffs and waterskins along the gunwales, narrowed the meagre space almost to nothing.

All those futile, tiny toys, against the glory of a dragon. Against the power of a wizard mighty enough to save one's life and hold it as his slave.

This is stupid, I'm not even mageborn . . .

In the days of the heroes . . . The story had gone on to relate that the mages, with the dragons who were their slaves, had conquered the land of Ernine, triggering a series of wars that had devastated the whole of what, by geographical references, seemed to have been the Bel Marches, and laid waste a dynasty and a civilization. Juronal had written centuries after the events, and much of what he said was clearly fantastic or borrowed from other tales. But thinking it over, as he had thought it over for days, readying his two machines, he was sure the account contained a core of truth.

He looked up at the *Milkweed*'s balloons, small moons in the first stain of the high summer dawn. The lights from the hall above were dim. The furnace's roaring heat beat against his body as he tonged the hothwais to the basket under the balloon valves. A hundred tiny tasks and checks, with the light wicker boat jerking on its moorings; with the ache of fatigue in his bones and scars, and the words of Juronal circling over and over in his mind.

The sky was bright. They'd all be waking soon.

He hugged Adric tight, fighting desperately against the desire to take the boy with him. For he would need help, he knew. It was in his mind also that it was very possible he was seeing his son for the last time. *Damn it,* he thought, *damn it, damn it, damn it . . .*

"Wherever she is, your mum'll know where I've gone," he said. His throat ached with the effort of keeping his voice from shaking. "We'll make out all right."

The balloons were dragging hard on the tiny craft. It was time to go.

"You pull that rope." John took a deep breath. "All the moorings'll let go at once." He swung himself up the rope ladder, scrambled over the gunwale and caught his boot on a curved metal segment of the dragon-slayer's steering cage, nearly precipitating himself ten feet to the ground. "You take care of your sister."

Adric raised his hand. "You take care of yourself."

"I'll see you when I'm back."

A cock crowed in the village. All over the moor birds were crying their territories. The dawn bells rang, calling those few who were interested to the worship of the Lord of the Sun. *Sarmendes, golden son of day . . .* But all John saw, as Adric gave a mighty and delighted yank on the mooring rope, was the faded lettering of Juronal's account that was embedded in his mind.

The dragons all died, and the mages also.

The Hold sank away below him. Wind took the sails.

The dragons all died, and the mages also.

John set the sails for the north.

CHAPTER NINE

Like its namesake, the *Milkweed* rode the silver dawn. Each tree and roof of Alyn Village passed beneath and John felt he could name every thatch and leaf. Fields he knew, walls, sheep and sheepdogs, the Brazen Hussy Inn, laundry, and cats on walls. Later he saw Far West Riding, and in the peat bogs that gleamed like flakes of steel farmers and peat-cutters shouted good-natured greetings: Would he need rescuing this time? Herd-boys pointed and stared, then cursed as their sheep fled. Later still, where the trees failed and only bogs and lichen and rocks rolled mile upon mile below, the great herds of reindeer and elk fled also, and hawks in flight circled near him to see, and then away.

It was a shining time. John felt as if his whole soul and body were permeated in light.

Early in the day, when the wind lay from the east, there was no sound at all save for the throb and crack of the sails, and the groan of the rigging in the gusts. Toward noon the wind came around from the west and the bitter north, and John let out some of his ballast—water from the barracks court well, dangling beneath the craft in rawhide sacks—looking for where the currents of the wind changed higher up, as eighteen months of experimental flights had shown him it did. He found enough of a difference high up that he could shift the sails to tack into it, for he was a good sailor, in water or in air. The beauty of the land below, dizzying and tiny, took his breath away.

Had it been his first flight he knew he'd never have survived. Like a child he'd have stared at the ground or the hills or the wonderments of the birds hanging so close to him in the air, and so have come to grief a thousand times. Heronax's notes about ballast and steering had been less than helpful. For most of the day he was able to pick out and name every stream and tor, every copse and ruined farm, but later he got out his parchments and drew maps with sticks of coarse charcoal and lead: silly and idiosyncratic, as were all his drawings, and he entertained himself by giving them absurd names.

When the winds turned completely against him, he took in sail and dropped the anchor into the trees near Gagney's Pond. He dragged the *Milkweed* down by main strength and a dozen pulleys and gears, for he didn't dare let out any of the heated air. The atmosphere was still closer to earth. He took on as much ballast as he could carry, cranked the engine to life, and the fanblades made a great clicking and whirring as they pressed the *Milkweed* forward.

He anchored at what had been a watchtower on Cair Corbie, barely a ring of stone now, and climbed down the ladder to build a supper fire. Wrapped in plaids and furs he sat cross-legged on the stumps of old walls and ate burned barley-bannocks, and gazed north across treeless barrens where the King's Law had never run, a million mosquitoes and gnats whining in his ears. According to Dotys' *Histories*, Crow Tower had boasted woodlots around its base, and there was always a pyre standing ready to be kindled in warning, though, maddeningly, the part of the volume that spoke of what the tower watched against was missing. Few trees grew hereabouts anyway, and as far as John could see through the moonstone light, there was no sign there'd ever been a wood about the tower . . . Still, he looked north and wondered.

Iceriders, probably. Or some of their long-forgotten kin. The Kinwars and the plague had drawn the King's soldiers south long ago. Something had certainly destroyed this tower and emptied all the lands between it and Far West Riding, which still boasted a formidable wall.

Probably, thought John, slapping for the thousandth time at a whining invisible attacker, the mosquitoes drove them back, or likelier ate them alive.

Weary though he was, he lingered for a long while, watching the lands lose their color. It seemed to him that he could descry their shape, formed of every shade of translucent blue, until the late moon rose and washed all things in frost and magic. He fetched out his hurdy-gurdy and played its great wild wailing voice in a song he'd written for Jenny, wanting her with him, not only because of what he knew he must face but to share this beauty with her, this nightfall and these sights, and the wonder of the day's flight. He touched the red ribbon, still bravely braided into his hair.

From high up, just before dropping anchor, he'd seen the horns of the Tralchet Mountains, white-crusted and cloaked in glaciers whose arms ended abruptly in the green-black sea. It was a desperate distance for the second day of flight, with the heat-spells of the hothwais slowly failing. The gnomes who'd given them to him had said they'd last for three solid days, but he had his doubts.

Still, there was nothing else for it. The gnomes of Tralchet Deep were his only hope of success in his quest, and he could only pray they'd heard his name from their kinfolk. In time he climbed the ladder, and with his telescope sought in the southern heavens the comet he'd calculated from ancient writings should be there but wasn't. Then he put in as much cranking of the engine-machinery as he could manage before rolling himself in his plaids and bearskins to sleep. It seemed to him that he lay awake a long time, watching the seven moon-white balloons jostle in the night breeze and, over the wicker gunwales, the dim-shining glimmer of the northern lights, blue and purple and white, rippling in the opal sky.

By morning the *Milkweed* had sunk a good twenty feet. This wasn't as bad as John had feared, but it wasn't good. Mist had come up in the night, so when he woke before dawn from exhausted slumber he had a moment's panic, unable to see, as if he had been struck blind. But the next moment the comforting icy clamminess told him that it was only one of the killer fogs of the moors. Mooneaters, they were called, or kidth-fogs, after the three magic sisters—or priestesses, according to the *Elucidus Lapidarius*—who were said to travel in them seeking to devour travelers' souls. In a way it was a comfort. He'd checked the vicinity of Cair Corbie very thoroughly for tracks and had found nothing more sinister than evidence of tundra wolves, but it would be a gie clever foe indeed who could find and climb the *Milkweed*'s anchor-rope in fog like this.

He felt along the gunwale to the ropes of the ballast bags. Kidth-fog seldom lay more than thirty feet high—he'd taken measurements against the side of the Alyn Hold tower for many years—so he emptied a little water from two bags on opposite sides of the boat, turn and turn, until the dim gray moons of the air bags slowly materialized overhead. Then, suddenly, as if rising through water, he was above the fog, vapors billowing around the wicker hull, through which gray stone hills rose distantly, islands in a lavender world of fading stars.

The black tusks of the mountains had become cliffs on the far shore of that numinous ocean. He let the ladder overside long enough to climb down and disengage the anchor, the boat drifting a little as he scrambled up again. It meant last night's cold burned bannocks for breakfast instead of something fresh and hot, but the thought of dawn over such a world of brume was worth the exchange, and he gave the engines a few final cranks and set the levers. The fan-blades turned, strangely flashing in the half-light.

If I die in the north, he thought, *at least I will have had this.*

He only wished Jenny were there to share it.

If Jen were here to share it there'd be gie less chance of me dyin' in the north, but there you have it.

Sunrise among the columns of rising vapors. Birds shooting through the surface like flying fish. The day moon glowing like God's shaving mirror. Beauty beyond beauty beyond beauty, as the mists thinned and lifted and then dispersed and all the lands lay untouched and unknown in the morning light below.

During the day John mapped, once the kidth-fog cleared, and set the sails, and assembled the vessel's weapons: five small catapults with crossbows of southern steel and horn, armed with six-foot harpoons. Some were poisoned, with the last of the batch he and Ian had made up. Others contained corrosives, or incendiaries such as he'd cooked up from his ancient recipes to use last year against the Iceriders. How much good they'd do he didn't know. Maybe none. If he encountered the wizard who had taken his son, they'd be useless.

Ian, he thought, *I'm doing the best I can.*

Sometimes he was able not to think about Ian's eyes as he came down the hill toward the dragon; was able not to think about the dragon's terrible gold opal gaze that turned to meet the boy. Sometimes he could think of nothing else.

He played the pennywhistle against the clicketing of the engines and the soft creak of the rigging. The twilight covered the mountains ahead in ghostly shadows, and in those shadows he saw spots of light, torches on the gates of Tralchet Deep.

In the dark that dwelled in the hollows of the hottest fire, Jenny saw him anchor his ridiculous craft and climb the road to Tralchet Deep. *Damn it, not NOW!* she thought. Thrice in ten years rumor had reached them that it was the gnomes of Tralchet who were behind the bandits' slave-raids on the farms, that the Lords of the Deep—Ragskar and Ringchin as they were known to humankind—used humans to work the deepest tunnels of the mines, where the air was foul and earth-skelks and cave-grues dwelled. John had not been reticent about speaking on the subject, even to the gnomes of Wyldoom whom he had served. It was this that had caused him to leave Wyldoom quickly and at night.

So tired that she could barely sit up before the brazier of coals, she saw the gnomes come out of the gates, squat armored forms with their fantastic manes of pale hair drawn through the spikes of their helmets; saw them surround him with their halberds and their spears. John, not the least discomposed, brushed aside the blades with the back of his iron-spiked glove and strode up to the commander of the gate guards, grabbed his hand and shook it; she could almost hear him exclaiming "Muggychin me old wart . . ." or Mouldiwarp or Gundysnatch or whatever it was, "how is it with you? And are Their Majesties in? Would you let 'em know John Aversin's here, there's a good chap."

The gates shut behind him, a black steel maw. She had tried before to scry within Tralchet Deep in search of the slaves and had learned that the Deep was surrounded by scry-wards and gnome-magic. She lowered her forehead to her hand.

John, she thought, *I hope you know what you're doing.*

All the day, and the day before, between bandaging men's wounds and weaving healing magic yet one more time, she had returned to her harp and the spells of music that she channeled through it, through the water in the moss-grown stone in the ash grove, to the witch-girl in Balgodorus' camp. The girl was still unconscious, she knew. Through the day she had glimpsed in her mind the orange smutch of torchlight on a tangle of thatch and poles, or in the midst of snatching a hasty meal of gruel and cheese had tasted in the cavities of her nose the harsh pong of smoke, and on her tongue a rude mix of herbs and cheap liquor. Then the vision would slip away, leaving her with a skull throbbing and a stomach queasy from shock.

Now, with the night's cool stillness whispering over the land, she put the vision of John aside, and with it all thought of him, as dragons did. Her harp slung over her back, she climbed down the rope on the wall and moved like a shadow into the woods.

Beside the moss-grown stone she dipped her fingers into the dew, stroked moonlight into silky filaments, as if she were spinning thread. From those fibers she plaited again her web of power and cast it around her in a shining curtain: moonlight and stillness, starshine and peace. And when that web was woven she took up her harp and sang gently, softly, about hope, about longing; about a sweetness drowned and buried, forgotten for years.

Child, she thought, *it isn't too late.*

Not long before dawn, she heard the whisper of rough wool against hazel branches and the tiny breath of grass beneath soft-booted feet. It was hard for her to bring her mind out of the music's dark-shining depths. She timed the girl's passage across the smaller spring, then the larger, heard when her jacket of pelts brushed the limbs of the birches just beyond the clearing.

The music, funneled through the pool on the stone, drew the girl's eyes to the stone first. Opening her own eyes, or rather adjusting them to common sight and common awareness, Jenny saw that she did not perceive her, thinking her only another tree, or a rock a little taller than the first.

The witch-girl was tall for her age, thin with the thinness of those poor trappers and hunters who eked out livings in the deep woods, barely seeing any but their families from one season to another. These people, though not quite sunk to the level of Mee-winks and Grubbies, were often brutish in the extreme. Jenny's

long acquaintance with their kind was studded with the knowledge
of bestialities, of casual murder and incest, of almost unbelievable
ignorance and want. The girl's long, narrow face was marked with
such crimes, sullen and dirty, great eyes peering from beneath the
coarse tangle of her hair. Her heavy lips were soft and sad. She
crossed the clearing to the stone and reached wonderingly to dip
her fingers into the hollow with its water, bringing them up to touch
the wet tips to her eyes, her mouth, her temples.

Knowing the girl to be still dazed by the blow to her head,
Jenny pitched her voice to the voice of dreaming, "What is it you
want, child?"

The girl shook her head. "Me ma," she replied, the truth of her
heart.

"What is your name?"

"Yseult." She raised her head then, blinking at the dark small
shape of Jenny in the darkness under the trees.

As a mage herself the girl could see through illusion, and
Jenny used none on her, only a gentleness she used for her own
sons. "Is Balgodorus good to you?" She was not, Jenny thought,
many years older than Ian.

The girl nodded. Then she said, "No. Not no worse than Pa
when he was liquored. Some of 'em's worse."

"But you don't have to let them hurt you," Jenny reasoned
softly. "That's what magic's for."

Yseult sniffled and rubbed her head, not the back of the skull
where Jenny's slung stone had cracked, but the temples. Jenny saw
the girl's days-old blacked eye and a triangular scar on the back of
her hand where it looked like a hot knife-blade had been laid. There
were older scars the same shape, and a mark on her chin such as a
woman's teeth make when a man punches her in the jaw. "I get
scared," she said. Her short square-ended fingers picked at the un-
tied points of her shift. "Men starts yellin' at me and knockin' me
about, and I can't think. I get angry, like I could call down fire and
fling it at 'em by handfuls, but then most times it don't work. And
Balgodorus, he says if any of the men, any of 'em, come to grief
it'll go the worse for me. I can't make it work all the time."

The bitten nails twitched and pulled at the tapes, and the
bruised dark eyelids veiled her eyes.

Improper sourcing, thought Jenny. *No sense of where the power's coming from, or how it changes, with the course of the moon and the movements of the stars. The poor child probably doesn't even know how to track her own moon-cycles to take advantage of her body's aura.*

"Would you like to leave him?"

The lids flicked up, a glance like a deer seen in a thicket for an instant before flight. The girl's body tensed, lifting on her toes.

"What is it? Don't go." She put Power into this last, a gentle touch that could have been shaken off like the touch of a staying hand. The girl's mouth trembled.

"You're from Rocklys."

Jenny shook her head. "I know Commander Rocklys," she said. "I don't work for her."

"You're with her men, them in the fort. You came with her soldiers. You want to take me away. I got to go."

"Please don't."

"You're a witch."

"So are you."

"I ain't! Not really." She'd backed almost to the clearing's edge. There were spells Jenny knew that might have constrained the girl, especially with her concentration shaken by fear and the dizziness of her wound. But Yseult would have felt them and known them for what they were.

"Would you like to be?" she asked instead. And when Yseult's eyes grew thoughtful, "Men don't hurt witches."

Yseult came down off her toes, and her breath went out. One grubby finger explored her nostril.

"You're a witch?" It was a question now, and Jenny had the sense that the girl was looking at her for the first time. Seeing her as she was, not as her fears had painted her.

Above the trees the dark was thinning. Jenny's dragon-senses brought her a tangle of voices, tiny and sharp as images in far-off crystal: "I'll teach the little bitch!" And, "You can't trust 'em, Captain, not a one of 'em!"

She kept her voice steady. "I'm called Jenny. If you like, I'll help you leave Balgodorus."

Sharp little white teeth peeked out, biting the scarred and chapped lip. "He'll catch me."

"He won't."

"He catched me before." She trembled, and Jenny felt a rush of fury at the man.

"You didn't have a true wizard protecting you before."

Crashing in the trees, boots in the stream, on the rocks. Impossible that Yseult didn't hear—hadn't she even learned that much?

"You're trying to trick me." The girl backed again, and the dark pupils of her eyes were ringed in white. "You're a witch for Commander Rocklys, and I heard what she does to witch-girls. I heard it from the Iceriders."

"She doesn't do anything," said Jenny. "She's trying to start a school, to help mages learn."

"It's all lies!" Yseult's voice edged with panic. "She lies to 'em to get 'em to come, so she can feed 'em to demons!"

"That isn't true." Jenny had heard that old tale a dozen times in a dozen different guises. It was a favorite with the Iceriders: John's mother had told Jenny as a child that the kings of old drank the blood of witch-born children, or sacrificed them to demons on the rocks beside the sea, or on the lap of an idol wrought of brass. Other tales said they used a magic spell to transform them into sparrows, or mice, or cats.

"She's never harmed me, nor my son, who is mageborn, too."

"You're lying to me!" Trapped between fear of Balgodorus and terror of the unknown, Yseult's voice shrilled with panic. "You just want me to help you hurt my man."

"He's not *your* man," said Jenny tiredly. "He's . . ."

Yseult's head went up. In the gloom beneath the trees voices cried out: "I'll skin the bitch! Answer me, you little whore, or . . ."

"I'm here!" cried Yseult desperately. "I'm here! She's tryin' to catch me, trying to kill me!" She flung a spell, rough and undisciplined, and Jenny's belly and bones gripped with nausea and pain. At the same moment Jenny heard one of Balgodorus' men cry out and fall retching among the brush. *Limitations.* Furious, Jenny flung off the magic, which had no more holding power than a child's hand, and faded back into the green-black shadows beneath the trees.

"Don't hurt me!" she heard Yseult scream. "She magicked me away! She went there, see her in the trees?"

She was pointing—her mageborn senses were at least that good—and Jenny turned and glided sidelong, wrapping the dark patterns of her plaids around her to break up the shape of her body. Balgodorus struck the girl, sending her to her knees in last year's dead leaves, and Jenny felt in her bones the desperate flutter of unformed magic that Yseult tried to fling at him: make him forget, make him love me, make him not hurt me, make him go away . . .

Nothing to the purpose, even had they not been shattered by the girl's fear: not only fear, but her desperation to be loved by someone, even the man whose boot-toe smashed into her ribs. "It was her that made them spells!" Yseult sobbed. "She put that pain on you just now!"

The men were spreading out, swords drawn, into the woods. Jenny remained still, veiled in mists and darkness, until they passed, while Balgodorus dragged Yseult to her feet by the hair, stripped her bodice from her back and welted her with his belt, new red marks burning on the white skin among the old. Only when he thrust her, shivering with her thin arms folded over her naked breasts, before him through the thickets toward the camp did Jenny finally turn away, and drift back to the manor.

"And damn me if it wasn't a thing like an iron wash-pot, and no dragon at all!" John leaned forward on the low cushioned divan and gestured earnestly with a handful of fish stew. Lord Ragskar glanced at Lord Ringchin, and then at the three gnomish Wise Ones who completed the circle at the High Table beneath an intricate canopy of pierced and fluted sandstone. All were still, startled, tongs and spoons of inlaid gold poised in their hands. Servants—gnomes all, in liveries of the bright soft silks woven beneath the ground and huge overelaborate jewelry—drew close to listen, and John pitched his voice into tones of deep distress.

"So here I am, sittin' me horse, feelin' a complete ass with all these harpoons and arrows and such—I mean, I'll go after any dragon in the northlands, but how the hell do you fight a wash-pot?—when me son come ridin' out of the gate, and yells,

I'll draw it off, Da', and goes after the thing with a spear. I shouted at him, but this sort of lid flips up in the thing and an arm comes out, a metal arm like a well-sweep, with iron claws on it, and grabs him, seizes him off his horse, and drags him inside it. And I'm throwing harpoons and firin' the crossbow and none of it's doin' a bloody thing, and the arm comes out again and whacks me silly off me horse, except I snagged me boot in the stirrup and the horse goes tearin' galley-west across the moor with me draggin' along behind . . ."

He saw the two gnome-kings clutch hard at their dignity and their manners and shut their mouths tight to keep from laughing at the image, and knew that he'd destroyed himself as any threat in their eyes. He glanced down at the hunk of pale flesh and sauce dripping in his hand, as if just remembering that he held it, and gulped it down, licking his fingers and then cleaning them fastidiously in the lotus-shaped glass goblet beside his plate. Tongs and spoon lay beside it untouched, the gems on them winking in the glow of lamps that hung on long chains from the ceiling. Clear pale light, far stronger than that of fire: hothwais charged with sunlight, beyond a doubt. John had always found his display of amiable barbarism—his dancing-bear act, as he called it—an effective means of getting people to underestimate him, particularly those who put stock in table manners. Or, in this case, those who had contempt for all of the tall men who lived above the ground. They didn't have to know that Aunt Jane would have worn him out with a birch broom to see him eat with his hands.

"I've been on this thing's track for three days," he went on after a time. "Did I say it had wheels? Well, sort of wheels—they were like two inside another three, and they moved . . ." He gestured vaguely, his hands trying to describe something that wouldn't tell them anything, really. He'd seen some fairly bizarre designs in his studies of ancient engineering. The less said the better to the gnomes about dragons, or about mages who saved their lives in order to enslave them. "Anyroad, the thing I'm using to track them with—this thing Jen rigged up that will smell out the magic amulet around Ian's neck—tracked 'em to the Gorm Peaks at the north of the peninsula here, or maybe to

Yarten Isle beyond. I can't tell, for it's too far, and this device of Jen's needs a thunderstone—a piece of a star—to work properly. And that's why I'm here."

He wiped his fingers on his plaid, propped his spectacles, and leaned forward, his face desperate with genuine anxiety and the feigned earnestness of the man he sought to make them think he was: barbarian, braggart, and not terribly bright. "I need magic thingies, y'see," he said. "Thingies to make this device of Jen's work, and to get close enough to where this wizard's hidden that I can find him and Ian. You know I've served your kin in Wyldoom, and served 'em well. And I've come to ask—I've come to beg—if there's aught I can do that'll get me these things from you."

Lord Ragskar's pale eyes slid sidelong to touch those of his brother-king. Lord Ragskar was the smallest gnome John had ever seen, barely over two feet in height and with a disturbingly babyish, beardless face. He looked in fact like a child—a wildly overdressed child, with his collars and bracelets of heavy gold and slabs of opal and turquoise, his rings of jewels faceted as the gnomes knew how to do—until you saw him move. Lord Ringchin was larger, fatter, and older, but clearly it was Ragskar who was the brains of the pair.

"In fact, there is." Lord Ragskar set down his tongs and wiped his fingers on a napkin: John had used his to wrap around his hand when he seized a joint of hot meat. "There is a bandit." He cleared his throat, and John leaned forward and did his best to look like he believed every word. "A robber, who . . . er . . . entered the Deep some weeks ago to steal. Eluding the guards, he took refuge in the mine shafts, but he has attacked a number of guards—to steal weapons, so he is now well armed—and has tried several times now to break into the food stores on the Twelfth Deep."

He nodded to the foremost of the Wise Ones, a hard-looking creature like a densely withered apple, pale gold eyes peeking from beneath brows long enough to braid. "Lord Goffyer here, Lord of the Twelfth Deep, has attempted to scry him out, but Brâk—this is his name—has stolen scry-wards and so protects himself from being found. Moreover, as a human, Brâk is able to move faster than we, particularly where the levels are flooded, and in a narrow way his strength is greater than ours in single combat. We would take it as a great favor if you would deal with this man. Then we can speak of reward."

"I'll do that very thing." John sprang to his feet and managed to knock plate, cup, and three pieces of cutlery off the low stone table as he did so, not bad for a single swipe. "Oops. Sorry." He held out his hand, grasping in turn the tiny, hard, muscular hands of each startled king. "You can count on me. Oh, and accordin' to Cerduces Scrinus' *Principles*, soda-water will take care of that stain."

John did not for a moment believe that any robber in his or her senses would attempt to thieve from the Deeps of the gnomes. In fact, he guessed that his target was the leader of escaped slaves. But simply having a square meal made him feel better, and afterward the Wise One Goffyer came to the guest chamber and gave him medicaments for his half-healed wounds.

Despite this helpful hospitality, the moment Goffyer was out of sight John went over the chamber very thoroughly, pulling aside wall-hangings and propping what few pieces of furniture there were in front of any part of the delicately hued wall that looked like it might conceal a doorway. He slept with all the lamps of green and gold glass left burning and his satchel of poisons tied around his waist. The Wise One had made two discreet attempts to get his hand on it and hadn't taken his eyes from it throughout the visit.

In the morning, after another good meal, John stated his demands: a star-fragment, or thunderstone, which he knew were powerful magic that the gnomes never parted with; a few ounces of ensorcelled quicksilver, something that the gnomes also guarded intently; and incidentally a hothwais charged with heat to keep the *Milkweed* afloat. The gnome-kings said they would consider the matter. Then he armed himself in his doublet of iron and grubby leather, his iron cap, dagger, and fighting-sword— his bow would be useless in the inky tunnels—slung the satchel of poisons over his shoulder, and set out for the Twelfth Deep, where the "bandit" had last been reported.

As he'd guessed, though only gnome-servants had been in evidence at dinner last night, at least some of the kitchen staff were human slaves, and they'd reported his presence to their brethren hiding in the deeper tunnels. Even before he left the passageways where the lamps burned bright he sensed himself being watched, though that might have been Goffyer. The Twelfth Deep was where the mine-workings began, both the active seams of silver and the abandoned ones that had been flooded or were infested with some of the more unpleasant creatures that dwelled below ground.

They'd given him a lantern, which burned oil rather than carrying a hothwais, and its light seemed to shrink as he passed into the less and less frequented realms. Somewhere a whiff of foulness breathed from a rock seam: damp stone, then the stink of scalded blood and sulfur. Among the rocks the last lights burned blue and small.

Passing these, he carried his single lantern far into the empty mines, then set down his weapons, and stripped off his doublet and cap. As he'd intended—and hoped—when he walked forward into darkness with his hands upraised, the escapees took him fairly quickly. Invisible hands seized him from the darkness and led him to Brâk, who was perfectly happy to bargain with him for enough soporifics to knock out the guards who prevented the slaves from escaping and a good map of the territory that lay between the Tralchet Peninsula and the first of the King's new garrisons.

"So it's true the King's sent his army again," said Brâk. His voice was deep and musical, with an accent like an educated southerner and a courtier's turn of phrase. "Good news, for everybody except the slave traders and the bandits and these pigs here." John heard him spit. "And what of you, my four-eyed friend? Is it true there's a mad wizard on the loose, raiding the garrisons and stealing horses in a magical iron wash-pot? Or was that just a tale to get old Ragskar to part with a thunderstone? He won't, you know. Those are strong magic, I've heard; strong enough from time to time to break the scry-wards we've surrounded our hideouts with."

"Oh, I knew that," John said cheerfully. "What I need is a hothwais, and a strong one, charged with heat to keep the air hot in my balloons. I had to say somethin', to let them talk me down."

Brâk chuckled, a deep rich sound in the blackness. "We have

hothwais here among us that will hold heat for two weeks before
we have to sneak back up to the forges and replenish their
strength. If we win through to the outer air, we'll need them less,
once we can be away where the smoke of fires won't show us up.
So you're welcome to them, my friend. We'll leave them where
you leave the maps, on the north side of Gorm Peak near the rear
gate of the mines."

So it was that John returned to the brother-kings and excused
himself from further search for their "bandit." "For from what I
glimpsed of them in the tunnels—and it was only a glimpse I
got—it seems to me there's a lot of 'em, and I'll not work to kill
my own people, who're only tryin' to free themselves."

"These are not slaves," said King Ragskar firmly in his
strange alto voice. "The bandit is a wicked man who entered our
realm with many followers."

"Be that as it may," said John. "I'll not be tricked into workin'
for the profit of slave-drivers, no matter what the cost."

That was the only time, in the Deep of the Gnomes, that he
genuinely thought he might have to fight his way out, which he
knew he was in no shape physically to do. He doubted that even
such heroes as Alkmar the Godborn would have been able to
fight their way through the corridors and guardrooms that separated him from the main gate, and Brâk had warned him of the
kings and especially of Goffyer. "Slaving and treachery is the
least of the evils to fear from them, my friend," the deep soft
voice had said. "Things we can scarcely guess at are done here.
It is best that you get out, and get out quickly. And if you see
Goffyer come at you with an opal or a crystal vial in his hand,
fight to the death."

But his performance of the night before had had its effect, and
he saw it in the contempt in the gnome-king's eyes. No one offered to demonstrate Goffyer's magic opal; they even gave him
food before they set him on his way. Regretfully John buried
the food without tasting it—*Let's not dig ourselves a grave with
our fork, Johnny*—and spent the next several hours and the remainder of the *Milkweed*'s lofting power mapping the countryside around the small rear entrance of the Mines of Tralchet and
down the vales below Gorm. He left these maps in the cleft of a

great gray stand of granite. When he returned to the place on foot the following day, he found a fist-sized pale stone there, and several smaller ones, the air around them shaking with the heat. Written on the granite below were the words, *Thank you. We will not forget,* in the hand and style of the Court of the south.

Alkmar the Godborn would probably have done it differently, John reflected with a sigh. *But we all do what we can.*

On the fifth day after his departure from Alyn Hold, therefore, he lifted off from the rear slopes of Gorm Peak, under heavy ballast, and set forth again to the northwest. By noon he passed the cliffs and glaciers of the hard and terrible peninsula and saw below the green-black water tossing with luminous mountains of ice. Then the land fell behind him, and he was over open sea.

Dark waves flecked with silver lace. White birds winging. Whiter still, icebergs carved and cut and hollowed by the action of the water, and the constant thrumming of the wind. Cold and the smell of the sea. Weariness and silence. Checking the compass and checking it again, and praying the adjustments the gnomes had made to the engines would last until he reached his goal. There seemed no strength left in him now, and he did not know what he would do if anything went wrong.

Sunset, and the dark backs of whales broke through the waves, blowing steamy clouds before they sounded again. The shadow of the *Milkweed* lying on the water for a time, longer and longer, and then twilight and the fairy moon.

Dreams of Jenny. Dreams of Ian.

A dawn of silence and birds.

And after another day of checking the compass, adjusting the engines and the sails and watching the whales and the birds, after another light-filled night, sunrise showed him the rocky fingers of cliffs spiking the sea before him, north and south and stringing away into the west, endless, tiny, dark, and rimmed with white. The new light smote them, seeming to pick glints of silver from the rocks, distant and pure and untouched. And above the twisted cordillera of the Skerries of Light, dragons hung in the air, bright chips of color, like butterflies in the glory of morning.

CHAPTER TEN

"M'am Jenny . . ."

She heard the whispering in her mind, the familiar call of scrying, and let the images of John in his fantastic vehicle fade. He had evidently come unscathed from the fortress of the gnomes, though she had no idea what he had done there.

"M'am Jenny, please . . ."

Balgodorus had attacked again, fire-arrows and catapults and more of Yseult's crude ugly spells of craziness and pain. Food was running low. Scrying the woods, Jenny had seen three more of Rocklys' scouts, hanged or nailed dead to trees. Scraped raw with strain, Jenny understood his strategy, the same strategy he used against the girl who was his slave.

Break her concentration. Wear away her ability to do her part in the manor's defense.

Rocklys is right, Jenny thought. *We do need more mages, trained mages, if we are to defend the Realm.* She reached out to the calling.

Yseult stood in the clearing beside the carven stone. The slanted light of evening brazed the unwashed seaweed tangle of her hair. She held her cloak about her, shivering, and glanced over her thin shoulder again and again. Outside her own window Jenny heard the outcry and cursing of the men on the walls, the bandits attacking—yet again, always again.

"M'am Jenny, please answer me!"

"I'm here." Jenny brushed her hair from her eyes, reached her mind through the scrying-crystal, through the water in the stone. "I'm here, Yseult." Sleepiness gritted on her like millstones; her eyes and skin and soul felt scorched with it.

"Come here and get me!" the girl pleaded desperately. "I'm supposed to be sleeping—he only lets me sleep when I'm not with him, with the men attackin'. I said I felt sick, and I do feel sick. He kicked me and said I better not be ailing. I can't stand it anymore!" She turned, scared, at a sound, eyes huge with terror and guilt. There was a fresh bruise on her chin, and the dark marks of love-bites on her neck.

"M'am Jenny, I'm sorry, I'm so sorry I called him after you!" Her voice was hoarse and shaking. "You got no idea what he's like when he's mad, and he's mad all the time now. Mad that you folks are holding out like you are, and mad because Rocklys be sending patrols and killin' his men, and spoilin' it for him when he tries to take food and slaves and that. M'am Jenny, I know I was bad but I was scared!"

"It's all right," said Jenny, her mind racing. By the noise outside it was a heavy attack, and Pellanor's half-starved defenders were at their last strength. "There's an old house where Grubbies used to live, on the edge of Black Pond, do you know it?" The girl nodded and snuffled, wiping her nose. "Can you get there? Did you take some food with you when you left?"

"A little. I got bread in my pockets."

Probably too frightened to hunt for any, and small blame to her.

"All right. When you get to the house, make these marks at the four corners. Make them slowly, and as you're making them, here are the words to say, and the colors to think about, and the things to hold in your mind . . ."

It was the simplest of ward-spells, the most basic cantrips of There's-Nobody-Here and Don't-You-Have-Pressing-Business-Elsewhere? Still, as Jenny outlined each guardian sigil, repeated the words of Summoning and the focus of power, she wondered despairingly how much of it Yseult's untrained and undisciplined mind would hold. A word said wrong, a sigil misdrawn or misplaced, would invalidate the spell, and Balgodorus' men, who surely knew the location of the ruined house as well as she and Yseult did, would find her. Jenny, worn down from battling the crazy effects of the girl's wild spells, felt a weary urge to slap Yseult senseless, to scream at her for being such a cowardly little fool as to do whatever her master said.

Of course she's a cowardly little fool, thought Jenny tiredly. *If you were unable to defend yourself with your magic two-thirds of the time, if you'd been convinced all your life that you needed a man, any man, to run your life and tell you what to do, how brave would you be?*

Where the hell was she going to get the strength to turn back the bandit attack enough to sneak out? How was she going to drive them away quickly enough that Balgodorus wouldn't find Yseult?

What had John learned, or guessed, or seen, that had sent him north in that crazy contraption to seek the dragons in their lairs on the Skerries of Light?

Ian . . .

She tried not to think about what might have become of Ian.

First things first.

"Mistress Jenny!" Someone pounded at the door of her room. "Mistress Jenny, I'm sorry to wake you, but you must help us!"

Smoke stung her nostrils. Jenny wanted to lay one vast comprehensive death-spell on them all.

First things first. She traced out a power-circle on the floor, shut her mind to the noises, the smoke, the cold tingling of fear under her breastbone. Brought to mind the place and phase of the moon, calling it clear in her heart and memory, circling it with runes. Brought to mind the magics of the three oak trees that lay due north of the manor, and the ash that stood due south, speaking their names and the names of their magics. Called on the silver energies of the stream, positioning it exactly in her mind, aligning it with the deep, still power of standing water, the courtyard well . . .

A little here. A little there.

The stars invisible overhead by day. The granite and serpentine of the rock beneath the ground.

Her bones, and the gold ribbons of dragon-strength that wound around them and through them, legacy of Morkeleb the Black.

The power of the earth and the stars, feeding the dragon-magic.

First things first. Find the girl Yseult and strengthen the wards around her, so that she would not be found—always supposing this was not a trap in the first place. Then redouble the attack against Balgodorus, sure now that her magic would not be counterspelled. It wouldn't be easy, and he'd be searching for Yseult. Too much to hope that Yseult would be strong enough to help them against "her man." Her man forsooth!

At least, without Yseult scrying the woods, a messenger could get through to Rocklys.

Jenny drew a deep breath, the slow fire of power filling her veins. A false glitter, she knew, and one that would take its toll on her later, but later was later. "Mistress . . . !" cried the voices outside, urgent, desperate. Her consciousness, altered by the concentrations of magic, heard them seemingly from a great distance away. Cold, as if, like the dragons, she floated weightless in the air.

She spun a final scrim of gold about herself, a protection and a balancing, a shawl of light. Reaching with her magic, feeling where the other woman's counterspells protected scaling-ladders, weapons, armor, and men. They had been at this game for weeks, shoving and scratching one another like animals in a pen. Counterspells marked the horses' bridles, the axles, triggers, ropes of the catapults.

The spells, thought Jenny, would have to be placed in the ground, or in the air.

This was more difficult, and far more complicated than the usual battle-magic; this was the point at which a mage of lesser strength, but greater lore, could win over a stronger but less skilled opponent. During all the years of knowing herself to be weak, Jenny had learned any number of work-around magics, in the knowledge that even the simplest counterspell could overset the best she could offer. She went back to them in exhaustion, calling images of the battle in her scrying-crystal and placing spells of fire or smoke or temporary blindness in the air where Balgodorus' men would cross them in their rush to attack, rather than on the men or the horses or the tools they used. The spells themselves were weak. Even her calling of power had not yielded much to her spent body and fatigued mind. But in her crystal's heart she saw one of the bandits spring back from the base of the wall as the scaling-ladder burst into flame in his hands; saw another go shrieking and waving his arms into the bloodied, ruin-choked slop of the moat.

She felt no triumph. Poor stupid louts, she thought, and pitied even their chief. To live as they lived, surrounded by brutality and hardship, seemed to her almost punishment enough for being what they were. Many of them had to die, for this would not cease their depredations on the weak; it was all they understood. But her heart ached for the children they had once been.

Not many minutes later Pellanor came to the door of her chamber. He was wounded in the head and blood smeared his armor, but he stopped, looking in silently, and made to silently go. Jenny raised her head from her scrying-stone, "No." Her mouth and face felt numb, as if speech were a great effort through the thick haze of power-spells and concentration. She raised her hand.

The Baron's grizzled eyebrows bunched down over the hatchet of his nose. "Are you all right? Can I fetch you something?"

She shook her head.

"They're wavering," he said. "They've broken, on the south wall. I thought you were spent, you need rest . . ."

"I did," Jenny said thickly. "I do. Not now." She got to her feet. "I must go. Outside."

"Now? Over the wall?"

She nodded, impatient at the flash of disbelief and anxiety in his voice. Did he think that after all this she'd run away? "Yseult," she said, hoping that would explain all this and then realizing that it didn't even come close. If the attackers were wavering before her renewed defenses, it wouldn't be very many minutes before Balgodorus went back to fetch his mistress; wouldn't be many minutes before the hunt was on. She had to reach Yseult and renew the warding-signs before then.

But she couldn't say it, couldn't say anything. Only shook her head and muttered with great effort, "I'll be back."

If Balgodorus even suspected Yseult had taken refuge within the manor, or changed sides to betray him, he would redouble his attacks and would never forgo his vengeance. She barely heard Pellanor's arguments and questions at her heels as she made her

way outside. Only once or twice she shook her head and repeated, "I must go. I'll be back."

Men milled about under the south wall. A siege ladder burned
in the mud of the ruined moat. Arrows flew back and forth, not
nearly as many as there had been earlier; one of the manor children scurried along under the protection of the palisade, pulling
out stuck enemy shafts for use tomorrow. Some of those missiles
had been back and forth between sides six or eight times. Jenny's
spells and Yseult's both marked the feathers. In spite of her
weariness Jenny had to smile. John would be amused by that.

"They're breaking." Pellanor looked behind him across the
courtyard, to a woman signaling from the opposite wall. "Old
Grond Firebeard's decided to give us victory at last. Can you tell
me where you're going?"

"Later." Jenny shut her eyes, called to mind the copse of trees
just opposite the northeast watchtower and summoned to it a
blinding burst of colored light, so sharp that the glare of it penetrated her eyelids even here. She heard the robbers yell—
although both she and Yseult had used such diversions on and
off for weeks—and opening her eyes, saw them running in that
direction. "Now!"

Pellanor dropped the rope. Jenny swung over the sharpened
stakes, dragged around her the rags of concealing spells, and let
herself down quickly. Someone cried out, and an arrow broke
against the stone of the wall near her shoulder. Too much to hope
the spells protected her, exhausted as she was. Rather than
strengthen them, which wouldn't work anyway as long as she
was still in their sight, she called instead the easier illusion that
she was an elderly man, low in value in the slave market and running for his life.

Someone shouted, "Don't let him get away!" and a couple of
arrows stuck in the earth, wide of their mark. Jenny tightened
her grip on her halberd and bolted for the woods.

Nymr sea-blue, violet-crowned . . .

And somehow the turn of that music, medium-swift, trip-foot
yet stately, spoke of the shape of the dragon John saw before
him, circling the bare pale spires of the rock near which the

Milkweed hovered, sixty feet below. Not dark like sapphires, nor yet the color of the sea—not these northern seas at any rate—more was he the color of lobelia or the bluest hearts of blue iris. But he was violet-crowned. The long, curving horns that grew from among the flower-bed mane were striped, white and purple; the ribbon-scales streaming in pennons from the shorter, softer fur gleamed a thousand shades of amethyst and plum. Long antennae swung and bobbed from the whole spiked and rippling cloud, and these were tipped with glowing damson lights. The dragon swung around once and hung motionless on the air like a gull, regarding him. Even at that distance John knew that the eyes, too, were violet, brilliant as handfuls of jewels.

Don't look at his eyes, he thought, bending his head down over the ebon and pearwood hurdy-gurdy, the wind gently rocking the swaying boat. *Don't look at his eyes.*

He played the tune that was Nymr's, fingers moving true with long practice over the ivory keys. A hurdy-gurdy is a street instrument, made to be heard above din and at a great distance in open air. The music curled from the rosined wheel like colored ribbon unspooling: blue and violet.

Nymr hung in the air for a moment longer, then tilted those vast blue butterfly wings and plunged straight down into the sea.

John saw the wings tuck back, cleave water. From overhead, for two days now, he'd watched the movement of the fish in the ocean, seeing down through the creeping waves to the schools of huge seagoing salmon, swordfish, and marlin, pale shapes that flashed briefly into view and sank away again. The gulls and terns, gray and white and black, that wheeled about the cliff-girt promontory scattered and circled, then returned to mew about the balloons. The dragon speared the deep, plunging away in a long spume of silver bubbles. *Creatures of heat and fire,* thought John. *How did they not die in the water's cold?*

Stillness and silence. The waves broke in ruffles of foam on the rocks, without the slightest roll that spoke of shelving shallows anywhere beneath. Rather the rock rose straight out of the water, all cliffs, line behind jagged line. Dwarf juniper, heather, sea-oats furred them with the occasional wind-crippled tree;

birds nested among them casually, like chickens on the rafters of a barn. The wind moaned through the rocks and John turned the fans of the *Milkweed* to hold the craft steady. The next island lay ten miles to the northwest. The sea horizon was pricked with them, thumb-tiny in distance. The gulls all opened their mouths and screamed . . .

Then the dragon broke the waves in an upleap of water, purple and flashing in the fountain brilliance directly under the *Milkweed*. John grasped and swung on the rigging, causing the fragile craft to heel, and the tourmaline wing knifed past close enough to douse his face with spray. It had only to spit fire at him and he was done, he thought, swiveling one of the small catapults to bear as the dragon vanished above the air bags. Sixty feet above water, any fight would be a fight to death. Shadow crossed him, light translucent through the stretch of the wings.

Then it was hovering in front of him again, rocking on the air as a boat rocks at anchor.

John stepped back from the weapon, picked up the hurdy-gurdy, and played again the pixilated threnody of the dragon's name.

The swanlike head dipped and angled. The eyes faced front, a predator's eyes. The entire great dripping body, thirty feet from beak-tip to the spiked and barbed pinecone of the tail, drifted closer.

John felt a querying, a touch and a pat, cold and alien as long slender fingers, probing at his mind. He concentrated on the music, wondering if indeed the dragon's name would keep the dragon from killing him. One of Gar's ballads had Selkythar the Golden writing the Crimson Drake Ruilgir's name on his shield, so the dragon's fire rebounded and consumed its creator—not a technique John was eager to put to the test.

Query again, sharper, pricking. He kept himself from looking up, knowing the amethyst eyes sought to capture his.

????, Songweaver.

His heart was beating hard. "I came to work no one's harm," he said, raising his head but keeping his eyes on the lapis claws, the beaded azure enamel of the leg-spines. "I'm here seeking Morkeleb the Black. Does he dwell on these isles?"

The mind slipped aside from his, indifference succeeding a

momentary spark of curiosity. Morkeleb the Black had spoken to him mind to mind, in human words or what had felt like human words at the time. All he sensed here was a tumbling surge of images that came and went. For a moment he seemed to see Morkeleb swimming in a thick green sea or flying in thick green air, Morkeleb indefinably different from his memory. Black wings, black mane, black horns; black scales like ebony spikes along back and joints and nape. Black claws reaching out, to slide through a thing that billowed in the water/air before him like a great gelid cloud of poisonous diamond.

Morkeleb in darkness, outlined by the light of stars. Reading the stars, thought John. Weightless in the Night beyond Night and scrying their light, seeing where each star lay and what it was made of.

Then Nymr's mind turned away, with an almost palpable shrug.

"I need to find him," John said and averted his eyes quickly as the dragon floated around to face him, reaching for him with those crystalline mulberry eyes. All that came to him through his mind was a sense of dismissal, contempt:

Tiny, peeping—the image was of a bird-baby in its nest—*nothing. A flower scent passingly pretty. Devoured.*

Nymr floated off. John saw the bird-head cock, rise, and fall on its neck. The star-drake studied the *Milkweed*, air bags and catapults and wheels and flashing fan-blades. He felt the traces and echoes of the dragon's curiosity, as if the creature were trying to fit together pieces of a puzzle. He felt it also when Nymr shrugged it away. Nymr's mind closed, indifferent again. No threat. Nothing that affected him.

Not a thing.

Meaning, as he had heard Morkeleb say, *Not a thing of dragons*.

John leaned on the tiller and put the *Milkweed*'s fans over a few degrees, strengthening their beat until the craft moved off around the towering crags, toward the next promontory, many miles away. Nymr hovered for a time, watching him—he was aware of the creature's eyes on his back as he had seldom been aware of anything. Then the dragon plunged down into the ocean again, to emerge a few minutes later with a twelve-foot swordfish struggling in its claws.

Jenny circled the Grubbie house three times before going in. The wards she'd showed Yseult glimmered on the slumped stone and mud of the walls, surprisingly strong. The girl had talent, and a genuine feel for the sources of power, once she had an idea of what they were and how to find them. Casting her awareness through the woods all around, Jenny detected no trace of ambush, no scent of men in the trees, no boot-broken twig or trampled mud. Yseult's tracks, too, had been eradicated where they crossed soft ground, or hidden in the leaves and stones. Crouched in the gathering gloom, Jenny breathed on her crystal and whispered, "Yseult?"

It was a few moments. The girl didn't have a scrying-stone of her own and, by the look of it, was bent over a puddle outside the back door.

"Yseult, I'm here. I'm coming in."

And if it's a trap, thought Jenny, with a twist of wryness to her mouth, *shame on me.*

The house had been looted years ago. The stone walls of the old dwelling, where the family had lived before they'd degenerated into night-creeping scavengers, were charred and smoke-stained. The dirty little hummocks and burrows all around it, where the Grubbies had actually slept and stored their food, appeared undamaged, but Jenny saw that all the entrances had been stopped, imprisoning the inhabitants to starve. Unlike the Meewinks, who took in travelers, then killed and ate them, Grubbies as a tribe subsisted on garbage, gleanings of the fields and middens, and the occasional pilfered chicken or cow. Yet in their way they were even more despised: inbred, bestial, with neither laws nor lore of any sort. Pellanor, who had begun with intentions of being a ruler to all he found in his part of the Wyrwoods, had ended by simply driving them out.

Jenny saw no sign of Yseult at first. But she waited patiently, showing herself to be alone. After a few moments the girl crawled out from one of the burrows, and stood picking dirt out of her hair. "Don't let him get me," she whispered and glanced around her. "Please." Both her eyes were blackened.

"I promise." Jenny saw by the tilt of the girl's head that *I promise* was something from her childhood, something that meant she was being lied to.

"Just get me away from here." Yseult shivered but made no attempt to escape when Jenny walked over and gave her a gentle hug. It was like putting her arms around a wooden doll. "I don't care if you take me to Rocklys or give me to the demons or what. I just can't be with him no more."

And if he comes back, thought Jenny, looking up into those shadowed eyes, *you'll fly to him again, and you know it.* Yet if she left Pellanor now, to convey this wretched child southwest to Corflyn, there would be only corpses at Palmorgin when she returned. She knew this as clearly as if she saw it in her scrying-stone.

"Can you stay here another night and a day?" she asked. "I can't leave my friends, not until I've made some provision for their safety. Balgodorus will think you've come into the fort with us. I'll make sure he thinks so. He won't be hunting you here. Would you be willing to travel with someone else to Corflyn Hold?"

Yseult looked scared, eyes showing white all around the rims; her blunt childish hands tightened on Jenny's plaid. "Can't I wait for you?" she asked. "If it's not too long? It wouldn't be. Them spells I puts on Balgodorus' armor and weapons and such, I have to put them on just about every day. They wears off that fast."

Of course they would, thought Jenny, with a rush of sympathy for the mind-breaking work of making and remaking all those spells. *She can't source power from one day to the next. She must be on the verge of collapse.*

"Will you be all right here?" she asked. "I'll try to get food to you, but I may not be able to."

Yseult shrugged and wiped her nose. "I been hungry afore."

"Whatever you do," said Jenny, opening her satchel, "don't go out of the circle of these walls. I'm going to strengthen the spells on them, so that Balgodorus' searchers won't see you in here. They won't even see this house or think about the house being here. They'll think they're in another part of the woods entirely

But if you go outside, not only will they be able to see you, but the spells themselves will be broken, and the house will no longer be protection."

"Why's that?" Yseult followed Jenny as she laid out her small packets of powdered herbs and dried wolf-blood, her silver-dust and ochre earth. The girl kept her hands behind her back, watching alertly as Jenny remade the guardians at the corners and began to sketch the power lines to source the magic of sky and stars and earth.

"Because the spells demarcate and stabilize a situation as it is," Jenny replied. "Power moves along the lines, in a flowing circle. Once the lines are broken, the power flows out."

"And you learned all this?" For the first time her expression showed something besides terror or apathy. "And can I learn all this, about witchery? How long did it take?"

"It took many years." Jenny traced a line in the air and saw Yseult's eyes follow. She must see, as the mageborn could, the glowing trace of the spell. "I started learning when I was a little girl. There was an Icerider woman, an Icewitch, living in the Hold . . ."

She hesitated, seeing as if it were yesterday, and not forty years gone, the elongated elegant face, the colorless eyes stony with contempt at Lord Aver's frustrated rage. "Bitch!" he'd screamed at her. "Hagwife!" Jenny couldn't recall what the fight was about, if she ever knew it. Now she understood that John's father had hated this woman because she had given him her body in derision. Because he could not turn away.

Why are you here? she had asked Nightraven once, with a child's frank curiosity. *If you know all this magic, why are you with Lord Aver?* Because even as a five-year-old child, she could see the look in Nightraven's eyes when she regarded her husband/captor, the man who had taken her at the point of his spear. *Why can't you just get away?*

Nightraven had folded those impossibly slender hands. In her height and her slimness, her sinuous bonelessness, she had always seemed almost like a drawing rather than a real woman; her black hair hung braided to her thighs. Her lips were very red, and though they were full and shapely, still they had that sensitive line, that reserve, that marked her son's. *I was cast out by my people, for my failure and my pride,* she had said. *They laid a geas on me, a spell of binding. One day they will send me word that my time of exile is done.*

And so they must have done. For one bitter autumn day when she was eleven Jenny had run from the Hold's kitchens where she slept up to the Lady's rooms and had found her gone, she and her frost-eyed wolf. Gone with no word, only a swirl of snow on the floor, leaving a baffled red-haired toddler motherless and a complex of love-spells on the man who had taken her prisoner such that he had never loved again, nor married any woman to be the stepmother of his child or the rival of Nightraven's memory in his broken heart.

"They's Iceriders with Balgodorus," Yseult ventured timidly, breaking Jenny's long silence. "One or two, that was throwed out of their tribe. They told me about the Icewitches."

"But none of them Icewitches themselves?" *That,* thought Jenny, *would be all we need.*

Yseult shook her head.

"Balgodorus has no other mages in his troop?"

Again the headshake. "Only me. He said . . ." She licked her lips. "He said he needed me." She sounded wistful.

"I daresay." Jenny tried hard to keep the sarcasm from her voice.

"Are there any but you, with Commander Rocklys?"

She sighed and traced the Fourth Guardian, connecting the links save the one through which she must pass when she left. The Sigil of the Rose, which drew the power of the moon, speaking to the others through the silver lines. "No. This would be easier if there were."

"I saw this other," said Yseult, and twisted again her chemise-points around grubby fingers. "Or dreamed about him, bringing a dragon back to life. Are dragons really beautiful, all different colors, with eyes like that? I thought they was green and ugly, and smelled of brimstone."

Jenny's hand froze in the air, and her breath in her lungs.

"He had a boy with him," the girl went on, groping at the recollection. "A wizard-boy, I thought—it was just a dream, I dunno how I knew—and he brought him up to the dragon, and they rode away on it together. I thought in my dream he might have been with Rocklys and was going to feed the wizard-boy to the dragon, and that's why I was afraid when I saw you. That you might do that to me. And there was something else there," she added, frowning. "Something I couldn't see. Something bad."

"Where?" said Jenny. "Did you see where this was? Or where they went? What the man looked like?"

Yseult only shook her head. "I didn't see his face at all. I couldn't. It was almost like he didn't have one. Or like it was a mask, and the eyes in it was a snake's or a dog's. Only the boy, and this dragon. And I was scared. But now I figure, even being fed to a dragon can't be no worse than staying with Balgodorus, if he's going to treat me like this. Can't you . . . Can't you take me not to Rocklys but just away from here? Can't you take me home with you, maybe, and teach me to be a witch and take care of myself? I won't be no trouble. I promise I won't steal from you or anything." And she crossed her heart like a child.

In the dark eaves of the Wyrwoods, Jenny heard the men searching, calling out to one another and cursing as they stepped in mud or on roots. She thought she could hear Balgodorus' voice, a roar of hatred against all things, perhaps women most of all. They'd be launching another attack, she thought. It was time to get back.

"When you meet Rocklys," Jenny said, "I'll let you decide, Yseult. But in the meantime, if there's a wizard out there who's kidnapping boys"—her voice seemed to strangle in her throat—"who's dealing with dragons, I think Rocklys ought to know about it."

CHAPTER ELEVEN

Not a thing of dragons.

That indifference, John reflected, might just be the saving of him.

The star-drakes were curious but unafraid. Reckoning perhaps that nothing human could do them harm.

God knows that's the truth. He lay on the palm of death like a thistledown on a still day. Like dolphins in the sea, or cows in a pasture, the dragons came to watch.

Two of them picked him up between Nymr's isle and the next, floating, as Nymr had done, weightless as kites above and behind him, following with slow lazy wing-beats above the winking sea. They were too far for him to identify them from the old lists. Likely not all the dragons were on the lists in any case, and only a handful of the tunes had survived. They were multicolored, iridescent as gems: the one to the north striped in yellow and green, to the south a marvelous jumble of reds and golds and blues. Later a third joined them, bronze spotted with blue like a peacock's tail, behind him to the east.

At the second isle he cast anchor, snagging the rocks above a little crescent of beach, and laboriously cranked the *Milkweed* down. This isle was perhaps thrice the size of Nymr's, with freshwater springs around which clustered twisted pines, heather, and hairy-stemmed northland poppies all pale pink and gold. Wild sheep roved here—John had seen them from the air—and birds without number, gulls and terns and pelicans, and some kind of fat gray flightless creature the height of his knee that waddled trustingly up to him as he dropped down over the gunwale and tried to eat the buckles on the sides of his boots.

Killing them would have been embarrassingly easy; so easy in fact that John couldn't bring himself to do it. Never having seen humankind, the mountain sheep would have proved scarcely less challenging targets, but he had no time to hang and smoke that much meat and was loath to waste it. He took his bow and shot gulls and terns; the bronze-dappled dragon flew in close, hovered and circled for some time around the *Milkweed* on its tether. It ignored John completely but reached out its long neck from time to time and bumped the air bags with its beak, like a dog sniffing at a floating bladder. John wondered what would become of him should one of the dragons decide to destroy the craft.

I suppose I'd live on fish and sheep till I'm an old man with a long beard, he thought, bemused by the image though by all rights he supposed he should be stiff with terror. He wondered if the dragons had the imagination to make the experiment, just to see what would happen. Since the dragons would do what they would do, beyond any ability of his to change, and since he had no other enemies in all the northern sea, he stretched out on the beach and slept, grateful not to be setting sail or charting a course or drawing maps or cranking the engine-pulley. He slept deep and did not dream, except for fragments of something about daffodils and Jenny braiding her hair.

When he woke a dragon was there, sitting on the rocks.

It had killed a sheep and was eating it, tearing it open to rip out the meat and entrails but leaving the pelt like a fruit-husk. John had seen such remains before, in the northlands. The dragon was yellow and black and white, with tiny complicated patterns of greens and purples worked along its back and down like a mask over its face. It ate cleanly, licking its paws and whiskers. He felt its mind touch and probe his, though he would not meet its eyes. Its thoughts came like music into his brain.

????—a question as much about the machine as about himself.

"Well, it's too long a way to come in a boat over the sea," pointed out John, sitting up and taking a drink from his water bottle. The dragon tilted its head and settled into a sort of resting crouch, watching him without movement save for the flicker of wind in the soft fuzz around the base of its horns. Gulls settled close to it. A piper ran up over the sand, and the fat gray dummies waddled near and pecked at the sheep's carcass as if they weren't aware of the dragon at all.

In time, keeping a wary eye on his visitor, John set a griddle over the embers of the fire, took a bowl and began to mix barley and water and a little salt, to make bannocks for his dinner. The white slip of the new moon set in the pale sky, the tide retreating from the shallow curve of beach. The world smelled of salt.

"I'm seeking Morkeleb the Black, who's said to be the greatest of the dragons; there's aught I'd learn of him. You lot have to admit it's the fastest way."

The dragon licked his whiskers again and combed them with his claws. John felt the strange-colored alien words tumble in his mind: *Hurrying always hurrying soon to die. Dayfly monkey-making-puzzle, seeking seeking always fiddling always. Learning why learning only to lose it all in the dark so soon?*

"It's just the way of us." John patted the bannocks into shape, dropped them onto the griddle. *And let's not forget and let them burn this time, you git.* "We build cities and tell each other tales, the way sheep climb the crags and birds fly."

Silly peeping. Morkeleb. Morkeleb.

And the thought entered his mind, not of Morkeleb's name but of the music that trailed behind it, and with that music the dragon's dark shape against the limitless stars. Black like the black of night, and misted with light.

Gone away. Gone away. Not a thing of dragons.

"Morkeleb's gone?" His heart sank. He had been prepared for a murderous attack by the black dragon, but not for his absence.

Not a thing of dragons anymore.

"D'you know why? And where he went?"

Indifference, like Nymr's, but tinged with something else. John realized the yellow dragon was afraid of Morkeleb.

Not get too near, not get too near. Always dangerous deep deep, falling into the stars. Black well in a black maze buried under a mountain, thoughts rising into his mind, cold darkness rising, then returning to the well. Shadowdrakes, dragonshadow, birdless isle in the west west west. Not a thing of dragons. This thing is made of what?

The dragon spread its silken wings, leaped skyward like a cat. It circled the *Milkweed*, and John called out the only name he knew—*yellow as the flowers, white and black* . . . "Enismirdal!" And when the dragon checked its flight, backing infinitesimally, he scrambled to his feet and pulled his pennywhistle from his pocket, forming shrill and thin the fifteenth of the dragon-songs, swift and pattering like the rain.

The dragon circled back. Flame and heat haloed its nostrils, and it hung in the air and hissed.

"Enismirdal," called John again, "if that's your name. The dragons themselves may be in peril. I need to find Morkeleb, or one of you who remembers a time when dragons were enslaved and made to serve wizards in the old days."

Peril? Dragons did not laugh, but there was a chiming in the air, like the falling ripple of ten thousand silver discs clashing. Enismirdal flung wide about him the net of his dragon-senses— John could almost see it, like a great cloud of golden spray on the air—and shivered all the defensive spikes of his body, from the horned and spired head down to the cruel mace of tail-tip. *Peril?*

Then it reached from the air with black enameled claws, and like a cat batting an insect in play caught John across the shoulders, lifting him and hurling him down into the sand. *Peril, Flying Man? Peril from that and you to star-drakes of the Skerries of Light?*

The silver discords burned the air, needled John's skull. Winded, bleeding, and covered in sand, John rose to his knees in the surf as Enismirdal wheeled toward the *Milkweed*, spitting fire.

"Ye stupid salamander, d'ye think I'd come here in this thing and warn you of it if the peril was from me and from that?" he bellowed. He wiped blood from his face. "Festering hell, I thought you drakes was supposed to be wise!"

Serpentine on flower-bed wings the dragon snapped around in the air, and all about it shimmered the scorch of its anger. *Wise? Wiser than some, who speak thus.*

It hung, a soundless cloud of brilliance above John, shadow lying on him where he knelt in the waves. The acid of its mouth dripped down to burn his face.

"You tell me if Centhwevir has been the same, since he returned from the lands of the east." John's breath rasped in his lungs; he squinted up at the creature. "And then kill me if you will."

The silence was so deep then that the crying of gulls rang loud, and the sough of the waves breaking behind him was a leisurely drum.

Not a thing of dragons, said Enismirdal's voice in his mind. *Others among us, each to his island alone. Centhwevir blue and gold*—and in the dragon's mind there was only the shape of the name, wrought of music—*nothing to me, nothing to me, where he comes or where he goes, and how he abides. Children of the stars, Flying Man; jewels of adamant, not slaves of Time as you. Not you, not me, none to say who we are or what we do.* The silver glitter of the dragon's anger chimed around him. *Being each of us—being. Remember.*

And he spit acid at him, flame hissing in the ocean inches from him, and wheeled in the air, then winged like a thrown spear to the south.

When he was out of sight, John became aware of the smoke from his campfire and the familiar smell of scorching barley. Shaking with shock he got to his feet, holding his arm where the blood ran down and limped up the beach to his camp. *At least,* he thought, shivering as he worked himself out of jacket and doublet and shirt to bind up the cuts the dragon had left on his arm and side, *he didn't destroy the* Milkweed.

But the incident brought home to him again the terrible fragility of his mission. As he packed up his camp—and ate the last of the stale bread he'd pilfered from the gnome-king's table—he found himself scanning again and again the horizons, knowing he was a fool and wondering whether he'd passed the degree of foolishness where it becomes not laughable but fatal. *Long ago, son,* he thought, resigned. *Long ago.*

He wrapped the gull meat in kelp from the beach and threw the burned bannocks to the dummies, who pecked at them once or twice and waddled disgustedly away. Though the sun was dipping toward the sea he unhooked the Milkweed's anchor and climbed the ladder as the wind took the silvery air bags, swinging out over the ocean. Once his engine was set he got out his charts again and scanned the sea with his telescope, sketching in the islands of the archipelago. He tried to give each its shape: domed skulls, spiring cliffs, here and there a shallow beach or the bright spangle of a spring. Between the islands the sea plunged blue-black, fathomless. Sometimes he could discern rock ridges joining one island to another: deadly reefs, ship-killers.

Whales sounded and played among the reefs and between the islands, great slate-blue shining backs arching clear of the water. Sometimes with them, and more often swimming alone, he saw other shapes, sinuous and snakelike, but it wasn't until one of these broke the surface with a long swan-neck and swam for some distance beneath the *Milkweed* that he realized these, too, were dragon-kind.

He dropped anchor at a small peak and spent the last of his strength winching the *Milkweed* down between the horns of its cleft. There he ate and in a cave in the rocks slept like a dead man; waking at noon, he brought down the telescope from the vessel and sat on the high cliff with it. Around a cliff-girt island not far off a dozen of the seagoing dragon-kind played. They were luminous dark purples and greens. Only when another dragon, black-figured crimson and gorgeous as a midnight rainbow, appeared in the sky and plunged down into the water with them did John realize that these were the females of the dragon-kind.

He journeyed on, following the Skerries west and north. In the light-drenched northern nights he traveled, searching at sunrise and sunset for the elusive comet Dotys had described. By day he slept, with the *Milkweed* drawn down as close to the rocks as he could force it so their shadows would render the craft less noticeable from a distance. Once he thought, looking through his spyglass at evening, that he saw Centhwevir, and discerned what might have been a man riding on his back. Once, making camp on an islet so isolated that the nearest neighbor was visible only when the *Milkweed* rode high above the crags, he found tracks: a dragon's claws, and a man's bootprints near the chewed and gull-torn bones of a couple of sheep. There were fragments of what looked like two seashells wrought of blown glass, but finer than any glass he'd ever seen, and near the remains of a fire carefully concealed with brush, a smaller print, a boy's boot with the nail-pattern characteristic of Peg, Alyn Hold's cobbler.

At last he came to the end of the Skerries and set out west over the open sea. For a day he was without any mark at all, as he had been when leaving the peninsula, and swept the horizon with his glass in vain. On the second day he saw peaks in the distance, wind-scoured, tiny, ringed all around with cliffs. When he came nearer, he saw that one of these islets had water, and it was there that he cast the *Milkweed*'s anchor and winched the craft down close to the blue-black rocks.

He rested, and ate, and searched until the light grew too dim for safety—the island was all rocks and little of it even flat enough to sit on. Nothing grew there. Not even birds nested on the high crags, though the big and the small islands to the south were alive with them. Only the keening of the wind in the rocks, and the gurgle of the stream, and the slow hammer of the waves broke the silence, and yet it seemed to him that he was never alone. At times this frightened him, at other times he felt he had never been in a place so peaceful in his life. In the morning he saw something like a shadow pass over the water, a gray flickering ghost that circled the rocks where the *Milkweed* was anchored. When he tried to look at it, there was nothing there.

Later he played on his hurdy-gurdy the tune Jenny had taught him, the air of the dragon's name, and the yowling voice of the instrument flung the notes against the cliffs and into the sky. Shadow covered him.

He looked up and saw Morkeleb the Black hanging above him like a nightmare kite.

John set down the hurdy-gurdy and shaded his eyes. The black dragon was not as large as some he had seen: forty feet from the smoking nostrils to the tip of the iron-barbed tail, and wings something close to twice that, outspread in the shining air. Mane, horns, streamers, and fur-tufts, scales above and below—all the things that on other dragons were saturated with color—were black, as if through the endless years the color had wearied him and he had put it aside. His eyes were white and silver,

Jenny had said, colorless as diamonds. He was careful not to look at them, or let them meet his.

He said, "Morkeleb," and the dragon reached down with its claws and settled, clinging to the rocks.

Dragonsbane. The voice that spoke in the hollows of his mind was such a voice as might speak omens in dreams. *Has someone paid you with books to seek me here, or with promises of men-at-arms?* As the dragon tilted his head to the side the whole lank rangy frame of him shifted, balanced on the rocks. The half-spread wings folded and tucked themselves against his sides, the long tail wrapped around the spire.

Though there was no particular inflection in the dragon's words—far more clearly articulate as words than any other dragon's John had encountered—he felt the simmer of irony and anger beneath them. The indifference and pride of the dragons, which had protected him thus far, was no protection here.

"No one paid me. I came of me own."

Seeking after knowledge, that you may better slay other dragons?

"Seeking after knowledge, anyroad," replied John. "But then I'm forever doin' that—and there's knowledge and knowledge. What I'm seeking is help." He raised his hand to shade his eyes, his spectacle lenses flashing in the sun.

"Well over a thousand years ago, it says in Juronal's *Moralities*—or anyway I think it's the *Moralities*, I've only got the back half of it—there was this wizard, see, named Isychros saved the life of a dragon. Now savin' a dragon's life involves learnin' its True Name—the true music of it, not the sort of tunes I've learned to play—and with that True Name, that true music, Isychros made the dragon his slave."

I am aware, Dragonsbane, how dragons are enslaved by their names. The anger in the air seemed to thicken, as if it were about to bead on the rocks.

John wet his lips. "Well, it seems Master Isychros didn't let it go at that. He sounds like one of those people that you lend him a horse to ride home on and he butchers it, sells the meat, sells the skin, stuffs a mattress with the hair, sells the mattress, and a year later sends you a silver piece to pay for it all—less interest, of course. This Isychros drove what Juronal calls a glass needle into the back of the dragon's head, which made the dragon Isychros' servant. And Isychros got a couple of pals of his—mages, they were—and ganged up to defeat and enslave other dragons as well, quite a lot of 'em in fact. He ended up with ten or fifteen mages, each of 'em holding sway over a dragon, and the lot of 'em went on to conquer the Kingdom of Ernine. Any of this familiar to you? I know Ernine *was* destroyed, way back in the days, but I don't know how."

What makes you think, Dragonsbane, that I was not there?

"Ah." John scratched his jaw, a scrubby brush of rusty red. "Well, it's good to know I haven't wasted the trip. It did happen, then?"

Silk-fine lids lowered over crystal eyes, and without actual words he felt the assent ripple and shiver in the air.

"And I read—at the end of Juronal's account—that they were defeated in the end, though it doesn't say how. Juronal wrote five centuries after all the shoutin' was over, and maybe all sorts of other stuff got mixed in with the story. But what Juronal says is that the wizards and the dragons all died." His heart was pounding, looking up at the dragon above him on the rocks. "Is that part true?"

That part is true, Dragonsbane.

A wave curled around the rocks below the snip of ledge on which he had slept. The rock feet, exposed by the retreat of the tide, were bearded with weed, alive with silver crabs. Turning his head, the dragon regarded the distance as though to scry the air.

It was not this wizardling's healing that bound Ramasseus and Othronin, Halcarabidar and Idironapirsith and the other star-drakes to the mages who rode on their backs. In his mind John heard the music of the dragons' names, beautiful and archaic as the songs of the stars, and knew without Morkeleb speaking of it that Ramasseus had been dark purple and green, Idironapirsith banded like a coral snake with salmon, yellow, and black.

This Isychros had a mirror, whose surface burned in darkness with a terrible light. Demons lived behind the mirror, and Isychros called them forth and put their power into devices of crystal and quicksilver, which he drove into the dragons' skulls. The demons entered into Isychros and burned out his heart, the core and essence of his being, and dwelled there instead in his flesh. Using his magic as a puppeteer in the marketplaces of men uses a puppet, they drove the souls out of the other mages whom Isychros touched, so that the mirror-demons could enter into their bodies and dwell there in their turn. Thus mage and dragon fused under the power of demons. This is the story of Isychros.

John's throat seemed to close, suffocating him, and he thought *Ian, no. It isn't true.*

His voice sounded like someone else's to him. "This isn't . . . isn't possible, is it? I mean, mages can deal with demons. Jen does. I've seen her."

There are demons and demons, Songweaver, as there are mages and mages. I only know that this was true, in that time and in that place.

"But he was defeated in the end, wasn't he?"

Some of the mages they cut to pieces alive and burned in fire, that the Hellspawn could not use the dead flesh as they had used the living. The mages of the city of Prokep in the desert found magic that would work against demons, withering them where they abode. When the demons were shriveled inside them, the dragons also died. The mirror was destroyed.

John found himself fighting for breath, as if he'd taken a blow to the pit of the stomach. "And was there no saving of any of them? No way to . . . to catch back the souls of those the demons had driven out? Or find them again where they'd been pushed out into the air?"

What is the way to catch back the souls of those that disease drives out, Dragonsbane? Or the violence that you practice against one another for sport?

No. No. No. He pressed his hand to his mouth as if trying to control his breath, or perhaps only to cover it from sight. When he took his hand away and spoke again, his voice was completely steady. "They've taken my son." He told what had happened at Cair Dhû, and what he thought he'd seen; the tracks at Frost Fell, and Rocklys' tale of a wizard with an outlaw band. "Centhwevir was bad hurt and came back here, I think, to recover. I saw Ian's tracks on an island three days' flight east of here, and those of this wizard with his bloody glass needles. There has to be a way to fetch Ian's soul back. I need your help, Morkeleb. I need it bad. And not only me."

And your Wizard-woman? The air rang with his irony and his anger, a cold sound like slips of glass breathed upon by wind.

John said nothing, but it was as if something inside him bled. *Not a thing of dragons anymore,* Enismirdal had said of the black dragon, and looking up at that cut-jet glitter John was suddenly reminded of his mother in her exile, alone on this birdless isle with whatever he had brought with him inside.

All that vast anger, colored by, John thought, years of silence and sea-winds, coalesced in that quiet level voice that spoke in the hollows of his mind.

I told her, when she turned from me, that there was a price for the loving of mortal things. This is that price. Had she remained with me—had she remained a jere-drake ... John heard and understood the word, a nonbreeding female—*you would not now need to seek me out. Were her son a dragon, there would not be this trouble.*

The dragon's anger was chill as flaying glass. John scratched his beard again, and said, "Well, at the risk of another dunking in the sea, I think you're wrong about that. If it was an accident that Centhwevir chose that time and that place to come raiding, I'll eat me gloves. This bloke in the pretty cap was Johnny on the Spot, waiting for me to do his job. It seems to me it won't be long before dragons'll be having as much of a problem as ever I am."

Dragons look after themselves. Morkeleb shifted his wings again and the early sunlight glistened on the bones of his pelvis, the ebon forest of spikes along joints and spine and skull. *In the days when Isychros formed his corps, we dwelt in the Mountains of the Loom, and in the caves of the mountains they called the Killers of Men; we dwell there no longer.*

Men are weak, Dragonsbane. When a man has been beset by a stronger man, he can run down the street of his smelly village crying, and others will come out of their doors and strike that strong man, for the weaker's sake. This is the way of men, who are always afraid.

John said nothing for a time, hearing on the rocks below him the voice of the surf. Trying to summon what to say that would draw this alien creature; trying with all the desperate knowledge that if he spoke wrongly, Ian was gone indeed. But all he could find to say was, "Don't let your hate for me rob her of the son she loves."

The dark head came swiftly around; John had to look aside fast, to avoid the diamond scintillance of the eyes. *You forget that it is not a man to whom you speak. Hate is not a thing of dragons.*

John said, "Nor is love."

No. With a snap like the strike of lightning the silken wings spread, catching the ocean wind. The dragon uncoiled his tail from the rocks. *It is not.*

A moment before the dragon had perched on his pinnacle, like some great glistening bird. Now it was as if muscle and scale and sinew had become shadow only, with no more weight than a scarf of thinnest silk. The wind lifted him easily, and he rose out of the shadows of the peak and seemed to flash all over with jewels as he came into the sun. John watched him with his whole heart crying out, *No!* The dragon's wings tilted; he swooped low over the waves, then climbed fast and steep, like a falcon rising above his prey. But he did not stoop like a falcon. He gyred again, high, high against the bright air, and flew west, dwindling to a speck and vanishing into the light.

CHAPTER TWELVE

I'll have to tell Jen.

The thought was almost more than he could bear.

And then: *I'll have to get the* Milkweed *back to land.*

In a kind of blank numbness John refilled every water container on the little craft at the spring, folded his blankets, and scattered the ash of his fire.

Ian was gone.

The demons entered into Isychros and burned out his heart . . . Using his magic as a puppeteer uses a puppet.

John touched the fading ache in his ribs.

Whatever was happening—whyever the demon mage had taken the mageborn boy—it was inevitable that they'd show up somewhere: demons, mages, dragon.

And at the moment, only he, John Aversin, knew.

He checked the *Milkweed*'s air bags and found them buoyant still. Scrambling up the ladder and over the withy gunwale as the craft lifted above the shadows of the surrounding cliff, he felt a curious sadness at leaving the birdless isle.

There was little charge in the engine, and he cranked for some time before it grew strong enough to turn the vessel's bow toward the largest of the three Last Islands. His first desire was to head east immediately: If the *Milkweed* came down halfway between the Skerries and the Tralchet peninsula he supposed he could sail her in to the sorry little cluster of huts and ruins on the estuary of the Eld River, but it wasn't anything he wanted to try. Yet his store of food was low. On the largest island he shot gulls and cooked them, gathered eggs to boil, and set forth again in the westering light. Mind and heart felt blank. He wondered if Jenny could see him in these dragon-haunted isles, and if so whether she knew what he did and what he had learned.

Ian was gone.

He closed his eyes and saw his son's boot-track, and the tracks of the man in the embroidered cap.

They were in the islands somewhere. *I could find them . . .*

He thrust the thought away. *They'll turn up,* he thought. *In the Winterlands, in the south, in the air above Cair Corflyn or Bel, spitting smoke and fire . . . They'll turn up.*

He prayed he could reach Commander Rocklys with the warning before they did.

In the pewter twilight of the northern midnight he saw a boy's face desperate with worry, dyed by the firelight and smoke of the lower court of the Hold: *I'm not inexperienced.* Saw a red baby's face no bigger than his own fist, ugly and frowning under a fuzz of silky black hair.

Oh, my son.

Demons.

His heart twisted inside him.

According to Dotys in his *Histories*, and passing references in Gorgonimir, the penalties for trafficking with demons in past times had included being skinned, boned, and burned alive. Gorgonimir listed an elaborate hierarchy of the Hellspawn ranging from simple marsh-wights, Whisperers, gyres, pooks, house-hobs, and erlkings to the dark-wights that bored their way into men's souls. *There are demons and demons,* Morkeleb had said. Reading the ancients, John had gotten the impression that most of them didn't know what they were talking about.

What is the way to catch back the souls of those that disease drives out, Dragonsbane?

He can't be gone. He can't.

Now and then a marsh-wight would take over a child and have to be exorcised. The task left Jenny exhausted and she always treated it with the greatest and most painstaking care, but it wasn't beyond her powers, and sometimes, if it were done quickly enough, the child's soul could be recovered, or part of it anyway. Even the little pooks of the marsh could be deadly of course. John knew that in Far West Riding, near the Boggart Marshes, funeral customs involved binding the corpse to the bier until it could be burned, for fear that demons would inhabit it.

A demon wizard. Demons more powerful than the spells that wizards used to protect themselves.

He shut his eyes, trying to will away the images that crowded and tore in his mind.

He had heard whisperers in the swamps take on the voices of Jenny or Ian, or one of his aunts. They'd call to him to do this or that, or try to lead him away into the marshes. Easy enough, he supposed, for a Hellspawn to speak to a mage through dreams. *Do this rite, speak these words, mix blood and pour it on a heated thunderstone—then you'll have the power you've been seeking* . . . Jenny was not the only one to have been taught that the key to more magic was magic. He knew there had been a time when she would have done anything to obtain greater ability in her art.

Only it wasn't power that would hiss up out of the steam.

Through the night and the next day and the night again he flew east over the empty seas, sailing when he could and cranking the springs of the engines taut. He watched the compass, and the spyglass, and consulted the charts he'd made, and betweentimes checked the swivels on the catapults and painted the harpoon-tips with poison. Twice he saw she-dragons, swimming and sporting with the brilliant males in the crests of the waves.

Being each of us, Enismirdal had said. *Being.* Whole galaxies of meanings and shades of meaning attached to *being*: a hot singular purity, like the dense core of a star, from which magic radiated as light. Dragon-magic such as Jenny had absorbed from Morkeleb in her days of dragonhood, sourced and rooted in adamantine will.

This, too, apparently, the demons could take.

At least I know more than I did, thought John. *At least I can go to Jen—if I make it back alive—and say, There was this wizard named Isychros, see, and he made a bargain with demons* . . .

But it was to Rocklys, he thought, that he would have to go first. To tell her that there was a Hellspawn at large wearing a wizard's body and wielding a wizard's power. There was a

Hellspawn at large, inhabiting the body and the growing powers of what had been his son.

He was a Dragonsbane. He was the one who understood, as much as any human understood, how to slay star-drakes.

He was the one they would call upon, when that unholy three—demon-haunted mage, demon-haunted slave, demon-haunted dragon—returned from their hiding in the Skerries of Light.

No, he thought, putting the understanding from his mind of what he would in all probability be called upon to do. *No.*

John put the *Milkweed* in at an islet shaped like a court lady's shoe, in the hot glitter of late afternoon, in time to see the bright blink of blue and gold skimming low and fast over the water, and, scrambling to the tip of the peak with his spyglass, discerned the two forms mounted on the dragon's back.

Heart hammering, he followed them with the glass and saw them settle on another isle perhaps twenty miles to the north. His hands were shaking as he pulled out the dozen scraps of parchment from his satchel: It was a C-shaped island with a central lagoon, according to his earlier glimpse, bright with waterfalls, thickly wooded, and populated by sheep.

Build a raft, cross the open sea, and take on the three of them with one fell slash of his mighty blade?

I'll write a ballad about that.

Wait until they'd gone on and then head east as fast as he could and leave his son, or what was left of his son, in the demon's hands?

He closed his eyes, his heart hurting more than he had thought possible.

Ian, forgive me.

Jenny, forgive me.

It was not something, he already knew, that he'd ever be able to forgive himself.

He remained on the peak, waiting, watching, wondering what he'd do if they didn't fly on, if he had to take the *Milkweed* up with them still there, through the fey brittle twilight.

Then in the morning he saw a flash of luminous blue in the

sky, and turning his spyglass eastward saw Nymr the Blue circling down toward the waves, where she-dragons dipped and swam in the lagoons among the rocks, sounded in depths a thousand times darker than the light-filled midnight skies.

Exhausted as he was, blinded and aching with grief, John couldn't keep himself from turning the spyglass to watch. Did the females come into season, the way mares and cows did, he wondered. Or were they like women, welcoming this male or that for other reasons more intricate and obscure? Why had he seen no babies, no dragonettes? Dotys—or was it Cerduces?—had said somewhere that the younger dragons were bright-hued but simply patterned, in bars and bands and stripes, like the black and yellow Enismirdal, the patterns becoming more and more intricate over the centuries, and more beautiful as the dragon aged. Morkeleb was black. What did that mean?

And what happened after black?

My son is dead, he thought. *I stand a good chance of coming down in the middle of the ocean halfway back and then if I make it to land walking from Eldsbouch to Cair Corflyn and THEN having to take on a demon mage and a dragon, and here I am wondering about the love-lives of dragons?*

Adric's right. Dad was right. I am frivolous.

Nymr circled over the sea again, wing tips skimming the waves. The air seemed wreathed with the garlands of the dragon's music, filling John's mind, twined with other, stranger airs. Serenading the girls?

But it was not the she-dragons that came.

It was Centhwevir.

Centhwevir dropped on the blue dragon like a stooping falcon, plummeting from the white crystal of the noon sky with wings plastered tight to his blue and golden sides, beak open, claws reaching, eyes blank and terrible. Nymr swung, spinning in the air, whipping clear at the last moment as the blue and gold dragon raked at him; Nymr hissed, slashing back with claws and teeth and tail.

And drove up, striking where Centhwevir was not. Was not, and had never been.

Color and lightning blazed and smote John's eyes, elusive

movement and a whirling of the air. Sometimes he could see the two dragons, other times three and four, images of Centhwevir or simply fragments of driving, spinning blue and gold and purple, like the aurora borealis gone mad. They ringed Nymr, who slashed and snapped futilely, furiously, at the air. But out of those planes and whirlwinds of color and lightning fire spewed, spattering Nymr's sides as he rolled in the air, and blood gushed from claw-rakes that appeared in his belly and sides.

The blue dragon fled. Centhwevir pursued, now visible, now veiled in crazy fractures of illusion, above and behind. For a moment, when the blue and gold drake came visible again, John saw then that not one but two figures clung to his back, wedged among the spikes with their feet hooked through a cable of braided leather passed around the dragon's girth.

His heart stopped in his throat, seeing the dark hair, the weatherstained plaid. The two dragons twisted and clutched, light, illusion, magic searing and glittering between them as well as fire and blood and the spray of the waves. They fell, locked together, spikes and fire and thrashing tails, plunging toward the sea. John bit back a cry. They were close to the whirlpools of the twelve rocks, if Ian came off there would be no saving him . . .

There is no saving him, thought John, but still he could not breathe.

Nymr made one final attempt to flee, racing south. Centhwevir fell on him from above and behind, tearing and raking, ripped himself by the great spikes and razors of the other dragon's backbones and wing-joints and neck-frill, and this time Nymr gave a thin hoarse cry—nothing like any sound John had heard from any dragon before—and plunged down into the sea, dragging Centhwevir and his two riders with him.

"Ian!" John stumbled panting to the cliff's beetling edge and knelt among the sea-oats and the poppies. He was shaking all over as he watched the sea where the two dragons, the wizard and his slave, had all vanished under the chop of the waves. *Too long,* he thought, sickened, unbreathing. *Too long to survive . . .*

Fire flashed in the waves. Centhwevir's head broke the surface, then his glittering back. The telescope showed John the gray-haired mage still clinging to the dragon's back, holding Ian by the collar of his jacket. Ian was gasping, choking, but he did not struggle. The man's face was grim but curiously uncaring, as if he harbored no fear of death. His eyes were fixed on the great blue shape of Nymr, whom Centhwevir had fast by the neck and one wing in teeth and claws.

Driving himself with his tail, Centhwevir made for the round island. Once John thought he saw Nymr struggle and move his other wing. But he was clearly dying as his attacker dragged him up on the beach.

It was hard to see. John looked around desperately, then ran along the cliff-top to a higher rock, thrust precariously out over the night-blue waves three hundred feet below.

Through the lens he saw the dragon-wizard's face clearly: a cold small mouth, and cold small eyes set close. A clean-shaven man, fastidious and rich—a man with a merchant's cold eye. He half-carried Ian from Centhwevir's back and laid him on the sand a little distance away. He didn't even cover him, just turned back to the two dragons, took from his knapsack the silver fire-bowls and the sacks and packets of powders needed for healing spells and began to draw diagrams of power in the sand.

The diagram incorporated Centhwevir, who sat up on his haunches and folded his wings. The blue and gold star-drake seemed unhurt, and settled more still, John thought, than he had seen other dragons sit. When he had accomplished the diagram and completed the sigils of power and of healing, the dragon-wizard—demon-wizard—drew from his knapsack another of the slivers of crystal and, as he had before, drove it into the back of Nymr's head. When Centhwevir turned his head and the wind caught the fur and feathers of his great particolored mane, John saw the blink of crystal there under the horned neck-frill. The dragon-wizard took something—some of the dragon's blood, John thought, but could not be sure—in a cup of gold and nacre, and carried it to where Ian lay. Opening the boy's wrist, he let the blood drip down to mix with that of the dragon, and from out of the cup took a talisman of some kind. It looked to John as if he pressed it to Ian's lips, and then to his own; then unfastened the breast of his robe and slipped the talisman he had made inside.

Probably, thought John with a queer cold dispassion, into a pocket around his neck, to keep it safe.

Ian lay where he was while the wizard bandaged his wrist. John could not see whether his eyes were open or shut, but as the wizard walked away the boy moved a little, so John knew he lived. The wizard returned to Nymr, this time crossing carelessly over the traced lines of power.

John lowered the telescope from his eye. He was sweating as if he had been struck with some grievous illness, and the only thing in his mind for a time was his son's face and the face of the dragon-wizard—demon-wizard—working over Nymr.

Demon or no, thought John, *he's wounded. Centhwevir's wounded. Ian, or what once had been Ian, is laid up as well.*

If I'm to kill them, now's my chance.

John unloaded the crates and struts and casings from the *Milkweed* through the white mild summer night, though weariness seemed to have settled into his bones. Twice he checked through his spyglass, but the blue dragon and the blue and gold still lay on the beach. Ian remained where he was, covered with a blanket.

Stay there, John whispered desperately. *Just stay there and nap. I'll be along in a bit.*

He didn't let himself think about what would happen then.

He assembled and counted out the various pieces of his second machine on the little level space at the bottom of the cleft that split the island. Toward midnight the twilight there deepened, but overhead the sky still held a milky light, and never did it grow too dark to see what he was doing.

Sometime after the turn of the night he lay down in the warm sand and slept. His dreams were disquieting, dark humped shapes scurrying through them, green pale eyes glistening and the smell of fish, scalded blood, and sulfur everywhere. He thought he saw things like shining lizards creep up out of the surf and dance on the narrow beach of the turtle-shaped island, thought he saw the dragon-wizard sitting in their midst, letting them drink from his cup of gold and pearl.

The old wizard first, he thought, rising from his sleep. He set in the plates of triple-thick crystal, the wheels and gears and the gimballed steering-cage that was the heart and core of the dragon-killing machine. *Maybe that'll end it.*

There was a demon in Ian as well, and he knew that wouldn't end it, but he tried not to think about that. He found himself wishing he'd been able to learn more from Morkeleb about the crystal spikes in the dragons' skulls, the nature of possession when it came to dragons . . .

They were going to strike somewhere, almost certainly before he could make it back to land himself.

Body and bones, his father had said. Body and bones.

He mounted the metal plates to the wooden ribs and transferred all but two of the *Milkweed*'s catapults to the Urchin's tough inner hull. It looked indeed like a rolled-up urchin when he was done with it, bristling with spikes as the dragons bristled. If he could not have the maneuverability and speed that a horse would give him, he would need armor and weight and surprise. Common sense told him that he needed to rest, to hunt, to eat. He felt the reserves of his strength trickling away as the moon set and the long summer morning climbed toward noon.

At an hour before noon he wound the gears and springs of the gnome-wrought engine and, in the great wheel of the guidance cage within it, urged it out onto the beach. The Urchin lurched and jolted, then spun in a small circle, refusing to move farther no matter how John swung and pulled his weight. Cursing, he threw over the brake levers, let the tension out of the springs, and dismantled the engine again. Surf beat on the rocks. Gulls cried. Shadows moved. He wondered what was passing on the turtle-shaped island but dared not stop to look.

The second trial worked better. The machine ran smoothly on its wheels, scrunching unsteadily in the soft sand. John had long ago mastered the complicated acrobatics of weight and balance needed in the cage. He turned, swung, swiveled the machine with its spines and its catapults, his half-naked body slick with sweat. *Right. When I build this thing for keeps, it gets vents.* He was gasping for air when he braked again, unlatched the lid and climbed the cage to put his head and shoulders out . . .

And saw, across the spaces of the water, two dragons rising from the island to the south.

Gold and blue they flashed in the light as they turned. Gorgeous as sunlight and flowers they wheeled, dipped low over the surf. Catching up his telescope John followed them, and saw the man with his embroidered cap tied close over his head and the boy with his cowl blown back, his dark hair blowing free.

"No . . ." John was shivering in the sea-wind on his wet shoulders and face. "Don't."

But they were winging away north again, and westward, not even stopping at the island where they'd camped.

"Come back here!" he screamed, dragging himself from the dragon-slaying machine's round belly, watching the great glittering shapes dwindle to hummingbirds. He was alone on his island, with the crabs and the dummies and the sheep. Bowing his head, he beat on the metal side of the Urchin and wept.

CHAPTER THIRTEEN

"Fool!" Commander Rocklys slapped the scroll down onto her desk so hard the sealing-wax shattered. "A thousand times a fool! Grond's beard, who the . . . ?" She looked up angrily as the chamberlain stopped short in the doorway, and her face altered when she saw Jenny at the man's slippered heels. "Mistress Waynest!" She sprang to her feet, reminding Jenny of a big tawny puma. "Thank the Twelve you're back safe!" Genuine concern twisted her brow. "Did you find this bandit wizard? Did you bring her here?"

Jenny inclined her head. "And I think you'll find her more than amenable to the idea of a school. Please . . ." She caught the Commander's arm as Rocklys made to stride past her into the anteroom. "She's very young," she said, looking up into Rocklys' face, "and she has been badly used. Be very, very gentle with her."

Rain pounded on the wood shakes of the roof. The parade ground beyond the window was a dreary piebald of rain-pocked gray mud in which the eight surviving members of Rocklys' original twenty-five unloaded their meagre gear. The Commander counted them with a glance, turned back to Jenny with shock and rage in her eyes. "The bandit Balgodorus . . . ?"

"Was gone the third morning after the mage left his forces," said Jenny. "I believe he still had nearly seventy men with him, out of close to three times that at the outset of the siege."

"Siege?" the Commander said sharply.

Jenny nodded. "At Palmorgin. We barely reached the walls before the bandits were upon us."

Rocklys began to speak, outraged, then seemed to see for the

136

first time Jenny's dripping plaids and drawn face. "You're soaked." She laid a hand on Jenny's arm, roughly solicitous. "Gilver . . ." The chamberlain disappeared promptly and came back a moment later with a servant, towels, a blanket, and a pitcher of hot mead. This last he set on the table while Rocklys steered Jenny firmly to the folding chair and brought the brazier over. "This bandit mage . . . she'll serve the Realm?" pressed the Commander, planting one foot on the seat of the chair opposite and leaning her elbow on her knee.

"I think so."

"Good. Good. Another came in yesterday—my cousin may be a fool, but at least he's had the sense to send out word in the south begging those with the inborn power to come forward. The old man kept it secret for years. As if anyone still enforced the old laws against wizards! Bliaud—that's his name, a decent old stiff—has been using magic to keep caterpillars off his roses and prevent himself from losing his hair. Idiots, the lot of them!" She shook her head in disbelief.

"And he came?" Greenhythe was a sleepy backwater of the southern Realm. Jenny couldn't imagine a retired gentleman undertaking the perils and discomforts of the journey.

"He took some persuading, and my cousin sent a decent escort." Rocklys made a face. "His family didn't want him to come—magic 'isn't done' by gentlemen." Her voice flexed with scorn. "Which was why I told Gareth that Cair Corflyn is the only place we could have such a school, away from the prejudices of the south. Can you imagine trying to teach anyone anything of magic with imbeciles like Ector of Sindestray—that's my cousin's treasurer-general—whining like frightened slaves about the old laws?

"The province of Imperteng in full revolt now—and that fool Gareth has taken the King with him to the siege camp at Jotham!—tax revolts in the Marches, upstart merchants in the Isles thinking they're aristocrats, a pardoned traitor, if you'll excuse me saying so, in charge of Halnath . . ." Her fist bunched in exasperation.

Jenny toyed with the idea of objecting to the term *pardoned traitor* in reference to the Master of Halnath, who had revolted against the takeover of the old King's mind by the witch Zyerne. Given Zyerne's abuse of power, in fact, the prejudices of the south were understandable.

Instead she said, as tactfully as she could, "Perhaps Prince Gareth thought his father would be safer with the army at Jotham if there are tax revolts along the Marches. The Marches aren't that far from Bel."

Rocklys' mouth hardened, but she said grudgingly, "Well, it's an argument. More like some fool thought the Twelve Gods wouldn't grant victory if his sacred hoary head wasn't on hand for their silly rites every morning." Her voice twisted with impatience and contempt. "The old man's so fuddled these days all a rebel would have to do is lay hands on him to convince him to oust Gareth from the regency and appoint his captor in his stead."

Behind her, through the open shutters, Jenny watched the red-hooded priests of Grond Firebeard, the Lord of War, process slowly into the camp temple, three and three, with a crowd of men-at-arms in their train. Their candles showed pale in the gloom beneath the colonnade. "All the more reason for us to teach mages to use their powers and use them responsibly, for the betterment of the Realm. Thank the Twelve . . . Yes, what is it?"

The red-robed priest in the doorway discreetly held out to her a beeswax taper, part of the ceremonial crossing the court: Jenny recalled that the Firebeard's altars needed to be kindled by the commander of the company that guarded His temple. Father Hiero had long ago given up trying to get John to perform the chore. Evidently Rocklys' Legalism was as entrenched as John's belief in the Old God, for the Commander simply stuck the wick into the stove.

"Well, mum for all that." The Commander waved the priest brusquely from the room and turned back to Jenny. "You got her here, and you'll be teaching her, and Bliaud . . . What's the girl's name?"

"Yseult."

"Yseult." The Commander dipped her hand into the tribute box, turned its stones over to catch the light. Jenny wondered what merchant she'd pried those gems out of. "If what your man told me was right, if there's a mage abroad who's managed to en-slave a dragon to his will, we'll need whatever help we can get."

Jenny listened to Rocklys' account of John's visit with a growing chill in her heart. She had watched John for days in her scrying-stone, in fire and in water, since she had seen him emerge unharmed from the Deep of Tralchet; had watched him turn, not south to Alyn Hold but west across the dark oceans, and guessed at last that he was bound for the Skerries of Light to seek Morkeleb for help or advice. *Dear Goddess, does he think Morkeleb will help him?* she'd wondered desperately. *What had he read that made him think that was the only way?*

Save a dragon, slave a dragon.

A wizard who had used John as a cat's-paw to harm Centh-wevir enough that the wizard could then save the dragon's life. Who had enslaved Ian and carried him away.

Rage burned her, prickling at her scalp. Rage and guilt that turned her sick.

And because there was no other help, not even novices here at Corflyn, John had sought Morkeleb.

Morkeleb would kill John on sight.

Ian.

She closed her eyes, the Commander's voice running on past her, willing herself to hear and not to think about the past. Not to think about years spent seeking her own powers, leaving the boys—whom she had never wanted to bear—to be raised by John. The years spent putting her magic before her love of John. *I want your children, Jen,* she heard John's voice. *I want any child I have to be yours. It's only nine months, not long* . . . And her own fears, her hesitations; her unwillingness to take the time, to spare the energy she knew it would demand. She saw herself standing by the hearth at Frost Fell, her back to him, arms folded stubbornly, shaking her head.

Oh, John. My beloved John.

It had been nearly three weeks since she'd last seen him in the heart of the fire, leaning against the mast of that ridiculous flying boat, gazing across the waking sea where dragons circled the spires of the shining islands. After that the dragon-magic foxed and splintered the visions, vouchsafing her only an occasional glance: John alone, patiently cranking his engines; John patting bannocks together beside a fire; John playing the hurdy-gurdy where dawn-tinted water curled to a beach. And once, terrifyingly, John with one knee on the *Milkweed*'s railing as a stardrake leaped, blue as lapis, blue as cobalt, blue and violet as the summer sea straight up out of the waves, and dove toward him in a sparkling maelstrom of music and spray.

"—be sending a messenger to Alyn Hold in the morning."

"What?" Jenny jolted back to the present, looked up to see Rocklys standing by her chair. "Oh, I'm . . . I'm sorry, Commander. I . . ."

The general's face, for a moment angry at her inattention, softened. "No. I'm sorry, Lady Jenny. I've been going on as if you weren't soaked to the skin and probably off your feet with fatigue." She flipped a pale green peridot in her fingers, tossed it sparkling back in the strongbox.

"Gilver, show Mistress Waynest to the guest rooms. I hope that man of yours had the sense to take to his bed, and stay in it. If ever I saw a man done up . . ."

"Don't trouble with a messenger," said Jenny, rising and gathering the blanket around her shoulders. "I'll ride out tomorrow morning myself."

"Yourself? Have you seen a mirror? You look like . . ."

"It doesn't matter what I look like." Jenny stood, the blanket drawn around her shoulders. She hesitated for a moment, on the brink of telling Rocklys what she had seen in stone and fire, and then said only, "I've been too long away. Yseult and I can be back . . ."

"Yseult?" Rocklys was shocked. "You can't be thinking of taking her with you! With Balgodorus still at large? Looking for her, belike? If you must go—and I don't like the idea of it at all, though I'll send a guard with you—by all means leave the girl here."

If she'll stay, thought Jenny, wondering how that bruised and abused child would react to being told she must remain, without the woman who had saved her, in an army encampment full of men. She hesitated, trying to decide where the girl would be safest.

"If she elects to stay here," said Jenny, "please promise me this. Keep her safe. Not just from the men in the barracks . . ."

"Of course she'll have her own rooms," protested Rocklys. "In the courtyard with mine. She'll never come near the troops. You can't . . ."

"Not just from the men," said Jenny quietly. "Whoever this dragon-wizard is, if he's kidnapping mages it's for a purpose. It may be we've brought Yseult here just ahead of his seeking her out himself. That goes for your little southern gentleman as well, and his sons. It may be best, until I return . . ."

Rocklys opened her mouth to protest, and Jenny went on over her.

". . . that they don't go beyond the fortress gates at all. I don't want secret messages arriving with Bliaud's sons' signet rings, and maybe their fingers, done up in parcels. With the revolt in Imperteng," she went on, "and the King not in fit mind to rule, I'm very curious about who this dragon-wizard is working for, and what his intentions may be. At the moment I'm the only trained mage in the north, and I'm a little surprised that I haven't been made a target before this. And maybe I have."

"And I sent you out with only twenty-five men. I'll organize a more substantial guard . . ."

Jenny shook her head. "I've traveled the length and breadth of the Winterlands alone all my life. By myself I can go quiet and unseen. An escort would just slow me down and tell Balgodorus, or anyone else, where I am. I should be back within a week, to begin teaching your little fledglings. But right now there's something I need to learn at the Hold."

Though he laded it with every ballast-bag he had, it took all of John's strength to winch the *Milkweed* down to the Urchin and lash the spiked machine to the empty wicker boat. He hunted gulls' eggs and boiled them with rock-anise. *Too long,* he kept thinking, *too long.* The eggs were barely cooked when he pulled them from the water, scuffed out and buried his fire, and, climbing into the wicker boat, dumped ballast and set sail for the west.

The winds were contrary but strong. He was awake, tacking patiently, through the night; he anchored at an islet that was barely a pinnacle sticking straight from the sea, slept an hour and woke to beat his way west again. He dumped ballast at noon and again a few hours later, but the *Milkweed* continued to sag. Then it rained, weeping gray into the empty sea, white bars of lightning leaping between the clouds and the waves, but the wind changed and drove him west through the night, and in the morning his telescope showed him the Last Isles rising through the lashing skirts of the foam.

From the south he saw, too, the dragons coming. Centhwevir and Nymr, flashing like perdition in the newly freed sun.

They must have seen him, but neither turned aside. The wind drove hard out of the northeast. John had to tack again, leaning on the ropes, watching the dragons ahead of him and dizzy with fatigue. He saw them dip and circle the birdless isle, then plunge suddenly down among the rocks. *They'll trap him in a cave,* he thought, almost too tired to think anything, and the *Milkweed* swung in a long sickening arc against the veering wind. *Dragons know what I know—that chances of a kill are stronger if the dragon you're attacking is on the ground.*

He yanked the air valve to bring the *Milkweed* down and cast anchor as close as he could, seeing among the rocks the sunburst and scramble of blue and gold. Nymr and Centhwevir, when he could see them through the blinding aura of lightning and illusion, had their wings folded close, necks striking in long fluid darts, and he could see that their prey was still trapped in its lair. For a moment John glimpsed Morkeleb himself, pressed back among the rocks. Bleeding—the black dragon's neck and face were scored and torn, and the dark gloss of him seemed to have paled, gray as cinder and ash.

He was fighting for his life. John could see that, in every desperate lashing of neck and claws. The two younger drakes seemed to appear and disappear in a chaos of demon-aura, and Morkeleb struck wildly, against air or rock or sand. With a prayer to the Old God, John swiveled one of the catapults and fired a harpoon into Centhwevir's back.

Centhwevir wheeled, mouth gaping, and John fired the second catapult. But the dragon seemed to split and whirl into three green-fire shadows, and the bolt went wild. Acid spattered on the wicker gunwale near John's hand, setting the rail aflame. Without any seeming transition, the crazy burning wildness of the air was all around the *Milkweed*, and through the smolder John had a momentary glimpse of a cold square face and pale eyes somewhere close to him, like an image in a migraine dream. Then Centhwevir screamed, the high metallic shriek of a dragon, and whirled as Morkeleb, slipping past Nymr, seized his flanks with those great black-clawed hands.

Centhwevir reversed direction like a cat, biting and lashing and spattering acid, but Morkeleb had hold of him, and that was not something that could be ensorcelled away. In that moment John flung himself over the *Milkweed*'s gunwale and slithered down the ropes to the Urchin, lashing and rocking below. He slashed the ropes and fell with the machine, grabbing the base of the nearest spike to keep from being jolted off; the drop was only a yard or so, but it jarred the bones in his flesh. Nymr and Centhwevir were fully occupied with their victim, whom they drove back against the cliff-face again. John slipped into the Urchin's hatch and slammed it shut, kicked his feet into the braces of the wheel and slapped free the brake lever. The Urchin swiveled; John fired another harpoon, this time catching Nymr in the flank.

He slammed his weight on the wheel to reverse direction but something smote it from the side; a tangled confusion of blue and gold all laced with green flame. He fired another harpoon but in that instant all the crystal ports that surrounded him shattered inward, tearing him with shards, and the pain of cramp and nausea seized limbs and throat and belly, as if he were being bitten by a thousand rats.

Pox-rotted demons . . .

The dragon smashed the Urchin again with his tail, splitting the casing, buckling the struts. John fired again, not letting himself think about where Ian was in this fray or what might happen to him. Panic filled him, as if he were in a nightmare—he seemed to hear his father screaming his name. More demonmagic, the kind of thing Whisperers did, only infinitely more powerful. Another blow flipped the Urchin off its wheels, slammed John hard against the hull. He yanked the last two harpoons free

of their catapults and slithered through the broken hatch as
Centhwevir seized the Urchin in his claws. The dragon dropped
it immediately, and John clung to the edge of the trap for balance. It was impossible to aim—there seemed to be five Centh-
wevirs coming at him from all directions—but as soon as he was
steady he flung the harpoon as the dragon dropped down over
him to smash the machine with his tail again. The weapon
missed, but Morkeleb, momentarily free from Nymr's attacks,
flung himself on Centhwevir's back, raking again at his wings.

Centhwevir writhed free, spitting acid, bleeding now from a
dozen wounds. Morkeleb flung himself into the air with a great
crack of dark wings, and as the two younger dragons whirled to
meet him, wounded and more visible through the flak, John
flung his last harpoon, lodging in Nymr's shoulder.

That seemed to decide the dragon-wizard. John heard him cry
out an order and, through the splintering firefall, caught a brief
glimpse of Ian clinging to Nymr's spiked back. Nymr slipped
from beneath Morkeleb's attack and sprang skyward, wings
flashing. Golden dragon and blue slashed the air, veering as they
caught the wind. Then they were away, dwindling over the sea
toward the skerries.

Morkeleb hovered for a moment above the rocks, a floating
shadow against the light, while near him the fire on the half-
burned *Milkweed* flickered sullenly and went out. John lay in the
sand, panting and half-blinded by the blood trickling from his
forehead. At least the internal pain was gone. The Urchin resembled nothing so much as a walnut cracked by a child more
interested in getting the meat than making a neat job of it.

Three weeks chasing cave-grues at Wyldoom, he reflected, *and
dealing with the gnomes into the bargain. This dragon-slaying is
getting just too bloody costly. I'll really have to give it up.*

He came to choking, drowning. Ice-cold seawater engulfed
him. As he tried to thrash to the surface, he felt the prick of iron
claws closing around his body and the next second was dragged
gasping into the air.

Hold still or I shall drop you into the sea. I am weary enough.
Though he knew perfectly well the dragon wouldn't let him

fall by accident, John hooked one arm around the black wrist nearest him, fitting his hand carefully among the blood-sticky spines. His spectacles had been knocked off: rocks, waves, and the great black dragon himself were blurred as Morkeleb circled back to the island and, stretching down his long hind-legs, settled on his haunches and laid John down on the sand.

They drank my magic. The dragon crouched among the rocks, a movement stirring his bones. Then stillness, and anger like the anger of a star. *They drank the magic from me—ME, Morkeleb the Black, the most ancient and the strongest, Void-Walker, star-rover, destroyer of Elder Droon, and there was nothing I could do against them, no hold upon them that my power could take.*

The word that came into John's mind as *magic* was not what Jenny meant when she spoke of it. It should, he thought, lying numb and dripping on the warm earth, be another word entirely, even as the word *being* that Enismirdal had spoken should have been something else. But he did not know what either of those words should be, and it might be that they were the same.

Like the slow pull of dark tide, Morkeleb's anger flowed through John's mind and, under that anger, fear. Fear of what could not be touched. Fear of singing shadows that killed. The steel-thin hoops of Morkeleb's ribs rose and fell, and the blood that trickled down his mane mingled with the dripping seawater, so the dragon seemed a black island in a lake of gore.

This is a thing of utter abomination, a thing of illness, spreading and eating. This is a thing that swallows the core of magic and fills the empty place with madness and death.

"Help me," said John. He brushed salt-gummed, blood-gummed hair out of his eyes, and every cut and abrasion of him burned with seawater and sand. "I saved your life."

The long birdlike head swung around, and John looked down quickly, lest he be trapped in the crystalline maze of the dragon's eyes. He could feel Morkeleb's fury, the fury of trapped pride and of fear. The fury of scorn, for himself as much as for John; the fury that he should be beholden to anything, much less to a bird-peep of a human meddler who wasn't even mageborn.

The fact was the same. The debt was the same.

Save a dragon . . .

Come then. The black claws reached for him again.

"We need the machine." John sat up painfully. His spectacles lay not far from him in the sand. They'd fallen soft. He brushed the sand from the lenses, but they were too dirty to put on, and in any case his hands were shaking too badly to manipulate them. "I twilkin' near killed meself getting the parts, and we'll need something of the kind."

Morkeleb opened his mouth and hissed with disapproval. *Gather it together then, Songweaver. We must be away.*

CHAPTER FOURTEEN

I saw this other, Yseult had said. *Or dreamed of him, bringing a dragon back to life. He had a wizard-boy with him.*

High summer twilight drenched the sky, though midnight was only an hour off. In that blue clarity even the desolation of Cair Dhû seemed beautiful. Jenny had reached the place to find a band of Iceriders camped among the shattered walls, with their scrubby ponies and their dogs, their silent blue-eyed children and low tents of reindeer hide. She had had to wait until night to send spells into their chieftain's dreams, warning him of terrible disaster coming to that place, and then it had taken them time to drill and shatter the oracle bones, exclaim over the results, break camp, and be on their way.

Nothing was left now of the battle John had fought with Centhwevir, save dark stains on the rocks. But there was no other place to start.

A wizard-boy.

Jenny stood in the place, eyes closed, breathing what had been. Dragons could taste the past, lift from stones and ground and the water under the earth echoes of all that had passed above them. But the echoes were in the form of dragon-senses, difficult for a mortal mind to sort. She felt/smelled/heard the dragon's mind, and John's, even the shrill panic of the warhorse Battlehammer. But there was nothing there of the mind of her son. Only the searing mind-taste of demons.

Jenny's belly curled in on itself. *Demons! Dear God.*

And not little ones either. No Whisperers or swamp-wights here, giggling as they lured travelers into the marshes for the pleasure they could drink from human pain and frustration and fear.

147

She felt stunned, as if she'd looked unexpectedly into burning light.

Ian. Oh, Ian.

The power of demons was Other. Demons came and went from another plane of existence, where magic was different. Everything was different. And these, she could sense, were more powerful than any she had heard of.

Would she have been able to protect her son, had she remained a dragon? Would she have wanted to?

As a jere-drake she had known intense and passionate desire, and the coupling of dragons was like being transformed into fire made of jewels. But that was not the same as loving, or caring for those one loved.

Patiently, her eyes the eyes of darkness, she searched, and in time she found the place where the dragon-wizard had drawn power out of the earth. At her summons the eroded ghosts of the power lines drifted to the surface once more, but they told her little she did not already know. The dragon-wizard had been trained in the southern traditions—the Line of Erkin, it looked like. But demon-fire had imbued and informed every trace and circle. Every exorcism she had ever performed—and they had been few enough—returned to her, the snaking insinuation of even petty pooks and gyres. The wormlike crawling to get inside a human mind, a human soul; to have a body whose pain the demon could drink. To have the ability to torment and hurt others, to generate more fear and more pain. They would inhabit even corpses, given the chance.

A tiny image came to her, the broken fragment of a memory: a big gray-haired gentleman walking on a beach at dawn. Walking after troubling dreams. Sea-wind lifted his dark scholar's robe to show the clothes of a wealthy merchant beneath. A scholar-dilettante, such as she had met in the Court of Bel. A man with a face too intelligent for the company of money-hoarders and counters-up of bales.

She saw him stop, look down at something—a shell? a piece of glass?—where the waves creamed on the pewter beach. He bent down and took it in his palm.

Oh, John, she thought, as the memory slid away. *Stay away from them.*

She drew her plaids closer about her, trying to still the dreadful hurting of her heart.

In her mind a voice said, *Wizard-woman.*

He was behind her, crouched on the smashed ruin of Cair Dhû's walls. His black bones folded together like a fan of sable silk, and the clear cold silver eyes seemed to emit both light and darkness. Her heart soared at the sight of him as a wave soars when it shatters itself on rock.

Love and wonder.

And as a wave shatters her first words ran away unspoken.

Your heart wept, he said.

They have taken my son. She spoke as dragons speak. *And John was hurt.*

Heat rose off him, and he turned his face aside. Wind shifted the black ribbons of his mane, the tufts of ebon feather. Curving horns striped black on black gleamed as if oiled.

Oh, my friend, she said. *I am so glad to see you.*

So. The heat seemed to spread and widen, but grew calm, like water deepening and deepening, stilling as it deepened. She had a sense of deadliness, of terrible things taking shape far below the surface, things that stared with mad silver eyes into the dark. Then slowly all that rage collected itself and vanished as through a hole in eternity, utterly away from this world.

So, he said again. *It rejoices my heart to see you also, my friend.*

Something in the air around him changed.

She said, *Forgive me.*

Forgiveness is not a thing of dragons. Each deed and each event exists forever in our minds as what it was and is. But what you speak of, when you ask forgiveness, is only a part of what you were and are, Wizard-woman, and what you will be.

He settled himself, a dense black shining shape in the thickening dusk. His eyes were cold twin moons, looking into hers.

Four years now I have dwelt apart from the star-drakes, seeking to understand those things in my heart that were no longer the things of dragons. When we came unto the Skerries of Light, there were Shadow-drakes among us, Dragonshadows, and they lived on the Last Isle. I went there seeking them, for they understand all things, and have in them power greater than that of the greatest among the dragons. They were not there.

For some reason she recalled the stone house on Frost Fell, autumn evenings when rain hissed down the chimney in the fire, when even her harp seemed a violation of the world's sleepy peace.

Yet I stayed in that place, he said. *And in these four years I have tried to do as they anciently taught, hoping that in the achievement of their power I would find relief from my pain. But the pain itself is no less.*

Her heart reached to him in wordless sorrow, but he rippled the dark scales of his back, putting her anguish aside.

It is not as it was, Wizard-woman. You have no need for grief for my sake. In this hour, as I see you, I find that indeed I feel differently than I did, although it was my hope then not to feel at all.

As if jewels shifted, catching a sharp blink of light, she felt his wry humor. *And so my wizardry, and my knowledge, and all the roads of the galaxy that I have walked have led me to this: a black knot that cannot be unraveled, an eyeblink in all the flowing years of time, and yet that I cannot put by. And I do not know whether this knot is a thing of men that came to me from your heart, Wizard-woman, or a thing that lies hid in dragon-kind as the eggs lie hid within the jere-drakes until it is time for them to transform into queens. Perhaps even if I could find the Shadow-drakes I would receive no answer. They do not give answers that make sense except to one another.*

She said, *Perhaps it is a thing that will come clear in time. Time was the thirteenth god, they say, until the other gods cast him out because he was mad. He carries all things in his pockets, but what he will take out, no one knows.*

And as she said it tears came down from her eyes, remembering again all those strange pain-filled gifts the mad Lord of Time had given her.

No one indeed, retorted the dragon. *Least of all did I ever conceive that I, Morkeleb the Black, would come down from the north drawing that silly toy boat of your Songweaver's by a rope like a dog with a string in its mouth.*

And Jenny laughed, delighted with the shape the dragon pu

in her mind: the *Milkweed* trailing with half-deflated balloons, its charred gondola piled with broken bits of machinery, at the end of a rope whose other end was gripped in the dragon's iron beak. On the heap of debris John sat cross-legged, telescope in one hand and map across his knees, making notes.

My poor Morkeleb! She held out her hand to him. *That was very, very good of you.*

Good is not a thing of dragons. His spikes bristled like Skinny Kitty when routed from a cupboard. *Your Songweaver is in his own walls once more being made much of by his fools of aunts. But it was not for love of you, my Wizard-woman, or for the sake of your brat, that I left the Last Isle.*

Half-rising, he exposed to moonlight the nacre of new-healed flesh on his belly and sides. *They are demons, who eat the souls of dragons and mages alike, as they ate the soul of this southern mage; as they ate the soul of your son. And demons will always seek to open the way for other demons. These have a strength that I have not seen since the Fall of Ernine, a thousand years ago. Whether these are the same demons or others with the same power I know not, but they can devour my magic—I, Morkeleb!—and they can and will devour yours, and anyone else's they so choose.*

Silent, they regarded one another for a time, the dragon black and glistening in the starry night and the woman small in her plaid skirt, her bodice of worn leather. All the old legends warned against meeting a dragon's eyes, but having been a dragon herself Jenny had nothing in her mind or soul that Morkeleb could trap. Rather she saw into his mind, to the will that was core and spine of dragon-magic: the magic at the core of dragon-flesh and dragon-dreams. It was like losing oneself in night sky.

For a moment more their minds touched, his bitterness and her sorrow that each person, each being, has only one future and cannot have two.

Things are as they are, Wizard-woman, he said at last. *Now come away. There is a man who awaits you at that stone hovel you call your home, and two others of your young. And we must speak, you and this Songweaver and I, of demons, and of what must next be done.*

* * *

"Where'd you spring from, me lord? And you too, Lady Jenny?" It was the same guard who had admitted John a month ago. He looked past them at the village street, mucky in the cindery dawn, then back, frowning in outrage. "By Cragget's beard, those bandits are getting above theirselves! Were you hurt? Not but that you couldn't take on any bandit in the country, either of you," he added hastily, touching his forehead in salute. "But a band of 'em . . ."

"We took no hurt." Jenny looked around as they stepped under the half-raised portcullis and into the empty parade court. Only a few servants and batmen stirred, though the smell of smoke issued from the bakeries. By the chapel two yellow-hooded priests and a flute player waited for the augur to proclaim the proper moment for them to go in to morning rites.

"Son, I'm a Dragonsbane—and not a very good one—not Alkmar the Godborn." John glanced in the direction of the chapel. "I'd thought the Commander'd be up at rites."

Morkeleb had set them down on the far edge of the hills, after flying most of the night. A day's rest at Alyn Hold had given John at least a chance to shave—he'd resembled some mad, bespectacled hermit two nights ago, when Jenny had run up the stone steps of the Hold to throw herself into his arms—but he still looked desperately thin, face worn down to its bones. His shoulders were pointier than they should have been through the patched linen of his shirt, and his hands bandaged.

Jenny was astonished that he wasn't dead.

"Nay, sir, it's the Iceriders, see." The guard touched his brow in apologetic half-salute. "Not that her La'ship ever puts foot in the Temple, but there! Old Firebeard gives her victory all the same. But yesterday half the garrison rode out, when word of 'em came. They burned out two farms over by the Eldwood . . ."

"There were more at Cair Dhû," Jenny stopped herself just in time from saying, *four days ago*. There was no way, short of riding a dragon, that she could have covered the distance. She concluded with barely an in-taken breath, "a week ago; a woman at the Hold saw them. Is Mistress Yseult still here?"

"Oh, aye. Though not up yet, of course." The guard got a

batman to show them to the kitchen, where the cook gave them bread and cheese and mulled cider and John shed his disreputable doublet, pushed up his sleeves, and lent a hand with breakfast porridge for the garrison. Jenny sat quietly in a corner, watching with some amusement his account of being robbed of their horses: " 'Master, master,' says this beggar, 'an entire army of three thousand bandits came down on me farm. They had to take it in turns to sack the house 'cause there wasn't room for more'n twelve inside at a time, and the line of 'em went right down the lane past two other farms. Me neighbor Cob Rushleigh's wife was out sellin' cider to the ones that was waitin' their chance . . .' "

"They're getting arrogant." Lord Pellanor stepped over to the bench and took a seat beside Jenny, a quarter loaf in one hand and a pitcher of cider to share in the other. "We'll keep a watch for them when we set out for Palmorgin."

"They're miles away." Jenny shook her head. She wondered at the Baron's presence here. He had given no indication of leaving his siege-damaged Keep when she departed it ten days ago. "But thank you just the same. I called their images into the fire as soon as we knew the beasts were gone and set Words to them, so the horses will come back to Alyn Hold, but there's no knowing how long it will take."

The Baron started, then grinned under his gray mustache. "The more fool me, forgetting. Maybe you can come out to Palmorgin again and put a little word on my cattle. Balgodorus hasn't been back, but the small fry are out in the woods. We lose a beast now and then still."

"I'll do that," promised Jenny. "I do it at Alyn. But Come-Back spells on beasts wear off quickly if they don't have an amulet to hold them."

"And of course the amulet's the first thing thieves would get rid of," sighed Pellanor. "Just a thought, my dear."

"Is that the type of thingummy you're going to teach old Papa?" A young man dressed for travel in extravagant yellow joined them—one who was clearly his brother stood drinking cider near the stove and laughing uproariously at John's imitation of himself hunting under rocks and behind bushes for the missing horses. Through the kitchen windows Jenny could see the grooms in the stable court, saddling horses and roping gear onto mules, under the grim eye of a grizzled sergeant, assembling the convoy that would take the latest installment of tax money to Bel in the south. A small, rather fragile-looking old gentleman, bundled in a coat of gray fur fussed around the perimeter of the action, now and then scuttling forward to scribble sigils on the baggage in red chalk—every time he did so the men visibly flinched, and the sergeant had to step in and tactfully draw him back. Bliaud, thought Jenny. Half the sigils were mismade and none of them Sourced or Limited. They would be dangerous if they weren't wholly ineffective.

Jenny laughed. "If he likes. It's just piseog—hedge-magic. I had to put a spell like that on John's spectacles so they wouldn't get lost or broken."

"Strike me purple, it sounds a damned sight more useful than some of those spells in Papa's books." The young man smiled— his name, Jenny recalled hearing somewhere, was Abellus, Bliaud's son. "I always thought them a bit silly myself, and *filthy* dirty and just *centuries* old, but they're nothing to what this fellow Master Caradoc brought in."

"Master Caradoc?" said Jenny. "Did the Commander find still another mage, then?"

"Came two days ago," said Lord Pellanor. "Rode out with her yesterday, after these Iceriders." In the courtyard Master Bliaud made impressive arm-passes over one of the mules, which promptly kicked its groom. The sergeant took the mage by the arm, explaining gently, and behind their backs the head groom bit his thumb and rubbed surreptitiously at the chalked wyrds. "He's from Somanthus Isle, across the gulf from Bel. One of the merchant princes. I think like Master Bliaud he kept quiet out of caution, when the Lady Zyerne was all but ruling in the south. But he and the Commander knew one another at court."

"The Commander said she nearly fell over with surprise when he disclosed himself as a warlock," Abellus laughed, unconsciously using the pejorative variant of the word. Bullion flashed on his glove as he gestured. "Of all the world, she said, he's the *last* she'd have guessed."

"Given that wizards can't hold property in the south, I bet he kept quiet about it." John came over to the table, licking butter off his fingers.

"Stuff." Abellus' younger brother Tundal stepped after him, wiping out his horn cup and hanging it back on his belt. Stout where his brother was willowy, he wore conservative drab, but like his brother expensive and well cut. "Nobody's enforced that wretched law for decades. And besides, what's a wizard? I mean, Papa could go on for days about the vapors of the air and the magical relationships between clouds and the rocks in the earth, but he couldn't so much as charm a wart. At least little Yseult can do that."

"How is Yseult?"

"Oh, she's well, she's well." Tundal impressed Jenny as the kind of young man who always believes others are well, whether that was the case or not.

"She keeps herself to herself," Abellus added, pitching a last scrap of manchet to the kitchen dogs. "I think she's still afraid of that *dreadful* bandit Papa said she was with, and who can blame the poor thing? She hasn't put a foot outside the compound, barely outside her rooms. But she told the Commander yesterday that our convoy needed to leave this morning, else we'd be caught by the most *ghastly* floods crossing the Wildspae. So we're on our merry way. Topping to have glimpsed your lovely countenance again, Mistress Waynest."

He performed an extravagant East Wind in Paradise salaam, and his brother an old-fashioned Greenhythe dip, with knees bent. "Curious," remarked Jenny, as the tall form and the slender made their way from the kitchen, slinging on their travel cloaks. She glanced at Pellanor. "The Wildspae's a good ten days' ride. I didn't think Yseult able to read the weather as far away as Nast Wall, where the river rises. Certainly not what it will be a week from now."

"Well, there's been some sign." Pellanor twisted the ends of his mustache. "I heard Yseult tell the boys that, and Bliaud said as much, too. Maybe this is something Master Caradoc taught them how to do."

"Been teaching 'em already, has he?"

"Some," said the Baron. "The Commander was anxious that

he begin, with the news of the Imperteng fighting getting worse. Damned hill-men—I fought them myself twenty years ago and they never seem to learn. She called me here to tell me the Regent wants me in the south. I'm bound back to Palmorgin to get my affairs in order, then I'll be marching out with my men."

John said nothing, but the antic humor that had been on him dropped from him like a wet shirt. Jenny felt his stillness, his silence.

Pellanor felt it, too, for he said, "Well, with the pirates in the Seven Isles and the troop levies coming up short from the Marches, there's folk in the council who say it's madness to keep garrisons here, with so little income from the north."

"Aye." The nimbus of anger around John reminded Jenny strangely of Morkeleb. "Aye, it is that."

"My dear Lord John." Gilver the chamberlain appeared, bowing, in the kitchen doorway. "And my dear Mistress Waynest. I beg a thousand pardons for not greeting you. Breakfast in the kitchen? I am so sorry."

"I'll be off." Pellanor clasped Jenny's hand in his gloved ones, then turned to John. "Don't think ill of me, Aversin. I'm the King's man, as you are."

"Aye." John returned the grip. "Just send me word who they're replacin' you with, so I'll know who I'll be dealin' with; and your people, too."

"I will." Pellanor forced a laugh. "And I'll call on you first thing, if we find we have a dragon to deal with."

"Oh, that'll bring sunshine to me day."

"This is most unexpected." Gilver hurried alongside them as they left the kitchen, crossed the muddy court where Bliaud was bidding an absentminded farewell to his boys. "Your business with Commander Rocklys was urgent?" He looked from John to Jenny, as if asking what could have brought them both away from Alyn Hold.

"Depends on what you think about Icewitches." John hooked his gloved hands through his belt. "We think the band of 'Riders Jenny saw a week ago had a sorceress among 'em."

What an undermanned garrison would make of a rumor about demons, wizards, and dragons, Jenny didn't like to think, especially considering the way the grooms of the convoy regarded Bliaud behind his back. She chimed into John's improvisation with, "There were signs at their camp that I couldn't interpret. I thought perhaps Master Bliaud might have more information, from the books he's read; this Master Caradoc, now, also."

"Ah." Gilver laid a finger beside his red-veined nose. "He's a wise one, Master C. The Commander spoke of you to him, and he wants very much to meet you, my lady. Handsome as ever he was when first he courted her—ten years gone that is now—and just as short-spoken." He chuckled. "And still won't make more of a salaam than a little twitch of his arm, not even to her—barely to the King himself. Flummery, he says. They should be returning tonight—Master Caradoc communicated just lately with Master Bliaud on that head. Shall I have a bath drawn for you? You must be shattered."

As they crossed the small inner court where Rocklys had her rooms, John remarked, "Has that gone bad, then?" A new wooden lid covered the well in the center, and rings had been driven into the stone lip so it could be locked down with a chain.

The chamberlain grimaced. "That was an unpleasant story," he said. "One of the men had a grievance—Dumpet only knows over what—" He named the southern godlet of chaos and anger. "He poured about three buckets of latrine-filth and dead animals into it, the Commander tells me. He's been triced and blistered, of course, but it's taken Master Caradoc these two days to cleanse it. Now, with being called away, he hasn't had a chance to finish the job. The Commander has ordered it be kept covered because some of the servants *will* try to use it still, since it's closer than the kitchen."

John and Jenny exchanged a glance. The wizards lived on this court as well.

Camp servants filled baths in Rocklys' private balneary. The room they were given was beside Bliaud's, on the other side of the chamber in use as a library and schoolroom. Bathed, combed, and refreshed—both turned down Gilver's offer of mulled wine—Jenny and John had a look at the small collection of books Bliaud had brought from Greenhythe and Master Caradoc had carried up from Somanthus Isle.

"Gaw, I never knew Dotys wrote a history of Ernine!" exclaimed John, turning one volume over in his hands. "Not that the old faker knew the first thing of what he's talking about, six hundred years later. Look, he says the kingdom came to ruin because the last monarch didn't worship the Twelve Gods properly and loved concubines to excess. That's what he says about 'em all, you know. And here's a complete copy of Ipycas' *Nature of Minerals*— I didn't think any were still in existence! And copied a treat. Those have to be Carunnus' illuminations—look at the mazework on the borders. D'you know, Jen, that according to Ipycas, or at least the pages I have of Ipycas, King Ebranck Ferrex of Locris used a combination of sulfur and quicksilver as an aphrodisiac and fathered fifty-three children, all on different women?"

"I presume," said Jenny dryly, "that the women had some pressing reason to assure him of the paternity of their offspring?"

"Well, he was gie rich."

"And not particularly bright, it seems."

"Now, Corax, the Master of Halnath, this was back when the Masters ruled Halnath in their own right, had a diamond so big it had been hollowed out into a bottle, like that dew-spoon of yours, and he kept in it what was said to be the tears of a sea monster, because those would dissolve ordinary glass and turn it and themselves into smoke . . . How'd they figure that one out, I wonder?" He perched on the back of a chair, his feet on the seat, lost in the wonder of antique trivia. "Gutheline II, it says, had cages carved for his pet crickets out of chunks of coal . . ."

"Lady Jenny." Yseult stopped in the doorway, startled to see them. She would, Jenny thought, have turned and fled had she been able to do so unseen. "I . . . I'm glad to see you. Did you find your boy?"

"We've found . . . word of him." Jenny drew her breath deep, trying to keep her voice from shaking. The girl looked better than she had a week ago, the food at Corflyn Hold beginning to fill out some of the hollows in her face and body. The dress she wore gave her a curious dignity, green wool embroidered with yellow flowers and quite clearly donated by the wife of a sutler or yeoman. Her oak-colored hair was braided and bound with ribbons of yellow.

But her eyes were downcast, avoiding Jenny's; the wary mouth settled to a neutral line. Jenny frowned a little and put out her hand to raise the girl's face to her; Yseult stepped self-consciously away.

"Are you all right?"

Yseult looked up quickly, the wide brown eyes determinedly smiling, cheerful as she had not been cheerful when Jenny had left. "Yes. 'Course. I'm fine, Lady Jenny."

"Is this Master Caradoc treating you well?"

She nodded, too fast and too many times. "He's good to me, m'am. Good to me, and teaches me everything, everything I always wanted to learn."

Jenny was silent, remembering her own desperate hunger to learn between Kahiera Nightraven's going and Caerdinn's grudging acceptance of her as his student. Remembered the magics she'd tried to invent for herself in those awful years, which almost never worked: the power that would not come. The nights weeping when the patched-together remnants of Nightraven's teachings turned out to be only mumbles of nonsense words.

Even Caerdinn's curses and beatings had been a blessing, then.

Men had called her whore and witch and hag in the streets when they saw her following after Caerdinn, and the children with whom she had once played ran from her. She reached out compassionately and touched Yseult's braided hair. "It isn't easy."

The girl's eyes flickered briefly to hers, then dodged away again. She shrugged and smiled. "You said it weren't going to be easy, m'am. But I've done harder."

"He isn't . . ." There was something very wrong in the too-quick replies, the casual voice. Something evasive in the studiedly averted face. "Are you all right?" she asked again.

"Oh, yes, m'am. Everything's fine." The girl produced a dazzling smile, as if for inspection. "Everyone's so good to me. There's not a thing amiss."

Everything in Jenny screamed at the lie, but she let it go. Quietly, she said, "And yes, we . . . we know what happened to Ian. John saw him." She nodded back to that lithe unlikely form, digging around in a volume titled *Revealed Geometries of the Planetary Movement*. She drew another breath, trying to steady herself against the memory. "Ian was taken—kidnapped—by a mage who appears to be putting together a corps of mages and dragons under the influence of demons. A wizard named Isychros did the same thing a thousand years ago. Has anyone come to you, or to Bliaud, trying to get you away from this Hold?"

"Oh, no, m'am." Yseult retreated a step, shaking her head. "Nothing of that. I stayed in the walls, like you told me to, and I been safe. Master Bliaud, too."

"And no one's sent you dreams, as I did, to try to get you away?"

"No, m'am."

It was on Jenny's lips to ask about the weather witchery, so improbably far in advance, but instead she asked, "Are you happy here, Yseult?"

"Yes, m'am." The girl dropped a quick curtsy. "I maun be going, m'am. 'Cuse me, m'am."

Jenny watched her worriedly as she crossed the courtyard, running a casual hand over the chained cover of the contaminated well, and vanished into one of the three shuttered rooms on its opposite side.

"What the hell are they doin' to the poor chit?"

She looked around. John was still perched on the back of the chair, the book on his knees, but he, too, followed Yseult out of sight with his eyes. "She acts like me cousin Ranny did when her mother's husband was comin' to her bed."

"Yes," murmured Jenny. She folded her arms inside her plaid. "Yes, that's what I thought."

"This old Bliaud bird wouldn't be witchin' her to him on the quiet, would he?" He stepped down from the chair, laid the book aside and came to stand beside her. "Or this Master Caradoc?"

"I'm not sure Bliaud could get the spells right." Jenny's brows pulled together, at the memories of the two or three village girls who'd crept to her cottage in secret, over the years, begging for charms to make "this man I know"—they never would tell names at first—"stop bothering of me." Without exception they pleaded that "this man I know" not be hurt, though Jenny knew perfectly well that those pitiful little cantrips for impotence or "have him be back in love with me mother again" wouldn't put an end to what was going on. "Though you never can tell. And of this Master Caradoc I know nothing."

"Nothing except that Rocklys is in no position to get rid of him, if he's able to teach the others. And that he was a suitor of hers she wouldn't have."

"That wouldn't stop her from sending him about his business."

"You think so?"

Jenny looked up into those sleepy-lidded cynical brown eyes.

"She's first and foremost a military commander, Jen, one of the best I've seen. She lets nothing stand in the way of good order and her objectives, whatever they may be. This school of hers means a lot to her. It may be she just doesn't want to know. If," he added, "that's what's goin' on. It may not be."

"But something is."

"Aye." John scratched the side of his chin. "Somethin' is."

Later in the day word reached Corflyn Hold that Rocklys' forces had been sighted from one of the signal-towers on the Stone Hills and would be at the gates by twilight. John and Jenny had spent most of the afternoon in the library, hunting for further mention of dragons, demons, or the long-forgotten incident of Isychros' Dragon Army, with no success.

"Dependin' on how many dragons this wizard can round up," John said, emerging from a slim and badly corrupted text of the Pseudo-Cerduces, "we're like to need somethin' along the lines of the Urchin. But we'll need to plaster the thing with spells if it's to be the slightest good."

"And I'm not sure ward-spells will work." Jenny laid aside a grimoire. "I have no experience with the magic of the great Spawn, but if dragon-magic won't touch them, I don't know what will."

"Well, they got rid of 'em somehow way back in the days," pointed out John logically. "Morkeleb spoke of desert mages from someplace called Prokep, wherever that was. And with Rocklys behind us we can at least prepare and get word to Gar, and see if there's anything of use in the archives at Bel or Halnath. This Caradoc may have heard somethin', too."

He stood and stretched his back, and walked to the window, where one of the camp washerwomen was crossing the courtyard with an armful of clothes. Fine linen shirts, stiff from drying, and on top a blue robe trimmed with squirrel fur, a south-erner's garment for the northern summers. Jenny, looking past John at the bright sun of the court, smiled.

Then she heard the intake of John's breath and saw his shoulders stiffen.

But he waited, silent, until the woman went into the third of the three shuttered chambers and reemerged without her burden. Then he caught Jenny by the wrist. "Come on," he said.

Silently she followed him across the court.

The room assigned to Master Caradoc was small, dim, and filled with half-unpacked boxes and bundles. The laundry lay on the neatly made bed, shirts folded, blue robe carefully spread out. And on top of the blue robe lay an embroidered cap.

Puzzled, Jenny looked at John, who was walking quickly from pack to pack, touching, feeling, manipulating the leather and canvas as if searching. "What is it?"

There weren't many bags. Some appeared to contain blankets, cookpots, and other articles of travel, others books. On the windowsill was what looked like a shell, wrought of thinnest glass and broken at one end.

John twitched aside the knots of one bundle, dug into it like a hound scenting carrion, and straightened up. In his hand was a cup wrought also in the shape of a shell, gold overlying mother-of-pearl as fine as blown glass.

"It's him," he said softly. "It's Caradoc."

Jenny frowned, not understanding.

"The wizard who took Ian. The mage I saw on the isles of the dragons." John raised the cup. "I saw this in his hands."

Jenny opened her mouth to speak, then let her breath out unused. Their eyes met in the shadowy chamber.

John said, "We've got to get out of here."

Book Two

THE BURNING MIRROR

CHAPTER FIFTEEN

Beneath a camouflaging plaid, John and Jenny passed the telescope back and forth and watched Rocklys and her men march into the fort with the setting of the sun.

Mailshirts made a muffled leaden ringing when the drums and pipes fell silent. In the back of her mind Jenny heard Caerdinn's harsh angry voice: *A great gray snake of men, with banners on its spine, they were.* Marching away to the south. Leaving us to our foes, and to poverty and ignorance afterward. Leaving us without law.

Rocklys rode ahead on her big stallion, and the smoky light made her helmet plumes and cloak dark as blood. John touched Jenny's arm and pressed the spyglass into her hand. Through it she saw the man who rode at the Commander's side.

Square-jawed, strong-built, his face was settled into lines of arrogance, the arrogance of money that has always bought unquestioning obedience. A fair match for Rocklys, if she had taken him. *Merchants wanting to be aristocrats,* she said in scorn . . . A maid of the House of Uwanë was perhaps the only thing he couldn't buy. On his hair he wore an embroidered cap; gloves of embroidered leather protected his hands.

The man who'd taken Ian.

Jenny shut her eyes. She should, she knew, feel only pity for the man himself, whatever fragments of his consciousness might still remain. She'd seen what even small wights did to and with those they possessed.

But she could feel no pity. *You arrogant, greedy bastard,* she thought, knowing she was being unjust, for he must have been as hungry for craft as she. *You heard the demon whispering in your dreams, promising power if you just did one simple rite . . .*

Didn't you know? Couldn't you guess?

Or didn't you want to know? Did you think you could control the situation, as you controlled all of your life before?

Her jaw ached and she realized her teeth were clenched.

"There." John nudged her. "Look."

The column was interrupted for a space, where prisoners walked, hands bound up to wooden yokes set over their necks. Women and children mostly, with the alabaster-fair skin, coarse black hair, and low flattened cheekbones of the Iceriders. But nearer the front, where Rocklys and the southerner Caradoc rode side by side, two prisoners rode bound on horses, a boy and a girl. Through the spyglass Jenny saw the silver chains, the sigils and wards that lashed their wrists to the saddlebows.

So John's mother Nightraven must have been brought to Alyn Hold, a prisoner of Lord Aver's spear.

Those, she thought, and not the protection of the farms, were the reason for Rocklys' pursuit of the band.

As Yseult must have been Rocklys' motive in convincing Jenny to seek Balgodorus, while Caradoc took Ian.

To found the Dragon Corps.

Only after the last of the army passed through the thick-planked double gate of the fort, and the gate shut behind it, did the two watchers move. Stealthy as hunters, they wriggled their way down the slope and into the trees, concealed under every ward-spell and guard and Word of Invisibility that Jenny could conjure around them.

"Where are they, anyway?" asked John, as he and Jenny worked their way through the undergrowth toward their camp. "I mean, it's a bit of a trick to hide a full-grown dragon."

"Morkeleb doesn't seem to have any trouble."

Morkeleb awaited them in the deep hollow where they'd hidden the blankets and food they'd taken from Corflyn in departing, though Jenny could see no trace of any living thing. Then something whispered in her mind, and what had been a spiky growth of holly was suddenly revealed, as if by a mere shifting of perception, to be blacker, glossier, harder than holly ever grew. What seemed to be tree branches took on the shape of tall spines and the bristling armory of joints and wing bones and tail. Two flashes of will-o'-the-wisp resolved themselves within a thicket of saplings, and the fireflies that had bobbed there took on the curious unholy glitter of the dragon's jewel-cold antenna lights. The smell of the pines and the water seemed to blow away, though there was no touch of wind, and the acrid, metallic stink they had veiled gleamed through like the blade of a concealed knife.

And so, Wizard-woman. Did you see your son?

"Ian doesn't ride with them. But Rocklys has taken two prisoners, Icewitches, to add to Bliaud and poor Yseult. That means Caradoc must make slaves of four more dragons or has already done so. I don't think Gareth and all the forces of his father can withstand a corps like that."

Jenny felt the heat of his anger again, rising through the accretions of shadow.

Not of dragons, he said. *And not if they are allied with the Hellspawn.*

"Can you bear us south?" she asked. "Take us to Jotham, where Gareth mounts siege before the fortress of the Prince of Imperteng? From him we can gain access to the archives of the Realm and the University at Halnath. Surely there is something that speaks of demons."

Do not count upon even that to help you, Wizard-woman, said Morkeleb. *Do you not know how it is among the Hellspawn? You, and cats, and whales, and ants, and every other being that has life: You are all beings of flesh in this world. And we, the star-drakes, we are beings of magic, beings unlike your flesh, bone unlike your bone . . . but still of this dimension, this plane of existence. We live and we die, and our magic is drawn from this fact.*

The Hellspawn are Other. Each Hell, each world, each of those separate and several planes from which they come is Other, from ours and from one another as well. All power is sourced from the things that surround us: Moon and Sun, the patterns of the stars and the way trees grow, our very flesh and the beat of our blood. They have Things in their worlds that are not stars. They have Things in their worlds that are not heat or

*cold, and to strike flint and steel in one of them will not make
flame, though in another perhaps it will. There is neither life nor
death in some of those Hells, and in some there is, and in some
there is something Else that has its own laws. Thus to do
the great magic here they must work through humans who have
that magic in their flesh, through dragons who are wrought of
magic—through those things attuned to the patterns of power in
this world.*

There was silence. Jenny touched with her mind the kindling
in the firepit, calling a small blaze to being. Though the sky
would hold light for hours, it was inky-dark under the trees, and
the damp close cold of the low ground rose about them. She un-
packed the food while John went down to the spring. Morkeleb
backed himself still farther into the dark woods, his thin bird-
beak laid upon his claws, and it seemed to Jenny that for a time
he ceased to be visible at all.

"I don't like it, Jen," said John when he came back. "And I've
been fair crippling meself tryin' to find another way. But I think
you'll have to go back into Corflyn Hold tonight."

Jenny was silent, gazing into the fire. Thinking of Nightraven
standing on the walls of Alyn Hold, gazing away toward the
north on nights of storm. Of the two little Icewitches bound on
their horses with silver chains. Ian running toward her through
the poppies that carpeted Frost Fell in the spring, and John's face
in the morning sunlight as he held his newborn son.

"And do what?" she asked softly.

"See the lie of the land." John set down the dripping water-
skin. "And that only. See who this Caradoc is when he's at home,
and how he and Rocklys get along these days. Any money she's
not twigged that it isn't him anymore? She may have her doubts
but not want to know it. It fair kills me to think Ian was in the
fortress when we were there this afternoon, but he must have
been. See if there's anythin' about the demon that would tell us
what counterspells to use, always supposing we find counterspells. If there's a book that says, 'Oh, yeah, Muckwort Demons
make their victims turn three times clockwise in a circle before
they fall asleep, and they can be exorcised by dandelion juice,'
we're gonna feel like a fair couple of clots for not countin' how

many times Caradoc and Yseult and Bliaud turned in a circle, and which way they turned.

"I don't know what you're going to do, love," he added softly. "I'd go meself—since I'm of no use to Caradoc if he does catch me—but he's sure as check got some kind of magic guard round the place and I'd never get past it. You can."

"Morkeleb? I'll go, but I will need all the help you can give me, to pass unseen. Will a demon be aware of me?"

Of you, Wizard-woman? Yes. Wind began to creep through the trees, a curious icy tugging, and beneath it the frightening undercurrent of heat that accompanies spells of transformation and change. *They smell blood. They feel the presence of human minds and human souls through the roots of their teeth.*

Leaves jerked and threshed on the trees. The fire in the pit leaned, flattened, stretching yellow fingerlets over the ground as if trying to creep forth from its prison. Rags of mist and smoke whirled among the tugging branches of the trees.

Only a few thousand of us made the journey from our home to this place, this world, to the Skerries of Light. We can ill spare the wisdom of their songs, and still less can we risk giving over those songs to those that dwell on the Other Plane.

The heat was suffocating, worse than the heat of age that periodically seized her flesh. The wind ripped at Jenny's hair and clothing, freezing where it touched, but doing nothing to dispel the brimstone in the air.

They will be aware of you. It may be that in spite of all that I can do to turn their thoughts aside, they will be aware of me. Wizard-woman, stretch out your hand.

The wind ceased. Fog rose out of the ground, black and impenetrable. Night-sighted, Jenny was barely aware of John's form beside her, and she saw by the way he reached out his hand that he was totally blind. She caught his groping fingers in hers, then extended her other hand, her left, to where Morkeleb's silver eyes had gleamed in the dark.

Something flashed and whirled in the mist, and hard strong claws closed around her wrist, dug into her shoulder. She half-felt, half-saw the dark beat of wings near her face. It seemed no bigger than a peregrine but sinuous and glistening as a snake.

Though gripping thorns pricked her wrist, there was no weight on her arm at all.

Give me your name, Wizard-woman, the voice said in her mind, *as once I gave mine to you when in the Deep of Ylferdun you saved my life.*

And she spoke it in her mind. There was a dragon-name, which he had called out of her four years ago, when she had taken on dragon form and flown away with him from Halnath Citadel, but that was not the name she now spoke. Around the spine of that music were woven other memories: Caerdinn cursing her, and John's hand lifting her hair; the lance of pain through her bowels when she bore Ian, and her laughter when lying in her bed in the house at Frost Fell, with her cats and her harp and the sunlight of a hundred summer mornings. The smell of roses. Autumn rain.

Pain in her wrist, then blood-heat on her arm.

Wizard-woman, what do you see?

Her eyes changed. She saw John.

Bent nose, round spectacles silvered over with mist, the alien contours of his face. A different perspective, like a doubled vision . . .

The mists dissolved. Perfect, glistening, deadly as a tiny knife of chipped obsidian and steel, Morkeleb sat on her forearm, no bigger than a hawk, silver eyes infinitely alien in the dark.

His voice was the same as it had always been, speaking in the abyss of her mind. *Open your mind to me,* he said. *Empty your mind to my voice. If I do not return, at least you will have knowledge of what it is that I see.*

He lifted his wings and, releasing her arm, rose like a scarf of black tissue on an updraft, hanging before her face.

What do you think dragons are made of, Wizard-woman? he asked. *Does magic have a shape, or a size? Can the will be bottled in a flask?*

Then he was gone into the dissipating vapors.

Jenny settled herself beside the fire to wait.

She had been a dragon. She knew what Morkeleb meant when he told her to open her mind to his, for it was a thing of dragons: One did not have to look into a dragon's eyes to hear its voice, or see what it saw. She waited, and her thoughts—which had circled a little around Nightraven, and Ian, and the old worn-weary track of her grief—settled, jewel-clear as a dragon's, interested without love or grief. She was aware of John sitting by the fire, drawn sword across his knees. Aware that his face was half-turned away, watching her, but watching also the woods all around.

She was aware of the forest, of the foxes creeping cautiously out, wondering if the dangers of evil heat and evil smell were gone; of the stupid, timid rabbits coming to feed. Of the smell of the pine-mast and the movement of the stars.

She saw Corflyn Hold from above, a quick glimpse of molten amber light cupped in lapis lazuli, and men moving about. Smoke and horses. Then gone.

Stronger to her nostrils came the smells of wood, dust, and mice; water and mold. She became aware of mouse-magic—she hadn't even known such a thing existed—and the darker stench that was the magic of rats. Morkeleb's spells, to keep even rodents from fleeing his approach and so alerting Caradoc.

Dark and mildew.

Firelight. The tawny radiance of pierced clay lamps, and the smell of burning oil. The room lay below her, foreshortened and changed but recognizable as the one in which she and John had been that day. Morkeleb must be lying along a rafter, she thought, with the same detachment she experienced when it crossed her mind to wonder whether John had remembered to put Caradoc's golden cup back exactly as he'd found it. Question and observation simply came and went.

Dragon-sight—mage-sight—showed her three-quarters of the room encircled by a spell-diagram, a vast sigil of power of a kind she had never seen. The glowing lines of it extended up onto the walls and, in a curious way, past the walls, through them, and down through the floor, visible for some distance into the foundations and the earth. Instead of Guardian Wards, thin wisps of greenish light burned at the diagram's five points, reflected in the frightened eyes of the black-haired boy and girl who sat bound in chairs within one of the figure's three circles.

Yseult, Bliaud, and Ian were there, standing behind the young

Icewitches' chairs. It was as if their eyes had been replaced with colored glass. Jenny observed this with a dragon's heart, the only way her own concentration would not be broken by the life-in-death of her son. On the table beside the box of jewels two more glass shells lay, broken and empty. Jenny understood without knowing how that demons wore those shells when they crept into this world through the Gate to their Hell.

Caradoc wore the embroidered cap that the laundress had brought in clean that afternoon. Interlocking circles of satin-work; stylized lilies. He'd bathed and washed his hair; Jenny could smell the camomile. Rocklys, standing before him, still wore her red military tunic and her riding boots, and her hair was flattened and matted from her helmet.

She said, "What is it that you don't want me to see?"

Caradoc sighed. "We've been through this before, Ro . . . Commander." His voice was a pleasant baritone, but the voice of a man not only used to having his own way but to being always right. "I told you at the outset that the presence of the untrained and uninitiated can completely nullify the effects of a spell."

"And I've heard since then that that isn't the case." Her colorless level brows pinched above her nose. She studied his face. Wondering, as John had said, and not really wanting to know.

"From whom?" His gesture of scornful impatience was, Jenny guessed, a perfect counterfeit of a familiar human mannerism, and one moreover with which Rocklys was well acquainted, for she seemed to relax. "One of the local hedge-witches? The only spells *they're* capable of wouldn't be affected by a brass band and a wrestling-match going on in the room. We're not charming warts here, Roc. We're not casting spells to win some bumpkin's heart. If you want my help, well and good, but you must accept that there is a reason for everything I tell you. There is a reason for every request I make. You don't explain everything to your troops—you can't, nor should you." He used the informal "you," as to a family member, and Rocklys' shoulders stiffened again, this time with familiar annoyance.

"Please understand that my wishes *must* be followed to the letter, else I cannot help you accomplish what you seek to accomplish."

For a time their eyes held, and the part of Jenny's heart that was human still saw the virile impatient merchant, newly come to court, and the granite-hard angry princess he had courted but could not win. It was an old clash of wills, and it served to convince Rocklys, had she in fact harbored doubts, that there was nothing amiss in this man she once knew.

Caradoc held out his hand peremptorily, and after a moment the Commander placed in it two jewels, dark faceted stones. The Icerider boy twisted against the bonds that held him to his chair, bonds twined with spell-riddled chains that glowed faintly to Jenny's mageborn perceptions, and began to weep. The girl, younger, round-faced, and cold-eyed, stared stonily before her, but behind her gag her breath was coming very fast.

"Were these the best you could get?"

"I have to send some taxes to the south, to justify our presence here." Rocklys' voice was cold, angry at being bested. "And I have to pay my men, and feed them, and keep the horses in oats. If word got to that bunch of painted twits the Regent keeps about him that I was purchasing gemstones, do you think"—and the pronoun she used was one of formal usage, of master to servant—"they'd leave me in command?"

"They wouldn't even care." Caradoc, who had glanced up in anger at her choice of address, turned with elaborate unconcern and held one of the jewels up, calling a spot of brilliant light into being, so that lozenges of pale purple were thrown onto his chin and brow.

"No," murmured Rocklys. "No, I think you're right. It would pass unnoticed in their silly quibbling about jurisdiction and whose rights overlay whose."

"So why trouble yourself?" Caradoc shrugged. "Amethysts are all right—these are of good quality and strong color—but if you could get another couple of rubies or emeralds we'd do better. They hold—" He hesitated, trying to answer the question that was in Rocklys' eyes without, it was clear, really telling her anything. "They hold certain spells more strongly. I'm not sure about that peridot—I think you were cheated by the merchant, but we can probably make do with it if we have to. And now, Commander . . ."

He walked to the door, only a step or two, and opened it to look outside and up at the sky. "The timing of these spells is very precise, particularly this close to mid-summer. It's full dark now, and barely time until midnight to do what must be done. Commander," he added, as she nodded brusquely and turned to go.

She turned back. The lintel of the door hid her face from Morkeleb's watching gaze, but every line of her body seemed to radiate discontent.

"Remember what I said about these practices remaining utterly unobserved. Neither of us can risk having one of these wizardlings incompletely given either to my will or to the bonding with the dragon. I tell you, if you or anyone watches what is done in this room or in the courtyard, I cannot promise that you will be able to conquer and hold the south."

The woman nodded and made again to go. Then she looked back. "And I have told you, Sorcerer." Again she addressed him as she would a servant. No wonder, thought Jenny, that wealthy suitor had gone away unwed. "I do not seek to conquer. Nor to wrest control of the Realm from its rightful King for my own pleasure or to satisfy some greed. I only seek to bring order. To make things as they should be."

Caradoc bent his head, and the lamp flames slithered along the embroidered lilies and across his silvery hair. "Of course."

She's lying to herself. The thought floated through Jenny's mind as Rocklys closed the door. *As he to her.*

And the thoughts were gone, put away to be regarded at leisure another time. Morkeleb's dragon-senses followed the Commander's boots across the court, hearing even the opening and shutting of her own door, and the creak of her desk chair as she sat. Aware, but setting the sounds aside.

Caradoc walked carefully through the gate in the magic circle and stood before the two young Icewitches. Morkeleb—and through him, Jenny—could feel the spells that Bliaud, Yseult, and Ian kept over them, spells worked through them, like magics worked through the bones of the dead. Caradoc asked, "Do you understand what I'm saying?"

The boy nodded. The girl said nothing, nor did she move. But she could not control her ice-gray eyes, and the sorcerer nodded briefly, satisfied that she could.

"I'm going to put one of these in each of your mouths." He held up the gemstones, burning purple in the lamplight. "If you swallow them, I'll take a knife and cut them out of your bellies and stuff the cavities with live rats. Do you understand?"

The boy was crying. The girl, bound and ringed and crippled by the spell-wards upon her, flung her hatred at the man, since it was all she had to fling.

Caradoc's broad shoulders tightened. Clearly he hated having his will crossed. "I see we're going to have to do this the hard way." He took the smaller of the two amethysts, a crystal the size of the end of his little finger, and, removing the boy's gag, put it into the boy's mouth, afterward gagging him again. The other stone was perhaps twice the size of the smaller, and a few shades paler in color. Caradoc handed it to Ian, who stood nearest him, as if the boy were no more than a table to hold things. Then he took a scarf of thin silk from his pocket and tied it around the girl's throat, pulling tighter and tighter until her back arched and thin, desperate noises issued from her throat. Leaving only the barest passage for air, he knotted it, then pulled down the gag. Her mouth dropped open, her chest heaving, and he dropped the jewel onto the protruding tongue. The girl moved her head as if in spite of all she would spit it out, but he shoved the gag into place again.

"One thing you will learn," said Caradoc, looking down for a moment into the bulging, frantic eyes and for a clear moment Jenny saw, not the man, but the demon that dwelled inside. "I will be obeyed."

Did he do that to Ian?

Jenny let the thought go.

The rite was surprisingly short. Jenny watched, dispassionately, through the incense-smoke and mists, recognizing more of the gestures and devices than she expected. There was a Summoning of some sort, but the Limitations set carefully around the two chairs seemed wrong to her. They were signs of protection, of the preclusion of demons rather than their calling. The power seemed wrongly centered, drawn in on the two children rather than on the sorcerer.

It was only when, in less time than it would take a loaf of bread to bake, Caradoc brought the rite to a conclusion and walked across the fading lines of the sigil to the young Ice-witches again, that Jenny realized what she had seen done. The boy had ceased his tears. The girl, though her eyes followed the blocky form of the man, showed no more hate, no more emotion of any sort, passive and empty.

Empty.

Caradoc removed the gags, took the amethysts from the mouths of each child, then walked to a strongbox. Lamplight flashed on its contents when he opened it, and with Morkeleb's eyes, Jenny saw what it contained.

Two rubies and a sapphire dark as the sea, clear, strongly colored, and without flaw. And in each jewel, it seemed to her, though they lay in the shadows, there burned a tiny, infinitely distant seed of light.

But only when she saw him pick up his cup of crystal and nacre and go to the door, only when she heard the chains of the well-cover clatter back, did realization strike her. She cried out, darkness swallowing the vision, the bridge between her mind and the dragon's collapsing. She cried out again, inarticulate, and felt warm strong hands grasp her arms—

"Jen!"

Her eyes opened and she saw John's face.

"Jen, what is it?"

She was trembling, breathless with shock. Having laid hope aside, she had no idea how painful it would be when it rushed back in; the agony of knowing that there might be something that she could do.

"Ian!" she said.

"Was he there?"

"Ian . . ." She swallowed. "The wizard—Caradoc—he didn't bring the demon into him, to drive out his soul and his mind. John, he took the soul of him—the heart of him—out first, and stored it in a jewel. Then he let the demon in. Ian's still there, John. We can still get him back."

CHAPTER SIXTEEN

"Why would he do it?" John spoke over his shoulder, not looking toward the fire that would dull his night-vision, keeping his eyes turned toward the dark woods. "Why would he want their souls kept around, once he's taken their flesh?"

"I don't know." Jenny glanced up from staring into the fire, from trying to reconnect her spinning mind with Morkeleb's. "It's a thing I never heard of. Usually, according to Caerdinn, anyway, the smaller pooks and wights don't . . . don't completely expel the mind, the soul, of their victim. Sometimes that soul can return when the demon is exorcised, if too much time hasn't passed. With the Great Wights it's different, of course. But this . . ."

She fell silent, remembering the demon blazing in Caradoc's eyes. The hell-light in Ian's.

"It was midnight when he met with the demons before, I think," John said, after a time. Jenny had opened her eyes, unable to find the dragon's mind with her own. "They came up out of the sea, silver and shining. Salamanders I thought they looked like, or toads, creeping out of little glass shells. Water must be one of their Gates."

They come from another place, Caerdinn had muttered to her, when they'd stood together on the edge of the Wraithmire watching the ghostly flicker of the fen-wights in the dark. *Since ancient days there have been men that would open Gates into Hell, in the hopes of finding power for themselves.*

They had been watching, Jenny recalled, for a wight that had seized a simpleminded woman, entering into her mind and dreams and causing her to kill and cut up her husband, children,

177

sister, and father before the villagers had summoned Caerdinn. Together, she and her master had exorcised the woman, but her own mind never returned. Perhaps that, thought Jenny, recalling the silent, bloodied hut, the creeping lines of ants and humming of flies, had been just as well.

Though she knew the presence of wizards in Corflyn Hold would almost certainly make it impossible to scry within its walls, Jenny took the finger-sized sliver of white quartz from her pouch and tried to summon images: the courtyard, Caradoc's chamber, the strongbox in its niche above the bed. But the place was written over with scry-wards, as she had written them everywhere on the manor walls at Palmorgin. All she could see was the dark bulk of the walls themselves, from a great distance off, and she realized from the look of the sky that what she saw was another night, another season, another year. An illusion.

Caradoc was in the courtyard, she thought. Summoning the Hellspawn from that other plane of existence. Summoning them through that distant Gate, through their medium of water, across whatever space lay between. Summoning them into the emptied minds, the emptied hearts, of those two poor children.

Yseult saying, "Yes, m'am," and "No, m'am," with that evasive, casual brightness, not meeting her eyes.

Yseult sending Bliaud's sons away, lest they see how their father had changed.

Rocklys asking her to stay, demanding that she take an escort.

"So it's been Rocklys all along." She folded her plaid around her shoulders and looked up again at the sky. The red star called the Watcher's Lantern stared back at her. Midnight chimed like cold music on her spine. *All doors open at midnight,* Nightraven had said to her once, separating her hair with a comb of silver and bone and plaiting the power-shadows called to being by that simple act. *All doors open at moments of change: from deepening night to dawning day, from fading winter to the first promises of spring.*

All doors open.

"I should have guessed it." Flames made slabs of fire in John's spectacles as he turned the log.

Jenny looked up, startled. Sometimes it seemed impossible to her that this man was Nightraven's son.

"The Realm as it's constituted drives her mad, you know. Each fief and deme with its own law, most of 'em with their own gods as well, not to speak of measurements. Everybody drivin' in all sorts of directions and not much of anythin' gettin' done, while them at Court make up songs and moon-poems and theological arguments these days, I'm told. Look at the books in Rocklys' library, the ones she keeps by her: Tenantius. Gurgustus. Caecilius' *The Righteous Monarch*. All the Legalists. Of course she's got no patience with Gar trying to do the right thing by old bargains and old promises. Of course she wants to step in and make it all match at the edges."

" 'I only seek to bring order,' " Jenny quoted softly, " 'to make things as they should be.' Gareth has to be warned, John. She has the biggest army, probably, in the Realm right now, even including the one he's taken to Imperteng with him. And whatever he has will be no match against dragons and wizards and demons working in concert."

"What I'm wondering"—John propped up his spectacles with a bandaged forefinger—"is what in the name of God's shoebuckles makes Rocklys think she can control Caradoc? Even given she doesn't know he's possessed by a demon, doesn't this woman *read*?"

"No," said Jenny. "Probably not. All her life she has wielded her own strength successfully, to her own ends. She is used to the struggle for mastery with Caradoc. If he appears to yield to her, do you think it's likely to occur to her that it's a trick? She . . ."

She raised her head, hearing the whisper of vast silken wings. "Here he comes."

And then, realizing that at no time had she ever been able to hear Morkeleb's approach, "The trees!"

At the same instant she hurled a spell of suffocation onto the fire and flung every ounce of strength she had into a great whirling tornado of misdirection and illusion around herself and John as dragons plunged out of the sky.

Lots of dragons.

John shouted, "Fire!" as he grabbed her arm, and claws raked and seared through the canopy of leaves above them. Snakelike heads shot through the branches, mouths snapping; green acid splashed a great charred scar in the pine-mast and Jenny cried out the Word of Fire, hurling it like a weapon at the rustling roof of the trees. The crown of the forest burst into flame, illuminating for a refulgent instant the primitive rainbow colors, glistening scales pink and green and gold, white and scarlet. One of the dragons screamed as the long scales of its mane caught and the scream was echoed, terribly, from the girl on the other dragon's back, Yseult with her skirts and her hair on fire. Then the two dragons were gone, and John and Jenny were running down the path to the spring, while all around them smoke billowed, flaming twigs and branches rained, and acid splattered in from above.

John dragged them both down into the water, the heat already blistering on their faces. The spring slanted away southeast to join the Black River two or three miles below Cair Corflyn. Jenny shucked off her wet plaids and heavy skirt, pulled her petticoats up high and began to crawl with the sharp stones digging and cutting at her knees and palms. John was behind her, holding his bow awkwardly over his back. Jenny drew the fire after them, Summoned the smoke to lie in a spreading pall over the whole quarter of the forest; it stung and ripped at her lungs, gritted in her eyes.

"Morkeleb will see the fire," she gasped.

"If he's alive." John slipped on a stone and cursed. The water was freezing cold underneath, though it had begun to steam on top. "If he thinks it's worth his while to take on four other dragons . . . Well, three, with the girl out of action . . ."

"He'll come."

Acid splashed into the glaring water in front of them. Through the steam Jenny saw the huge angular shape of a dragon framed in fire, crouched before them in the bed of the stream.

John said, "Fester it."

It stood just beyond the ending of the trees, where the spring ran into a marshy meadow. Wings folded close it bent down, darting its head under the fiery canopy. The flames gilded its scales, blue on blue, an iridescent wonder of lapis, lobelia, peacock; outlined the small shape on its shoulders, among the spines. It opened its mouth to spit again and John, knee-deep in the steaming water, already had his arrow nocked and drawn when Jenny saw the rider's face.

She screamed *"No!"* as John loosed the shaft. *"It's Ian!"* She flung a spell after the arrow, but it was an arrow she had witched herself, months ago. Ian rocked back as the bolt hit him; caught at the spikes around him and slowly crumpled. The dragon backed into the darkness.

"Now!" John grabbed her wrist, dragging her. "There's caves along the river."

"Morkeleb . . ."

"What? You don't think I can take on two dragons by myself?"

And Jenny heard it, the dark dream-voice calling her name.

They stumbled from the burning woods and saw him, a whirl of sliced firelight edging blackness in the air, tearing, snapping, swooping at the gaudy barbaric shapes of the red and white dragon and a sun-yellow splendor that Jenny thought must surely be the dragon Enismirdal. Morkeleb was faster and larger than either, but as the other two rose toward him, fire and darkness seemed to swirl up with them, splintering image and illusion into threes and fours. Jenny narrowed her mind, focused it to a blade of light, and flung that blade toward Morkeleb in spells of perception, of ward.

She saw, for a flashing instant, through his eyes. Saw the other dragons fragment and scatter, now into five or six discrete attacking shapes, now into rainbows of horrific color—maddening, camouflaging—and shot through with splinters of a ghastly and wicked greenish flame. Jenny redoubled her concentration, drawing power from the unchecked rage of the fire, from the granite and dolomite deep beneath the stream's bed. Through the dragon's eyes she saw the shape of an attacker come clear, and Morkeleb struck, black lightning, raking and tearing.

Then the image splintered again, and Jenny gasped at the sudden cold terror that took her, as if a silver worm had suddenly broken through her flesh, creeping and reaching for her heart and her brain. She called on all her power, guarding herself, guarding Morkeleb, but it was as if something within her were bleeding, and the power bleeding away with it. The discipline that Caerdinn had beaten into her took over, systematically calling on the other powers alive in the earth—moonlight, water, the glittering stars—and her eyes seemed to clear. Morkeleb had gotten in another few telling rakes with claws and teeth, driving them back. Blood rained down onto Jenny's face, and droplets of searing acid. The silver hemorrhage within her did not stop.

Morkeleb plunged down, black claws extended. She felt herself seized, ripped up from the earth. Her head snapped back with the shock of the parabola as he swept skyward again, a razoring cloud of wings. Around them both Jenny flung the holed nets of her guardian-spells and felt as her magic locked and melded with his that his power, too, had been drained and drunk away. They were flying east, flying fast, and she was aware of wings storming behind them, of a madness of pursuing color and rage. Rain clouds draped the high bleak shoulders of the Skepping Hills.

Into these Morkeleb drove, and Jenny reached out with her mind, Summoning the lightning and drawing around them the wardingspells to prevent their pursuers from doing the same. In the event there was nothing to it: Caught between conflicting powers, the lightning only flickered, sullen glares illuminating the cottony blackness around them.

In time the dragon gyred cautiously to earth.

"John?" Jenny rolled over, wet bodice and petticoat sticking to her limbs. The cave the dragon had brought them to was so low-roofed that only Jenny could have stood upright in it, and narrowed as it ran back into the hill. Rain poured bleakly, steadily down on the slope outside. She could hear the purling of what had to be Clayboggin Beck somewhere close and almost subconsciously identified where they were, and how far they had flown.

Witchlight blinked on glass as John turned his head. She marveled that in the midst of the chaos of fire, blood, and magic, Morkeleb had managed to seize them both.

"I'm sorry about Ian, love."

She drew in a deep breath. "Did you know when you shot?"

"Aye." He sat up cautiously. The tiniest blue threads of light showed her the glint of old metal plated onto his doublet. Behind him, flattened unbelievably, like a bug in a crevice, Morkeleb lay at the back of the cave, a glitter of diamond eyes and spines. "I knew he would be riding Nymr, see."

Jenny turned her face away. The knowledge that Ian was alive, and could be brought back, burned in her: rage, resentment, horror at what John had done.

"Caradoc won't let him die, you know," John went on. "There's too few mages in the world, and he had to pull both of 'em, Nymr and Ian—all three, I should say, if you count whatever goblin's riding 'em—out of the fight, as he pulled Yseult."

"And if your arrow had killed him on the spot?" Her voice was shaky. "We can bring him back, John, but not from the dead."

"If we'd died then," said John softly, "d'you think Ian would ever have been anything but a slave to goblins, a prisoner helpless in that jewel, for as long as his heart kept beating and his lungs kept drawing air? Watchin' what they did, while they lived on his pain? Sometimes an arrow to the heart can be a gift, given in love."

Jenny looked away. He was right, but she hurt so deeply that she had no words for it. John took off his doublet and lay down, pillowing his head on a soggy wad of plaids. His shirt steamed faintly in the heat-spells Morkeleb called to dry their clothing. There was only the sound of breathing in the cave, while the gray light struggled outside. In time Jenny got up and went over to lie beside him, holding his hand.

Given the rugged and heavily wooded terrain of the Fells of Imperteng, and the possibility of rebel guerrillas there, neither John nor Jenny considered it safe to be put down in the dark several miles from the camp of the King's men. Moreover, as John pointed out, there was no telling whether one of the dragons had followed them, waiting to pick him and Jenny up the moment Morkeleb was out of sight.

Thus the dragon flew straight to the camp below the walls of Jotham and circled down from the evening sky on the second day after their escape. Jenny spread out around them a great umbrella of Lousy Aim to deal with the consequences.

It was necessary. Men came running, shouting, from all corners of the camp—camps, for it was clear from above that each of the King's vassals pitched his tents apart, and there was no intermingling of the striped tents of Halnath with the cream-white if grubby shelters of the Men of Hythe. Jenny saw them clearly, as a dragon sees, the cut and color of their clothing as diverse as the variety and size of their bivouacs. Their voices rose to her, along with the wild neighing from the horses and the frantic bleat of sheep, racing in wild circles in their pens. Arrows soared in a futile cloud. Then spears, brushed aside by Jenny's spells. Then men ran away in all directions as they had run in, pointing and crying out as they saw that the dragon clutched a human being in either claw.

John, being John, waved and blew kisses.

Balancing on his great wings, Morkeleb extended his long hind-legs to earth, then folded himself down to a crouch. By that time two men stood on the edge of the drill-ground where he settled, tall thin young men, the red-haired wearing a black scholar's robe, the fair one's spectacles a note of incongruity against the red military tunic, red breeches, and elaborately stamped and tassled red boots.

It was this bespectacled crimson figure who cried, "Lord John! Lady Jenny!" and strode forward, holding out his hands.

There was a time, Jenny remembered, when he would have run.

She made to curtsy in her ragged petticoat and John's grimy plaids, but he caught her in his arms, bending down his ridiculous height. Then he turned and embraced John, breathless with amazement and pleasure, while Morkeleb folded himself a little more comfortably and regarded the scene with chilly sardonic unhuman eyes. Forty feet seemed to be his true size, larger than which he could not go, but it was difficult for Jenny now to be sure.

"What are you doing here?" demanded Gareth of Magloshaldon, son of—and Regent for—his father the King. Even as he spoke, Uriens of the House of Uwanë appeared, a tall man who in his youth must have looked like the statues of Sarmendes the Sun-God: inlaid golden armor, crimson cloak, his great jeweled sword hurling spangles of light. "It's all right, Father," Gareth said quickly, going to him as the King, seeing Morkeleb, raised his weapon and began to advance.

"Lo, it is the Dragon of Nast Wall!"

"It's all right," Gareth repeated, catching his arm. "He's been conquered. He's here as a . . . a prisoner."

Morkeleb opened his mouth and hissed, but if he said anything Jenny did not perceive it, and Gareth gave no sign.

"He's a dragon." The King frowned, as if there were something there that he could not comprehend. His servants and batmen hurried up around him, tactfully taking him by the arms. "Dragons must be slain. 'Tis the duty of a King . . ."

"No," said Gareth. "Lord Aversin—you remember Lord Aversin?—and Mistress Waynest have taken this dragon prisoner. I'll sing you the song of it tonight, or . . . or the night after." He turned back to John, frowning as he saw the burns and blisters of acid-seared flesh. "What happened?" He looked, too, at Morkeleb, as if knowing that only direst emergency would bring them to the camp.

"Rocklys is a traitor." John tucked one hand into his swordbelt and with the other scratched his long nose. "And that's the good news."

Without comment Gareth heard John's tale, though when John spoke of the Skerries of Light the Regent's eyes glowed with longing and delight. Sitting quietly between John and the red-haired Polycarp, Master of Halnath and Doctor of Natural Philosophy—and clothed in an overbright and too-long gown lent by an officer's wife—Jenny understood then that only part of Gareth's obsession with tales of the ancient Dragonsbanes stemmed from more than a gawky boy's craving for heroism and deeds of courage at arms. What Gareth loved was that they were tales touching on dragons.

As John, she realized, had come to love dragons as his understanding of them grew.

"She always looked down on you, you know," Polycarp said to Gareth. He set aside his note tablets. "She and I spoke two or three times when she was in command of the troops besieging Halnath. When word reached her that your father had become . . . ill"—he glanced at the tall man, seated in the chair of honor at the center of the table—"her first reaction was horror that you would be ruling the Realm."

"I'm not ill." King Uriens, who had listened to John's recital with the grave wonderment of a child, sat back a little, frowning. His hair, which had been the gold of ripe barley, was now nearly white and had grown so wispy that it had been cropped short. Coming out to slay the dragon earlier, he had worn a flowing golden wig.

Other than that, Jenny thought, he looked hale, with the good healthy color of a man who eats well and spends part of each day outdoors. Every time Jenny had seen him, since the death of the sorceress Zyerne who had drained away so much of his life and spirit, the old King seemed a little livelier, a little more aware of his surroundings, though he still had a child's fascination with every flower and button and pulley, as if he had never seen such things before.

And it was discouraging to reflect that Rocklys had probably been correct: If Uriens were separated from his son, he could easily be persuaded to forget him and make anyone—Rocklys or the Prince of Imperteng or John or even Adric—Regent in the young man's stead.

The King went on, "I just get sleepy, but I can still be King even if I get sleepy, can't I?" He turned anxiously to his son, who smiled and laid a hand over the big brown fingers.

"No one better, Father."

"It was mean of her to say that." Uriens turned back to Polycarp. "I wouldn't have thought it of her. She was always such a fine warrior, such a fine fighter. I remember I gave her armor for her thirteenth birthday. You asked for books." He regarded Gareth with mild puzzlement, though with no animosity in his voice.

By the flush that crept up under his thin skin at his father's words, Jenny guessed that his father had had a good deal to say on the subject of boys who asked for books rather than armor.

"Why doesn't she like us anymore?" Uriens said.

"She doesn't like us because she's not getting her own way," said John, with a wry sideways smile, and the King nodded, understanding this.

"Well, that's why she didn't marry that merchant fellow. All for the best, of course."

From outside the plain, dark walls of the tent came the barking of the camp dogs, the caw of rooks about the midden. Very little other noise, thought Jenny. No slap of arms or calling-out of orders. Morkeleb, crouched in the midst of the main parade ground in sinister, glittering silence, seemed to have damped every sound.

What would the spies and scouts of the hill-men make of it, or the Prince of Imperteng, for that matter?

"She told me," said Gareth quietly, "that she hadn't liked the idea of my regency but she was willing to learn different. After that she always treated me with respect."

So maybe even then, Jenny thought, Rocklys had begun to think of taking the throne.

"She spoke out half a dozen times in council against letting the fiefs and the free towns keep their own parliaments and maintain their ancient laws," the young Regent went on. "She said it was foolish and inefficient. But what could I have done? The Princes and Thanes acknowledge me King in part because they are allowed to *have* their own laws, to live the way their ancestors bade them live. A king can't tell his subjects—his *willing* subjects—that he knows more about how they should live than their ancestors did."

"Evidently," John said in a dry voice, "she thought you could."

"As for Caradoc," said Polycarp, long fingers toying with his stylus, "I remember him. About five years ago he came with a dozen copyists and offered me their services in repairing and replacing some of the oldest manuscripts in the library, if I'd grant them permission to make him copies as well. I always thought he was too fortunate in trade to be quite honest."

He glanced over at the King, but His Majesty had become absorbed in contemplating the gold beading around the edge of a plate that held cheeses, sweet breads, and the intricate savories of the south.

John sniffed. "Now we know where he got the fair winds and the good tides from."

"More than that," said Gareth. "In the past two years there have been enough . . . well . . . accidents . . . to shipping in the islands that a motion was made in council to revive the old laws against wizards holding property or office. Only no one knew who the wizard was." He glanced apologetically at Jenny, then went on quickly, "Tell us about your dragon-slaying machine."

John obliged him, keeping the exposition short and business-like, as he could when need arose. "I've been working on it for owls' years," he said, when he was done. "I got the idea from somethin' in Polyborus—or was it Dotys' *Secret History*?—but most of the actual design came from Heronax of Ernine, except I used the steering cage from Cerduces Scrinus' designs for pa-rade floats." He tapped the drawing he'd sketched in chalk on the tablecloth, surrounded by half-empty goblets.

"And I was trading with the gnomes for pieces for years and driving poor Muffle mad with all the little locks and levers that hold the thing together, so it can be took apart. It's a heavy little bastard."

Gareth and Polycarp exchanged a look. "The Lord of the Deep of Ylferdun would make us more," the Regent said, pol-ishing his spectacles with the tablecloth. "The last thing he or any gnome wants running around loose are dragons."

Four years, Jenny thought, had sobered and quieted him. When she and John had come south two years ago, for the naming-feast of Gareth's daughter, Jenny had seen that the im-pulsive, sensitive boy who'd come north to beg John's help had settled into a young man well aware of his limitations and willing to ask help, deferring lovingly to the shadow of the war-rior king his father had been and granting him every show of royalty and state.

Gareth settled his spectacles back on his nose. "How long do we have, would you say?"

"Depends," replied John. "If Rocklys has all the dragons she wants—and they must take a twilkin' bit of fodder—then we've maybe three weeks. Maybe more, depending on how bad Ian and Yseult were hurt, and how fast Rocklys wants to march her men south. She knows we know of her, and she knows Jen and I got away. My guess is she'll gather her troops and head south as fast as she can"—his eyes narrowed and an edge crept into his voice—"and bugger the bandits and the Iceriders that'll strike the new settlements."

He averted his face to hide his quick anger, but Jenny saw the sudden fisting of his hand, and how his mouth hardened and thinned. Between them, King Uriens had slipped into a doze again.

"I'm sorry," Gareth said quietly. "I'm sorry about this." He straightened the plate and the crumbs before him with embarrassed care, trying not to meet John's eyes. "She . . ."

John shook his head quickly. "She was the best thing going, son, and you'd no reason to doubt she'd keep her trust," he said. "And she's a damn fine commander. I suppose the things that made her good are the very ones that turned her against you: the need to see everything done the way she feels is right. And not hearing excuses for why it can't be done the quickest way. But I tell you," he went on, "and I know, because I've tried doin' both: You can't be a commander and a ruler at the same time. You need to see different things and be two different people. Maybe more. Rocklys would have found that out if she'd ever gotten to try, which we'll make bloody sure she doesn't."

"My lord . . ." A soldier-servant appeared in the doorway of the tent, barely sketching a salaam in the direction of the dozing King. The open flap let through the chill scent of the forest beyond the wooden palisade, and the sound of the River Wildspae roaring through the arches of Cor's Bridge. "My lord, the men are asking all sorts of questions about the . . . the dragon." He lowered his voice as if he feared that Morkeleb might hear, and of course, thought Jenny, he could. The man's mistake was in thinking the star-drake would care.

"They don't like it a bit, and that's a fact, my lord. They say there's witchery in it." He glanced at the King and then at Jenny, and Jenny could almost hear him remembering Uriens a few years before, in his warlike prime. Before the sorceress Zyerne.

"Well, it's good to know your men are up on the obvious, anyway," John said. "You'd better be damn glad that dragon's there, son," he added, addressing the soldier. "And if you'll excuse my sayin' so"—he glanced at Gareth, who nodded, bidding him continue—"if you'll excuse my sayin' so, you're gonna be a whole lot gladder in about three weeks."

CHAPTER SEVENTEEN

It was agreed that John would ride east with Polycarp and a small guard to Halnath Citadel, leaving Jenny with Gareth. Rocklys had spoken of the camp as lying "before the walls of Jotham," but Jotham lay in fact in the rough country where the Trammel Fells butted up against Nast Wall. It was impossible to make a camp closer than two miles from the city's gate and thus impossible, too, to mount an effective siege. Here in the flats beside the River Wildspae forage parties had little defense against the tough fell-men and mountaineers who slipped through the forest. Cor's Bridge commanded the road to Belmarie in the south, whence came the army's supplies, and that was something. Now, too, the guards watched the road that lead from the north.

The Wildspae was deep here and dangerous. It grew wider farther west, so Rocklys would have to come through here.

Morkeleb remained close, but displayed a surprising facility for being unnoticed. There were times when Jenny, speaking to the servants in the kitchens or the soldiers who worked frantically to dig underground shelters against the coming of dragons, realized that people didn't even remember that he was there.

Does this surprise you, Wizard-woman? The dragon stretched himself along the ridge that shouldered against the camp's eastern wall. Caves were everywhere in these limestone foothills, and without altering his size Morkeleb seemed able to fit, as a rat can, through crevices barely a quarter his apparent girth. The dragon would simply appear among the clumps of hemlock and maple, shake out his mane and resettle his wings.

We are travelers, we star-drakes. When we come to a place

190

where none of us has been before nor glimpsed even in our dreams, we conceal ourselves in the strongest places we can. There we breathe, and sleep, and cast forth our dreams around about us, drinking in the air until it tells us what creatures walk the stones and ride the winds. There are worse beings than dragons in existence—and behind the worst, creatures even more terrible than they.

And his mind brought not only words but images to hers, images that she could little understand: landscapes of black stone under red and swollen suns; worlds of thick, rank mist whose cold carried over thought, where shambling dreadful things roved half unseen among glaciers of purplish ice. She turned her eyes from the digging and building in the camp below and asked him, *Morkeleb, where do the dragons come from?*

And he only said, *Far away.*

Far away. A hole in her awareness of how the world was constituted, infinities of darkness she had never suspected, unimaginable corridors stretching into the night sky and beyond.

Dragons from stars in an empty sky.

Far away.

Is there magic there? she asked. She sat against his shoulder, feeling the heat of him through the enameled iron of his scales. It was unlike the warmth of any other creature, a glowing sense of power. *The place you come from, and all those places that lie between?*

Ah, Wizard-woman, he said, *there is magic everywhere. It breathes from the ground like dew. We drink it; we wrap ourselves in it as if it were a blanket of music; it is of us.*

And having once been a dragon, Jenny understood. And for a moment she ached with the ache of wanting power, power to wield the magic that she knew was abroad in the world. *If I had only been strong enough,* she thought, *Ian would be safe.*

From this hill also they sometimes saw the woodmen or the fell-dwellers in their green jackets and baggy striped trousers, sliding silently through the trees to observe the camp by the river. They were little dark men with thick black hair, and their ancestors had held these fastnesses from time immemorial against the fair-haired race of Belmarie. Twice Jenny watched them attack the men who labored to strengthen the fortifications on Cor's Bridge itself or the redoubts that were being raised to dominate the road beside it; twice saw the warriors of Bel stream from the main camp's gates crying, "Uwanë, Uwanë for Bel!"

The second time, Jenny slipped into the camp as soon as the fighting ceased and made her way to the Regent's tent, knowing that she'd find him curled up on his bed, shaking and sick.

"Were there any way of dealing with them other than subjugation, believe me, I'd try it no matter what Father says—or said—about the honor of the Realm." Gareth dragged in his breath in a shaky sigh and ran a hand through his fair hair—the dyed pink and blue lovelocks thinned almost to nothing and pointy with sweat. Thanks to John's teaching, the young man was capable now of leading men into battle, though he took care to appoint able officers and to stick close to them and to their advice.

"I take it they're less than pleasant neighbors?" Jenny fetched a basin of hot water from the pavilion's outer chamber. She'd seen the King in the battle also, leading the soldiers with a ferocity startling to one used to seeing him as only a smiling elderly man.

He was the Lord of the House of Uwanë, raised to war; Gareth had only to tell him which way to ride. The men followed him gladly, crying out his name, and told themselves afterward that he was himself again or nearly so.

Gareth shook his head. The greenish pallor was fading a little from his cheeks. "There's always border raiding going on," he said. "Prince Tinán claims his lands stretch all the way down to Choggin, though they never were farmed by anybody before our people started to settle there. It's been owned by the Thanes of Choggin and their people for more generations than you can count. And of course now everything's complicated by bloodfeuds. No, just the tunic," he added, as Jenny brought fresh clothing from the press. "And the mantlings—those green ones—and the hood. I have to change and get out there for the victory celebration."

"That was victory?" It had not had the look of victory to her.

"We have to call it one." Gareth pulled off his tunic, spattered with gore, and reached for the fresh one. He flinched as he handled the soiled cloth, fingers avoiding the blood. "Thank you," he added, as she gave him a cloth to wash with. "Dear King of the Gods, I wish I didn't have to do this. I wish I could just . . . just lie down." He swallowed hard. "Father's the Pontifex of the Realm, but I have to be there because he forgets. And truly, if there isn't some show of strength against them, the fell-men only push harder. It isn't . . ."

He hesitated, his thin height drooping over her, gray eyes blinking nakedly, for it does not do for a commander to appear in spectacles before the assembled armies of his Realm. His shoulders, under the purple wool of the tunic, had lost some of the weediness Jenny had first known, and his arms had strengthened from diligent sword practice, but there was a terrible sadness in his face. "I wish it wasn't like this," he said softly. Then he turned away and made a business of fastening his sword-belt, stamped in gold and set with cabochon emeralds; of adjusting the elaborately dagged and ribboned mantlings that spread like a butterfly's plumage over his back and made his shoulders seem wider. "I wish it was all as easy as it was when we only had to defeat and drive out a dragon. Like all the ballads, about Alkmar and the other heroes of old. I wish . . ."

He half-turned back to her, gloves of bullion and velvet and agate in his hands, and she saw what he wished in the weary grief of his eyes. She smiled, as she would have smiled at Ian, encouraging him to go on when the road was difficult.

"I'm glad you're here." He put his arm around her again in a bony hug. "I've missed you."

But as Gareth passed through the tent doorway for the procession to the altar of the Red God of War, Jenny sat on the bed again, the memory of her son piercing her heart.

He was alive. Trapped in a jewel, as this boy was trapped in the gem of kingship, his will no longer his own.

She pressed her hand to her mouth to stop her tears.

"Shall I bring you gold?" she asked Morkeleb later. She lay against the curve of the dragon's foreleg, a harp she had borrowed from Gareth resting on her shoulder. In its music, and in the magics the star-drake had shown her, she was able for a time to rest from the nightmare of Ian's enslavement, to put from her mind Caradoc's grim little smile as he thrust the jewel into the strangling Icewitch's mouth. "There is gold in the camp. I can get Gareth to contribute a few golden plates and cups, so you can have the music of the gold."

I am aware, said Morkeleb's dark slow voice above her, *of the gold in the camp, Wizard-woman.* He arched his long neck, and the night-breeze that trailed down from Nast Wall stirred the gleaming ribbons of his mane. *There are days when I am aware of little else. I saw what gold could do to me four years ago, when the sorceress Zyerne trapped me through the gold in the gnomes' deep. Sometimes it seems to me that if I accept even a cup or a chain, or a single coin, the longing for gold would conquer me, and I would not stop until I had devastated these lands.*

The glowing bobs of his antennae drew fireflies from the twilight woods, and the voice that spoke in her mind had a strangeness to it, as a man's would have, did that man grope for words. But Morkeleb never groped for words.

Gold laces the rocks of the Skerries of Light, Wizard-woman. Those of us who dwell there breathe our magic into that gold and bask and revel in the wonder that chimes forth. As we travel from world to world, gold is not the only thing we seek, but it is one of the things. When we come to a place that has gold, we remain a long while.

On the Last Isle, there is no gold. I find that I think differently away from its presence, and meditations become possible to me that were not even conceivable before. This was something that the Shadow-drakes told me, years ago. They said that to become one of them one must put gold aside. I did not see why it was necessary that I should, and so I did not. But after Zyerne and the Stone in the heart of Ylferdun Deep made me a slave, I thought again.

He fell silent, the run of his thoughts sinking down below words, like the heartbeat of the sea.

Finally he said, *The Shadow-drakes said also that they gave up their magic, as well as gold. This I do not understand. Magic IS the thing of dragons. Without magic, what would I be?*

Each night, and many times during each day, Jenny scried for sight of John. Frequently she saw him in the great library of Halnath, a maze of chambers and shelves that had been a temple of the Gray God lifetimes ago. Sometimes she saw the Dragonsbane with the Master of Halnath in the Master's private study, a round chamber whose walls were lined with books and with lamps of pierced work, scrolls and tablets and books and bundles of pages spread out between them on the table. But sometimes, late in the night, she saw him alone, sitting on the floor, surrounded by volumes or scattered handfuls of notes in unreadable old courthand. Candles stood fixed in winding-sheets of drippings on the shelves or the floor, their light outlining his gleaming spectacles and making shadows in the quiet set of his mouth. Once she saw him press thumb and forefinger to the sides of his beaky nose, eyes closed and face still, as if even in solitude he would show no one what he felt.

In the daytimes more often John and the Master were with the gnomes of Ylferdun Deep, who had for centuries maintained close ties with the Master and the university. Occasionally these glimpses were fragmented or obscured by scry-wards, for the exquisite stone chambers in the Deep of Ylferdun were guarded like those of Tralchet. She recognized Balgub, Sevacandrozardus the Lord of the Deep of Ylferdun; and others, too, of the gnome-kind, engineers by the way they looked at the drawings and diagrams John unrolled before them. They shook their heads and fingered their heavy, polished stone jewelry, and John hurled his diagram on the floor and stormed from the room. Later, she saw him half-naked and covered with grime in a deserted courtyard of Halnath Citadel, checking over the metal shell of a half-built Urchin. So they must, she thought, have come to a compromise. They guarded alloys and engines and secrets jealously, but dragons were dragons.

One of the engineers was with him now, a tiny gnome-wife whose vast cloud of smoke-green hair was pinned up in spikes tipped with opal and sardonyx. She pointed out something in the coldly glittering engine and touched a crank. John shook his head. He asked about something, and held up his fingers to demonstrate an item the size of a gull's egg. A hothwais, Jenny guessed, charged with some form of energy. The engineer glanced at the two gnomes with them—lords of high rank, whose jewels were even more ostentatious than hers—and all shook their heads again.

John gave up, disgusted, and climbed into the interlocking double wheels of the steering cage. He hooked his feet into position and grasped the steering bars, and said something, gesturing, to the gnomes. The engineer patted the air reassuringly with her little white hands.

John yanked off the brake.

If it was power John was concerned about, he could rest easy on that score. The Urchin, which had a dozen small wheels instead of the four of the original design, leaped away like a racehorse from the starting-post, John clinging to the steering-bars with an expression of startled horror and the gnomes racing behind.

John caught at a lever. By the way it simply gave, Jenny guessed at a serious design flaw. The Urchin whirled like a mad bull for the courtyard wall, and John twisted at the steering bars, sending it smashing into the gate instead. The gate crashed open in splintering gusts of wood; the Urchin rolled down the ramp beyond into the dairy yard, milkmaids and cows and chickens scattering in all directions. It crashed through the wooden water trough, hit a dropped dung fork just right, and sent it pinwheeling through the air; John flung his weight against the steering cage in time to avoid a barrow full of milk buckets and then, with the Urchin headed full-bore for the dairy-house itself, wrenched the cage with all his strength as if to turn.

The Urchin rolled, flipped up on its back with its twelve wheels spinning crazily in the air, and slid into the midden piles with John hanging upside-down in the cage. Even after the thing came to a stop, half-buried in dung and soiled straw, the wheels continued to churn.

John calmly unhooked his feet from the straps and turned in a slow somersault from the bent steering cage to sink knee-deep in muck. The gnomes ran up to join the ring of children, dogs, dairymaids, scullery help, and guards and the still enthusiastically whirring Urchin. John wiped the slime off his face and adjusted his spectacles.

Jenny could read his lips as he said, "You're right; works fine. Fix the brake, though."

"Which is as well," she said, when she told Morkeleb of it later. Another evening, after another day of waiting, another day of scrying landmarks to the north and finding that she still could see them, which would be impossible when Rocklys' legions approached. Though she would not use her magic against the soldiers of Imperteng—and indeed, Gareth never asked it of her—she did this for him and also laid spell-wards and guards on the new fortifications his men were building on Cor's Bridge and the dugouts.

With the coming of evening Jenny's anxiety for Ian always grew. To assuage it she had climbed the hogback ridge behind the camp and sat gazing out over the slow-slanting smoke of the cookfires into the light-drenched distance of fading woodlands and shining streams, her fingers finding almost unthinking solace in the ancient tunes summoned from Gareth's harp. Old ballads and old tears, the laments of ladies long dead for lords whose names were forgotten. Pain and sweetness rolled together like a southern candy. Darkness filled with the promise of light. In time, the dragon had come.

"Spells of some kind must be laid on the Urchins," she said at the conclusion of her tale, "if they're to withstand the magic of the demon mages. The magic of the gnomes is different from that of humankind. It may serve . . ."

It is not different. The dragon shifted his hindquarters and scratched like a dog at the cable of braided leather he had begun to wear about his body, just forward of the wings. *Different to you, yes, as an ass differs from a horse, or a chicken from a hummingbird. But to a demon they are the same. And such a demon as I think these are will breathe them aside, as a child breathes away the flame of a candle.*

Sometimes she watched the affairs of Alyn Hold through her crystal; called the images of Adric and Mag while the boy trained in weapons and the girl plagued her nurse and John's aunts half to death, slipping out to be with her friends or to rig elaborate experiments with pulleys and pendulums in the hay barns. At such times the pain was the worst, for the children were deep embedded in the pattern of her life, and it was hard to be away from them. Ian she tried and tried to see, using all the methods that Morkeleb could teach her. She knew that if she succeeded it would only hurt her worse, but still she made the attempt. Nor would she put it by with failure, but spent weary nights at it, until she fell asleep to the dawn-callings of the birds.

Then one evening she summoned John's image in the crystal and saw that he'd tied a red ribbon through the epaulet of his disreputable old doublet. She said to Gareth, "I have to go. He must have found something."

"I thought these all were burned." Polycarp of Halnath unlocked the inner door of his study, revealing a secret chamber, furnished only with a chair, a small table over which a lamp hung, and two shelves of books, each volume chained to a ring in the wall. He cast a nervous glance at Morkeleb, who had reduced himself in size and perched like a jet gargoyle on Jenny's shoulder. Morkeleb turned his snakelike head and returned his gaze: the Master quickly averted his eyes.

"I came across them in a volume of Clivy." John crossed to the table and lowered the lamp on its counterweighted chain. "Clivy's the world's prize idiot on the subject of farming and from what I read of this book he knew even less about women—it's called *Why the Female Sex Must Be Inferior to the Male*—but it was one I'd never read before. These were stuck in the middle."

Four sheets of papyrus lay on the table, tobacco-colored with age and cracked down the center where they had been folded.

"As far as I can guess from the date of the handwriting," said Polycarp, closing the door behind them, "those have to have been written by Lyth the Demon-caller. He was a priest of the Gray God here at the time of the Kin-wars. The Master at the time had him carved up alive for trafficking with demons, and all his books and notes were thrown into the same fire with the pieces. According to the catalogs that particular volume of Clivy was one of the original manuscripts in the library, so it would have been there then."

"There was any amount of dust on it," added John, and

perched on a corner of the table. "No surprise, considerin'. If I had incriminating notes about me, Clivy's where I'd stick 'em."

"And did this Lyth traffic with demons?" Jenny touched a corner of the papyrus. Caerdinn had taught her three or four styles of writing, including the runes of the gnomes as they were used in Wyldoom and in Ylferdun, but the old man's own scholarship had been grievously limited. A word or two of the jagged script leaped clear to Jenny's perusal—"gate" and "key" she knew, and "erlking," a word sometimes used for the Hellspawn in the Marches. But more than those, she felt the paper itself imbued with a darkness, as if it had been in a room thick with the smoke of scorching blood.

She drew her hand back, her question answered.

"They kept the matter quiet because of the upheavals," said Polycarp. "But yes. There were two gyre-killings here in the Citadel, and two recorded during that same time in Ylferdun Deep. One of those was after Lyth was taken prisoner, but when the Master's men went through and smashed or burned everything in Lyth's house, there were no more."

"So he used something in his house as a gate," said Jenny.

"By what it says here"—John nodded to the four sheets of paper—"it seems to have been a glass ball floating in a basin of blood, though God knows what the neighbors said about the flies. Not that they'd say much to his face, I don't suppose. But he says as how there were other demon gates, and that one of 'em lay in a sea-cave on the Isle of Urrate . . ."

"Urrate?" Jenny looked up sharply. "That's the sunken island—"

"Just north of Somanthus," finished John. "Somanthus, as in where Caradoc hails from. Lyth—if it is Lyth—says that particular gate was blocked when Urrate sank in an earthquake, but it accounts for the things I saw comin' out of the sea in me dream, and out of the well in Corflyn's court. Anythin' that'd hold water could be sorcelled into a gate."

Morkeleb had crept down Jenny's arm and now crouched on his haunches on the tabletop, his head weaving above the papers like a serpent's, the diamond reflections of his antennae making firefly spots in the ochre gloom. He hissed, like a cat, and like a cat his tail moved here and there, independent of the stillness of his body.

"Sea-wights, Lyth calls them in his notes," Polycarp said. "He doesn't describe them—they weren't the things that came to him out of the glass ball and the blood. And this is the only other mention I've ever seen of the Dragons of Ernine."

"It doesn't give Isychros' name," said John. "But it says here that 'an ancient mage' enslaved dragons—no mention of wizards—by a bargain he struck with demons he summoned out from behind a mirror. But this is the most interestin' thing." He propped up his spectacles again and hunted through the manuscript. "Here we go: *Demons are ever at war with one another, for the demons of one Hell will torment and devour the demons of another Hell, even as they torment and devour men. Thus the magic of the Hellspawn can be used, one against another.*"

He looked across at Morkeleb. "Had you ever heard that before?"

I had heard it, the dark voice of the dragon murmured in Jenny's mind. *The Hellspawn seek always to find ways into this world, for the hearts and the bodies of the living are to them as gold is to dragons, the medium of an art that gives them pleasure. They drink pain, as the dragons drink the music that dwells in gold. And I had heard also that the demons of one kind can— and do—drink the pain of the demons of another kind.*

"Then that may be what the mages of Prokep did, to defeat the dragon corps. Not used human magic at all, but made a bargain with . . ."

The dragon's antennae flicked forward, and his eyes were tiny opals, terrible in the gloom.

Do not think, Songweaver, to ride to the ruins of Ernine and seek behind the mirror of Isychros. It is a bad business to have any dealings whatever with the darkling-kind. They give no help without the payment of a teind in return, and the teinds they require imperil not only those who bargain but everyone whose lives they touch.

"Ernine?" Polycarp turned his head sharply. "No one knows where Ernine lay. The records speak of it, but—"

After the fall of the city to the dragons, it was destroyed, said

Morkeleb. *But later another city rose on its ruins. It was called Syn after the god that was worshiped there.*

"Syn? You mean Sine, the ruins where the Gelspring runs out of the hills?" Eagerness charged the Master's voice. "That was Ernine? You're sure?"

Morkeleb swung his head around, and again Polycarp had to look aside quickly, lest he meet the dragon's eyes. Jenny saw the ember-glare of Morkeleb's nostrils and felt the heat of his anger pass like desert wind through her mind. *This is what comes,* said the dragon, *of making myself the size of a ratting dog; grubs whose memories barely compass a single round of the moon's long dance with the sun ask if I am sure of cities that I saw founded, and laid waste, and founded and laid waste again. Pah!*

Thoroughly embarrassed, Polycarp apologized, but Jenny barely heard. She had barely heard anything, beyond the words *the magic of the Hellspawn can be used, one against another.* Her breathing seemed to her to have stilled, and her heart turned cold in her chest.

Ian.

Quietly, John laid a hand on her arm. His voice was a murmur in her ear. "He's right, love."

She looked up at him quickly.

"Whatever we do to deal with Caradoc and his wrigglies, playin' one tribe of demons off against another will only make it worse, for us and for everyone who comes after."

She looked aside. "I know."

But through supper and into the night, reading the scrolls and tablets and books of the library of Halnath, she could not dismiss those words from her mind, nor the thought of Ian, a prisoner in his own body and in a sapphire in Caradoc's strongbox. When she slept, the thought of him, the image of him, followed her down into her dreams.

CHAPTER EIGHTEEN

In her dreams Jenny came to Ernine, the yellow city where the Gelspring ran out of the mountains, where orchards flowered in the fertile lands of the river's loop. In her dreams she saw it as it was in the time of the mage Isychros and the heroes Alkmar the Godborn and Öontes of the singing lyre. She passed through the market that lay before the citadel hill and climbed the curved path to the palace of sandstone and marble, where the Queen's ladies with their gold-braided hair wove cloth among the pillars.

It seemed to her that someone who walked at her heels asked her, "Did you ever wonder who this Isychros was, Pretty Lady? Where he lived, and what kind of a man he was? He was a prince of the royal house, you know. And his eyes were like bright emeralds that catch the sun."

When she turned to see who spoke there was no one there. Nevertheless, as she hurried on, Jenny felt a hand brush her arm.

She was afraid then and wanted John. But John lay asleep beside her, far away in their borrowed bed in Halnath Citadel, and she was here in Ernine, a thousand years ago, alone.

She passed down shallow steps and saw the plastered stone blocks of the walls give way to the raw hill's bones. Gazelles were painted on the plaster, the big black Royal gazelles with six-foot back-curving horns, the kind that were never seen close to Nast Wall anymore. Somehow she knew that herds of them roved within a few miles of the city walls. Close by, someone played the harp, a gentle tune that made her want to weep. As the hotness welled behind her eyes she heard a soft chuckle behind her, laughter at her weakness, and something more. She put the tears away.

A corridor was cut in the rock, constellations painted on its
ceiling. A comet hung among the stars, trailing its harlot's hair.
Curtains covered the corridor's entrance, and others blocked it a
few feet farther on; still more covered the door at the end, layer
on layer. The round chamber beyond was draped with them, all
save the ceiling, where the night sky again was painted, and the
comet, brighter and colder than before.

The mirror was in the chamber. It was bigger than she'd
thought it would be, five feet tall at least. It was wrought of the
curious blue-pink opaline glass that one found in the oldest ruins
of cities in the south, and what it was backed with she did not
know. Whatever it was, it seemed to burn through the glass, so
threads of steam rose from the surface, though when she came
near there was no feeling of heat. The mirror's sides were framed
in soapy-looking silver-gray metal—it had a disturbing sheen in
the dark. Curves and angles drew the eye in an unfamiliar
fashion, as if to darkness previously unseen.

The flamelets of the bronze lamp that hung from the ceiling's
center doubled in the burning depths. Beneath them she saw reflected the table under the lamp, and the chair that faced the
mirror across the table, and Jenny herself in her borrowed red
and blue dress. Though she heard the chuckle of laughter again,
close to her ear, the mirror reflected no one else.

But someone said—or she thought someone said—*Put out
the lamps, Jenny. You know mirrors turn back light and blind
those who look in them to all but themselves and what they
think they know.*

She reached with her mind and put out the lamps.

Then she saw, in the darkness, what crowded against the glass
on the other side. Watching, and smiling, and knowing her name.

She awoke screaming, or trying to scream, muffled incoherent
whimpers, and John shook her, pulled her out of her terror and
her dreams. She clung to him in the darkness, smelling the comforting scent of his bare flesh and hearing his voice say softly,
over and over, "It's all right, Jen. It's all right," as his hand
stroked her cheek.

But she knew that it wasn't all right.

In the morning, after scrying deep and long in crystal, water, wind, and smoke for any sign of Rocklys' army advancing beyond the Wildspae, she flew with Morkeleb south to the Seven Islands. Because they passed over the heart of the Realm, Jenny cloaked herself and the dragon in spells of inconspicuousness, something humans were better at than dragons; Gareth had problems enough. In the Wildspae Valley, and the green lands of Belmarie, where the Wildspae and the Clae joined, the farms were rich and the harvest ripening, and Jenny compared them to the Winterlands with bitterness in her heart. Then they passed over the sea to the six fertile islands that constituted the greatest wealth of the Realm, and the spine of gray rocks that marked what had been Urrate.

Morkeleb lighted among the broken pillars of a shrine, all that was left of Urrate's acropolis. Waves crashed barely a dozen yards below. Seabirds wheeled and yarked about their heads, and perched again on the lichen-cloaked shoulders of the Great God's statue. Poppies and sea grass swayed in the wind. Jenny could see the gleam of marble for some distance under the dark of the sea, white as old bones.

The dragon rocked on his tall haunches, swaying his head back and forth above the waves, balancing with wings and tail. Jenny kicked her feet free of the cable around his body, slid from his back, and settled herself in the chill sunlight. She closed her eyes, listening with the deep perceptions of the dragon-mind beneath the surge of the waters. Feeling, scenting, following Morkeleb's mind deeper and deeper, among the waving leathery kelp forests and the shards of the city's drowned temples and walls. Scenting for the stink of infection.

But there was nothing. Above her she heard Morkeleb singing, stretching luminous blue music into the abyss where the sunshafts faded, and in time she heard music answer him. Pipings and hoonings, deep echoing throbs. With Morkeleb's mind she saw shapes rising, black-backed, white-bellied, wise ancient eyes glittering in pockets of leathery flesh. Great fins stroked the water, guiding as Morkeleb used his wings to guide; great tails that could smash a boat thrust and drove. They all breached at once, fourteen slate-dark backs curving out of the sea, fourteen plumes of steam blown glittering in the sun. Then they rested on the surface, rolling a little, loving the warmth after the cold currents below, perhaps thirty feet from the rocks where the dragon sat, and the eldest of them asked Morkeleb why he had called.

Demons—Morkeleb framed them in his mind. Jenny, watching and listening, absorbed the images and the way the black dragon arranged them: different, very different from the dark voice that spoke to her in her mind. Long slow images of ugliness and hate, of bitter green magic like poison spreading in the water. Sickness, pain, blindness, death. Soul-drowning as a trapped porpoise drowns among the deep kelp. Dark rocks far down under the isle? Heat without light? Steam pulsing out into the sea?

The calves of the abyss replied. Not on Urrate but under Somanthus, far down where the western side of the isle fell away into a great deep: There was the burning gate. Dreams of wisdom for the taking. Dreams of power to summon at will the great warm shrimp-tides, and promise of new stories to tell, rich new songs beautiful and strange. Dreams rising to the men of Somanthus. A man used to walk on the shore to study the waves, or to learn the ways of the dolphins, or with a little sky-tube gaze at the stars. The whalemage Squidslayer did not know what to do, but it was clear, he said, that something must be done, lest greater ill befall.

Will you come, Wizard-woman, and see these things?

She surrounded herself with a Summoning of Air and clung to the leather cable around his body as he slid from the rocks. The water was colder than she'd expected. Her hair floated behind her like the kelp, and the whalemages surrounded them, not ponderous at all in their element but weightless as milkweed and swift as birds. They passed through the avenues of the sunken city, where weeds reached up through windows of toppled houses and the marble door-guardians gazed sadly through masks of barnacles and snails. The deeps beyond were icy, and very dark.

They did not go too near the abyss where the demons dwelled. Jenny could smell them nevertheless, feel them through the water, and her flesh crept on her bones with loathing and terror. Far down the endless cliff-face a kind of greenish light played around the rocks. On rock-ledges all the way down she could see the little glass shells that the sea-wights shed, and she thought she could see things moving, bloated and spiky, very different from the shapes they took in the upper world.

Chewing through the rocks, she heard Squidslayer's thoughts in her mind, like slow silvery bubbles. *All the underpinnings of Urrate, cut, eroded, dissolved. Years on years on years. Island falling, shutting dark within. Vast ecstatic sobbing of sea-wights at the deaths.*

And Jenny felt its echo, through the whalemages' minds, the thunderclap of pleasure at devouring such terror and pain.

Morkeleb turned beneath her like an eel. Surrounded by the whales they gained the surface again, and the wind dried her clothing as they flew through gathering dusk to Jotham. Neither spoke. That night Jenny dreamed again of the vault below ruined Ernine, seeing the things that watched from the other side of the burning mirror. Waking alone and cold with sweat in her little tent, she rose and climbed the hill behind the camp in the warm summer darkness, until against the blue-black sky a blacker shape loomed. She lay down between his great claws and slept, and the dreams of the things behind the mirror left her in peace.

John came into camp two mornings later, driving a flatbed wagon drawn by ten mules with the first two Urchins. He was accompanied by the little green-haired engineer Jenny had seen in her scrying-stone—Miss Tee was her name among humankind—and by the gnome-witch Taseldwyn, called Miss Mab among men. Gareth's treasurer, Ector of Sindestray, accompanied them, bearing documents any courier could have delivered, and also a very young warrior of Polycarp's guard who'd been trained, more or less, to operate an Urchin.

From the edges of the woods the warriors of Imperteng watched with suspicion as John and Miss Tee and Elayne the Halnath guard demonstrated the Urchins to Gareth. *Probably still believing,* Jenny thought, *that these things concern them.* The horses snorted and pulled at their tethers as the squat, spiked oval whirred and clicked around the parade ground, firing harpoons in all directions: Gareth flinched and ducked down beside Jenny in the shelter of the heavily fortified earthwork, then emerged to touch the tip of the harpoon. It had pierced two layers of target planking, thicker than the length of Jenny's finger.

"Ingenious, of course," approved Lord Ector temperately, "but expensive." He was a small man, stout and dark, and younger than his defeated hairline led one to think at first, and he wore a courtier's blue and white mantlings even in the camp's dirt. There was about him, though, none of Gareth's air of loving display for its own foolish gorgeousness. He was one, thought Jenny, who sought by the courtier's garb to establish birth and rights beyond all possible questionings of lesser men.

"Cheap at the price, though." John swung himself out of the Urchin's hatch and slithered rather gingerly to the ground among the spikes. "Long as we can keep the things wound, we're fine." After him came the young Halnath archer. At Polycarp's suggestion, the Urchins had been made large enough to accommodate a second person, both to fire the harpoons and, if necessary, to crank the engine. "And you can just hike the taxes on the Winterlands a little higher for 'em, can't you?" he added maliciously and flicked Ector's mantlings.

Ector glared.

"We have people working on poisons for the harpoons," said Gareth rather quickly, nodding back toward the camp. "I've sent two messages to Prince Tinán, warning him about an attack by wizards and dragons, and offering a truce in exchange for help, but I've heard nothing."

"Stubborn bumpkins," said Ector.

"Have they been lured into traps before?" John smote the dust from his patched sleeves, and the Thane of Sindestray fanned irritably at the billowing dirt with a circle of stiffened silk. "You have to admit that with garrisons from everyplace in the Realm on the march for here, professions of friendship don't have much of a true ring."

"It wasn't me who went back on the last truce," blurted Gareth, flushing. "That was—"

"And it wasn't Tinán, probably, who burned out the farms that got his dad killed," John pointed out. "In my experience, anyway, that's how these things work, son. Jen," he went on, "can you and Mab lay death-spells on that many harpoons?"

Jenny nodded, cringing inside at the thought.

Like Gareth, she thought—like Ian, like John—she, too, was trapped in this jewel of necessity.

She drew a deep breath. "This morning when I scried the fords of the Catrack River I saw nothing: fog, broken images, the woods ten miles away. They are close. And she'll send the dragons ahead." Ector looked skyward as if expecting to see it filled with fire-spitting foes.

"You'd better send for all the Urchins Polycarp has in readiness."

While Gareth dealt patiently with the council's messages, Jenny drew circles of power around the Urchins themselves in the parade ground, under the distrustful and disapproving eye of the troops. She summoned what power she could from the earth, and from the pattern of the waters below—from river's currents and the exact combinations of rocks in the hills—from the turning of the unseen stars. These spells she imbued meticulously in the stubby little machines. Her spells of human and dragon power she braided with the gnomish wyrds of Miss Mab, both on the machines themselves and then on the fierce barbed points of the poisoned harpoons.

"I always hate the death-spells," said Jenny, straightening her aching back and brushing aside the tendrils of her hair. Sunset turned the air to copper around them and the poison smoke burned her nostrils; the anger of the sullen soldiers who brought up wood for that endless boiling muttered at the back of her mind like the pull of an unseen stream. "And it seems like the older I get the more I hate them. And yet"—she gestured wearily at the pile of iron bolts—"and yet here I am working them again."

Her hands trembled as she spoke. She had returned twice in the last hour to the sanded flat behind Gareth's dugout to remake her own circles of power and draw into herself, and into her spells, more of the strength and magic she needed. Mab had worked her magic all afternoon without pause. Jenny couldn't imagine how she was doing it.

The gnome-witch, seated on a firkin, tilted her head a little, looking up at the woman with one round hand shading her pale-blue eyes. "It is because thou lovest," she said simply. Her hand was smaller even than Jenny's, smaller than Adric's, but thick and heavy as a miner's. Both women had shed all jewelry, braided up their long hair, and changed for the work into coarse linsey-woolsey shifts that could afterward be burned. Beneath the hem the gnome-woman's bare dangling feet were like lumps of muscled rock.

"The more years thou see, the greater grows thy love: for this John, for thy children, for Gareth; for thy sister and her family and for all the world. And as thy love grows, so grows it for every woman and man, for gnomes and whales and mice and even for the dragons." Miss Mab set aside the harpoon she had held on her knees and reached for another. They were stacked all around the two women like corn, tips and edges black with the sludge of the poison dip.

Jenny's voice was unsteady, remembering John between walls of fire, the black horn bow steady in his hands. Aiming at their son. "Is there another way?"

Mab's wide mouth flexed in what might have been a smile. "Child, there is," she said. "But not for a woman of bare five-and-forty, standing at this crossroad. Time is long," she said. "Love is long." And looking up, she smiled and waved as John strode across the sanded death-field in his shirtsleeves, a clay pot of lemonade in his hands.

The dragons dropped from the sky in the dead of the night.

Knowing that mages and dragons both could see in darkness, Gareth kept the men standing to in shifts through the night. Bending sweat-soaked over the reeking harpoons, Jenny heard in the dark of her mind Morkeleb's voice: *Wizard-woman, they come,* and a moment later saw the black soaring shape of him against the stars.

"They're coming," she said, her tone perfectly calm. Miss Mab looked up. Jenny was already turning to the nearest wood-bearer. "They're coming. The dragons. Now. Tell His Highness to alert the camp."

The boy stared at her, openmouthed. "What?"

"Tell His Highness—*now.* I'm going up."

"What?" Then he swung around, fist to his mouth in shock and horror, "Beard of Grond!"

Morkeleb hung, a nightmare of firelit bones, above the smoke-wreaths.

"Uwanë!" The young soldier snatched at the nearest harpoon—Mab yanked it impatiently out of his hand.

"Not that dragon!"

"Get His Highness!" repeated Jenny and gave the youth a shove. "Now! Run!"

Wordlessly Mab gave her the harpoon and caught up two others in a leather sling. Men were already running about, crying and snatching up weapons; the cry of "Dragons! Dragons!" and *"Uwanë!"* fractured the black air. At least, thought Jenny, Morkeleb's appearance would rouse the camp.

Then the dark claw reached from the darkness, closed around her waist.

See, to the northeast, said Morkeleb as they rose, and the hot circle of smoke and fire around the cauldrons shrank to the red heart of a burning flower, ringed with circles of tinier lights. *Along the rim of the Wall.*

And Jenny saw.

There were seven of them, seven dragons, hugging close to the shape of the mountains, taking advantage of shadows. With the far clear sight of the dragons she saw them, even in darkness knowing their colors and the music of their names: Centhwevir blue and golden, Nymr blue upon blue, Enismirdal yellow as buttercups, Hagginarshildim green and pink. The other three were too young to have their names in the lists, but she recognized the white and crimson jere-drake Bliaud had ridden to attack the camp in the Wyrwoods. The other two, younger still, were marked by gorgeous rainbow hues, not yet having begun to shape and alter the colors of their scales to chime with the inner music of their hearts. It seemed to her, even miles away, that she could see their eyes, and their eyes were dark, like filmed and broken glass.

Ian was riding Nymr. The knowledge went through her heart like a spear.

Do not think the boy on the Blue One's back is your son, Wizard-woman, said Morkeleb. *It is only a demon that wears his flesh.*

If the house is burned, said Jenny, with her harpoon resting upright on her thigh and the other two heavy on her shoulder, *the traveler will have no home to return to.*

There was no time for further words or further thought. She locked her mind and heart together with the dragon's, fusing the iron and the gold of their joined powers, and so fused, they attacked.

Jenny flung about them both the spells of concealment, of remaining unnoticed and unseen. But Centhwevir and the others split and fell upon Morkeleb from all directions, clearly able to see. The young fry hung back—Jenny wondered what wizard Rocklys had found to give to Caradoc as the seventh rider—letting the larger and stronger drakes, Centhwevir, Nymr, and Enismirdal, take on Morkeleb. Centhwevir was larger than the black dragon, but Morkeleb much the swifter and more agile. Morkeleb spat fire at the riders, forcing the star-drakes to back and veer to protect them, himself looping and diving to rip and tear at their underbellies, where no spikes protected the shining scales.

Clinging among the spikes herself with her feet hooked through the leather cable, burned by the acid of the other dragons, Jenny watched and waited, drawing power around herself and trying to use it as a shield and a blind. But every spell of evasion and concealment she used slid away like water, as if she only threw handfuls of leaves and dirt at the other dragons. Through Morkeleb's eyes she saw the dragons fragment into whirling flames of color, arcs of burning motion that were now here, now there, impossible to see. With Jenny concentrating, drawing on all her power, she resolved them now and then into their true shapes, allowing Morkeleb to attack, but he was only fending them off and falling back.

Behind them, below them, the camp was arming. Men's voices cried out, tiny as insects' on the walls. How long had it been? And how long would they need? Time dissolved and fractured, whirled like the attacking dragons.

And she felt in her mind, gripping and scratching, the strange wailing strength of the sea-wights, drawing at her, tearing at her thoughts. Wanting her. Knowing her.

And the worst of it was that in the depths of her bones, she knew them, too.

She called on her power, summoning it from her heart and marrowbones. But the magic only seemed to feed that need, and the demon songs grew all the sweeter, waves of sleepy strength. Brilliant wings sheared out of the blackness, claws raked down. Once she saw a pink dripping mouth snatching at her and thrust a harpoon into it with all her strength, but as if a veil dropped over her head she did not see whether she wounded the dragon or not. She only knew she was still alive afterward, and the harpoon gone from her hand.

The camp was under them. Fire and men shouting, arrows flying up, falling back spent. Her mind burned with the effort of calling up power, drawing on her own strength, on Morkeleb's strength, all the magic of their joined souls a wall of holed and acid-eaten bronze. The world swung sickeningly, and she clutched tight at the cable. Wheeling stars, smoke and the reek of death-spells biting at her lungs. She glimpsed the Urchins below, saw their harpoons slam upward as the dragons descended on the camp—saw by the way the harpoons went that the men inside the machines struggled too against demon-glamors and spells of ruin.

Blue on blue, drenched and dyed with firelight, firelight reflected in dead golden eyes. Wings hammering, claws descending, then the still white face, black hair like her own flying, blue dead eyes in which a single frantic spark remained.

His heart was locked in the dragon's heart, his mind in the dragon's mind. And with her dragon mind Jenny called out to him, *Ian!* Desperately willing that he hear. *Ian!*

And like hooks in her mind she felt the demons catch her. Through all her wardings, through all her defenses, as if they had not been there. Like nothing she had expected, nothing she had prepared for even in her craziest dreams, a power sourced from something she did not understand. Like nothing she had ever heard spoken of.

As love had been.

That was what they never told you about demons.

In her flesh. In her mind. Drinking her magic and Morkeleb's magic like maniac glutting swine. Without pain.

No one had ever told her, no account had ever hinted, how deep the pleasure of it went. How utterly right it felt.

Somewhere she heard Morkeleb cry, *Let go! Jenny, let go!*

And she felt his magic vanish. It dissolved and dispersed like smoke, leaving him defenseless—*Without my magic,* he had asked, *what am I?* As the magic swirled away it was as if he turned first to smoke and glass, and then winked utterly from sight.

She cried out again, *Ian!* Reached with all her magic, all her strength, all her will. Trying to grasp and hold the boy's mind and drag it to her, to safety.

And the demons inhaled her strength like smoke, swallowing it away.

The last thing she heard with her own thoughts was their laughter.

Pretty Lady, he said. *I am Amayon.* And he possessed her, in spite of herself, for there was nothing that she could touch or thrust from her. Those who saw her later described the rips and scratches where she had tried to gouge and dig the thing she felt spreading through her flesh, but of course she could not. She could no more excise it thus than she could have picked one drop of her blood away from another drop. It was a heat devouring her. All she knew was that flame overwhelmed her body as if she burned with fever, and when the flame reached a certain hotness, silvery explosions of what she could not identify as either pleasure or pain: the intensity of sensation on that borderline where the two fuse. And Amayon, like the odor of brimstone and lilies.

She was aware, later, of being with Ian, beside him with the wind slashing and streaming through her hair. She felt wild and light and mad, like the young girl she had never truly been allowed to be, watching hilariously as men below poured out of a burning bunker. The white and scarlet dragon Yrsgendl slashed at them with his iron-spiked tail as they stumbled and fell. One of the spiny Urchins raced and trundled toward the dragon, firing its harpoons, silly as a toy. The air seemed colored to Jenny's eyes, rich greens and purples, luminous, everything edged with colored flame. She could see her own spells woven around the

Urchin, a net of dancing light. Pain rose from below, a shiveringly glorious song: music and warmth and love and well-being and power, heady beyond any joy she had ever known.

"I'll bet they'd run if we pulled those spells away," she laughed, and Ian joined in her laughter. His eyes were no longer dead, but aglow with lively fire, more alive than she'd ever seen him before. She sensed his forgiveness for all the years of her neglect, sensed his admiration, his approval, his love.

"How about it, Nymr?" he called down to the dragon, and the dragon—both were mounted on the same one, Jenny didn't remember how—stooped like a falcon. Snatching away the net of spells was as easy, and as fun, as whipping a string away from a cat. The gnome-wardings tangled in the spellwork raveled away as well, and with a whoop of glee Bliaud—or Bliaud's demon, mounted on Yrsgendl—tossed a Word of Heat at the lumbering machine.

It lurched to a stop, whirled, and rocked comically as smoke poured from every vent and crack. Jenny, clinging to her son's shoulders, hooted with laughter, mirth that was echoed from the others: Bliaud, Yseult, Werecat, and Summer . . . A man tried to get out, and Yseult drove Hagginarshildim in close, spitting fire at him as he was caught in the hatch. It was like tormenting a snail, distant and ridiculous in its futile tininess: "Whoa, that'll cook his cockles for him!" whooped Ian, and Jenny laughed until she ached. Firelight flashed on the man's harpoon-tip and spectacles as he struggled to get free.

The second Urchin was flipped on its side, wheels spinning helplessly. Enismirdal and Centhwevir had ripped the earthen roofs from the bunkers, the men inside churning about like maggots doused in salt, terror and agony billowing up like the bouquet of a summer garden. Laughing, calling out to one another, the raiders spiraled upward into the night, gaudy leaves borne by the updraft of fire.

"We'll be back!" yelled Yseult, at the confusion of the camp. "Don't go anywhere!"

And pleasure washed over Jenny, deep caressing waves that penetrated the most secret caves of her body and her mind: contentment, belonging, the promise of reward and the drunken hi-

larity of power. Power and pain. This, truly, was life. The men in
the broken camp raced madly here and there, funny as ants when
the nest drowns, trying to put out fires or pulling vainly at the
arms and legs of the injured. Dozens more of them simply fled
toward the hills— "Do they think the fell-men are going to let
them through?" shouted Bliaud, his long gray curls whipping.
"I'd like to be there when they try!"

One man, the man who had wrenched himself free from the
burning Urchin, got slowly to his feet, leaning on his broken harpoon. Jenny was aware of him watching the dragons as they
swirled triumphantly away into the night.

CHAPTER NINETEEN

They gave her a young girl, all for her own; probably one of the camp servants or whores. By being judicious in her applications of pain and terror, Jenny managed to keep her alive most of the night.

Deep inside, Jenny was aware of her own horror, aghast, disgusted, sickened at what she saw herself doing to the weeping child. But she was aware that Amayon supped and munched and reveled in her emotions, her revulsion and pity, as much as in the victim's uncomprehending agony. And Amayon—as is the way of demons—routed his pleasure and delight back into Jenny's body and mind. Riven and battered, Jenny tried to find some way to fight, but it seemed to her that she could only watch herself performing upon the girl a violent parody of what Caerdinn had done to her when she was that age; watch herself as if she were someone else.

But you're not someone else, whispered Amayon. *That's you, Pretty Lady, my dearest Jenny dear. I don't make anything from whole cloth. No demon does. Admit it. Ever since Caerdinn beat you and harried you and demanded of you that you do what you couldn't do—*

"What do you want from me?" the girl was crying, blood coursing down her face. "What do you want?"

—you've wondered how it would feel to have that kind of power. You wanted to be him then. And now you are.

I'm not! screamed Jenny desperately, her voice tiny as the peep of a cricket in a crack. *I'm not, I'm not, I'm not!*

And the demon drank up her tears, mixed with the little whore's blood, and smacked his lips in delight.

The girl died toward dawn. The sensation was beyond description, a ringing climax of physical pleasure and emotional satisfaction that left Jenny shattered, confused, wrung out like a rag washed up on an unknown beach.

The dragon-mages had tents set a little apart from the rest of Rocklys' forces, in the camp where the Wildspae curved through the bare gray hills. Lying on the soaked carpets of the tent floor, breathing in the thick blood-odor that permeated them, Jenny—the tiny part of Jenny that huddled weeping like a ghost still clinging to her own flesh—wondered what else had gone on in the mages' compound, what rewards they had been given for their nights' work. What Ian had done.

The blue and yellow curtain rippled back. Bland and fresh-bathed, Caradoc stood in the opening, his hard mouth relaxed a little as if even he had been pleased and sated in the night. He went for a minute to the body of the girl, turning it over with the goblin-curved tip of his staff. Jenny heard Amayon—or maybe it was herself—chuckle, and sat up, aware that her face wore the smile of a woman yawning tousled in the bed of a hated rival's husband or son.

"*What* a little spit-cat she was." She stretched luxuriously and shook back her matted hair. "Have they got the balneary set up? I'm absolutely sticky."

Caradoc grinned with the side of that grim mouth, and impure fire flickered in his eyes. It crossed Jenny's mind, Jenny's own ousted and terrified mind, to wonder how long the real Caradoc had lasted, held by slow-dissolving ghostly bonds to his own flesh and screaming with horror that this wasn't what he'd meant when he asked the demons to give him power.

Or maybe it was. Maybe after enough time passed you could no longer tell the difference.

He chucked Jenny under the chin, as a man would a whore in a tavern. "How'd you like it?"

Monster, Monster! she screamed at him, or maybe at herself, desperate and tiny and unheard. Except, of course, by Amayon, who giggled in sated delight that she was still capable of emotion, and savored her horror like a piquant dessert. The demon in her laughed for answer to Caradoc's question, and Jenny's hand stroked down her own body in a caressing expression of total satisfaction. Somewhere she heard Amayon reply to the demon—its name was Folcalor, she somehow knew, a bloated thing in which struggled the half-digested whimpering remains of a dozen other imps—that lived behind Caradoc's eyes. *You know how delicious it is, to bring a new one to it for the first time.*

And Caradoc—Folcalor—laughed appreciatively. "Roc's getting on the road soon," he said. "We'll hit them again tonight." Something changed, shifted in his expression, and with a casual air he took from his pocket a green gem, a polished peridot the size of a quail's egg, which he held out to her like a sweet to a child.

Bastards, bastards! Jenny cried, trying to summon even a fingerhold of power over her own body, trying to thrust Amayon out of her self, her heart, her mind. Though she knew that without this she, the Jenny part of herself, would die, long before anyone could exorcise Amayon, if in fact anyone could do such a thing, still terror gripped her at the thought of being forever their prisoner.

Amayon did something to her, almost thoughtlessly, as a man would strike a child to hush it, something that left her gasping with pain. *And what's this?* he asked, eyeing Folcalor, eyeing the jewel.

"I have my reasons," the dragon-mage replied, and flipped the jewel in his palm.

All the teasing, playful cruelty vanished, and Amayon was suddenly cold and deadly as a cobra. *Reasons that the Lord of Hell knows about?*

The demon-light changed and flickered in Caradoc's dead eyes. "My dear Amayon . . ." The voice was a tiger's purr in her mind, velvet sheathing the threat of razor-clawed violence. "You don't think I'd do anything here without Lord Adromelech's knowledge? He is my lord, as he is yours—and if he hasn't opened his mind and his plans to you, he has at least to me. Adromelech has his plans. Now here, precious"—he held out the stone to Jenny again—"have a little sweet."

Jenny blew a kiss at him (*Filth!* she screamed at him, at them both, at them all), opened her mouth to receive the stone, and sat smiling and making little faces and playing with it with her tongue while the dragon-mage made magic circles around her, and drew together the curves of power. Inside herself Jenny wept, with what last strength was in her, trying to call together enough power to resist.

She felt herself go into the stone.

Rocklys' army broke camp with the coming of full light and marched through the day under the wood of Imperteng's somber boughs. Caradoc, and Jenny, and the other mages summoned an unseasonable fog to cover the land to the foot of Nast Wall. Through this the dragon-mages glided silent as shadow, just above the trees, gray cold wetness hemming them in. Through the latticed structure of the jewel Jenny felt the touch of magic trying to disperse the fog, and she and the others renewed their spells, drawing the vapors thick. When the dragon she rode, a lovely green and gold youngling named Mellyn, descended, Jenny could see with her demon eyes the Commander herself, riding fully armored on her sleek bay stallion, with Caradoc at her side. Now and then they spoke, Caradoc explaining matters in the smooth comforting voice that Rocklys had known for all those years, little realizing that it was the demon Folcalor who actually did the talking.

"This is the way many wizards are, Commander." The moon-stone flashed softly on his goblin-carved staff. "You have to humor them if you want their help. Of course I'm as appalled as you are, but . . ."

Two or three times in the course of that morning Jenny was troubled by something, some watchfulness she felt turned upon them; she didn't know what. Scanning the fogs around her, with the magic of the demons that now filled her heart and body, she detected nothing. Yet in that separated part of her, that heart imprisoned within the pale-green crystal in the flat silver bottle that hung around Caradoc's neck, she knew, and whispered the name.

Morkeleb.

He was there. Somewhere. She had seen him vanish, dissolve into smoke, even as her knees and thighs had still felt his scales and spines.

And her imprisoned heart, looking out through her own eyes in the fog as she had once looked out through Morkeleb's, knew

something else as well: the jewel in which she was imprisoned
was flawed.

Through the long day she grew to know that jewel as inti-
mately as she knew her own body. In a sense, this was now what
it was. She remembered seeing it in the strongbox in Rocklys'
chamber at Corflyn, and she familiarized herself with every
molecule of carbon, every milky impurity, every fracture line
and energy fault. Knew them and hated them. *These were the
best you could do?* Caradoc had complained to Rocklys. And, *I
think you were cheated . . .*

Caradoc was right. Rocklys was a warrior, not a mage. Faced
with the need to conserve money for her soldiers' pay, faced with
a clever gem merchant and a handful of brilliant stones, she
wouldn't have known how to check each jewel.

Jenny could not have said exactly why a diamond or a ruby
was better for the imprisonment of a disembodied spirit than a
topaz or a peridot. Nor could she have explained to a layperson
why magic must be worked with pure metals and flawless gems
in order to be itself flawless. But within her crystalline prison
she was able to move a little, and carefully—gently—she began
to draw power through the stone's threadlike fault.

And all the while she was aware of herself, and Amayon,
riding the green and gold jere-drake overhead, braiding and
gathering spells. Half-seen in the misty world below, the army
crept, drenched, as the drifting shapes of the other dragons about
her were drenched, in the feral sparkle of demon fire. She was
aware that her spells—the demon's spells—made her beautiful,
and being forty-five years old and never a pretty woman, she reveled in that beauty and that power. She rejoiced in the pert
breasts and silky skin, in the sudden absence of any need at all to
fight migraines, hot flashes, aches, indigestion. She was young
and could do whatever she pleased, for none could touch her.
And she smiled at the thought of that haughty bitch Rocklys'
surprise, when the time came for the demons to take their pay.

The ground below them sloped gradually toward the river.
Above the soft-rolling grayness of the fogs, the sun stood high.

All together, demons, mages, dragons spoke a word, and the
fog sank into the ground like translucent dust. Gareth's camp—

blotched with the burns of acid and the soaked blood of the men killed last night—lay naked under the dragons' shadows.

The army of Bel was ready for them at the outlying defenses of the bridge. The spikes of the gutted Urchins had been laid over the two main bunkers of the camp, and from these, harpoons slashed upward from a dozen salvaged catapult slings. Two wounded the little rainbow-drakes ridden by Werecat and Miss Enk—that semi-trained gnome adept Rocklys had brought in at the last minute from the Deep of Wyldoom—before all the demons, all the wizards pulled about themselves the spells of illusion and confusion, the fractioning of colors, images, shapes. At the same moment there was a great sounding of horns and drums on the northward road, and Rocklys' mighty voice roaring her battle-cry, "Firebeard! Firebeard!" The paean shook the air as they attacked the redoubts of the bridge, while the dragons struck at the defenders as they tried to rush from the main camp.

The battle was short, for the clouds that had lain on the mountain flanks stirred and swirled, and cold winds blew them down above the river and the camp. Thunder roared, lightning striking at the dragons, and rain streamed down in torrents. *Gnome-magic,* Jenny heard Folcalor say in her mind, with a curse. *They can't keep it up long.* She was hard put to turn aside the lightning bolts that struck at Mellyn's wings, and she felt her own rage rise, that squatty ugly creatures like the gnomes should dare defy them: *We will make them pay for this,* she said.

Wind howled and twisted at her long black hair, and below by the river fortifications she saw Rocklys' troops struggling against mud and rain. Rocklys stood at the top of a siege-ladder, sword in hand, waterfalls of rain hammering in her eyes. Wind swept away her shouted commands, and rage and pride came off her in such waves that Jenny laughed.

Behind her she heard a hissing and a shriek. One of the rainbow-drakes writhed, twisted in the air. Its rider, the Icerider boy Werecat, was thrown clear, dangling by one leg caught in the leather cable hundreds of feet above the ground. Jenny thought the young dragon must have been struck by lightning, for blood poured from its opened belly and sides; she could hear the cursing of its demon from where she sat. Dragon and boy fell, the dragon already dead, the demons drawing back to savor the desperate terror of the youth, imprisoned in his crystal, watching his last hopeless hope of freedom plunge away. The young dragon sprawled wrecked and bleeding on the earth, and she thought it bore less the marks of lightning than of attack by another dragon. But she had seen nothing.

Yet in her jewel, in her heart, in the part of her that was still Jenny, she knew.

They can't keep up the storm forever, she heard Folcalor say in her mind again. He was a big demon, and an old one, swollen with the hearts and lives of other demons he'd devoured; his mind was like a cesspool, stinking as he spoke. *And when they tire, we'll still be here.* He added, *Gnome-bitch.*

The troops retreated from the defense-works, back beneath the eaves of the woods, and made camp in the rain. Above the trees the lightning continued to flash in a sky turned to night. Rocklys deployed her forces around the wall of Gareth's camp. The demons settled in to amuse themselves, asking for soldiers or camp-slaves or the captives Rocklys had taken. Pain sometimes, or lust, or terror, usually all three: It was an art form, rendered the more entertaining by the echoed outcry from the imprisoned hearts of their hosts.

The demons grew drunk with delight.

You can't say you don't enjoy it, Amayon whispered to Jenny when she tried to look away, to will her awareness away from what was being done with her senses and her power and her body. *An ugly little thing like you never wanted to have all the men you could manage? To have them worship at your feet and beg for your favors? To have them see you as beautiful, as desirable—and then to punish them for it? To make them weep?*

Locked in the heart of the jewel, Jenny could only plead, *Let me alone.*

Your son's a better student of these arts than you are. The demon was disgusted. *Would you like to get him in here? Would that be fun?* And he laughed at the pleasure he made her feel.

The soldiers wore out, and left, or passed out drunk on the fouled carpets of the tent floor. Jenny lay for a time in the tangle of silks and furs on the tent's divan, drinking straight brandy and savoring the afterglow. Ian, the demon part of her knew, was still engaged in his own practices, but it would be good to go over there in time. It had been Ian's idea to weave the illusion that Bliaud's sons had been taken in the onslaught and tortured to death and to send this illusion to Bliaud where the old man was trapped in his ensorcelled gem. They had all laughed fit to split their sides at the father's pitiful weeping. She stretched, rolling her head in the sable pillows of her hair.

And turning her head, saw there was another man in the tent.

For a moment she recognized him only as the warrior who'd been trapped half-in, half-out of the burning Urchin, a lithe tallish man with brown hair rain-lank to his shoulders. Wet leather, wet plaids, polishing the rain from his spectacles with his torn shirttail. She was smiling, holding out an inviting hand, when she realized it was John.

She turned her face away, hand pressed to her mouth in shame and horror, and with her other hand drew up the sheet to cover herself. For a moment her throat locked shut, her whole body twisted with the pain. Then she heard Amayon laugh and the thought came to her that it would be entertaining beyond words to bring John to her—her magic would easily overcome his revulsion, but it might be more amusing to simply use a spell to bring him against his will—and then call for the guards while he lay in her bed.

Stop it! she screamed. *Stop it, stop it, stop it!*

And the demon roared with laughter. So loud did it ring in her mind that for a time she wasn't aware of how silent the tent was.

Her face still averted, she said, "Leave here, John."

"Am I talking to you, Jen?" he asked. "Or to the demon? Not that I'd get a truthful answer from whatever took possession of you."

Jenny faced him, and as the strength of the demon closed hard on her soul and her mind she forced it back with all the power she could draw through the flawed prison of the crystal, all she could still numbly wield. She trembled and could not speak, but she saw the hard wariness in John's eyes change. He stepped forward, as if he would have taken her hand, and she drew back.

He looked around at the soldiers sleeping on the floor, and the two snoring grossly beside her on the divan. His voice was very steady. "I understand it wasn't you, Jen."

She fought back the throaty chuckle, the words, *Then you can't have known me well, all these years,* and, *You should go over to the next tent and have a look at our son.* Fought them back so hard her jaws ached. And felt the sudden furious stab of Amayon's anger in her bowels.

Her hand drew back from his reach again, and she huddled the sheet around her, "It isn't that." The words were like gagging dry stones from her throat as she reached through to take fumbling hold on her flesh. "I—know—I pray—you understand."

The pain redoubled, twisted and dragged at her; pain worse than any she had known. She dug her nails into the back of her hand until blood came, to hold control against Amayon's terrible strength. "I can't—keep the demon—at bay. Go now."

"Not without you."

"You can't help."

"Mab, and Morkeleb . . ."

"Stay away!" Fire flared in the air between them as he stepped forward, driving him back. She had to back away again, put the divan between them, to keep herself from hurting him, from sending the second flash of demon-fire into his body. Agony ripped her and she half-doubled over, clinging to the head of the divan. Morkeleb's magic, all that was left of her own, burned her like a poison as she turned it against the thing inside her body, the thing that was fighting now like a tiger to take her over again.

Her breath came in gasps and she brought the words out quickly: "John, get out of here. Trust me. Don't try to help me and whatever you do don't try to find Ian, just get out . . ."

Her voice choked off as one of the soldiers on the divan sat up, eyes staring madly: "Spy!" he roared, and lunged at John.

John stepped back, tripped and elbowed him, sending him sprawling to the carpets, but the damage was done. The other men lurched to their feet, grabbing swords and knives. There was an outcry from beyond the tent wall, and the clashing of metal. John sprang over the divan, catching up the tawny fur coverlet and throwing it around Jenny's body, muffling her arms, lifting her from her feet. Jenny twisted, mute as a snake, kicking and butting with her head. John set her down at the back of the tent, drew his sword and turned to face the soldiers closing in around him. In Jenny's mind Amayon's laughter grew louder and louder, drowning thought, drowning resistance.

What kind of a ballad does he think he's in? Folcalor, Goth-pys, come here, you have to see this!

John hacked, gutted one man, kicked another in the belly and sent him sprawling into three more, then turned and sliced open the back wall of the tent. He swung back around to catch the blades of those who'd come in from outside—armored, these warriors, and two of them had pikes—twisting, cutting, dodging, backing toward the spilling rain of the outside.

He was here, you know, Jenny; he saw you with the soldiers. You really think he doesn't think it was you?

A man fell near her, flopped and gasped and tried to close up the gaping sword-slash in his breast with his hands; his sword lay at Jenny's feet. Pain clawed her, the terror that she would die if she didn't pick it up, drive it to the hilt in John's back . . .

She kicked it from her with all her strength and with everything left in her, called a slamming burst of lightning down on the attacking soldiers, and darkness that swallowed the lamps. *"Run!"* Handfuls of wet leather, bloody plaids, the familiar scent of them ripping her heart . . .

"Run!" She thrust him through the slit in the tent, whirled back and flung fire at the men coming through the flap. Ian, Caradoc, Yseult naked and wine-soaked . . . A blast of light, darkness, power throwing them back, then she fell to her knees, balled tight on the squishing rugs, sobbing, emptied, pain and more pain through which the unconsciousness she prayed for never came . . .

Stop it, said Folcalor harshly.

Amayon's reply was beyond words, beyond even the concept of words. Raw violent hatred at being defied. A beast lifting a bloody mouth from its prey.

STOP IT. You'll kill her.

She's safe in your hellfestering little jewel. Only it wasn't words, just a river of poison poured over the raw pulp of her soul. *She can't die.*

Don't think it, snapped the other.

Doesn't matter, laughed Gothpys wearing Ian's body as he returned through the slit in the tent. There was a spear in his hand running with rainwater and blood. *He's dead.*

And Jenny saw the scene in her mind. John kneeling in the soup of rain-thinned blood where they'd hamstrung him, trying to fend off their pikes and swords and harpoons with his hands. Wet hair hung down over his broken spectacles and he tried once more to get to his feet, tried to crawl away; looked up, and saw Ian with a spear in his hands, rain sluicing down his black hair, looking down at him with smiling hell-blue eyes.

Jenny's heart seemed to shut in white blank horror. *You're lying!* she screamed at them. *You're lying! Like you lied to Bliaud!* Her grip over her body slithered away again as the last flame of her resistance died.

On the third night after that, two horses picked their way through the bracken-choked rubble and inexplicable gashes of darkness that filled in the cup-shaped valley on the eastern rim of Nast Wall's foothills. Feathers and fragments of blue-white light drifted along the ground, and now and then showed up, among the skeins of wild grape and ivy, a startling white stone hand or incised lintel. High thin clouds hid the pale fingernail of the slow-waxing moon.

The rider of the smaller horse, a coarse-maned mountain pony, drew rein where fallen pillars marked the gate of what had been a path to the citadel on the hill: "Art determined to do this thing, man?"

Aversin's voice was weary, beaten with three nights of broken sleep and foul dreams. "Show me any other way and I'll do it, Mab. I swear to you I'll do it."

She sat silent, night wind lifting the ghostly cloud of her hair.

"The penalties are terrible for those that seek the spawn of Hell."

"More terrible than havin' seven wizards possessed? Seven dragons at their beck?"

She said nothing for a time. Then, "Understand that my spells may not protect thee beyond the Gate of Hell."

His spectacles flashed as he bent his head, rubbed his fore-head with a gloved hand. The horses fidgeted, uneasy at the smells in this place. At length he said, "No spells protected Jen, did they?"

"Never since the Fall of Ernine have demons so strong entered into our world." The gnome-wife's deep voice was troubled. "No lore I have studied touches upon the case. Yet the dragon says it was through her magic that they entered her soul."

"The dragon wouldn't bloody well get his whiskers singed to take his own child out of the fire," John retorted viciously. "The dragon's got no bloody room to talk. He wouldn't even bring me past the spell-bounds set around Rocklys' camp . . ."

"The dragon is right," Mab said quietly. "And the dragon did save thy life." In the flickering witchlight the shapes of the hillocks altered, and one could see in them the echoes of temples, palaces, market-halls long crumbled.

"Then it looks like I'm a fool, doesn't it?" John swung down from his horse and knotted the rein angrily around a sapling. "Only since I'd sooner be dead than live without her, I haven't got a lot to lose now, have I?"

Mab sighed. The will-o'-the-wisp coalesced into a glowing ball, shining in the air before John's knees. It illuminated a face drawn with exhaustion, eyes bruised with weariness and flaming with anger. Beyond them the gnome-witch evidently saw some-thing else, for her voice gentled. "Thou hast no knowing, man, of what it is thou stand to lose. Still, for her sake I will do for you what I can."

She dismounted and held out her hand. After a moment John knelt before her. "No spell of this world can touch the Spawn of Hell themselves," she said, "nor yet turn aside the illusions and the ills they send within their own Hells. They are of a nature that we do not understand, and it seems that now they have found some new power besides to grant them greater might. Yet can I strengthen thine eyes against the blindness that is one of their en-tertainments. Greater discernment I can give to thy mind, that thou might find thy way back to the Gate that I shall make in the burning mirror; and give that thy heart beat stronger, that thou remember thy love for Jenny, and put aside the desire to remain

in Hell forever. I can strengthen thy flesh, that it will not die behind the mirror unless thou so wish. But remember, man, if thou
diest, thy soul shall remain there a prisoner, unable to travel on to
where the souls of men return."

While she spoke, she touched his eyelids with her thick little
thumb and marked rune signs on his temples and breast. John
thought he should have felt something, some warmth or strength
or increase of power, but he felt nothing, not even the lessening
of his fear.

Don't do this, Johnny ... He could almost hear Muffle
screaming the words at him. *Don't do this* ...

"These signs and this strength will not hold long in the world
behind the mirror," said Mab's voice. He looked up at her,
hoping his terror didn't show in his eyes. "Beware of what thou
sayst there, and beware more than all else what promises thou
make to them. They shall try to hold thee in their world and make
thee their servant; departing, they shall try to put thee in debt
to them, owing a teind of your loyalty and all you possess, to
serve them here in this one. This above all things thou must not
permit. My blessings go with thee." Her hard hand ruffled his
hair. "Good luck."

He rose. "Does 'good luck' mean that I find the place or that I
don't?"

Unwillingly, the old wrinkled face returned the smile. "In Ernine of old," she said, "they worshiped the Lord of Time, who
saw forward and backward, and knew answers to such things.
But it is the nature of mortals, of gnomes and of men, that they
could not abide this knowledge, so they turned instead to the
worship of the Twelve. Even the Twelve ask no questions of the
Lord of Time."

Leaving the gnome-wife standing like moonlit rock, John followed the path Jenny had described to him, when she'd waked
moaning from the horrors of her dream. A second palace, and a
third, had been built over the Citadel of Ernine since the days of
the heroes, but once past the gates there was only one way to go.
Under knee-deep ivy and grapevines the very sandstone of the
stairway was grooved and smoothed by water and the feet of
long-dead servants and kings. In the courtyard where the queen's

ladies had worked their looms, a fountain still gurgled from the broken basin. Mab's pale guide-light drifted and flickered over the dark laurel, thorn-bristling roses, and wisteria grown monstrous with age that perfumed the night.

Shallow steps led him down. Under faded and fallen plaster, blacker shadows seemed to take the shapes of great-horned gazelles, and beyond an archway that had once been filled in with layer on layer of brick and mortar the witchlight showed him a rock-cut corridor whose ceiling still bore constellations of stars and a comet with trailing hair.

The door at the corridor's end had been closed with bricks also. But shifting in the earth had cracked them, and water and age had done the rest. *The Lord of Time strikes again,* thought John, regarding the crevice.

The witchlight flowed through ahead of him. He saw something silver in the dark.

He found the circular room Jenny had described. The witchlight shone on the mirror's tall frame, cold and strange in the light. Thunderstone, he thought, and written with runes against the mirror's breaking, for instead of destroying the thing, someone had covered over the glass with what appeared to be black enamel, hard and shiny as Morkeleb's scales. Steam rose off it, drifting in the light.

From the breast of his doublet John took the square of parchment Mab had given him, written with a sigil that could have been either an eye or a door. His mouth felt dry and his hands icy. He remembered again how Jenny had waked in the night, crying and clinging to him. But that memory brought him another, her eyes in the lamplight of her tent in Rocklys' camp, her hair pointed and sticky with blood and wine. She had told him not to look for Ian, not knowing he had already seen his son—or the demon that lived in his son's flesh.

I'd sooner be dead than live without her, he had said to Mab. But it wasn't the whole truth. If the recollection of what he had seen in the camp—of Jenny a vicious whore, and Ian . . . He shook away the thought. If that memory was going to be part of his life, together with the knowledge that they were possessed, forever subject to the demons that made them do those things, death looked good.

Only, he thought, as he spit on the back of the parchment and stuck it to the mirror's enameled face, *it might not be death.*

That was the tricky part.

He didn't know how the tiny sigil was big enough to admit his body, but it was.

He closed his eyes, said a prayer to the Old God, and stepped through.

CHAPTER TWENTY

They were waiting for him, right behind the glass.

Well, there's a brave one, said the Demon Queen, and took his face between her hands. Her hands were cold as marble in winter. Her lips, when they forced his open—tonguing, nipping, tasting—were icy, too. A dead woman's lips. Her tongue a serpent's probing tongue.

But heat burned under the chill. Heat flowed into his palms, though he felt how cold her flesh was under the clinging silk—if it was silk. The dark of the place was the purple dark of nightmares, where flesh glowed strangely and all things were outlined in fire. Scents and noises hammered and whispered in his brain, as if sound and odor were in fact designed for other organs of sensation than those he possessed. For a time he struggled only to adjust his awareness, and it came to him that the Demon Queen's blinding, blood-pounding kiss was a way of making sure he didn't adjust.

He caught her wrists, pushed her back, though she was tremendously strong. "Say, you aren't married, are you, love?" he asked her, and it took her by surprise. He fished through his pockets. "I had a ring . . . Here it is." He produced a cheap bronze bearing that had gone into the Urchin's engines and caught the Demon Queen's hand. "You'd have to talk to me man of business about the dowry—we're that set on dowries where I come from—but you and me together, we'll talk him down to not more than half a dozen feather beds and a set of pots. Can you make lamb and prune pie? The last lady I thought to marry was a tall bonny girl like yourself, only couldn't find her way about the kitchen with a map of the place and one of the scullery boys for a guide. She ended up cookin' a horse-head in mistake for a turkey-poult, stuffed with oats, for a Yule feast, and I had to call off the match . . ."

You're a fool! The Demon Queen stepped back from him and pulled her hand from his attempt to slip the bronze ring onto her finger.

"That's what they all said," agreed John, "when I spoke of coming here." He was careful to put the ring back in his pocket.

She looked like a woman to him, a tall woman, slim as a catkin but for the lush upstanding heaviness of her breasts. Luminous white skin seemed to shine through the garment she wore, smoke-blue shot through with fire when she moved; winds that he could not feel rippled and lifted and turned the fabric, as it rippled her hair. Black hair drawn up and back, strands and braids and swags of it falling around her face, down her back, glittering with gems as the manes of the dragons glittered. Her eyes were a goat's eyes.

And why did you come here?

He'd made her angry, breaking the falseness of her welcome; he saw that falseness return as she took him by the hands. He saw now they were in an enormous chamber: smokes, and lights, and portions of the floor that flowed like glimmering water. He could not tell whether he was hot or cold—both together, it seemed, and both unbearable—and it was difficult to breathe. Difficult, too, to decide whether the smells that freighted the air were sweet or nauseating. The Queen's courtiers who ringed in behind him had the appearance of men and women until he took his eyes off them. He knew they changed then and almost saw them at it.

He sensed them following as the Queen led him down corridors and stairs, through arcaded terraces where it was sometimes day and sometimes night, past windows where snow fell, or rain, or slow flakes of fire.

"Gie nice furniture," he remarked and paused to trace a line of porcelain flowers set in the C-curved ebony of a chair-leg. "I saw stuff like this in the palace at Bel two years ago, though how they got the wood to bend like this was more than I could learn. Still it's all the newest fashion, they say. How'd you come by it, if you've been locked up behind a covered mirror for the past thousand years?"

You are a fool, she said again, but this time there were a thousand undertones of other things in her voice. Her hand on his arm was the stroking of feathers on bare flesh, and he had to look aside from her lips and her breasts. The room was filled with pale mist and scented with applewood and burnt sugar. Oddly, through the mists, he could still see Miss Mab's sigil, burning like a distant lamp.

Lamps surrounded a divan, haloing it and seeming to hold the mists at bay. The floor was green marble, scattered with almond flowers.

"Why did you come?" She spoke as humans speak, through those blood-ruby lips, and her long ivory-pale face was sad.

"To ask your help, love."

"Alas." She drew him onto the divan beside her. Her voice was deep, and the note of it was like a warm hand curled around his manhood. "Would that we could offer it. But as you see, we cannot help even ourselves. That I, Aohila, should have been betrayed and imprisoned so, for things that were none of our doing."

A grave-faced child emerged from the fog, wearing nothing more than a garland of roses and bearing an enameled tray. Glass vessels on it held wine, clear as the last slant of afternoon light, dates, figs, cherries, and a pomegranate.

"You're hungry," said Aohila. "You've ridden a long way."

John shook his head. Mab had warned him about this, if he hadn't already encountered it in a hundred legends and songs. On that, at least, they all agreed, if on little else. "Narh. I had a meat-pie in me saddlebags, and the last time I took wine I made a fair disgrace of meself, dancin' on the table at me aunt Tillie's wedding and making that free with the bridesmaids. Aunt Tillie was like to die of mortification." He took the cup that she raised to his lips and emptied it out onto the floor. "But thank you all the same, love. And you really ought to get some socks on that page. She'll catch her death, runnin' about on the stone floor. Who was it covered your mirror over in black like that?"

Her eyes changed, losing the faint illusion of humanity, and green flame wickered and threaded through her hair. She said nothing.

"Not humans?" he asked.

The red lip lifted a little from her teeth, and he felt the blood start, where her nails cut into the flesh of his arm.

"These wizards of the desert are supposed to have done it, but it was other demons, wasn't it?"

It was like entering the cave of a poisonous serpent, naked and with bound hands. Hearing the movement of dry silken coils in the dark.

What do you know of it?

"Not much." His heart pounded. The fog behind him stirred, but he dared not turn his head; he caught the movement of light, and shapes within the light, from the corner of his eye. "I think I know which of the Nightspawned Kin it was, though."

She pressed him back on the cushions of the divan, and her fingers closed around the back of his neck, strong and cold, like a metal garrote. He realized she was strong far beyond the strength of the strongest of men. *Why are you here?*

"Because the sea-wights from the foundations of the Seven Isles are doin' exactly what you tried to do here, a thousand years ago," said John. "They've tempted a mage to his fall and are using him to manipulate a pretender to the local throne. They've got up a corps of dragons and mages, the same way you did for Isychros. Only instead of tryin' to set themselves up, they've got some poor sap of a human to rule for them, while they hang back and kill and fornicate and torture. I think that's been in their minds for a thousand years, since they helped the Lords of Syn to close you off in here."

What do you know, whispered her sulfurous voice in the hollows of his mind, *of the minds of the seaspawn?* Her nails dug into his flesh and he could feel the others behind him, a wall of slow-burning bones. Coming closer, smelling his blood. *And how do you know it was they who closed our door into the world of men?*

"It's not somethin' I can discuss."

Her body stretched out on top of his, fingers cold through his hair. Her lips were cold, too, brushing his, but they kindled a fire in him, like a drug. What had been fog seemed now to be enclosing walls, bright with frescoes and the light of a few candles, and she drew the jeweled pins from her hair, and from the knots of silk that held her robe. *What is your business, then?*

Her breasts were round as melons where they pressed his flesh, silk-soft and heavy, and again he was conscious of the underlying warmth, not of her flesh, but of some core of flame deep within. The scent of her intoxicated him. His hands closed hard over hers, stopping their caress. "To do a bargain with you, Lady," he said, his voice husky and dry. "Nothing more. I'm an old married man with children."

If he took her, he knew, it would give her power over him, as surely as if he had eaten or drunk in the realm of the demons. But it was hard to speak, difficult even to think, with his need for her blinding and burning and hammering in his blood.

"I came to ask help of you against the seaspawn, lest they do to you what they do to us."

She twisted her wrists from his grasp—it was like trying to hold on to the foreleg of a maddened horse—and reared above him, black hair swirling around her and the gold and crimson silk of her dress falling around her hips.

Bargain? BARGAIN? With US?

He saw when the red lips lifted back from her mouth that her teeth were fangs; and in any case he knew she didn't look like a woman when he closed his eyes. Still the desire to seize her, to crush her beneath him, to force her mouth and her thighs apart, overwhelmed him, so that he rolled swiftly off the divan and stood, shaking, behind its head.

"It's a fair bargain," he said. "Bein' your servant isn't in it."

Their eyes met and locked, and he saw that he'd guessed truly: that it was less the blow to her pride that a man would bargain with her than that he acted as a free agent, unswayed by her will. Her mouth pulled back in a snarl again, and for a moment he saw her as she was.

Then the demons seized him from behind: pain, and cold, and the breath ripped from his lungs. Black blindness, and the roaring agony of fire.

If I die in this realm, thought John, *it's here I'll remain, forever.*

Mab's spells had strengthened his flesh, but according to Gantering Pellus, demons seldom or never killed those who went to their realms, though how the encyclopedist had obtained that information wasn't mentioned. Chained naked between pillars of red-hot iron, his flesh being cut slowly to pieces by the whips of the demons, John didn't take much comfort in the *Encyclopedia's* assertion even if it was true. If he couldn't die, he couldn't faint either, and the servants of the Demon Queen were ingenious in how they used the razor-edged whalebone and leather. Dotys, or was it Heronax of Ernine?—he forced his mind to pursue the reference—wrote that sages of the old Kingdom of Choray had used certain incantations to keep pain at bay, but John was forced to conclude that this was probably a lie.

All you need to do is ask, whispered the Queen in the screaming core of his mind. *All you need to do is ask.*

Ask my mercy. Ask my favor. Ask my love.

He was lying, it seemed, in the open, under a white dimpled horror of sky. Chains held his wrists and ankles to what felt, under his bare back, like a circle of stone, though beyond his outstretched fingers he saw thin gray grasses moving in windless alien wind.

Silk blew over his face. He turned his head back, squinted up—he could not remember what had become of his spectacles—and saw Aohila standing just behind his head. He knew that what was going to happen next would be worse than the previous illusion. He said, "You know they'd never have sent me to bargain if there'd been any question of opening the mirror again. There isn't. It can't be done."

She was holding a golden cup. She dipped her fingers into it, brought them out wet. "Why then should we help you?"

She dripped the liquid from her fingers onto his body. Where it struck it was deathly cold, then at once began to itch, and slowly, to smoke and to burn.

"Because what you're doing to me, the seaspawn can do to you, and for the same reasons. Maybe the pain of demons is tastier than the pain of men. I'll look it up when I get back—it's probably in Gantering Pellus, or maybe Curillius, though Curillius isn't even accurate about how many horses you need to go on a quest across the Marches. But if they take over the southern kingdom, they'll be able to get at your mirror, you know."

She dipped out a handful of liquid from the cup and dribbled it down over his face. He jerked his head aside and got the splash of it down his cheek and neck, burning away the flesh, eating deeper and deeper.

"You don't think we can take care of ourselves?"

"I think you can." He had to fight to keep his voice steady, to keep the terror of more pain from dissolving his thoughts. "But I think there'll be evil and horror if a demon war is fought in the lands of men. I'm bargaining not so that you can get out, but so that you'll at least be left in peace."

"It isn't peace that we want, man." She squatted behind his head and, reaching over, pulled his chin back, setting the rim of the cup to his lips. "It's revenge on those who imprisoned us here." She pinched his nostrils shut, forced his mouth open and poured the poison in, so that he choked, gagged, swallowed. "All we need is one servant in the realm of humankind to start with. And it need not be unpleasant." She smiled and dipped her finger into the cup. Slowly, sensuously, she drew spells on his body, lines of fire and pain that ate into the flesh until his mind blotted with agony that never quite swallowed up his ability to feel. Then she emptied the remainder of the cup on the stone beside him, and rising, walked leisurely away across the endless gray grass.

He came to lying on her divan again. Raw inside and out, as if all that illusion had been done to him in fact. With his eyes closed he was aware of the other demons crowding around, whispering, but when he heard the dry friction of her silks and her hair beside him, and opened his eyes, it was only she. The mists were gone and the room had frescoes of deer and fishes on the walls; its windows opened into a darkness of jasmine and orange-trees.

She asked him again, "What do you want?"

What he wanted most was a drink of water, but he stopped himself from saying so. Not having drunk the poison willingly he supposed it didn't count, if it hadn't in fact been illusion. He sat up and coughed, the pain of just that was excruciating, as if he were all scar tissue inside.

"I want a spell that will defend machines against the magic of the sea-wights," he said. He rubbed his wrists, felt the raw galls of shackles, though the skin was unmarked. "We've built a number of 'em—machines, that is—and we need to protect 'em all."

"Done." From the folds of her gown she produced a vial of red-black glass, like something carved out of ancient blood.

John grinned shakily, "Surely you don't have pockets in that frock, now, do you, love?" and was rewarded with a stab of pain, as if she'd driven a sword into his belly and twisted it.

No sense of humor, he thought, sweating, as soon as he could breathe again. *It'd never work out between us.*

He blinked up at her nearsightedly and almost asked for his spectacles back. She'd probably count that as one of the traditional three requests—*why was it always three?*—and anyway, oddly enough, he could still see Mab's sigil shining somewhere beyond the wall. Maybe the wall didn't really exist. "I want a spell that will free both mages and dragons from the thrall of the sea-wights and restore their own minds and wills to them again."

The goatish eyes narrowed, under the jeweled swanks of hair. But she said, "Done." She produced a seal cut of crystal, cold and tiny and greenish-white, and laid it beside the vial on the cushions.

A wight the size of a chicken ran up to the divan and leaping up, caught John's wrist and drove its proboscis into the flesh. With a curse he shook it off, feeling the blood hot on his arm, but not daring to take his eyes from the Queen's. The wight lunged at him again; the Queen caught it by the neck, casually, and bringing it to her mouth bit through its throat, her head jerking aside and back like a dog's, to rip and kill.

With blood on her face, on her breasts and garments, she asked him, "Is there anything else?"

"And I want a spell that will heal them of any damage they've taken."

"Well." Her red lips curved in scorn. The dead thing in her hand had ceased to twitch, but the blood still ran out of it over her fingers. "Done." She dropped the dead wight to the floor, and something ran out from under the divan and began to gnaw it with thick little ripping sounds. With sticky hands she produced a blue stone box, soapy to the feel and heavier than it should have been as he took it in his hand. "Now let us talk of the teind you will pay me in return."

His hands closed around the box, the seal, the vial; he could not stop them shaking. He got to his feet and backed from her, and she lay back along the divan and smiled.

"I'll even let you out of here, for as long as it takes for you to take my revenge on the sea-wights," she said.

"Thank you," he said.

"Afterward . . ."

"No afterward," said John. "I'll pay whatever price you ask of me, but I won't be your servant in my own world. I hired my sword to the gnomes for a price, but when that price was paid I went my way. Sooner than that I'll remain here."

She sat up, angry, her lip raised a little to show a fang. He saw now that things lived in her hair—or maybe they were a part of the hair: eyeless, darting, toothed. *I don't think you've thought about what that will be like, o my beloved.*

Sweat stood cold on his face, because like the dragons her mind spoke in images and sensations, and he could see what it would be: agonizing and without any end. Ever. He made himself meet her eyes, and though the runes and sigils she'd traced on his flesh began to burn with the memory of the poison, he did not look away.

God of Time, don't let her take me up on it, he pleaded, in the deepest hollows of his heart. *I don't think I could do it . . .*

They faced one another for some minutes in silence.

Very well, she said softly. *We shall speak of terms, then.*

The walls behind her shifted, and he could see the Hellspawn through them, like fish in murky water. He recognized the two with the whips. Others held bits and pieces of a man's body—entrails, a hand, a foot. A long hank of bloodied brown hair with a faded red ribbon braided into it. A pair of spectacles. He looked back at the Demon Queen's eyes and saw lazy amusement in them, and something else that frightened him badly.

Since you will not be my servant, in exchange I will ask tha
you bring us rare and precious things.

His mouth felt like flesh long dead. "Name 'em."

Her smile widened, as if he had walked into a trap. "Even so
You're a scholar, Aversin. You found the mirror here; you make
machines that will slay dragons or fly with them across the skies
Therefore I name as your bond that you bring here a piece of a
star, a dragon's tears . . . and a gift given to you freely by one who
hates you. That is your teind. If you do not redeem it by the las
full moon of the summer, the one they used to call the King's
Moon, then you will return to this place and come through the
mirror again, to become my bondsman indeed."

Bugger. Dizziness swept him, and the knowledge of what she
was asking, of what she would do. *Dragons don't shed tears. No
a thing of dragons, Morkeleb would say . . .*

"And if I don't come?"

She got to her feet. He could not tell if she were clothed or
naked, but only sheathed in moving light. He had backed to the
wall and felt behind him sometimes plaster, sometimes picking
bony hands that caught his wrists when he tried to sidestep her
languid advance. She had a jewel in her hand, small and coldly
sparkling, he could not tell its color. He tried to flinch aside but
could not move in the grip of the things behind him, only turned
his face away. For a moment he felt it burning in the pit of hi
throat. Then it was gone.

Her hand crept down the side of his face, along his throat, and
he felt the scratch of her nails on his breast.

"If you don't come," she said softly, "we will assume that it i
not your intention to redeem your bond. Then we will take you
wherever you are. Your flesh will be our gate. Living or dead."

His mouth was dry. He felt Mab's spells fading, colder and
colder in his flesh. His breath dragged in his lungs. Too soon, he
thought desperately, too soon . . .

He only said, "Done," forcing his voice to remain as level and
calm as he could. Turning, he reached over and took the spec
tacles from the demon that held them. There was blood on them
and from the thing's mouth dangled strings of sinew and part of

hand whose scarred fingers he refused to recognize. "Now I've taken up enough of your time . . ."

It was getting hard for him to see, his vision tunneling to gray. In the mists that parted before him he saw black glass, and tiny in its midst the inverted silvery sigil of the door. "Until the King's Moon, then." The Demon Queen drew him back to her and pressed herself to him, kissing his lips. The desire to stay with her, to throw her to the iron earth and take her then, rushed back onto him, consuming him like a flame.

To hell with Jenny, to hell with Ian, to hell with the outer world . . .

He thrust her from him and walked toward the sigil, with the wailing sweetness of her singing in his ears.

"Better than your little brother, aren't I?" whispered Jenny into the ear of the man who grunted on top of her and laughed as she felt his body tense, chill in horror as he reared back from her, whiskered face aghast. How she knew about the incident she didn't know—the distant, locked-up part of her assumed it to be some knowledge of Amayon's—but she saw that the clear tiny incident was in fact true. The guilt of it had driven this poor soldier all his life, and lived, cruel as a snake in his vitals, even after all these years.

"What was it he said to you?" she purred, as the man tried to throw himself from her couch. "*Bultie*—he did call you Bultie, didn't he? *Bultie, don't hurt me anymore, don't hurt me . . .*" Her mimickry was flawless; it was as if the seven-year-old's voice flowed out of her throat as she held onto Bultie with iron strength.

"Whore bitch!" he yelled at her, struggling, and Jenny laughed again at the comical revulsion and nausea that contorted his face.

"What, can't take it?" She shook back her hair, lovely and thick as a cat's pelt. All around the canvas walls the camp echoed with men's voices, jesting and laughing over the latest triumph, and saying *it won't be long now*. The dragons had burned the Regent's camp and scattered most of his men into the woods. The Regent himself, and his father, and a small remnant held out in the devastated fort. In celebration Rocklys had distributed an extra rum ration to the men. Jenny hadn't found it difficult to entice them one after another to her tent. Stupid fools.

"You know what happened to him, to little Enwr, after you were done? When he ran to your papa and tried to tell on you? Oh, don't worry, Bultie, your papa didn't believe him—"

"Stop it, whore!"

She raised her perfect eyebrows mockingly. "What, didn't you pick Enwr because you knew your papa wouldn't believe him?" Her perfect fingers toyed with the silver collar about her throat, a silver and crystal dew-spoon hanging like a gem below. "After your papa beat him—"

"Stop it!"

"—little Enwr ran away—"

"Be silent or I'll kill you!"

"—and met some bandits in the road . . ."

With an inarticulate cry the man dragged his hand from her, bloodied from the grip of her nails, and stumbled toward the door, sobbing. He didn't make it, but fell to his knees vomiting wine onto the carpets, cursing weakly and weeping while Jenny crooned in little Enwr's voice, *"Oh, Bultie, that hurts! Oh, it hurts!"*

She nearly rolled off the divan, laughing, as Bultie crawled out of the tent. And turning her head, saw a man standing nearby, half in shadow.

She knew him. She'd never seen him before, but she knew him.

She held out her hand—Amayon held out her hand—and said, "What, you've never seen a woman before, handsome?"

For he was handsome, in a curious thin-boned way. Long gray hair framed a narrow face marked with fresh cuts, as if he'd seen recent battle. Shadow concealed his eyes, but in the dark under those brows she thought there were stars shining far off. His long thin hands were folded under a cloak like a black silk wing. He said, "You can call fire with your mind, Wizard-woman, and salt with your mind. Call them through the flaw in the jewel and ring the flaw with them, to guard you as you reach through it, and to sustain you there."

She heard Amayon scream, felt the stab of pain, the flush of heat, rising and rising . . .

"You are dragon as much as you are woman," said the stranger, and his voice was dark echoes in her mind. "There is a dragon within you . . ."

"Pig! Bastard! Catamite!" It was Amayon screaming, Amayon who flung Jenny's body against the stranger, clawing, biting, gouging.

But the stranger was strong, astonishingly so. He caught her wrists, held her hands from his eyes, eyes that, she saw now, were white as stars. "You are dragon," he repeated, and the words shone through the flaw in the jewel, through into her heart. "You have no shape, no body of this world. Slip through that flaw as water slips through the crack in a jar."

Nausea gripped her, wrenched her; nausea and pain, pain that took her breath. She—Amayon—began to scream at the top of her lungs: "Rape! Murder! Help! Save me!" And outside the tent men cried out, running.

The stranger flung his cloak around her, dragged her through the tent's postern door. Frenzied, Jenny sought to break his hold on her, flung out a wailing, desperate cry for Mellyn, for Folcalor, for anyone to help her . . . And at the same time, gasping in pain, deep in the lightless jewel's heart, Jenny gathered the dragon-strength, drew and drew at the essences of fire and salt. Though the pain hammered her, she formed them in her mind, and they whispered through the flaw in the jewel, real, as she was real, only without physical body, as she had no physical body . . .

The strength of a dragon stirred in her, reached out to fight Amayon . . .

Water, whispered the voice in her mind. *Become water, Wizard-woman. Do not fight him but flow away. Turn to steam and let the wind take you.*

Men ran from the tents to drive them back from the camp's palisade. Jenny saw with her wizard's sight the rope that hung down against the logs. The soldiers didn't. Laboriously, as if gathering seeds of millet with hands stiffened by cold, she formed spells of Look-Over-There, spells of Kill-Fire that doused the torches among the tents, spells of clumsiness, of inattention, of trailing bootlaces and dropped weapons. Smoke from the snuffed campfires mingled with white wet unseasonable fog that lifted from the river . . .

And she felt Folcalor's spells. The demon-spells of the gross, great thing that rode Caradoc like a dying horse, the thing that she had come to hate in these past five days only slightly less than she hated Amayon—that she loved with Amayon's bizarre and carnal passion. Spells dispersing the fogs and the smokes, illuminating cold flares of marshlight around them.

"Stop them!" Rocklys pounded out among her men, her great black-horned bow in her hands and Caradoc at her heels. Soldiers fell on them, soldiers whom Jenny had taken into her bed for four nights now. The gray-haired stranger was armed with a staff; he used it to fell the first man, and Jenny caught up the soldier's fallen halberd and dagger. Spells tangled like glowing wool around her, and she fought them off; opened one man's face from brow to chin, reversed the halberd and broke the jaw of another, clearing the path to the wall.

Overhead she heard the soft deadly beating of wings and knew the dragons were coming.

Up the rope, said the voice within her mind.

Kill him! screamed Amayon, and the muscles of her arm cramped with the effort not to drive a blade into the stranger's back. Arrows thudded into the wall. Mellyn's voice cried *Jenny!* despairingly as Jenny groped through the flaw in the peridot, grasped the rope, the silk cloak whirling about her as she climbed. Her rescuer struck and slashed with his staff, and looking down, she bent her aching concentration against his enemies. He would, she knew, have to turn his back on them to climb.

She stayed her climb, sweating, shaking, forming in her mind all the limitations, all the power lines, all the runes of a spell of fire and lightning. She felt the demons drag and drink at the magic, tearing at the spells even as she formed them; saw Caradoc, on the edge of the phosphor-lit clearing among the tents, raise his hand.

Unarmed men, she thought; *if not unarmed, at least not ready for magic . . .*

Still she flung her power down on the circle of soldiers around her rescuer, and even with Folcalor's power fighting hers, even with Amayon dragging and tearing at her mind, fire exploded from the air. Men screamed and fell back, dropping their weapons to claw at their burning clothes. The gray-haired man leapt for the rope, and Jenny saw him climb behind her, bony and lean as if his body had no weight at all. Rocklys' black-feathered arrow slammed into his shoulder, hurling him hard into the wall. Jenny reached down, grasped his hand, and dragged him up beside her to the top of the wall. Wind slashed and tore at her hair, at the swirling black silk cloak, and she barely dodged aside as a greenish gout of acid splattered on the wall, the wood hissing as it began to burn. Another arrow struck inches from her knee, and Mellyn's voice cried to her mind in music that ripped her with grief.

"Jump!" Jenny said.

But the stranger caught her around the waist and threw himself not down from the wall but up. And up, wings cracking open, bones melting and changing. The hands that held her turned to claws. Above her Jenny saw the black glister of scales, the swirl of stars and darkness, mane and spines and iron-barbed tail.

The campfires fell away. They plunged up and still up, into the lightning-pregnant clouds, arrowing away to the east.

CHAPTER TWENTY-ONE

It was like being pregnant with some carnivorous thing that gnawed at her womb, seeking to eat its way out.

It was like standing guard on some rocky place alone in the freezing rain, on the second night without sleep, knowing there would be no relief.

It was like lying in bed with a lover in the hot flush of first youth, knowing that to embrace him would be death.

Amayon knew her very well. He had had time to familiarize himself with every flaw in the imprisoning jewel that was Jenny's heart and body, and it was only a matter of time, she knew, before he triumphed.

The Lord of Time was her enemy, as he was of all men. He was the demons' friend.

Thunder ringed the citadel of Halnath. Jenny felt in the rain that sluiced her face the Summonings of wizards and welcomed the protection of the lightning and the storm. As Morkeleb descended to the wet slates of the topmost court through the flaring glower of morning, the soldiers around the wall looked askance, but they raised their spears in salute as she walked past them. Someone gave her a cloak, for she wore only the silken rags of her nightgown.

The Master waited in his study. "Jenny—" He held out his hand. He wore battered mail over a black scholar's robe and didn't look as if he'd slept the previous night.

She gestured him back. The wet wool cloak stuck to her bare flesh underneath, and her wet hair to her face. She must, she knew, look every day of her forty-five years and more, haggard and puffy-lipped with debauchery, weary, soiled. It was hard to

ring out the words. "The demon is still in me," she said. "Don't
ust me. Don't trust what I say."

"It takes one to know one, love."

She turned, startled, at the voice, and fought to maintain the
ncaring dragon-calm that did not release its hold on power for
nything. *Don't let yourself feel,* she commanded, but it was
ie hardest thing she had ever done. *Amayon is there waiting*
r you . . .

John went on, "I'll know if it's you talking, or him." He sat
umped in a chair by the hearth. He looked more tired than she
ad ever seen him, even more weary than when he returned from
ie Skerries of Light. The skin at his throat was marked, as if hot
ietal had been laid there, and deep slits and scratches etched his
ands and neck. But it was in his eyes themselves, half-hidden
y his straggling hair, that the real damage showed.

They lightened and brightened when they met hers, however;
ie old gay madness, and the trust of love. He was glad to see
er, and it made her want to weep with shame and joy.

"They told me you were dead." She did not add that it was Ian
ho had said so. She thought about the way she had dealt with
iat grief, losing her mind to the demon, uncaring.

Then, "You went to the ruins." She didn't know how she knew it.

"I couldn't think what else to do, love." He got to his feet and
ame to her, carefully, not trusting himself nor wanting to break
er concentration. His fingers shook as they touched hers. She
new her own were cold, after the long flight over the bitter
iountains, but his were icy against them.

She thought about the things she'd seen, gathered behind the
iirror in her dreams. Thought about what she'd read of demons
i his books.

"He lay unconscious in the mirror chamber for many hours."
Iiss Mab rose from her little tussock before the fire, her thick
xquisite jewelry flashing like a dragon's scales. "Barely was the
iell I laid upon him sufficient to bring him forth again." She
anced back at Polycarp, who looked quickly away.

"I made the best bargain I could." John propped up his spec-
cles. "I never was any damn good at the market—you re-
ember that time I bought the stone nutmegs from that feller

with the monkey?—but I did try. Miss Mab's been tellin' me
what exactly I've got myself into, and all I've got to say is, tha
Demon Queen ought to be ashamed of herself."

He turned away from her, fumbling with the battered pouch a
his belt. When he turned back, he had something that looked like
seal in his hand, wrought of crystal or glass. At the same momen
Miss Mab came from the other side to take Jenny by the wrist.

It was well she did. Within her jewel-bound mind Jenny fel
Amayon drag and lurch at her arm, and she was overwhelmed
with the desire to flee the room, to hide, to use her will and her
magic and never be found. She twisted, pulled away, and other
hands caught her from the other side. She had a glimpse of the
gray-haired stranger's pale face, the eyes that were nothing bu
shadow and starshine: Morkeleb in his human guise, stepping
through the terrace doors.

She understood—Amayon understood—what the crystal sea
John held was.

Hatred, treachery, poison, murder, pain . . .

The demon's voice screamed in her, and like a dragon, she
sheathed her mind in diamond and steel.

Leave you, leave you, leave you . . .

Waves of unbearable pleasure, indescribable pain, swept her
She clutched at John's arm, at the corner of the table, as she
doubled over, sweating, nauseated.

"Hold on, love." His hand touched her chin, raising her head
she saw he had a white shell in his hand, a common one from the
beaches of Bel, and Amayon's voice within her rose to a shriek.

DON'T LET HIM . . .

A child within her. A desperate, terrified lover-child . . .

Her mind shut hard, Jenny opened her mouth as the shell wa
put against her lips. Closed her eyes on the sight of Polycarp
holding a candle to an ensorcelled stick of crimson sealing-wax
Held out her hand obediently, for Mab to slash her palm and smea
the crystal seal with blood. The little gnome-witch had to step up
onto a chair to press the bloodied sigil to Jenny's forehead.

THEY WILL TORTURE ME THROUGH ETERNITY!

Jenny remembered the nights of her own torment and replied
calmly, *Good.*

And Amayon was gone.

Desolation swept her. She was barely aware of Mab taking the shell from her mouth. Jenny turned away and put her hands over her face, brokenhearted, and wept.

"The demons have asked of Aversin that he bring them certain things." Miss Mab sat forward in the Master's big chair, and Polycarp, seated on the floor beside her, brought up a footstool again.

Nearly twenty-four hours had passed. The gnome-witch wore silk slippers of an astonishing shade of blue, emblazoned with rosettes of lapis and gold and bearing on their toes little golden bells. They jingled when she crossed her ankles. "That was the price he paid for these."

On the study table the crystal seal lay, cold greenish-white, as if wrought from ice. Indeed, by the frost upon it, in which any human touch left a print, it might have been so. The vial beside it had a slippery feel, and Jenny could see that it had burned rings in the tabletop. Now it rested on a saucer of glass. The blue stone box between them, though more prosaic, seemed somehow darker and heavier than any stone of the world she knew, and it was difficult to look at it for long at a time. Dark marks crusted it. Blood, she thought.

The white shell should be there, too, Jenny thought. *Amayon's prison.* She was ashamed of her desire to see it. To know if he were comfortable.

Absurd, she thought, burning with embarrassment. *Absurd.* As if John were not in desperate peril, as if Ian were not still a demon's slave . . .

After leaving the study last night she had slept and wakened to find John lying beside her. He had cupped her cheek in his hand and touched his lips to hers, and it was as if all the filthiness and cruelty and lust Amayon had dragged her through were washed from her body and her mind. She wasn't beautiful—she knew this and had always known it—but she saw her beauty in his eyes, and that was enough.

Her mind still felt detached, as it had when she saw Cair Corflyn through Morkeleb's eyes. She dwelt still, she knew, within the ensorcelled peridot, and that jewel lay in the silver bottle around Caradoc's neck. Her hold on her flesh, she sensed, even without Amayon in occupation, was tenuous. The difference was that no demon dwelt in her abandoned flesh, and she could operate herself, like one of John's machines, through the flaw in the jewel. The relief was greater than anything she had known.

Later they'd slept again, but John still looked tired. There was a haunted look in his eyes, as if he glanced always over his shoulder for something he expected but never saw.

"There shouldn't be much of a trouble about the first." Sitting on the floor at Jenny's feet, John squeezed her hand. "There'll be thunderstones in the treasuries of the Deep, won't there, M'am?" He glanced over at Miss Mab. "I've heard as how the gnomes treasure 'em up. I reckon me credit's good enough with old Balgub after this that he'd sell me one for not much more than a couple pounds of me flesh."

He spoke with a quick grin, but the gnome-witch looked away. Jenny felt John's sudden stillness through her knees against his back.

"No thunderstones lie in the Deep of Ylferdun," said Miss Mab and looked away from his eyes.

"Don't be daft, M'am," said John. "Your old pal Dromar spoke of 'em to me, four years ago . . ."

"He was mistaken," said the gnome-witch. "All have been sent to Wyldoom, in payment for a debt. And such things are far less common than rumor makes them. And in any case," she added, as John drew in his breath to speak, "none would they surrender to thee for this matter."

Her old pale eyes met John's squarely. Silence fell like a single water drop in a dream that spreads out to form a pond, and then a lake, and then an ocean that swallows the world.

"It is from the metal of the thunderstones, you see," she said, "that the Demon Gates are wrought. The metal from the stars holds spells as no other can, to render the Gates impervious to harm."

"As for a dragon's tears," said Polycarp, "I think that's simply fanciful, for dragons do not weep."

Did Mellyn weep, Jenny wondered, *when I escaped from Rocklys' camp?*

And from that her mind turned again to Amayon, and she

averted her face, ashamed that the others would see her own eyes fill.

The silence in the small library was like crystal poison in a cup. The pierced lamps salted the Master's foxy, pointed face, the old gnome-witch's wrinkled one, with patterns of topaz flecks.

John took a deep breath. "I see." His voice was deadly level. "I'd thought to pay the third part of the teind with me own hair and nails, they bein' the gift of me mother, who, barrin' Rocklys herself, probably hated me most in the world. Everybody always tells me I have me mother's nose but I need it meself to keep me specs on. Or do you plan to take that away from me as well?" His glance cut to Polycarp.

The Master met his eyes squarely. "If we have to."

"Thy hair and nails will confirm the Demon Queen's hold upon thee, Aversin," said Miss Mab, turning the rings on her stubby fingers. "She counted upon just such a reading of the riddle, I think, divining as demons do in the shadows of thy mind the hatred thy mother bore thy father's son. Of them could she fashion a fetch, to send into this world in thy stead. Perhaps use them to control thy heart and thy mind as well."

"Ah." Jenny felt the tension in all of John's muscles. Anger first, and then fear.

"Was that somethin' you knew, when you made me the spells to pass into the world behind the mirror?" he asked at last. "What they were likely to ask of me? Or that nobody here had the slightest intention of helping me pay this teind?"

"I told thee they would trick thee, John Aversin," Miss Mab said steadily. "And that it was not likely that thou wouldst leave the mirror with thy life."

"But you didn't bother mentionin' that all anyone would say about it was, *Oh, sorry, son, can't pay your teind, bit on the steep side.*" He stood, dragonlike himself in his spiked rusty doublet. *"But we'll take the protection and the freedom and the healin' nonetheless, thanks ever so, and we'll see to it that your name lives forever. So just lay right down there and wait while I get the ax."*

He swung angrily to face the Master. "Tell me one thing. Those guards who've been hangin' about every time I turn around today—they're to make sure I don't leave this place, aren't they?"

Polycarp looked away.

Face rigid, John looked down at Jenny, who had half-risen in shock and horror and rage. He bent to take her hands, his fingers like ice, and kissed her lips. To her he said, "Well, and they're right, love." There was a scathe of bitter rage in his voice. "Can't let the demons into this world, but somebody's got to go in and get the things to fight them with, for the sake of the King, and for Gar, and for the Law and all me friends. But it was for you, love. It was all for you."

He strode from the chamber, and the blue wool curtains lifted and swung with his passing. Polycarp rose at once and went to the door, and Jenny, reaching with her mind, heard him say to the men outside, "Go after him. You know what to do, but be quiet about it."

The Master caught Jenny by the wrist as she tried to follow. For a moment they looked into one another's eyes, bright blue into blue, understanding and not wanting to understand. "They won't hurt him," said Polycarp. "Just escort him to his room. Please understand, Lady Jenny. We cannot let him go free. No one who has had dealings with the Hellspawn, who owes a teind to any of that kind, can go free."

She jerked her arm against his grip, but he did not let go. Furious, she demanded, "Or me either?"

His blue eyes were sad. "Or you either, Lady Jenny. Think about it."

She pulled away and stood in the lamplit study, trembling.

"The Law holds harmless those who have been possessed," said Polycarp, "because in any case they seldom survive. But those who go willingly to the Hellspawn and bargain with them cannot be trusted, nor let to live. It is the bravest thing I've ever seen a man do, but it remains that he owes them a teind he cannot pay, and in the end he must be theirs. That we cannot allow. Not in life, and not in death."

Jenny looked back helplessly at Miss Mab, but the gnome-witch met her eyes with calm pity and grief. "Thou knowst it for truth, Lady. I helped him, that they would have one less mage within their thrall, knowing that you, as mage, would understand. With the King's Moon he is theirs; when the breath goes out of his ribs he is theirs; and by the demons that seized thee, the demons that hold thy son, thou knowst that he cannot pay them what it is they ask. This is how demons work, child. Through terror, and love, and fear to let the worst come to pass."

"There has to be a way."

The last New Moon of summer had set almost three hours ago. Even so far to the south the sky held a lingering indigo luminosity in which each star, like a dragon, sang its own name in music undecipherable to the human heart. From the battlements Jenny looked up at them in a kind of horror, and then beside her, into the white eyes of the gray-haired man who had come silently to her side.

Her voice sounded steady, detached, unreal to her own ears. "John tells me that the King's Moon was what they called the season when the King of the Long Strand, where Greenhythe is now, and the lords of the little realms of Somanthus and Silver and Urrate Isles were killed to pay a teind to the gods for harvest."

I know. The dragon tilted his head a little to one side, a characteristic movement. She could almost see the glowing bobs of his antennae. *I was there.* His gestures were not human, nor was there anything resembling humanity in the structure of the narrow, odd-boned face. It was curious to see him as a man, though no stranger, she thought, than the days she had passed in the form of a dragon. If he could transform himself into a dragon no larger than a peregrine, surely this matter was little to him.

Yet still it gave her a strange feeling, looking into those diamond-crystal eyes, alien and without pity.

She repeated, "There has to be a way."

It would be ill done, Wizard-woman, to cheat the demons, as though we were petty gamesters plying ruses with fake gems in the marketplace. Morkeleb laid his long white hands on the stone of the parapet. Only his nails were unhuman, black curving claws like enameled steel. His shoulders seemed stick-thin, like a doll wrought of bird-bone.

Honor is honor, whether one bargains with the honorable or the dishonorable. This is what the Shadow-drakes said. Once I did not think so. But to take freedom and healing, and return to them only charred bones; this is theft. Moreover, I do not think demons would be deceived even by the slyest of illusion.

Sometimes, Jenny, there is no way.

"Easy words," she cried, thinking of the means by which demon-callers were killed. And her mind formed the shape, if not the words: *You do not love.*

The white eyes regarded her, and hers fell before them.

It is true that loving is not a thing of dragons. Yet sometimes we do not only because we do not know how. I would not have entered the Hell behind the mirror, Jenny, because I know the hopelessness of it. Yet he, too, knew, and here you stand in the hope of being freed. I could never have done such, for I did not— I do not—know how to perform acts of such foolishness. Yet I am grateful to him that he did what I, Morkeleb the Black, the Destroyer of the Elder Droon and the greatest of the star-drakes, what I could not and would not have done because it is not a thing of dragons.

He turned his eyes from her, to the velvet gulfs of Nast Wall and the thin red flicker of John's comet burning low above its ridges. His brows pinched above the thin birdlike nose.

Now I am not even a thing of dragons, for I surrendered my will—surrendered my magic—that the demons should not trap me through it, and I do not understand now what it is that I am.

Morkeleb, my friend . . . She touched his shoulder, and he regarded her with eyes that were no longer a crystalline labyrinth, but a straight road infinitely distant, vanishing into colorless air.

Morkeleb, my friend, you are what you are. I treasure you as you are, always. Whatever you do and are, or whatever you become, I will be your friend. Maybe not what you wanted, once on a time, but the best that is in me to give.

Not once on a time, he said, *and not always.* And she saw on his face the cold crystal track of tears. *For you will die, Wizardwoman, as humans die, and I will become what I will become, and what will exist of what lay between us?*

He looked away, unwilling that any should see his tears or his heart. He had loved gold with a deep and terrible covetousness, and he had loved power and the knowledge that power opened to him. She sensed in him the grief of knowing, as she did, that there was no going back to what he had been.

She put up her hand to brush away his tears, and he stayed it with his long cold-taloned grip.

Touch them not, Wizard-woman; they would burn your hand.

So she took the crystal dew-spoon from around her neck and caught the tears in its bowl, and set it aside on the parapet.

What exists of the worlds that once you visited? she asked him, and gestured to the darkness and the stars. *They are still there, living in your heart.*

The hearts of dragons are not as the hearts of men. They are of a different composition, like their tears. I can return unto those worlds whensoever I choose. But you will be lost to me in the dark oceans of time, and there will be no calling you back. It was for this reason that I sought the Birdless Isle, and for this reason that I remained.

Nothing is ever lost, said Jenny. *Nor ever forgotten. And who knows what lies in the hearts and the dreams of the Dragon-shadows? When the Twelve Gods drove the Lord of Time away from them into exile, it was because they had forgotten that they were only things that he had himself dreamed. Nevertheless he let them drive him away and surrendered his godhood to them. He knew that they would always have existence in his heart for as long as it mattered either to him or to them.*

He said nothing for a time, but wept, and she stood silent beside him, holding his hand, and now and then gathering his tears in the crystal spoon. And it was true what he had said, that they blackened the silver handle where they touched it, as if, though the body he wore was that of a man, it was like his dragon-shape, formed of elements unknown on the planet of oceans and trees.

In time he looked at her with a glint of his old amused irony and said, *Vixen, that you turn even my grief into a present for your husband's sake,* and she heard under his wryness a new understanding of what it is to be human.

She picked up the spoon, which had a pool of tears in the bowl perhaps the volume of the first joint of her thumb. *I will throw this over the parapet, then,* she said, willing in her heart that she would have the strength to do as she said. *I would not rob you of your grief, my friend.*

Nor I rob you of your husband, he said, *my friend.* And he took the spoon from her hand and laid it carefully down on the stone once more. *Nor yet would I rob my friend of his wife, for whom he did what I have neither the courage nor the foolishness—love, as you term it—to know how to do.* He touched her cheek and her hair, as John did, and looked into her eyes with eyes that were not human and had never been. *I understand now why we startreaders do not take the semblance of humankind more often.*

She shook her head, not understanding, and he drew her to him and kissed her lips.

Because it is not a semblance, he said. *And we are not fools. There. Now I have done.* He reached up one hand with its long black nails and touched aside the tears that ran down her own face. *Is this why the God of Women is also the Queen of the Sea? Because tears are as the ocean is, salt?*

She smiled a little. *I do not know. Maybe because they are as the ocean is, endless.*

As is all human grief that waters the roots of loving. And his words in her mind encompassed the great stretches of time he had seen, before her birth or her mother's birth, and long after she and John and Ian would be dead. He nodded toward the spoon with its thin, glimmering pool. "If you will send that to the Demon Queen, look that the vial you choose is wrought of crystal, not glass." He spoke now as men speak, though in her mind she still felt the moving currents of his thought. "The tears of dragons are dangerous things. They will consume ordinary glass. Even crystal they will burn away in time."

She had been reaching toward the spoon but now stayed her hand. In Morkeleb's star-dark eyes she saw the echo of her own thought. And because she had lived many years with a naturalist who tinkered with flying machines and chemicals and clockspring toys, she asked, "Exactly how much time?"

CHAPTER TWENTY-TWO

"My only love," breathed the Demon Queen, and her mouth, like a black blood-ruby, touched and traced John's lips, the shape of his nose and the oval scar in the pit of his throat. "My servant and my love." Her hand slipped down his arm, his flank; her skin under his answering caress was pale pink as the hearts of lilies, flawless as that of a young girl, and scented of sweet-olive and jasmine. Her hair was a coiled ocean of sable silk.

She had the look, Jenny realized, of Kahiera Nightraven.

Her body laid over John's in the ember-cave of red velvet and candle flame, sinuous as a snake's. Jenny tried to shut her eyes and look away. Warm arms embraced her, and Amayon's voice breathed in her ear, *I had to show you this, my darling. For your own good I had to show you. He turned from you, the moment he entered her realm.*

You are lying. Jenny tried to call to her memory the image of John dying in the rain, run through by Ian's spear. She couldn't. It had never happened and the lie had never been told.

You are lying.

But her body ached with the memory of Amayon's pleasure-heat within her, with the gold-stained glory of domination and power. She struggled to wake but sank into memories of other embraces, delicious and degrading, and through them heard Amayon's voice calling her name. Calling from the white shell where he was imprisoned, as her own heart was imprisoned in the flawed jewel in Caradoc's silver bottle.

I can still come back to you. I can still love you, as he never loved you. How could he love you, he who never understood?

"Love?" came John's voice softly through the haze of th
dream. "Love?"

She woke up with tears on her face and a desperate urge t
know where exactly Amayon's white shell was being kept. Joh
was bending over her. And her first thought, swiftly shove
aside, was rage that John was there to keep her from going t
search.

His finger brushed her face. "You're crying."

I'm crying because you lay with the Demon Queen!

But that had been her dream, not his. Or maybe not his. Or sh
could not prove it had been his.

She drew a shaky breath and wiped her face, which wa
indeed wet with tears. John had kindled the lamp beside his nar
row bed, but the heavily latticed square of the chamber window—
he was not yet being kept in a barred cell—was cinder-gray wit
dawn. "I'm beginning to understand why dealing with demor
kind is always an ill thing," she said. "They don't leave yo
alone. Not in sleep, not in waking, not in death."

His jaw tightened, and she saw the oval scar where the Demo
Queen had marked him. Last night, after he had fallen asleer
she had turned back the blankets, and it had seemed to her tha
his body was marked with half-visible silvery traces that disap
peared when she leaned close to look. The marks of the Queen
lovemaking. The lines of possession.

"We'll get through this." He cupped the side of her face i
his palm.

But in her heart she thought—or perhaps Amayon whispere
to her, sometimes it was not possible to tell—*They're onl
waiting for you to leave, to get out the acid and the ax.*

"Miss Mab's outside," John said softly. "She says she's sorr
it's so early, but she's got word calling her back into the Deep."

Jenny pulled a voluminous robe over her head and sat up a
the gnome-witch came in, followed by a servant. The servar
bore a tray of braided breads, honey, clotted cream, and apple:
"You lads all right out there?" John put his head out through th
door to address the guards in the gallery. "Gaw, Polycarp shoul
at least send you what I get in here," he added, inspecting th

bowls of porridge the men had before them. He went back and fetched a couple of apples from the tray.

"No, thank you, sir," said one of the soldiers, studying the fruit with a wary eye.

John stood for a moment, the apple in his hand; Jenny saw the change in his eyes.

Demon-caller. Trafficker with the Spawn. Helltreader.

"Aye, well, then," he said. And then, "I'm not their servant yet, y'know."

"No, sir," said the man stolidly.

John returned quietly to the room and bit into the apple himself. Miss Mab had opened the blue stone box. It contained white powder, which she touched with her spit-dampened finger and used to mark Jenny's wrists, eyelids, and tongue. "How well this may work I know not," said the gnome-witch, brushing back Jenny's hair to peer into her eyes. "Thy heart is still prisoner within the talisman jewel, and it may be that nothing can be cured until it be freed."

Jenny nodded. She didn't think she could endure another night of Amayon whispering to her in her dreams. Of the knife-crystal visions that had visited her: her own drunkenness, cruelty, and rut; Ian grosser, more sarcastic, more filthy of mind and more ingenious at the giving of pain to people and to animals as each day passed. Ian trapped in a jewel as she was still trapped, weeping in agony and humiliation, begging his demon to let him die.

John in the arms of the Demon Queen.

She shut her teeth on the pain and made herself nod.

"Perhaps you can apply it again tomorrow," she said. "With some spells I've found repeated applications to have effect when a single occasion has not the strength."

"Indeed I have so found," replied the old gnome, carefully closing up the box. "I shall try again at sunset, if thou feel no better through the day. I should return from the Deep by that time. And in my home warren I shall try to weave other spells for your comfort, until such time as the healing takes hold. The Talking River beneath the ground is a stream of power, and its power grows as it flows deeper into the earth. By the time it passes singing over the Five Falls on the ninth level, where my warren lies, its influence can be woven into wreaths and braids and such I will bring to you, to help you sleep without dreams and Aversin also."

Jenny glanced quickly at those wise old pale eyes, praying that the gnome-witch could not read those dreams, but she could not interpret what she saw in Miss Mab's wrinkled face.

A guard came to fetch John, for the half-made Urchins were being brought into the courtyard. Jenny, who had dressed by that time in a plain brown and yellow dress such as servants wore, gathered her magic within her, to witch the senses of the guard that none might see her pass. But as she did so she felt Amayon's mind, the strength of his will, redouble within her, in response to her calling of power. She felt, too, that curious dislocation, as if all things were seen through a fragment of glass—through the green crystal of the imprisoning jewel.

Morkeleb had spoken of the Shadow-drakes putting aside their magic. It was hard to do. She simply walked as quietly as she could from the room in John's wake, and the guards, having had no instructions concerning her, let her pass.

It was said in the north that everything that could be bought and sold, was bought and sold in the Undermarket beneath Halnath Citadel, where the Marches of the Realm met Ylferdun Deep. The giant cavern, cut into the cliff on which the citadel stood, was the gate-court of the gnomes. Legend said they could seal that opening with a stone wall in the space of a night. The gates at the inner side of the huge chamber were certainly solid, closed fast night and day and guarded from four turrets. As she entered the Undermarket, Jenny could see in the stone floor the metal tracks on which the little gnome carts ran to carry goods in and out of the cavern.

The gnomes mostly sold silver and gold, gems and objects wrought of rare alloys, or ingenious machines produced by their incomparable skill. In exchange, merchants brought spices and herbs, rare chemicals and salts. There was silk from the Seven Islands and the stiffer, drier silks of Gath and Nim; rare birds and the feathers of birds completely unknown in the north; jade and porcelain and musk. In another part of the market oxen, pigs and sheep were penned. These the gnomes bought with silver and copper, for they were fond of meat and in their caverns had only white cave-fish and mushrooms.

The merchants set up tables in long rows, their wares laid out on blankets or bright cloths. Some erected booths or pavilions of wood, with flowers or bundles of fresh greens tied on the posts. Others put up tents, and near the front of the cavern, where the wind drew off the smoke, hawkers fried sausages and river fish or steamed sweet dumplings and custards. Thus the whole vast gloomy space smelled of hot fat and fresh flowers, of crushed greens, spices, sweat, stone, lamp oil, animals, dung, and blood. The noise in the vaulted space was terrific.

Jenny walked from dealer to dealer in vessels of stone and glass, and finally settled on a snuff-bottle of alabaster as thin and brittle as paper—"So fine you can tell whether it contains nut-brown or betel, my lady!" enthused the huckster. Then she found a worker in colored glass who, after turning the bottle over in her calloused fingers, nodded and said, "Aye, I can enclose it in a vial, though the work of it's so fine t'were a shame to hide it."

"It's a riddle," said Jenny. "Designed for one who is clever enough to remove the glass without damaging the alabaster inside."

She paid for it in silver that Miss Mab had given her—neither she nor John had a penny of their own—and promised to return the following day for the finished vessel. Then she ascended the endless wearying flights of stairs, pausing to rest on the frequent landings where benches were set and vendors of lemonade and felafel plied their wares. At the citadel again she sought out the courtyard where John and Miss Tee, the gnome engineer, were instructing several dozen of the Master's warriors in the use of the dragon-slaying Urchin machines.

"It doesn't need a deal of strength to haul the cage around," John was saying. He stood on the wheeled engine platform surmounted only by the steering cage itself, stripped like his audience to singlet and breeches. Miss Tee—Ordagazedgwyn was her name among her own folk—worked among the craftsmen at the side of the court, assembling the other machines.

"Keep your arms and legs soft—it'll gie kill you if you go

heavin' about with all your might when you don't have to. Jus
swing your body's weight, and harden up at the end, like this . . .'
He moved, the characteristic shift of weight necessary to guide the
cage, and as he positioned each soldier, made sure they under
stood the balance necessary, the peculiar use of momentum.

Watching him, Jenny's soul seemed to knot itself behind he
breastbone. He bore the demon's mark in the pit of his throat
and the knowledge in his heart of what humankind would do
to him before the ripening of the moon. But he was making
sure these children—in their youth they seemed no more—
understood enough about the machines that they'd stand a
chance against dragons and magic.

Jenny crossed to him, through the dust and clanging of
hammers. She was half the courtyard away when he turned his
head, his eyes seeking hers. It was as if his whole face grew
light. "Jen." He stepped down and took her hands and kissed her
"Miss Mab was out here before daybreak, Miss Tee tells me
markin' each of our Urchins with magic chicken-tracks in what
ever was in that red vial." He gestured toward the dusty confu
sion of machinery. "She left the vial with me, for you to finish
up. We've gie little time."

He glanced past her at the two bodyguards, leaning stolidly
against the wall. Polycarp himself stood in the colonnade, blue
eyes bright and filled with envy. Jenny felt it when John's gaze
crossed that of the Master. For a moment it seemed to her that
she could see, with the thin slip of the waxing day-moon over his
shoulder, the marks of the Demon Queen's patterns down his
arms and across his shoulders: Runes spelling out words that she
could almost read. They faded the next instant, but his face
looked as if he had not slept.

But he asked her only, "How is it with you?"

"Well." She made herself smile.

Shadow fell over the court; soundless dark wings. The stu
dents looked up, crying out and reaching for swords that no
longer hung at their belts. Someone made a move for one of the
catapults set up nearby, and John said, "Don't shoot at you
dancing-master, son; y'know how far in advance I had to book
us the lesson?" He swung up into the unprotected cage and

settled his feet into the straps. "You, Blondie. Up here with me, and hold tight. We'll make the lot of you Dragonsbanes before the full moon."

Morkeleb circled high once, then dropped, striking and snatching. John whipped and jerked on the steering cage, spinning the platform clear of the blow. "You got to watch for his tail," he called to the students who scattered in a wide, fascinated ring. "Head and tail, like right fist and left fist. Don't waste your shots on his sides." Morkeleb dove and snatched, slashed and hissed, and beside her, Jenny felt Polycarp shiver with awe and delight.

It was, as John had said, a dancing lesson, a game of cat-and-mouse: graceful, deadly, and astonishingly agile and swift. Once Morkeleb got his claws under the platform and flipped it; John kicked his feet free, swung his weight on and under the cage, and with a lurch and a jerk got the platform on its wheels again. *They must have counterweighted it,* thought Jenny, *after the battle at Cor's Bridge.* "Watch how the dragon moves," panted John, waiting while the tall blond girl scrambled back onto the platform. "They have no weight, but they use their wings to balance and turn, see? When they shift, that's when to try to get a shot off under the wing." Only Jenny felt the steaming mental ripple of Morkeleb's ire and felt in her mind the unspoken words that he did not send to John:

Beware, little Songweaver. I teach you that the demons' hold may be broken, but I learn from you, too.

She remembered his human face in the starlight, the lonely grief in his labyrinthine eyes. And it seemed to her that as the dragon passed before the afternoon sun, bone and muscle and sinew were momentarily only a trick of the light. She seemed to see not the black steel and enamel of muscle and bone, but only smoke shot with starlight, half-visible.

Not human, she thought, and now not of dragons either. But he understands. *Sometimes there is no way . . .*

Only trust in the mad Lord of Time to sort it all out.

Oh, my friend, she thought. *Oh, my friend.*

"Up you get." John slapped the blond girl's flank. "Feet in the straps. Grab the handles—one of you, get up here and let me show you how to crank the engine. They need a deal of that. There. Now. Off we go."

Polycarp crossed to where Jenny stood, slipping the black robe from his shoulders to stand in his singlet and hose. "I have to learn this," he said, breathless with delight. "I have to try."

His young soldiers applauded wildly when they saw him coming, laughed and called out. Spread-eagled motionless in the Urchin's cage against the pale sky, John regarded him in silence, then tilted his head a little and said, "You've your nerve."

The Master of Halnath looked away. The two bodyguards glanced at one another, started to speak, and then stopped. There was a silence, too, among the young warriors. Obviously none of them knew that John stood under sentence of burning alive the hour before the teind came due.

Polycarp looked up again. "Do you understand?"

"Aye. I understand." John stepped from the cage and handed the Master up onto the platform, to the soldiers' renewed cheers. Only afterward, when Jenny was examining the spell-wards Miss Mab had laid on the other Urchins, did John come over and take her aside. Morkeleb was patiently working with another pair of students, slowing his slashes and feints; Jenny could hear the rumble of his thoughts in the back of her mind, like a wolf-killer hound grumbling about being put to watch pups. The liquid in the Demon Queen's vial, like the vial itself, was dark red, shiny, and thick. Miss Tee told her it had been thinned with water and painted on the frames with a doghair writing-brush, but the liquid did not thin. Rather, it seemed to convert the water into itself. It was as if the runes of safeguard and countermagic, traced up the ribs and across the spiked plates of the Urchins, were drawn in blood.

"Are you all right, love?" John took off his spectacles and with the back of his arm wiped the sweaty dust from his face. "Listen. Don't be angry at the Master—about those two blokes, I mean." He jerked his head at the bodyguards. "And don't . . ." He hesitated. "Spells or no spells, they're going to need all the help they can against Rocklys and her dragons." His eyes met hers, peering and naked without the protective lenses; made as if to flinch away and then returned. Knowing she knew. "It'd be good if you went with them."

Don't fight him, she saw in them, behind the fear of what he knew would happen when she left the citadel. *Don't widen the gap, for demons to come into the world. Don't leave yourself open to them by craving power or revenge.*

"It was stupid of me, bargaining with the Demon Queen. It's not like I hadn't read a thousand books and scrolls and legends sayin' *This is a bad idea.* I"—he swallowed hard—"I'll pay this teind somehow. I won't go back and be her servant, you know."

"No," Jenny said, "and I think I've found the way."

While they ate supper in John's chamber and waited for Miss Mab, Jenny told John of what Morkeleb had said the previous night, and what she had purchased that day. "According to Morkeleb, a dragon's tears are corrosive. They combine with glass, volatilizing both, so neither the glass nor the tears remain. The alabaster they'll eat through in, I calculate, about thirteen days—the time that lies between now and the full moon. We can . . ."

There was a scratching at the shutters of the chamber's single window. Jenny went to open it; Morkeleb slipped through. Strangely, Jenny found the sight of him in miniature more disturbing than at his true size, like jeweler's work come alive. He spread his wings and floated to the back of her abandoned chair, wrapped his long tail about one of the back-supports and cocked his glittering head.

Victorious in your seeking, Wizard-woman?

"I was. The glassmaker should have it ready tomorrow. Is there something that can destroy a thunderstone in the same fashion, minutes after we render it over to them? Before they can use it for their own purposes? What destroys iron?"

Water, said Morkeleb in her mind. *Rust. Time.*

"It always comes back to time." John picked out a fragment of pork from the stew and offered it to Morkeleb with his fingers. "If the Lord of Time were to return with a bag of the stuff for sale he'd make a bloody fortune."

Only among men, replied the dragon. *It is said the Shadow-drakes play with it, make music from it, as we make music from gold. Keep your scorched and lifeless pap, Dreamweaver; it is not a thing of dragons to eat such stuff.*

"Polycarp's cook'll slit his wrists with grief if he hears." John popped the meat into his own mouth. "Is it true thunderstones are bits of stars?"

They are pieces of what men call Falling Stars, the dragon replied. *No more true stars than this comet you have been seeking. In truth, they are balls and fragments of rock that float in the dark between worlds. Thus human magic cannot weave spells to destroy or change them, for you do not know the world whereof they come. Most are covered with ice; between worlds it is very cold. They drift in great shoals, like north-sea pack-ice in the spring. The young sport among them.*

Into Jenny's mind came the image of drifting chunks and towers and fortresses of ice, glimmering in the starlight, and the rainbow shadows of dragons flickering among them, no bigger, it seemed, than dragonflies. In the void between worlds the dragons did not have the same shape that they wore in the world of ocean and trees, and this, too, she found troubling.

Stars themselves are not what they appear. They consist solely of fire, and heat, and the light they emit. There is no "fragment" of a star.

"Aye, well," said John softly, "she didn't say 'fragment,' now, did she? She said 'piece.' Which could mean the star's light itself, couldn't it? Gathered in a hothwais, like the fire's heat that kept the old *Milkweed* in the air, or like the air the gnomes use when they go into the levels where the air is foul."

They looked at each other, with uncertainty and hope. "Miss Mab will know," said Jenny. "It would take the magic of the gnomes to prepare one. No line of human wizardry ever understood how to source magic to alter stone. What about the gift from an enemy?"

"Well," said John softly. "I've had a thought or two about that. And I'm afraid you're going to have to break me out of here so I can collect that one meself."

The moon had long sunk below the citadel walls when Jenny emerged from John's room. She nodded to the guards and felt their eyes on her the length of the battlement: *the Demon-trafficker's woman. Maybe a trafficker in demons herself. Like that woman a year ago in Haylbont Isle who cut her children to pieces.*

Jenny found herself praying that Miss Mab had returned with the spells against dreaming. The prospect of another night like the last made her frightened and sick.

The narrow stair at the end of the gallery—the dark arched doors of the empty Scriptorium, then down the winding servants' ways. Storerooms and kitchen wings. Gnomes never liked to be housed in towers. There was a small courtyard at the citadel's lowest level, near the bronze doors that led to the Deep stairs. From the cobbled pavement Jenny descended a further half-dozen steps to an area barely larger than a closet, from which several doors let into a suite of subterranean rooms. She saw no light in the round window she knew was Miss Mab's, but this meant nothing. Mageborn and a gnome, Miss Mab could read in the dark if she chose. When Jenny tapped at the door and spoke the gnome-wife's name, however, she received no reply, and the door gave inward with her touch.

"Miss Mab?" She stepped through, looking around at the darkened room. "Taseldwyn?"

The cupboard stood open and empty; the blankets had been stripped from the bed. Where Miss Mab's enormous jewel box had stood on the end of the table there was nothing, no combs or brushes, no blue satin slippers. Puzzled, Jenny stepped out into the areaway.

"What is it? Who comes?" Light flared topaz behind the glass of another door. The door opened wider and revealed the wrinkled face of Miss Tee. "Ah, the magewife!" The door opened wider. The engineer was dressed for bed, in tucked and embroidered linen. Her pale-green hair lay braided on her thick breasts, and she had removed all her many earrings for the night. "Didst come for Arawan-Taseldwyn, dear? She has gone."

"Gone?"

Miss Tee nodded. "The Lord of the Deep sent this morn, bidding her return to Ylferdun. Word of this traffic of demons reached him, I think. She has gone to be tested by the other Wise

Ones of the Deep." She clicked her tongue disapprovingly and shook her head. "Fools. As if any would think Taseldwyn would have aught to do with such, or that I wouldn't know of it, I wouldn't see it in her eyes."

"Tested?" Jenny's heart turned chill. "You mean she's a prisoner?"

"They're all fools." Miss Tee shrugged. "And so they'll find, the Wise Ones, Utubarziphan and Rolmeodraches and the rest of the mages, but only after they've wasted a year . . ."

"A *year*?"

The green eyes blinked up at her. They were the color of peridot, a stone Jenny had come to hate. "This is the length of time, they say, in which a demon's influence will show itself." She set down the lamp she carried and took and patted Jenny's hand in her own hard muscular ones. "Worry not on this, child. She is only held in her own warrens on the Ninth level, under guard to be sure, but she will be well treated. Thou canst be sure of that. She is of the Howteth-Arawan, and they are powerful in all the Deeps of the Delver-Folk. Their Patriarch will never let the council condemn one of theirs. Even for humans a year can't be that long. Sevacandrozardus, Lord of the Deep, is a fool and a twitterer on the subject of demons. Dost know he wished even to have the doors to the citadel shut, because of that vial, and the seal, and the box? Because thou who wert possessed of a demon still walked unhindered? Yes, great ill came of the demons in times past, but just because man or woman touched an object that was touched by Hellspawn does not mean they will become corrupt themselves."

Climbing the stair to the citadel's upper levels, Jenny wasn't so sure of that. Throughout the day, the reminiscence of Amayon had returned to her, over and over again, like an itch that could be neither scratched nor salved. It came back now, the frantic desire to know at least where the shell had been bestowed.

She put it aside. It would do no good, she thought. She was reminded of her sister, when Sparrow suspected her husband of carrying on an affair with Mol Bucket: Sparrow had followed Trem one night and had seen him go into the bold-eyed cowherd's house. There were some things it was better not to know.

Miss Mab in prison. Even in her own chambers a year would be a long time. Would the Lord of the Deep or the gnome sorcerers whose magic was the true heart of the Deep permit Jenny to see Miss Mab? Would they even let her into the Deep?

At the dark archways of the Scriptorium she paused. Jenny could see a line of brightness framing the door of Polycarp's study. On impulse she hurried across the cold tiles. A thunderstone that could be used to form a demon-gate was one matter. A hothwais, which, for all the understanding of the nature of stone that lay at its creation, was at bottom a low-level spell, was another. Even if it retained within it the light of the stars, it could not be used by the demons for any purpose whatever.

When she reached the door, she found it open a little, the lamp inside sending a slice of yellow light across the octagonal tiles. Jenny touched the door, pushing it farther ajar. Within she saw Polycarp seated at the pickled oak table where she had so often scried him in conference with John. The fire burned low in the round hearth, mingling its glow with that of the pierced lamps to thread the Master's mop of curls with amber, edge the bony arch of the nose, and tip the lashes of his shadowed eyes with brightness.

His arms were stretched out on the table and cupped in his palms he held a small white conch-shell, mottled with pink and stoppered with crimson wax. He bent his head, as if listening to a voice whispering almost too low to be understood. His eyes were half-shut, concentrating on everything that was being said.

Jenny stepped back, cloaking herself automatically in darkness and glamour. She almost threw up with shock. *No,* she thought. *Polycarp, no. Put it down. Put it away.*

She thought, *No wonder the Lord of the Deep suspects Miss Mab as well. No wonder he speaks of having the Deep locked.*

No wonder they want to kill John.

Morkeleb spoke truly. This is an infection spreading poison to whatever it touches.

The Master's thin fingers stroked the shell delicately. Then his mouth flinched in revulsion, and he put the thing on the table and pushed it away. He rose so suddenly that he nearly overset his chair, and stood for a time, breathing hard and shivering in every limb. With convulsive speed he snatched up the shell and carried it to the black iron cupboard on the wall. He thrust the shell inside and slammed the door with a clank. His fingers fumbled with the key, the brass glinting fiery in the lamplight. He twisted it hard and crossed the room in two strides to his desk, flipping open a box of carved black oak, as if he would put the key into it.

But he didn't. He put it in his pocket.

Jenny melted into the shadows and fled to John's room with cold dread beating in her heart.

CHAPTER TWENTY-THREE

"Destroy her."

It was Ian's voice.

He lounged in a camp chair in Caradoc's tent, though Jenny couldn't see the rest of the tent; it was as though the wicked ur-light shone sickly only around the table where the boy and Caradoc sat. His long black hair was oily and unwashed, and his face was not the face of a child.

"And find another wizard where?" Caradoc's shirt was open and the silver bottle that he carried around his neck now lay on the table. Eight jewels were scattered across the table. Each flickered in the wasted light.

"We can't risk it."

"Scared?"

Ian's eyes narrowed. He turned his head and looked through the wall of green crystal that separated them from Jenny. The jewels on the table seemed more alive than his eyes. "Concerned," he temporized, and through the double and treble meanings in his voice Jenny sensed—felt—remembered from Amayon's mind the shape and terror and darkness of the Hell from which they'd come, a cold place where soft things shifted and mutated, feeding upon one another and living in fear of the formless awfulness in the Hell's heart.

"Don't be." Caradoc held up a bright green jewel and, with it in his hand, walked over to the crystal wall behind which Jenny crouched, naked and shivering.

He smiled, his broad, clean-shaven face curved with contempt. She saw again, through the human arrogance, the face of the demon Folcalor: more intelligent than the others of his kind, sly and greedy and watchful. "It's this easy." He raised his staff with its moonstone head.

Jenny cried, *Don't! No!*

He struck the wall, struck it on the great fire-rimmed flaw that ran from the floor to lose itself in the darkness above Jenny's head, and at the blow she felt faint, as if she were bleeding.

John! she screamed, but John was asleep—she could see him sleeping far off. Her own body lay curled at his side, the body she could no longer reach, no longer touch. Though the moon had set early, Jenny could see, as if by its pallid light, the patterns that traced his flesh like the slime-track of some unspeakable thing; the pale mark left in the pit of his throat. As she watched John turned his face away, his expression taut with pleasure: *Aohila,* he said.

Help me!

He reached out, and she heard the Demon Queen laugh.

"Mother?" For a quick second she saw through the crack the bright summer night in the Winterlands, and Adric's stocky form against the backdrop of battlements and stars. "Mother, is that you?"

Then Caradoc's staff smote the crack in the wall like an ore-crusher's hammer, and Jenny staggered back and fell. Blood from a hundred painless cuts was sticky on her hands. She tried to crawl away from the wall, but the demon loomed there in the darkness, striking the crack again and again. Splinters burst and flew from his knotted staff and from the wall itself, like chips of glass. Rage contorted his face; when he opened his mouth, green light came out, and curls of smoke. Unable to breathe, Jenny crept toward the farthest wall, but her own flesh was too much for her to endure. She sank to the floor in her own blood, covered her head with her arms, and waited.

She woke sometime after, exhausted.

Caradoc was gone. The circles he had drawn glowed faintly still in the darkness. Something told her that it was mid-morning in the world outside, the world most people knew as real.

Aching with weakness, she dragged herself to the flaw in the jewel and through it poured her consciousness into her distant body again.

* * *

There was a very old spell Jenny had learned from Nightraven—not that Nightraven had ever used such a cantrip herself. But the women of the Iceriders sometimes used it, in the places where their magic feathers told them their lovers were meeting with younger and better-favored girls. It was a spell that could be worked with very slight power.

Exhaustion weighed her down, beyond anything she had felt in the hard days at Palmorgin. Food lay ready on a tray for her: John had used the bread, the boiled eggs, the fruits, and the salt fish to create a dumpy little lady all stuck together with jam, "I love you" squiggled in honey around the rim. But though she laughed, she was barely able to eat, and the bitter memory returned, of John whispering the Demon Queen's name, oblivious to Jenny's cries for help.

She washed and dressed and collected what she would need for Nightraven's spell: a curtain weight for a spindle and a basketful of weed-fibers, dust, lint, and the combings of her own hair. These she carried down to the Undermarket. Spreading her cloak in a corner behind the booth of a woman selling gourds— cut and glazed and painted as bottles and dippers—she began to spin thread, and with every turn of the spindle, with every twist of her fingers, she daubed a little magic into the air.

Morkeleb joined her, guised as a gray-haired man. Jenny did not know when. Maybe some spell of unseeing cloaked him; she did not know. But none spoke to either of them, and when the town merchants packed up their goods and the market wardens came around the hall making sure the last stragglers departed, they passed them by as if they were not there.

Once the hall was cleared, the bronze doors at its inner end opened. From the hall beyond those doors, carts were trundled out and loaded. Jenny used little magic, but only sat and spun and watched. And in time it was obvious that no one was looking at the end cart of the line, so she gathered her spinning into her basket and slipped into that cart, covering herself with her cloak.

She didn't know where Morkeleb hid, but after the carts had all been rolled into the inner hall and the doors closed and locked for the night, the dragon was there. Guards sat at a little table playing dominoes near the outer doors. The click of the dominoes sounded very loud, and the smell of the cocoa they drank filled the dark: rank, sweet, spicy. There were few lamps in the hall, and they hung on chains dozens of feet from the high stone ceiling. The night below the ground lay heavy on most of the chamber, among the looming shadows of the neatly packed carts. It did not take much magic to collect it a little thicker about herself as she crossed to the doors that led into the Deep.

Morkeleb met her there. He seemed uneasy, drawn in on himself: *It is troubling to me,* he said, *to become of humankind. The things of humans speak loudly in my flesh and my mind, anger and envy, sloth and fear—above all other things, fear. I ask myself things I would never ask: What if we cannot leave this place? What if I do not recall the turnings of the passageways and stairs? What if we are found, or my magic fails me, or we return to discover that this Master of Halnath has indeed listened to the demon in the shell and freed it to take over his flesh? Do men and women truly live in such fear?*

Most do, said Jenny. *And most of the ills and griefs of humankind arise out of it. And at the bottom of all fears is the knowledge that all will one day end.*

Morkeleb said, *Ah,* and fell silent for a time. At the foot of the stair they crossed a bridge, lacy stone grown in a thousand turrets and columns. Water thundered far below them in darkness. *And magic is the anodyne to those fears? The way to braid and weave air and fate and time? Or to give oneself the illusion that one does so?*

I suppose it is, said Jenny, startled. *I had not thought of it before, but yes. Magic is the weapon we wield against chance and time.*

And does it succeed? asked the dragon.

She said, *I do not know.*

The world beneath Nast Wall was crossed and woven with rivers, gorges, and bridges where lamps of silver burned. Everywhere, as they descended deeper, Jenny saw latticework windows looking out into those gorges, or opening from smaller dwelling-caverns into larger. Each passageway, each stair, each road was dimly illumined with globes and tall thin chimneys of colored glass, and by the light they shed the gnomes passed by on their business, their long ghostly hair wound up in jeweled sticks and combs and frames, or else left to trail over their bowed shoulders like clouds. None spoke to Morkeleb and Jenny, or seemed to see them. The dragon's cold hand, with its long claws, held Jenny's, and he led her unerringly through the ways that he had traversed with his mind and his dreams, when four years ago he had lain in the upper reaches of the Deep on the far side of the mountains, whispering music to be whispered in turn from the gnomes' gold.

There is too much gold here, he said, pausing to get his bearings at the head of a road through a cavern where the very stones sparkled. *The Shadow-drakes were right. I find now that its mere presence is a taste in my heart, a sweetness remembered, and it is difficult.*

Do any legends speak of where the Dragonshadows might have gone? asked Jenny, to distract him. To distract herself maybe, from the memories of her fear and her dream. *Could they have departed entirely from this world?*

I think . . . The dragon began and stopped, and Jenny could feel the currents of his thought check and swirl, like water around rocks. His profile shifted slightly as he looked at her sidelong. She saw in her mind what John had told her of, the Birdless Isle under the crystal brilliance of new morning, heard the slow heartbeat of the sea and the breathing of the wind. Felt their presence as a core of peace that plumbed the foundations of the world.

I do not think they would have departed this world, said the dragon, a new thought naked as a bird-peep, *without telling us.*

He led her between sparkling mountains of sinter and great pools that stretched like glass. In time they came to a place where a small river fell singing over five ledges of corrugated white limestone, overlooked by balconies cut and fretted into cavern wall. *They will be watching her,* said Morkeleb. *The Wise Ones of the gnomes.*

She said once that she comes forth often on her balcony, said Jenny. *We will wait.*

The dragon looked at her sidelong again, as if he sensed her weariness and hunger, but he said nothing. While they waited, a little to Jenny's surprise, he told her stories after the fashion of dragons, by speaking in music and images and scents in her

mind, as if he would distract her as she had him. She saw
mingled wonderment of violet suns and gray oceans beating
endlessly on lifeless shores, felt the different forms of magic
sourced from all those different stones and suns and those dif
ferent patterns of stars. He told of worlds where livid-colored
plants fought and devoured one another, of raindrop and seagull
and the creeping life of the tide pools on the Last Isle. He spoke
of the Dragonshadows he had known long ago, their deep power
their wisdom, their peace.

They are like the wind and the air, he said. *And yet now that
look back I see that they loved us, all of us who thought we chose
our own way here.*

His hand, white and thin with its long black curving claws, lay
on hers, and looking at his face she could not tell whether she
saw a man's face or a dragon's.

In time Miss Mab came out on her balcony, clothed in a red
robe. Morkeleb and Jenny climbed up to her, quietly, through the
soft murmuring of the water and the smooth snow-and-salmon
curves of the rock.

"A hothwais," she said thoughtfully, curling her short legs
under her robe and looking from woman to dragon and back.

"Would this be safe?" asked Jenny. "Could demons turn a
hothwais to harm, were one given them?"

"The very grasses of the field can demons turn to harm, child
I am not sure but that they cannot turn to harm the starlight thou
wilt give them, in this hothwais, though I know not any way they
can do so. And indeed, anything will be of lesser harm than what
they might do with a true thunderstone. Is it true," she asked
turning her wise pale eyes on Morkeleb, "that stars be as thou
sayest, vast storms of light and fire, not solid anywhere? This be
a marvelous thing."

"Would it not be possible," asked Morkeleb after a time, "to
place a Limitation on the hothwais itself, that its essence, its na
ture, fades with the fading of the starlight it holds? Thus the
Demon Queen would be left with only a stone, of which one pre
sumes, even in the realm of Hell, they have sufficient for their
needs."

Miss Mab was silent for a long time, turning her huge, heavy rings on stubby fingers. Below the balcony the waterfalls gurgled a kind of endless, ever-varying music. As she had said, there was great power in the stream, power that Jenny felt even sitting on the terrace. Close-by someone played a harp, very different from the gnomish zither, and a woman's voice, unmistakably human, lifted in a sad and wistful song.

Here, too, thought Jenny, *they keep human slaves.*

"It should be so," Miss Mab replied slowly. "The nature of hothwais is permanence, not evanescence, so such is not commonly done. Yet I know of no reason why it could not be done. Let me see what I can do. I will send thee word, Jenny Waynest, at Halnath."

"I misdoubt this will be possible." Morkeleb spoke up quietly. "With Mistress Waynest's absence overnight, I think she may not return openly to the citadel. The fear of the Hellspawn is very strong, and she bears their mark."

Jenny looked, startled, at the dragon, and he returned her gaze with strange galactic eyes.

"It is true," said Miss Mab, "that mine own people have imprisoned me for a year and a day for even entering the Mirror chamber in the ruins of Ernine."

"Then send this thing to the camp at Cor's Bridge," said Morkeleb. "For there under the Regent's protection we will surely be."

Upon those words Miss Mab returned to her chamber and brought out honey-bread and curdled cream, strong-tasting white cheese and fruit, and light woolen blankets, for the air in the caverns was clammy and chill. Jenny slept uneasily, and woke, it seemed to her, more weary than when she had lain down. Morkeleb she did not think slept at all.

The dragon's prediction about Jenny's absence overnight turned out to be alarmingly true. When she slipped out of the merchandise cart into the Undermarket shortly before dawn, it was to find the citadel's soldiers searching the corners of the great cavern—perfunctorily, it was true, as if they truly did not expect to find anyone there. "What would a witch possessed of a demon be doing sleeping here anyway?" demanded one warrior of another, disgustedly pushing back his visor. "She's probably in Bel by now. And anyway, would we be able to see her?"

Probably, thought Jenny, settling into the darkest corner she could find and freezing. Despite Miss Mab's spells of dreamless rest the demon Folcalor had returned to her in the night, drawing circles of violation around the jewel that housed her true self, and the effort to keep his power at bay had sapped her strength badly. Still she managed to remain unseen until the guards had gone, then slipped out of the market cavern on their heels and up to the citadel again.

She did not know when Morkeleb left her. It was less magic than simply quiet and remaining unnoticed that got her through the service quarters, down the guarded passageway ("I've a bit of food from his Lordship the Master for Master John," she said to the guards, displaying a pot of honey and several rolls on a glazed tray borrowed from the kitchen) to the cell where she guessed, even without reaching forth her mageborn senses, they would be holding him chained.

She was right. Morkeleb was right. The chains were long enough that he could lie down, and the cell dry and provided with a pallet, but it was heavily guarded. The chains themselves were wyrd-written to render them proof against all but the most powerful spells. Weary as she was, spent as she was, it took Jenny nearly three-quarters of an hour to fashion a tiny cantrip that would send the guard outside to the privy, where she was able to abstract his keys when he set aside his belt.

"Jen!" John sat up, startled, as she entered his cell. He'd been sitting on his pallet, his back against the wall, reading—Polycarp had left him an enormous pile of books, but because of the manacles on his wrists he had to prop his hands and the book with his knees. "I was afraid some guard hereabouts took it into his head to kill you out of hand. They said you'd been missing overnight."

"I was in the Deep. They have Miss Mab a prisoner—"

"Gah!"

"They're afraid of the demons, John, and they've every right to be so." She was unlocking the ring of iron around his neck, the spancels on his wrists, as she spoke. The Demon Queen's mark stood out like a wound. She forced herself not to think about her

ream, about the visions of him in those white serpent arms.
Miss Mab is going to make a hothwais to hold the light of a star.
harmless gift for the Demon Queen. But as to the third part of
e teind . . ."

"I'll settle that." John stood up, hesitating with the book in his
and, clearly loath to abandon it. Then he shrugged and stuffed it
to the front of his doublet, adding for good measure another
ne. "But to do it we'll have to go to Jotham."

The camp at the bridge bore every mark of hard usage under
e bitter gray downpour of guardian storms. Its palisade pro-
cted the stone span but was black with fire, save where new
ood gleamed yellow under the wet. And yet the banners of the
ouse of Uwanë flew over the charred dugouts. As Morkeleb
wept in low from the cloud-choked canyons, Jenny saw that few
nts remained standing. The blackened ground within the de-
nsive work was gashed with trenches, the earth above them
ving them the look of long, twisted graves.

John, held in the dragon's claws, waved a white sheet taken
om the citadel laundry at the men who came running from the
enches, crying out and pointing their arrows skyward. Only
hen Jenny saw one man, taller than all the rest and thinner,
ectacles flashing in the pale day, emerge from underground at
run and wave his arms at the men did she say softly, "That's
m. We can go in."

It is a trusting Wizard-woman.

"Even so," said Jenny. She felt the wave of Morkeleb's cyni-
sm pass over her, as if he'd plunged through a wall of dark
ater, but he spread wide his wings for balance and drifted
ward the ground. The men below jockeyed for position, but
areth gestured again. A sweep of fugitive sunlight riffled his
air. The storms were definitely breaking. Flying through the
sses, Jenny had felt it—the clouds dissolving, the magic that
ld them failing at last.

Morkeleb stretched out his hind-legs and settled on the earth.

"My lord, really!" Ector of Sindestray exclaimed angrily as
areth walked forward, his hands outstretched.

"Jenny. John."

"Polycarp get in touch with you?" John asked jauntily.

"My lord, this man is under sentence of death . . . !"

"One of his pigeons came in this morning." Gareth's eye flicked to the demon mark, then away. He looked unhappy. "H said Jenny had vanished. He said he was putting you unde guard—"

"Ah. You haven't had the one about us stealing the vial and th seal and the box, then? You'll get that one tomorrow."

As he spoke Jenny touched the satchel she had tied around he body, the satchel Morkeleb had given her just before he resume the form of the dragon. *I think it best we have charge of these instead of Master Polycarp,* he had said. *They are, after al Aversin's, purchased with the costliest of all currency.*

"This is outrageous!" insisted Lord Ector. He still wore cou mantlings—Jenny couldn't imagine how he kept them properl folded. "My lord, you're aware of how demons influence men minds! How they take over men's bodies! You can't pretend yo trust these . . . people."

Gareth reached out, then drew his hand back without touchin the satchel. "Polycarp wrote of these things," he said. "And what you did to achieve them." Ector cleared his throat signif cantly but Gareth would not meet his eyes. Wind flicked the pin and blue ends of his hair. He had a fresh wound on his cheek, an his thick spectacles had been broken and mended, and there wa a hardness to his face, a grim set to his mouth.

"It wasn't you by any chance who told him to chain me up?"

There was long a dreadful silence. Gareth shuffled—*No balla of old Dragonsbanes,* thought Jenny, *provided guidance on situ tions like this*—then at length said quietly, "No. But you yourse know all the legends, the histories, involving demons. Polycar isn't the only one who favors invoking the penalty, you know."

John glanced at Ector and said nothing. Gareth flushed.

"I've told Polycarp, and others on the council, to wait. That trusted you."

John bowed his head, but his mouth was wry. "Thank yo But you really shouldn't. If it weren't me, you shouldn't. An with Jen vanishing as she did I can't blame him, I suppose, fo lockin' me up. Mind you, I'm not ettlin' to walk into the rest of i but I'm workin' on that." He propped his spectacles on his nose. "Poly'll be here . . . when?"

"Tomorrow," said Gareth. "They're taking the Urchins through the Deep of Ylferdun today. Reinforcements from Bel have been sighted—the rain that protected us slowed them down." Another sweep of sunlight sparkled on the soaked and puddled earth of the camp, and Gareth and every warrior there looked uneasily at the sky.

"Played hob with your harvest, too, I'll bet." John shoved back the long hair from his eyes. "They'll be on us tonight, you know—Rocklys and her lot, I mean."

"I know. They have to, if they're to take the bridge. I'm having the men stand to . . ."

"Nah." John shook his head. "Let 'em eat their dinners and catch a bit of kip. Nuthin'll happen till . . . eighth hour of the night, I'd say. Halfway till dawn."

"Why halfway?"

"Because that's when men who've been standing to since the eighth hour of the afternoon slack their guard and figure nothing's going to happen till dawn. That's when they take a bit of a doze or sneak off to the privy, or start lookin' about the camp to see who else is on watch they can talk to."

Lord Ector opened his mouth in indignant protest as Gareth and John brushed past him, side by side. "Have you got flares built up, ready to burn? They can see in the dark as well as in daylight, so the bigger the pyres you can torch the better."

Gareth nodded. "We've kept the wood dry as best we can, and we got oil in yesterday's convoy. When the clouds clear, we'll need the light. The moon won't rise until mid-morning tomorrow, and anyway it's only three days old."

"Son," sighed John, "I can tell you to three-quarters of an inch how far the moon's waxed since I rode to Ernine. Now show me where you've got the Urchins from the first attack. Are they put back together? Good. Jen, d'you feel up to a bit of magic?"

True to John's prediction, the dragons attacked between midnight and morning. Jenny was dozing in John's arms in the dugout of Gareth and his father the King, reveling in the peace of being left alone by Caradoc and his spells of intrusion and domination. Curled in the heart of her jewel, she was aware that Folcalor had other fish to fry and assumed her, probably, to be still in Halnath Citadel.

Dimly, very dimly, she seemed to see Caradoc himself, the man who had truly once loved Rocklys, who had sought learning and power and walked along Somanthus' northwestern strand: a broken, white-haired man sleeping, dazed, in the heart of some far-off jewel.

But she felt no pity. Now and then she would reach out through the crystal's flaw to her body, to feel more closely the warmth of John's arms, and the tickle of his breath in her hair. Time seemed to her very fragile then, very precious—later she would look back on those moments with an aching longing, as a traveler lost on the winter barrens dreams of warmth. She knew the sentence of death to be a reasonable one, having seen Polycarp alone in the dimly lit study with Amayon's prisoning shell. She knew, too, that even the manner of death prescribed was necessary, given the power demons could wield over the dead.

But not John, she thought, closing her hand tight over his. *Not John.*

Then in her mind Morkeleb's voice said, *Jenny. It is now.*

She flowed through the fault in the jewel like water. Flowed into her flesh, her bones, her mind.

John was already sitting up, hair in his eyes and groping around for his spectacles. "Here we go, love," he said, and slung around his neck the frosted crystal of the Demon Queen's seal and a little stone knife to draw the blood for freeing. He gathered her to him, his hands cupping her face, collecting together the night of her hair, and kissed her lips. "You know what to do?"

"I know." There were crossbows stacked in the corner of the room, horn reinforced with steel. The poisoned bolts were so long and heavy she could barely lift the weapons. John slung three of them over his own back, and two over hers. She felt the touch of his hands adjusting the straps; his heart and hers already armored, drawn apart into the fight.

Not good-bye, she thought. *Not good-bye.*

Above, at ground level, men were shouting, boots pounding

by the dugout's opening. The orange glare of torches flashed and juddered along the wall. The King sat up and called out a woman's name, confused; Gareth was holding his hands and talking to him gently, telling him that all things were well. "Use them carefully," John said to her, "but if you get the chance, don't hesitate for anything. Understand?"

He was talking about Ian. She thought about the drunken, slack-mouthed boy fumbling at the bound bodies of camp whores, tied up for his pleasure; thought about the sickened, weeping child she had sometimes glimpsed, a prisoner as she was a prisoner, in her dreams.

"I won't."

"Good lass." He slapped her flank and followed her up the ladder to the slit under the earth-heaped roof. As they made to part he caught her hand; already, against the darkness, the black skeletal shape of Morkeleb had risen. "You haven't . . . There isn't some spell you can lay on me, to keep me from . . ." He hesitated, then said, without change of expression, "If I die in the fighting, I'm theirs, y'see."

Jenny hesitated a long time, weighing what she knew of her waning strength against her love for this man. She knew that though destroying his body afterward would prevent his returning as a fetch, if he died in the fighting there would be no way of retrieving his naked soul from the Demon Queen's hands.

She said, "I can't. Not and lay the spells I'll need for the battle." She didn't even know if she'd be able to summon sufficient power to protect herself and Morkeleb against the magic of the other dragons. Weaving the wards would take all she had, after laying spells upon the Urchins and these crossbows in the afternoon.

"Aye, well," he sighed. "I'll just have to manage to not get meself killed, then." He kissed her again. "You don't get yourself killed either, love."

John caught a soldier outside the trench and handed him the three crossbows, to follow Jenny. They parted in the firelight, John to the squat glittering ball of the Urchin, and Jenny to the smoky shadow of the waiting dragon.

CHAPTER TWENTY-FOUR

Jenny wove the wards of protection around them, listening for the first beating of dragon wings in the dark.

Put all of your magic into it, whispered Morkeleb's voice in her mind. *Leave none for yourself, none in your flesh, your bones, your heart. It will do you no good in any case, and the demons will take you again through it. That is the secret of the Shadow-drakes.*

Jenny said, *I can't. We'll be in danger . . .*

Trust, said Morkeleb. *The whalemages have laid on us spells of warding as well, as good as yours or mine.*

Jenny's hands shook, and the circles of power and energy and Limitation with which she had surrounded herself and him waned in the jumping torchflare. The crossbows hung on their straps from the cable that ringed the dragon's body, the spiked and terrible shape of them blending with his spines. She tried to call on the dragon within her soul, but since her escape from Rocklys' camp, it seemed to her that that portion had been left behind. *I can't.*

Trust.

She thought she saw the flares and torches through his body, as if he were insubstantial, wrought of smoke himself. His eyes, and the bobs on the ends of his antennae, were a glitter of stars in the darkness that thinned away like smoked glass.

But his voice remained strong in her mind. *Trust.*

She surrendered the last of her magic, pouring it into the spells that would guard them both from delusion and panic. Without it she felt empty, cold, and naked as she climbed onto his back.

His wings unfurled without a sound. He lifted as the fire showed them the first of the attackers. It was Yrsgendl, white and scarlet, with Bliaud on his back. Silently they rose, higher and higher, fading into the dark.

Jenny saw the dragons winging from Rocklys' camp: pink and green, gold and green, yellow, rainbow . . . blue. *Oh my son,* she thought, as she hooked her feet hard through the cable and slung the first of the heavy crossbows into the cradle of her arms. *Oh my son.* Only the discipline of having studied magic let her close her mind.

Yrsgendl plunged, spitting fire and acid onto the camp. From all around the redoubt, from every trench and dugout, arrows spired up, fell back . . . And a single black heavy javelin slammed up straight and hard from the trundling Urchin that suddenly swung to life, pinning the dragon through the left wing.

It was a lucky shot, taking him through the widest portion of his silhouette against the dark. Morkeleb plunged from above, and Jenny swung the crossbow to her shoulder and fired downward, and that arrow pierced the younger dragon's back among the spines. Yrsgendl whipped around, mouth opening in a furious hiss, and Jenny felt/saw the demon illusions shiver and spatter around the wardings laid by the Demon Queen's vial. She fired again, driving the red dragon down, and a second harpoon from the Urchin knifed upward, burying itself in Yrsgendl's breast.

Yrsgendl wheeled, heading for the darkness, and again Morkeleb drove him down. Spitting, hissing, Enismirdal and Nymr plunged out of the sky above Morkeleb, but he slithered unseen from beneath their attacks, snapped and fastened on Yrsgendl's wing, dragging him back. Yrsgendl flapped and fluttered, weakening, and the Urchin, breaking through the damaged redoubt, trundled with surprising speed toward where the injured dragon would fall. Hagginarshildim, green and pink, and the surviving rainbow drake swooped on the machine, but John whipped and dodged, ducking from under the lashing tails, and the rainbow drake tore its own flesh open on the Urchin's spines. When Hagginarshildim attacked a second time, she received a harpoon in her foreleg; Morkeleb drove her down, too, forcing her to remain at the scene of the action.

Yrsgendl was on the ground, sick with the effects of the drug on the harpoon's tip. This, Jenny knew, was the tricky part, for the harpoons were tipped not with poison but with a powerful serum of poppy, and the dragons would be able to shake it off quickly. The rainbow drake spat fire at John as he rolled free of the Urchin, dived across the intervening ground to where the red and alabaster shape lay. Jenny saw firelight flash in the crystal seal that John pulled from his doublet.

Then Nymr was attacking, and Morkeleb whipped around to evade, and Jenny saw nothing of what passed below. But a moment later, as her own drugged crossbow bolt sank into the flesh of the blue dragon's neck, she saw from the corner of her eye a slither of dark-red flame, and as Nymr lashed at Morkeleb, teeth and tail gleaming, Yrsgendl whirled up from below and sank his teeth into the blue dragon's tail, wrenching and tearing at the flesh.

Jenny heard a dim shrieking in her mind, the cursing and wailing of a demon disembodied, but could not spare a thought to the matter. Nymr was a big dragon, too big to be easily driven into range of the Urchin's bolts. As he fought, Yrsgendl released him, only to circle and plunge on him from above as Morkeleb held him in combat. By the glinting torchlight Jenny saw who rode the white and scarlet dragon, and her heart stood still. Had she had any magic remaining she would have stretched it forth—

Don't do it! she thought wildly. *Don't do it!*

John unhooked his feet from the braided cable around Yrsgendl's body, and as the younger dragon fastened for a third time on the spiky ridge of Nymr's spine, he slid down and caught his footing among the bristling spears.

John . . . !

Ian swung around, the thin hollows of his face transformed by exhaustion into a man's. The blank blue eyes widened as he raised his hand, but John was quick and very strong. He caught the boy's wrist, and Jenny saw, lashed to his palm by a thong, the pale cold seal of the Demon Queen.

Ian screamed and gasped, his head falling back; Nymr gave a great frenzied thrash in the air, and John grabbed the cable, hooked his arm through it as he swung free and fell. Below them whirled darkness, flares, and the spinning shapes of dragons: Morkeleb said, *Stay where you are, Wizard-woman! I'll catch him should he fall.*

But John didn't fall. Entangled in his two captors, Nymr could only thrash, and Ian reached down, grabbing his father's arm, dragging him back onto the blue dragon's back. He moved clumsily, for it took far greater effort for him to reach out from an unflawed crystal, but he managed at least to hang on. Dimly, Jenny could hear Morkeleb calling out instructions to Yrsgendl, or rather using the younger dragon as another limb of himself, so powerful were the wordless impulses of his mind. Morkeleb's teeth shifted from Nymr's foreleg to his neck, and held the bigger dragon immobilized while John worked his way, hand over hand, to Nymr's head. In her mind Jenny could hear the screaming of demons, furious, dispossessed, thick as whirling leaves in the air: Gothpys, and Bliaud's demon Zimimar, and the one that had held sway over Yrsgendl. Among the torrents of cobalt and peacock Jenny glimpsed silver, like a ball of glass, and this ball John seized and drew out, dripping with the dragon's blood.

Then he flung his other arm around Nymr's neck, pressed his face into the swirling ribbons of the mane, and held on, as Morkeleb and Yrsgendl released their hold and floated back, and the blue dragon began to circle, slowly and carefully, to the earth.

Jenny could hear Ian crying out, "Father! Father!" Desperate, terrified, but with enough sense to simply hold fast to the cable and let Nymr bring them both to ground.

John and Ian were clinging together, the boy weeping, John stroking black handfuls of his son's hair, when Morkeleb lit nearby and Jenny all but fell from his back. "It's all right," John whispered to the boy's frantic sobbing, "it's all right, you're all right now," as Jenny threw her arms around them both.

"It's all right," she said—foolish, she thought, but the only thing she could say, "Ian, the demon is gone . . ."

"You saw," he whispered, choked. "Mother, you saw . . . I . . . I . . ."

And he had seen her.

Above! cried Morkeleb, and Nymr and Yrsgendl launched themselves skyward again, as the rainbow drake and the surviving Icerider gyred down on them, spitting and slashing.

Jenny flung herself back to Morkeleb, a barely visible starwraith in the smoke and dark, and John dragged his dazed son to the protection of the Urchin, half-lifting him through the hatch. Then the Shadow-dragon leaped skyward again, with Jenny slinging to her shoulder another of the double-weight crossbows, and Nymr and Yrsgendl sweeping out under Morkeleb's command to gather in the next dragon to be driven into the Urchin's line of drugged fire.

Together they drove down Mellyn, numbed with poppy. The screams of the demons echoed in Jenny's mind when she heard a hissing shriek above her and, turning, saw Caradoc himself and the golden drake Centhwevir streaking down on them like aureate lightning. Below her, from every ravine of the hills, rose the throbbing of drums and the braying of Rocklys' trumpets as her forces advanced.

They had, Jenny thought, intended to hold off their attack till dawn, when the dragons would have reduced Uriens' camp to confusion. But with the dragons slipping out of her grasp, it was now or never, and she threw her forces toward the fortress wall. As the other dragons closed protectively around Morkeleb's flickering shape, Jenny heard the deep battle-cry, "Uwanë! Uwanë!" and knew that Gareth had been ready, waiting for this.

John, get Ian out of there! It occurred to her to wonder where Bliaud—as clumsy at working from his prison as Ian—had hidden himself, and if they could get themselves out from between the hammer and the anvil in time.

Then dragons closed around Centhwevir, catching and dragging at him, trying to force him to earth. The rainbow drake was down, twitching faintly on the ground—Jenny got the barest glimpse of him as Hagginarshildim, green and pink, circled back from spreading havoc on the camp, and Enismirdal winged out of the passes of the mountains at Caradoc's call. Jenny wasted two of her three remaining shots trying to hit Centhwevir but buried the third bolt in Enismirdal's primrose neck. In the vast rout of slashing wings and snapping teeth that followed, she saw the yellow dragon veer and falter as the drug took its effect. Dimly she could hear Folcalor calling on his forces, trying to rally the remaining dragons and wizards, while the furious shouting of men in battle rose from beneath them.

A heaving sea of forms struggled blindly in darkness below. Blood on steel, and now and then pale faces contorted in pain. Flares threw some light, but mostly it was primal chaos, the confusion as legend said had reigned upon the waters of the ocean before the Old God sang sea and sky apart. On a hill above the road a ring of fire had been established, and in its golden crown she glimpsed Rocklys on her horse, her standard-bearers around her signaling the corps commanders to their positions. Then the rainbow drake rose, with more crossbows, more heavy drugged bolts, and two of the great dragon-killing harpoons in her claws.

An outcry from below made Jenny look down again. Through the striving knots of warriors the Urchin was moving, cutting down all in its path with its spikes, and Jenny saw it was heading straight for the lighted knoll where Rocklys sat. The Commander turned her head. She said something to an aide, who handed her her bow, and the men afoot closed up around her with their spears. Still the Urchin advanced, and there were soldiers running behind it, slipstreaming through the carnage where none dared stand in its way. Jenny was aware of Caradoc hurling spells at it, spells that glanced off the Demon Queen's wards.

Bolts shot from the Urchin's forward ports, striking among Rocklys' guards. Still she remained where she was, watching it come, mechanical and strange. She had chosen rocky ground, too steep for the Urchin to climb readily, though Jenny thought later that it could have done so.

But it stopped. The hatch flipped open, and John emerged, his bow held in hands bloody from Nymr's spines. He nocked an arrow, but he was slow—exhausted, Jenny thought.

And Rocklys was not slow. She never was.

Her arrow took John in the chest, the impact of it jarring him back, out of the Urchin's hatchway. He fumbled, caught at the spines behind him, trying to get down unhurt. Jenny saw the blood, saw the fire gleam on his spectacles.

Then he fell. With a roar of rage, the men who had run behind the Urchin surged up around it, cutting and slashing their way through Rocklys' guard.

Centhwevir wheeled and fled.

Take him! Jenny cried. *Follow him! Stop him! He has the prison-jewels!*

But the other dragons—Yrsgendl and Nymr and the young rainbow drake—circled and turned to the business of driving to ground Enismirdal and Hagginarshildim; Jenny thought she heard a voice in her mind say something about Time. *Time. Follow and time.*

The prison-jewels, the talismans! Folcalor can still use them!

Ian, and Bliaud, and the other mages—and she herself—were still prisoners.

But Morkeleb was streaking after, leaving the battle behind in the night.

We can't let him land! How long, she wondered, could Ian maintain the connection between his imprisoned self and his body? Could his demon retake him before it was trapped, as Amayon had been trapped? Could another demon step into its place?

Would he be strong enough to use magic to save his father's life?

John falling with an arrow in his heart . . .

She thrust the thought aside.

The demons would not have John's body—Lord Ector would certainly make sure it was burned before it could be put to demon service—but his mind, his consciousness, would be forever behind the mirror, the prey of the vengeful Demon Queen.

But of course, she seemed to hear Amayon saying it, of course, she herself could save him, if she turned back.

Centhwevir winged on into the night, with Morkeleb and Jenny hard on his track. They passed over the wood of Imperteng and the Wildspae's ebon curve; passed over the formless lands of Hythe and Magloshaldon and the farms of Belmarie. *The sea,* Jenny thought. *They are going to the sea.* To the Gate of Hell that lay below Somanthus Isle. She was desperate, terrified, when she felt the alien consciousness of Squidslayer and the other mages of the deep, rise out of that blue-black abyss.

Rims of silver on the black waves and rocks. Centhwevir striking water, gold and blue shining for a moment. Then gone, and a moment later Morkeleb, plunging from the sky like invisible lightning, and the cold living impact with the sea.

The spells of the whalemages enveloped her in air. She saw Centhwevir, wings and legs folded flat, a vast sea serpent lashing sideways as he dove.

Frantic with horror, Jenny saw the Gate, the green glow deep within the rocks; saw herself, prisoned in the talisman jewel. All of them—Ian, Bliaud, Yseult ... And deep in her mind the memory rose of the half-glimpsed horrors of that lightless watery Hell, of the thing the other demons called Adromelech, a silent, terrible darkness at its core. . . .

Jenny sensed the whalemages following but afraid to reach forth with their magic lest they be taken, too. Green things, vile and deformed, floated in the water or reached from holes in the rocks: endlessly long tendrils of seaweed that finished in grasping hands, fish with glowing mouths and twisted, vestigial wings. These swarmed around Morkeleb, biting at him, tearing at Jenny's shoulders and arms.

Among the rocks, a hundred yards above the Gate, Morkeleb cornered Centhwevir, cutting him off from the sicklied glow beyond.

The blue and gold dragon belched fire—not the acid of true dragons but demon-fire that enveloped witch and dragon in a searing cloud. Morkeleb rocked back, then attacked again, lashing and snapping, quicker than the larger drake and more able to slither through the holes and canyons. The deformed fish of the deeper trenches near the Gate rose up, but the whalemages and the dolphins formed a protective ring around the struggling dragons, driving the infected monsters back.

Jenny fired her crossbow bolts into Centhwevir's breast and neck, but the bubbles in the threshing water spoiled her aim, and the water itself slowed the missiles. At last she kicked her feet free of the cable, and with one harpoon in hand and the other slung on her back she launched herself across the black space toward the dragon and the demon-ridden mage.

Caradoc saw her coming. She felt the burning weight of the spells that for three nights had dragged her strength. His shirt was torn, and his cap gone; the silver bottle floated behind him on its ribbon, and his gray hair lifted like seaweed in the swirling water. His eyes opened wide, and there was in them nothing but greenish light; his mouth opened, and like the dragon he blew fire out of it, transforming the water around her to searing steam.

Illusion, pain, death, like the illusions of a dream. The demon Folcalor reached into her and tore at the roots and stumps of her magic for a handhold, but these she let go of, dragon and human alike, trusting only in the whalemages' spells. With vicious demon wisdom it snatched at her dreams, the ancient longings and fears, and these, too, she released, letting them go. There was nothing in her mind, and only a clear whiteness in her heart, as she drove the harpoon with all her strength into Caradoc's body, pinning him to the rocks against which Morkeleb had forced Centhwevir. Then, while Caradoc thrashed and picked at the harpoon and blood poured from his working mouth, she turned like a fish in the water and plunged her hands into the waving particolored glory of Centhwevir's mane.

As she drew out the crystal spike, the demon behind her hurled lightning, power, blasting her body away and against the rocks, driving the breath from her lungs. Cold claimed her, heat and cold together, and then falling darkness that seemed to stretch to the abyss beneath the world.

CHAPTER TWENTY-FIVE

She came to herself with the sounding of the ocean in her ears. She lay on a bed of something soft and damp and smelling of fish; morning sun sparkled in her eyes.

Is it well with you, Jenny?

Well? asked a number of other voices in her mind. *Well?*

She sat up, and something rolled off her chest and plopped onto the stuff on which she lay—seaweed, she saw. When she reached down for it, she saw that her hand was crinkled and shiny, red with the scarring of burns. Though the pain was suppressed by spells of healing and of nepenthe, she was aware of it, as if her very bones had been cored with a red-hot rod.

Everywhere that the rags of her burned clothing did not cover, her skin was the same, wrinkled and stiff with scars.

Her hair was gone.

So was her magic.

Morkeleb asked again, *Is it well with you?*

She could barely make her stiff fingers undo the stopper of the silver bottle still clutched in her hand. From it she poured seven jewels into her palm: two rubies, two amethysts, a topaz that had clearly been pried out of another setting, a sapphire, and a flawed peridot. As if in a dream she put the peridot into her mouth and felt herself flow through the flaw and into her body again. Her pain redoubled at once, so she bent over, gasping. Her hands trembled as she spat out the jewel and cast it into the sea.

She said, *It is well.* And she wept.

All around her on the rocks the dragons perched, like winged jewels themselves, gorgeous in the morning sun. The air was filled with their music, music that had been silent the whole of the time Jenny had seen them at Rocklys' camp, the whole of the battle. It whispered on the air, like the sea breeze or the salt smell of the ocean. Seven dragons, and there was a sort of glitter over the sea, a smoky darkening of the air that Jenny knew was Morkeleb.

Nymr bent his azure head, *Tears/distress/thing of men?* He had a voice like distant wind in trees.

And Morkeleb formed a thought, a silver crystal of loss and necessity and the ongoing tread of time, which Jenny saw that Nymr did not understand. And patiently, Morkeleb explained, *Thing of men.*

Save a dragon, slave a dragon, said Centhwevir's sweet voice in her mind. *Debt.*

My magic, said Jenny, raising her scarred face from her ruined hands.

Dragon-magic.

It is only possible, said Morkeleb, *if you will become a dragon; for in your human self there is nothing now that magic can fasten on. It is all burned away.*

And John's life with it, she wondered, if the mages back at the camp can't save him?

She said, *I free you then, all of you. Morkeleb, take me back.*

The music circled her round, and she saw how all the airs and threads of those so-different melodies were in truth part of a single enormous singing. She didn't know why she hadn't been aware of it before.

Dragon-friend, said Centhwevir, the soft clashing of a universe of golden chimes. *Dragon-friend.*

Then he spread his wings, a field of lupine and daffodils, and let the wind lift him. They all lifted afterward, pink and green, white and crimson, blue on blue on blue . . . Lifted, and spun like a drift of leaves over the ocean where the whales rolled and spouted, and swirled away to the north.

Morkeleb said, *The whalemages sent fishes to tear Caradoc's body to pieces, that the sea-wights could make no use of it. Likewise they have heaped stones before the demon Gate. There is nothing further for us here, Jenny. I will take you back.*

* * *

"Some general she was." John grinned weakly as Jenny came into the infirmary tent. "Couldn't hit a man in the heart at less than fifty feet? The country's well rid of her." And he held out his hands to her. "Ah, love, don't cry."

He gathered her gently to him and hesitantly ("Does this hurt too bad, love?") cradled her scarred and hairless head to his shoulder. "Don't cry."

But she could not stop. And neither he nor Ian, who came out of the shadows to awkwardly pat her back—he had grown, she saw, two inches in his time with Caradoc—could ease the pain that encompassed all her being.

Rocklys was dead. "When the reinforcements arrived, we called on her to surrender," said Gareth, who came in, battered and blood-streaked, some time later, in attendance on his father. Uriens, resplendent in his golden wig and armored and cloaked as befit a King, walked among the wounded who had bled for his sake. Now and then he would bend down and speak to this man or that. Once he held the surgeon's implements when a dirty wound was cleansed and stitched; when Pellanor of Palmorgin was carried in, bleeding from wounds he'd taken fighting at Rocklys' side, he took his hands and sat beside him until the Lord of Palmorgin whispered, "Forgive me," and died. Men reached from their beds to touch the King's cloak, and Ector of Sindestray, walking in his wake, made nervous approving noises in his throat and tried to get him to finish up and leave.

Cringing with shyness, Gareth brought up a stool and sat, barely noticed, beside John's cot. He fished out his bent and broken pair of spare spectacles and perched them on his nose, taking care around a place where a blow had opened the side of his face.

"She called for her sword and rode straight into the thick of the enemy," he went on unhappily. "I wouldn't have executed her, you know."

"She would have executed you." Polycarp, who had come in just after him, gingerly eased his left arm, which he wore in a sling. His red hair was sweaty and flattened from a war-helm, but looking up into the Master's eyes, Jenny could see no trace of the demon. In any case she would have known it, had Amayon gone into another. Would have known and died of jealous grief.

"That doesn't mean I'd have . . ."

"No," said the Master. "I mean that she knew what she would have done to you and expected the same."

A shadow fell across the lamplight. "Why is this man here?" King Uriens stood looking down at John.

Gareth stood, tangling the stool in his military cloak and knocking it over. "Father, you remember Lord Aversin." He scrabbled awkwardly to pick it up. "He defeated the dragon . . ."

"He didn't kill it." Uriens folded his hands before the ruby buckle of his sword-belt and frowned. "He's a trafficker with demons. Ector said so. I think the demons must have helped him drive the dragon away the first time, and now it's come back."

"That's right, your Majesty." The Lord of Sindestray appeared at his elbow again like an overweight blue-and-white butterfly. "And the woman, too."

John's eyes blazed dangerously. "Now wait a bloody minute! I hadn't so much as heard about the demons four years ago when I . . ."

"He'll have to be locked up." Uriens spoke with the self-evident logic of a child. "If he's trafficked with demons, he'll have to be done away with. He'll try to destroy the Realm. They all do."

"Father . . ." Gareth straightened protestingly.

"I'm sorry, my son. I know he's your playmate but he'll try to destroy the Realm."

"And the woman," Ector reminded.

"He's a Dragonsbane! He fought the dragon for the sake of the Realm . . ."

"Of course we know how Prince Gareth feels about Dragonsbanes," Ector said smoothly. "Naturally, any demon who wanted to gain influence with him has only to . . ."

"If you say one more word about how I've sold me soul to demons," began John, half-rising, then sinking back with a quick intake of breath. Guards in the white and azure of the Lord of Sindestray stepped out of the shadows. Jenny raised her hand, furious, conjuring in her mind the Word of Fire and Blindness . . .

And it was only a word. A cast dry chiten in her mind. Dead leaves falling from her hand.

A guard took her by the arm. Jenny whirled, yanking free, but there were other guards, coming from all directions. John somehow had Polycarp's dagger in his hand, sitting up again with blood staining the bandages on his chest, and Gareth stepped forward and caught his wrist.

"John . . ." He turned his head and caught Polycarp's eye.

The Master looked aside. Jenny couldn't find it in her heart to blame him; he knew, too well now, the strength of the demon whispers, the terrible temptation of those promises.

Gareth's eyes met John's. Desperate, pleading . . . *Trust me. Trust me.*

John glanced at Jenny. Then he opened his hand and let the knife be taken from him.

Guards brought a litter: "Take him to the dugout His Majesty slept in last night," instructed Ector, for the King had wandered away.

"You mean the one he doesn't have to sleep in now?" demanded John sarcastically. "Because the dragons have all been sent on their way and the wizards who rode them cured?" His voice was shaking with anger.

"I will not be drawn into controversy with a demon," Lord Ector said primly. "It is well known they twist any argument to their advantage."

John looked at Gareth, who averted his gaze. Jenny watched as John was lifted onto the litter; while Ector's attention was on that she stepped back into the shadows. Gareth was right, she thought, in not forcing an issue. She would be of more use free than if Ector remembered her presence and persuaded the King to have her imprisoned as well. But John's face, still as marble, struck in her heart like a dagger of accusation, and the torchlight made a dark patch of the Demon Queen's mark on his throat.

As the curtain fell behind Ector and the guards, Jenny saw Gareth return soundlessly and slide his hand under the pillows. He took out a piece of iron, an arrowhead, she thought. This he slipped into the breast of his tunic, out of sight.

* * *

That night the surviving mages came to the Regent's tent. Bliaud seemed the most alive, the most sure of himself, but even he was vague; Miss Enk and Summer the Icerider girl were little more than sleepwalkers until the talisman jewels were put in their mouths and their souls returned to them. And then, because Jenny was keenly aware of Gothpys and Zimimar and the other demons lingering and whispering outside the tent, all the mages joined together in using the Demon Queen's seal to draw the disabled demons back through the bodies to which they had once been linked and imprisoned them in shells and pebbles and snuff-bottles.

Afterward they went out, by the flickering witchlight summoned by Yseult, and cast the emptied talisman gems into the River Wildspae, where the current roared strong over the rocks. The amethyst that held the soul of the Icerider boy Werecat, his sister Summer smashed to pieces with a hammer, her face void of expression. Polycarp did the same with the topaz that was among the talismans, which they guessed contained the soul of Caradoc himself. Jenny made herself hope that the merchant prince's soul would find peace.

Her magic did not return. Bliaud and Yseult both treated Jenny with the Demon Queen's powder, but it had no effect. She remembered the demon Folcalor biting and chewing and ripping like a maddened rat at her mind; remembered releasing into the ocean anything that he might have seized to draw her into his power.

There was nothing inside her.

Only an aching longing that slowly crystallized: a longing for Amayon. For the fire and color, the power and joy, of the demon within her.

This was insanity, and she knew it, yet the longing did not go away. In her emptiness it glowed like a gentle comfort, and it seemed to her that even John's love was a pallid thing beside the wisdom and understanding of the demon who knew her so well.

She nursed John in the days that followed, in the guarded dugout under the eyes of Uriens' and Ector's warriors, and it tormented her soul to see Ian and Yseult and Bliaud able to work

he magic of healing on him. Tormented her, too, to imagine
hem looking aside from her while she performed the humbler
asks, fetching water and grinding herbs. Pitying her. The world
urned to poison around her, and she found herself thinking—
gainst all reason and experience—that Amayon alone would
are and understand.

The moon burgeoned fatter and fatter in the afternoon skies,
ike a white flaccid creature drawing nearer each day to be
lutted on the flesh of dying kings; Ector's men built a pyre on
he other side of the bridge. One hot afternoon Jenny could smell
he oil they soaked it with. Ector glared at the mages whenever
e passed them, for the laws in the south had been made with the
nderstanding that those who had been possessed against their
ills by demons, once exorcised, never really returned to their
ight minds. There was no legal provision for mages who had
een taken against their will, for at no time in the history of Bel
ad demons appeared strong enough to do so. All this Jenny
limpsed through the curtain of obsession, of weariness, of pain.

That night Jenny met Gareth and Ian beside the dugout prison
nd took the keys from the sleeping guards. The silence of that
nchanted sleep lay over the whole camp as Gareth descended
he ladder and came up again with John leaning heavily on his
houlder.

"I'm sorry I couldn't . . . couldn't stand up for you," said the
oung man. "I did everything I could to get Father to change
he sentence. It's abominable after what you've done for the
Realm!"

"It's good sense." John had shaved that morning for the first
ime since the battle, and looked haggard and thin. The burn on
is throat stood out dark where his doublet and shirt were un-
aced; the blazing moonlight seemed to pick out threads of silver
vhere the Demon Queen's other marks crossed his collarbone
nd neck. "Meself, I wouldn't trust a soul who'd gone and made
leals with demons. For you to do it, Regent as you are for your
lad, you'd have every lord in the land in revolt, and me among
em. Have you got it?" he added, and Gareth handed him the
iece of iron he'd taken from the cot the day John had been
laced under arrest.

"Ian?" John held out his hand to his son. But Ian turned away without speaking. He'd worked quietly, steadily, to heal his father's wounds, and with Yseult had put spells of healing likewise on Jenny's burned and crippled hands. Yseult had even done what she could to alleviate the migraines, the hot flashes, the aches and griefs that flooded back to Jenny once the magic that held them at bay had gone.

But through it all Ian had been silent and avoided his mother pitying her, she thought—or worse, repulsed by what he had seen in the days when both had been the slaves of their demons.

Jenny could not watch when Gareth handed John a satchel containing the shells and bottles and pebbles, stopped and marked with sealing-wax, that contained the souls of the demons. She'd spent a week trying not to give in to the desire to scour the camp for them. Under her linen sleeves her scarred arms were welted with the marks of her own fingernails, when the pain of wanting to search grew too bad. For three nights now Amayon had shown her in dreams what would be done to him through all eternity once he was sent behind the mirror, and it was nothing she would have done to her worst enemy—not even to the Demon Queen whose name she had heard John murmur longingly in his dreams. Some of it she hadn't conceived of any sentient being doing to anyone or anything.

Let me out. Let me out. Let me out before they send me there.

She must not free the demon into this world. She knew that— digging her nails once again into her own flesh she knew it—and knew, too, that there was no chance of sending him back to his own *(Yes, there is! I promise I'll go back there!)*. And he had done terrible things to her, degraded her in ways she sometimes found it difficult to recall. *(When I'm gone, you'll remember them! In every detail in your dreams forever! Unless you set me free . . .)*

But still . . .

The worst of it was that the aching hollow where her magic had been left her desperate for something to fill it. Amayon's presence had been comforting. With him occupying her, she had never been alone.

If you take me back, Pretty Lady, my adorable one, you will have your magic again.

Be silent. Be silent. Be silent.

"What was that he gave you," she asked John, as they drifted to where Morkeleb waited for them at the edge of the camp. "The first thing, the arrowhead?"

"This?" He drew it from the pocket where he had also concealed the hothwais of starlight and the glass and alabaster bottle of the dragon's tears. He held it up, a savagely barbed war-point with an inch or so of shaft still attached.

"A gift from Rocklys," he said. "Maybe the last one she ever gave—anyway the most wholehearted. Unless there's a way you can draw off some of the pain I'm in and put it in a vial to throw in for good measure. I count that as her gift as well."

"No." Jenny looked away, hating him suddenly for reminding her of her loss. For speaking so casually of her pain. Amayon, she thought, would never have harmed her so. "That's not something I can do now."

CHAPTER TWENTY-SIX

On the last night before the King's Moon, two shadows made their way down the painted corridors of the old temple of Syn, in what had been the city of Ernine. Their lantern threw swaying light over the painted gazelles and brought the stars depicted overhead into alternating brightness and obscurity; the comet seemed to wink and follow them through the corridor and into the round room. Along with the hothwais of starlight, Miss Mab had smuggled to Jenny a diagram to follow and the correct powder of mingled silver and blood: *It'll never work,* whispered Amayon in her mind. *Not without my help. Nothing you do will ever work again.*

What would I be, Morkeleb had asked, *without magic?*

That was different. He was a dragon—whatever, she thought a dragon was. She was only a woman, left with nothing.

She wondered how she could face life without magic. How she could face life, face John, face her children, with the memory of what she had done. And of what she had lost.

Somehow she made herself draw the sigils of power on the floor. Her twisted fingers trembled as she arranged within it the bottle of glass and alabaster, the softly glowing hothwais of starlight, the arrowhead. Behind them in a semicircle she set out the seven demon prisons and the seven spikes of glass and mercury that had been extracted from the heads of the dragons, grimly sealing her mind to the far-off howling of the spirits imprisoned within.

The dreams of their upcoming torment were fresh as a new brand on her: agony, nausea, shame. How could she turn Amayon over to that?

It took her some time to realize that it was John that she'd saved from it.

Still, she couldn't set down the white shell. He'd been difficult, yes. But at other times he'd been so good to her, so considerate. The pleasure he had given her could never be duplicated. It wasn't something she'd turn to often, of course, but to know it was there, now and then when things were bad . . .

A warm hand closed over her scarred one. "Better leave it, love."

He was right, but she pulled her hand away from his, slapped the shell into it, hating him. "You do it, then," she said. "You'll be glad to see it, won't you?"

He looked for a long time into her eyes. "That I will," he said gently. "That I will."

She turned away, shaking all over, and would not look. It was John who completed the sigil and spoke to the seal still printed on the mirror's burning darkness.

"It's the Moon of Sacrifice, love," he said, "and here I am. And here's all the rare and precious things you asked me for: a piece of a star, a true star, caught in the stone of the gnomes; and a dragon's tears." He smiled. "And the arrowhead was given to me gie hard by one who wished me ill, and if you like I'll show you the hole to prove it. And to show you I've no ill will, you can have a baker's dozen and one of the rest of 'em, to serve as you served me; and as they'd have served you."

Jenny heard the voices of the things behind the mirror. The slurping of their tongues, and the long, thick breath.

Then the Demon Queen said, "And you, beloved?" Her voice was roses and smoke, amber and the whisper of the summer sea. "Will you not leave that scarred dwarf you've been tupping all these years and come, too? She's protected you for the last time—dried up now, and bitter. Think carefully, my love. In another year she'll be a screaming hagwife, if she isn't one now. You may not find it pleasant to live with what the sea-wights left behind."

Jenny turned and left the chamber, fumbled her way through the anteroom, and along the painted hallway in the dark. She stumbled out into the thick liquid warmth of the night and crumpled on the step, her shoulder against the stained marble, the strange sweetness of the Marches swamps filling her lungs and her mind. She doubled over, trembling, hurting inside and knowing what the Demon Queen said was true. Seeing what she would be, what she would become, without magic, without music . . . without Amayon. She buried her face in her crippled hands.

Jenny, don't! Go back there! Stop him, beloved, enchanted one! Amayon's voice screamed all the more clearly in her mind. *Pretty Lady! Heart of my hearts! Do you know what they'll do to me? Do you know what demons do to other Hellspawn, when they get hold of them? I'm immortal, enchanted one, I can't die, but I can feel—I can feel . . .*

She closed her mind, dug her nails into the papery scabs on her wrist, and his voice went on, desperate, frantic, like a fist beating at a door.

Don't let him! He's jealous, jealous because he cannot give you what I gave! You think he'll want you in his bed, knowing what you were to me?

Don't answer, Morkeleb had said—and so she did not. But the memory of the pleasure was a torment in her flesh, rising to drown her.

Jenny! JENNY!

She knew when the Demon Queen reached out and claimed him—claimed them all. All the payment of John's teind. The screaming rose to a crescendo in her mind, so she crushed her head between her slick scarred hands and closed her eyes, trying not to hear, trying not to know. Trying not to call out his name.

Amayon . . .

And he was gone. The desolation was worse than when his hold over her had been broken.

She wrapped her arms around herself, shivering and trying to breathe, and was still shuddering when she heard behind her the slow drag of John's staff; the sliding thud when he fell. She knew she should get up to help him, but she could not. The black hollow within her was too deep.

In time she heard him crawl to his feet again.

"Why'd you leave?" His voice was very quiet behind her.

She didn't look up, scarred head bowed, scarred hands folded on her breast. "Because I couldn't stay."

She heard his breathing, saw her own shadow thrown by the lantern, a distorted rumple on the worn sandstone steps.

"Aye, well, then," he said in time. "We'd better go."

Morkeleb bore them back to a vale not far from the Jotham camp. Gareth and Ian were waiting for them in the cold glimmer of moonset and dawn, with horses and mules laden for the journey north.

"Yseult hanged herself," said Gareth, when John and Jenny came near enough to him to speak. "And Summer, the Icerider girl." He glanced at Ian, seated silent and alone on a fallen tree, and the boy looked neither at him nor at his parents. "About midnight."

Jenny remembered Amayon's scream, still bleeding in her heart. The gods knew what Ian's demon had said to him, promised him, pleaded with him to stop John from ridding the world of them. From sending them behind the mirror. The gods knew what Ian had been going through, while she, Jenny, longed for and hurt for Amayon—did he want his own demon's return as desperately?

He couldn't, she thought. He has his magic to comfort him. Her jaw ached from clenching and she put her hands before her mouth.

John said nothing. Armored in his silence, he helped Jenny onto the mare Gareth had provided, swung to the saddle of a gray warhorse, and bent to clasp the young Regent's hands. "Thank you," he said.

"I've arranged for Master Bliaud to go quietly back to Greenhythe," Gareth said. "He has estates there, away from his family, where Lord Ector won't find him if he decides to make trouble. Once you and Jenny are north of the Wildspae I don't think you need have any fear of . . . of my father's sentence against you, or of Lord Ector and the council. What Rocklys left of the garrison at Corflyn won't have the strength to go against you, and when I replenish it I'll speak to the new commander."

"So you're going to replenish it, are you?" John tilted his head a little, expressionless, suspicious.

Gareth looked shocked. "Of course I am. As soon as the men can be organized to march."

John inclined his head and bent from the saddle to kiss his lord's ring. "Then I thank you again. For all."

But all these things Jenny saw only from a distance, as if through a thousand layers of dark glass. Amayon's absence was a blackness and a weariness, the leaden loss of everything that had made the world magical and colorful and wild. Her head ached, her burns throbbed, and the hollow from where her magic had disappeared was a chasm in her soul.

In all the ballads, evil was vanquished, order was restored, and the shining hero prince wed his lady, both beautiful and young. Neither, apparently, had nightmares afterward or dreamed of what they had lost. All wounds healed cleanly and no souls were broken by longings or obsessions or mistrust.

Jenny dreamed about the Mirror of Isychros. Saw again the sigils drawn on the stone floor in blood and silver: the bottle of tears and the softly glowing hothwais of starlight, the arrowhead stained with John's blood. Amayon's voice screamed in her mind again, but beneath it, in the still quiet part of herself, she thought, *I missed something.*

Something important.

She looked back at the scene again.

Amayon's white shell seemed to drag her attention to it, to be the only thing she could see. She forced herself to look beyond: There was a snuff-bottle holding Bliaud's demon Zimimar, a pebble that prisoned Gothpys. Miss Enk's demon had been trapped in a perfume vessel, and Summer's in another shell. Yseult's demon was in another perfume bottle, that one of alabaster.

Six demons. Eight cold silver spikes.

Better leave it, love.

You'll be glad to see it.

That I will.

And Amayon screaming, screaming as he was thrust into the Hell of those who hated him, who would torture him beyond the imaginings of humankind, forever.

Six demons. Eight silver spikes.

Caradoc and Ian sitting at a table, eight jewels scattered between them. *Destroy the jewel,* Ian said, and Caradoc shook his head.

I have my reasons . . .

What reasons? Jenny asked.

Pretty Lady! Heart of my hearts! She heard Amayon's voice again in her soul, drowning out all thought. *Do you know what they'll do to me? He's jealous . . . He's jealous . . .*

John turning his face away from her as he whispered Aohila's name.

It will pass, Morkeleb said.

Jenny leaned her head on his shoulder, where the steel scales were smooth as glass.

How can you be sure?

His warmth came through ironclad bony angles, comforting in the thin autumn chill. Predawn mists filtered both the night's dark and the light of the breakfast fire, where John was mechanically burning bannocks. Jenny supposed she should care, for Ian's sake, but Ian had eaten almost nothing for three days that she knew about and almost certainly for longer than that . . .

And that, too, she found hard to care about, to think about.

It was difficult to think about anything but her loss and her pain.

She had dreamed last night, something, she couldn't remember what, and upon waking had felt only bitterness and despair. She knew she was behaving like an insane woman, that her longings for Amayon, her obsession with her demon, was disastrous, blinding her to something only she could remember . . . Something she dreamed, she thought, back at Halnath perhaps, but it was beyond her power to wrest herself free. Ian was silent, drawn in on himself and more so every day that passed. And John . . .

She found she could no longer think very clearly about John.

All things pass, Jenny, the dragon said. *That is the one fact about all things.*

As my magic passed? She threw the words bitterly at him, though she told herself daily that she must accept it and make an end of self-pity. But when John had lashed at her to do so, only a few minutes ago, she had snapped, *I'll stop pitying myself when you stop dreaming about the Demon Queen!*

The days without her magic had been torture, redoubled by the shame she felt when resentment scalded her at the sight of

Ian kindling the campfire with a gesture or healing his father's wounds. Last night, seeking respite, she had attempted to play the harp Gareth had given Ian, but her crippled hands were slow to respond despite Ian's healing, and when her son had reached to touch her she had stiffened, so he shrank away.

Morkeleb said nothing. In the darkness he seemed a thing of flesh still, ebony and jet. With the coming of dawnlight, she knew she would be able to see through him, a strange beautiful clearness that held within it both darkness and light.

He had guided them now for three days, scouting through the tangled ravines and thick woods where the men of Imperteng still made war on the Realm. Only an hour ago he had returned to tell them that the road to the north was clear and that he himself would take his departure for the Skerries of Light.

Now he said, *It is only magic, Jenny. One thing among a thousand things of life.*

Her head jerked up and she hated him, hated him as she hated John and all other things, and her painful stiff little hands tried unsuccessfully to ball into fists to strike him. *So he says,* she lashed at him, *he who never tasted it, never knew it! Easy for you, who gave it up and got wisdom in return, or the illusion of wisdom! It was the core of my bones, the heart of my mind, and I do not know if I can live without it!*

Without it? he asked. *Or without the demon?*

She tried to draw back within herself, where everything gaped and bled. Where everything daily, hourly, spoke Amayon's name.

Amayon was not the only one, she realized, who knew her well.

Go to him! John had screamed at her as she fled the camp. *Become a dragon-wife if you're going to leave me, but leave me or return for good! You go and you come back and I don't know if you're going to stay next time or not!*

Tears ran down her face, a river like the blood of pain in her mind. She said, *There is nothing for me, when I gave everything to save him. To save them.*

And he, said the dragon softly, *to save you.*

But she could only close her eyes and rest her head on the strength of his bones. She thought that something touched her hair, though whether it was a dragon's claw or the semblance of a man's hand she could not tell; only that it brought her comfort, and peace such as John had said that he had felt on the Birdless Isle.

What would you, then? he asked.

The words fell into the hot aching blackness of her soul like glowing diamonds, stilling the roil of her thoughts. It seemed to her that whatever she asked—to go with him to the Skerries of Light, to find peace and healing, to simply be turned to stone until all this had been worn away by a thousand years of rains— whatever she asked he would do.

Peace seemed to come into her mind. She drew breath, and sat up, and ran her hands over her bare, scarred scalp. *Once before you asked me that,* she said. *You gave me a choice: to become a dragon, and to live forever in magic. It would be easy, I think, to do that now.*

He sat still, like a great cat, his forepaws crossed and his diamond eyes glimmering from the transparencies of dawn. Smoke from John's campfire momentarily delineated him, becoming for an instant the curve of the horns, the riffle of the beribboned mane, then dissolving to a skeletal ghost.

Maybe I've been with John too long for my peace, she went on. *It will be hard to go back, now, as I am. To be pitied by those who knew me when I had power. To see Ian in pain, and John . . .* She shook the thoughts away. *And I'm not . . . able, really, to cope with what I think may lie ahead.*

Because Folcalor didn't die, Morkeleb. Folcalor wasn't one of the demons we imprisoned and sent behind the Mirror of Isychros. And Folcalor is more intelligent than the other demons; slyer and more patient. He had some plan, some intention, beyond the dragons and the mages whose bodies he enslaved: something that involved the mages' souls. If I went with you now, if I sought peace now, I would not be in the Winterlands when he comes again.

Morkeleb said, *Ah.*

Do you understand?

It is not a thing of dragons, said Morkeleb, *to serve, and to risk, and to bleed for others. It may be that I, too, have associated too long with your Songweaver, my friend. Because I understand. Will you be able to endure?*

Jenny looked down at her scarred hands. Thought about Yseult, and Summer, whose despair at losing the sweet poison of their demons had cost them their lives.

Thought about John.

I will endure, she said. *I will trust the Lord of Time, as humans must, who cannot will pain away by magic, nor seek relief either in illusion or immortality. This is what I am.*

Even so, said the dragon. *I have lived for many years and have seen those things that humans receive, who trust the Lord of Time. And whether those things are bitter or sweet, or whether they are all only illusion—this I cannot tell. I would that I could heal you, my friend, but this is not possible: I, who destroyed the Elder Droon and brought down the gnomes of Ylferdun to ruin, I cannot make so much as a single flower prosper when frost has set its touch upon it.*

His warmth surrounded her, velvet against her wasted flesh and peace-filled as the sunlight on the Skerries of the north. *Therefore I can only say, Live however best you can. Watch for these evils, and seek healing for yourself, even when the darkness and the pain seem unending. I will come back to you, my friend, to your help or to your rescue or only to sit on the hillside and gossip, as friends do.*

She smiled as he spread his ghostly wings and lifted from the ground as mist lifts, an unearthly glitter of starlight and bones. *I will be there when you come, Dragonshadow.*

He thinned away into the silver morning and was gone . . .

To be continued in
The Knight of the Demon Queen